BLOOD
FOR OUR
FUTURE
"DOM LATED SHLANO"

Paul E. Vallely
(MG, US Army, Ret)

Dr. Kevin Collins
D.P.A.

4/21/08

Tom
You and I know freedom
is never free
God Bless America
Semper Fi
Kevin "Coach" Collins

Blood for our Future

Paul E. Vallely
(MG, US Army, Ret)

Dr. Kevin Collins
D.P.A.

ISBN # 978-0-6151-9688-6
Published by Stand Up America, USA
Bigfork, Montana
Printed in the United States of America

We wish to thank our families: Marian "Muffin" Vallely ,
Dana Vallely and Scott Vallely
and
Jane Marone Collins, Kevin Collins jr. Kerrin Collins, Jessica Collins,
Liam Collins, Amanda, Abby and Kevin Patrick Collins
for their love and support.
We wish to offer a special thank you to Joan Collins La Chance for her tireless editing and encouragement in the process of producing this manuscript.

We also wish to thank our team, Heidi Roedel our graphic designer
and Victoria Creamer our editor and formatter.
Without them this book would not be possible.

We extend our thanks to Norm DeForrest for his help and guidance with our cover design, as well as Lt. Col. Oliver North and
Lt. General Thomas Mc Inerney for their support and kind endorsements, and Ms. Lee Kessler for her support in the production of this manuscript.

CONTENTS

PART ONE
PRELUDE TO A SHOWDOWN

CHAPTER 1

SACRIFICES BEGIN:
DOM LATED SHLANO

BY LATE MAY 1942, Amos Stegman admitted the truth to himself. He had come to understand that he had to get his family out of Germany, and he had to act very quickly. As much as he tried to ignore them, Amos had to finally allow himself to recognize the truth: the rumors and reports of the Nazi's plans to kill every Jew in Germany were true.

As a bookkeeper in a copper wire manufacturing plant, Amos had the time and the opportunity to gather the type of information he would need. Chilling stories about relocation camps springing up in Poland were confirmed to him by Jewish laborers who had been forced to load and unload freight trains carrying supplies to German troops on what was to become the *Eastern Front.* Strong men would shake as they described the unmistakable smell of burning bodies in towns near the camps.

During the first days of June, fear started to grip his almost every waking moment. It pushed him to get his plan in place. As quietly as he could, he sold everything, sometimes for less than ten percent of value. Amos methodically moved from one family member to the next begging for whatever money they could give him. When he finished his own family he went to his wife Ester's family.

At each home tears and hugs filled the air. The exchange he had with his own parents was especially painful. His father had been a Captain in the German Army during the First World War. He could not accept the idea that the German government would turn on its own war veterans, Jewish or not. Amos's mother was more practical. She was born in Odessa Russia and very clearly remembered the Cossacks raiding her family farm. She remembered seeing her older brother's head fly off of his shoulders from one mighty swing of a horseman's sword. She knew Jews always have to stay on guard. She knew it was not just Germany where Jews could be legally killed. She knew the world was against her and her people. Rose Stegman was always suspicious of government, any government. When she heard her son speak, she knew he was right. She also knew the world she and her family lived in was quickly coming to an end.

Without hesitation, Rose gave Amos her blessings and whatever money she had. As she handed over her money, tears streamed down her cheeks. She and her only child realized that once he left, they would never see each other again. Remorse and shame gripped Amos immediately. His chest began to heave, and his body began to shake as his breaths came in a short and shallow rhythm.

"No mother, I can't take this. You and Papa will need it to escape yourselves. They will soon be coming for all old people. Keep your money and run." Amos said in a whisper as he tried to force his mother's hand open. Suddenly, Rose smacked his cheek with a stinging stroke. A small drop of blood formed in the left corner of his mouth. "Don't be a fool! Amos, you and your family must live! Young Jews must live. It is our duty to God. Your father and I... we have had our time. If our people are to survive we can not save the old and watch the young die. We, the old must be willing to shed blood for the future of Jews all over the world. Now stop this foolishness and please, Amos, please let us do our duty to God and to our people." She tenderly took her son's right hand and folded a small velvet pouch of rubies into his palm. "Dom lated shlano" (which means blood for our future, in Hebrew) she said in a low whisper, her voice cracking with a flood of emotions.

Amos held his mother and father in a long quiet embrace; then turned and left without making eye contact. His parents' gaze never moved from the floor as he walked away. As best they could, each wanted to remember the family's faces from the good times. They wanted no sad faced memories if they could help it.

On June 4, 1942, the worst possible news spread like wildfire through the

European Jewish communities. Adolph Hitler's sadistic SS Chief Reinhard Heydrich had died from the wounds he received in an attack by the Czechoslovakian underground. The Nazis were enraged. They swore to avenge his death with the blood of as many Jews as they could get their hands on. Men, women and even some children were rounded up and summarily shot by young Nazis blinded with a flaming irrational hatred. They murdered with no fear of having to answer to anyone for their crimes.

The "Final Solution to the Jewish Question" was slammed into high gear and it was eating through Europe's Jews like a flame through paper. With terrifying speed whole communities of Jews, who had lived in their hometowns for generations, were simply disappearing. The few, who could, packed up and ran to save life and limb.

On Friday morning June 12, 1942, Amos woke earlier than his usual 6:15AM. He had to get every detail worked through before he could go to work. There was no time to waste. He could not be late. He could give no sign that he was aware of the danger he and his family were in, let alone that he fully intended to escape to safety. At 4 o'clock that morning, Amos and his wife Marte made a series of painful decisions. They carefully examined each of their possessions deciding which they could take with them and which they would have to leave behind. The weight of carrying her three-year-old twins Judith and Ruth, and their infant son Noah would be enough to deal with. Their trip to freedom would allow them to take very little besides the clothes on their backs and Mama Rose's rubies.

Amos's workday started as usual. He made tea for the Nazi appointed manager of the plant and settled in to finish the weekly reports. As a worker at a plant with a mostly non-Jewish German work force, he enjoyed Saturdays and Sundays off. His Fridays always consisted of hours of carefully prepared reports detailing the week's output. Since the plant chronically failed to meet its real production quotas, Amos had to be especially creative to cover for the manager's incompetence. For this service, the manager allowed Amos to credit himself with overtime hours he had not worked. This little extra pay helped Stegman gather up the bribe money he needed to get his family out of Germany.

As the hours dragged by, Amos went over the plan again and again. He and Marte would bring their children to a small out of the way café just across from the fishing boat that would be smuggling them out of the country. They would pay the owner his bribe, then once safely inside the café, they would wait out of sight in his kitchen. At dawn they would meet the boat captain, pay him his bribe, and slip away.

After a day that seemed one hundred hours long, it was finally 6 o'clock; quitting time at the plant. The Nazis had set the workday to go until then in an effort to make life as difficult for their few observant Jewish workers as possible. Getting home by sundown as required by Jewish law, is difficult for most of the year, although June presented no problem. Friday evening, services had an extra meaning for Amos and Marte. Their prayers for deliverance were deeply heart felt.

SATURDAY MORNING

The first hours of that Saturday were gray and rainy. That was good news. It would be less dangerous making their way to the docks because the dreary weather and people's fear of the Nazis, kept the streets virtually empty. At 1:45 AM they slipped onto the street and headed for freedom.

Nevertheless, empty streets can be dangerous streets. Amos wished there were more people walking through town. Empty streets make seeing the few people who *are* out that much easier. They offered no protective crowd cover, but at that time in the morning he could expect little else.

"This would be a dangerous move at any time of the day," Amos thought and prayed. At last, the family somehow made it to the café without being discovered. To the end of his life, Amos firmly believed the hand of God Himself guided their steps in and out of the shadows at just the right moment. The rain held off for the 20 minutes it took to make their way to the meeting place. They had just slipped into the café when the skies opened.

Thunder and lightning frightened the children. The girls could be silenced with hugs and kisses from their loving parents, but baby Noah seemed inconsolable. As the hours passed Amos and Marte took turns alternately trying to sleep, but neither could. They always kept one eye open, watching over their children, watching for menacing uniforms. At 5:15 AM the kitchen door was yanked open. Fear shot through both of them as they draped themselves over their children in an effort to buy them even one more minute of life, if their worst fears had been realized and they had been discovered. It was the shop owner's teenaged son.

"Time to go, Jews!" he growled like the sick mongrel he was.

Once they were back on the street they could see the boat captain frantically waving his arms, calling to them to hurry in a hushed voice. Amos could smell the sea. He had never noticed its smell before, but now it smelled like freedom.

"Yes, now I know what freedom smells like. It's a mixture of salt air and rotting fish, but it is delicious," he thought clutching baby Noah with one hand and little Ruthie's hand with the other.

Boarding the swaying and bucking fishing boat, they were both surprised and horrified. They were surprised to see there were seven other people who would be making the trip and they were horrified at the accommodations, or lack of accommodations to be more precise.

In spite of its fancy sounding name, The Hans Kessler was anything but fancy. Barely seaworthy, it would never have been allowed to sail in ordinary times. Like its captain and owner, the Kessler had long since seen its best days. It was now a creaking pile of timbers that looked like the day's storm would be the last one it could survive.

The smell of rotting fish and diesel exhaust were almost enough to make them turn around and take their chances in Germany. Of course, that was never really an option. The captain was a crude and angry man whose greed had just barely overcome his fear of discovery as a smuggler of Jews. He actually hated Jews as much as any Nazi and would have been a Nazi if he were younger and had more to offer them. Now it was only through a twisted sense of honor that he was keeping his commitment to sail his passengers to freedom. The heat was on. The streets of Germany were now much too dangerous for people who helped Jews. He promised himself he would never try this again. This would be the last boatload of Jews, for any amount of money. The

Nazis were killing those they even suspected of helping Jews. That made even the handsome bribes he was getting for each passenger look insignificant.

"Schnell! Schnell!" the captain kept saying as he directed them into the fish hold and reminded them to be quiet. Thunder and lightning made the scene even more frightening. Baby Noah awoke with a cry loud enough to almost be heard above the storm. The captain glared at Marte and snarled: "Shut it up or I'll throw it over board."

"It?" Marte thought, "what kind of people are these Germans?"

Somehow Noah calmed down and they all settled in, deep in the darkest corners of the ship's hold. There were no seats; they were left to sit on the slimy fishy deck. Standing in the small hold of the pitching and heaving, Kessler was not possible. They had to plant themselves in the slippery goo of yesterday's catch, like it or not.

All seemed well until one of the captain's men, a boy barely 12 years old, yelled down, "The harbor patrol is coming! Quiet or we'll all be killed." The passengers held their breath and waited. They could hear the putter of the small patrol boat then an officer ordering the captain to stop and prepare to be boarded. Next they could hear Nazi Coast Guard sailors walking on the deck just above their heads. Every step chilled the passengers with fear.

One of the sailors shined a light into the darkened hold. The hand of Providence rocked the Kessler just enough to keep the light from hitting the corners where the frightened Jews huddled for safety.

The water became increasingly choppy. A lightning bolt lit up the sky. The following thunder sounded like a cannon had been fired from the deck. Noah began to cry. It was not a baby's cry for food or changing. It was primal and filled with the fear that gripped his infant mind at its core.

The other adults in the dark hold whispered: "Shut that child up or we're all doomed."

"What's the matter with you? Do you want to get us all killed?"

Amos held his baby son close to his chest and began to rock, desperately trying to quiet him and end the danger his crying represented. Nothing worked. Baby Noah would not be calmed.

Now Amos could feel the eyes of the other passengers on him. They were becoming like laser beams burning into his flesh. Finally he reached into his pocket for a handkerchief. With his hands shaking, Amos stuffed the cloth into Noah's mouth. Immediately, a tiny hand reflexively came up and wrapped its fingers around Amos's pinky. Tears fell heavily from his eyes as he held his infant son closer and closer, tighter and tighter until there were no more cries, no more clutching little fingers. Lighting and thunder filled the air. Amos felt his little Noah slowly go limp; his life ebbing away. A minute later he was gone.

As the creaky old fishing boat made its way out of the harbor, Amos passed his son's lifeless body to Marte. They fought back their emotions as they passed Noah between them, each feeling for the final flickers of his warmth as it drained from his little body. Each knew the warmth would never come back. As the heart broken Marte held her tiny son, a small drop of blood fell from the baby's lips.

"Dom lated shlano." Amos said brushing away his tears.

Chapter 2

A Very Secret Assignment

When the call came Eli Schulman was puzzled. He couldn't think of a reason why he should have been summoned in such a formal and secretive manner, to the meeting he was about to have with his cousin Aaron Stoller. Stoller and Schulman had not been particularly close for number of years. They weren't enemies, but they had drifted apart since their grandfather, Amos Stegman, died ten years earlier.

As young men in a young Israel, both of the cousins served proudly in the Israeli Defense Force. They were military men willing to fight and even die for Israel.

Amos thought of his grandsons as his gift to the nation that had taken him and his family in when they had nowhere else to turn. Having no surviving sons of his own, his Eli and Aaron were the pride of his life. He drew deep satisfaction from seeing them rise in rank year after year. Amos loved his new country, and would do anything for Israel. For him Israel was everything he dreamed it would be when he and Marte arrived with nothing but their twin daughters to settle in Haifa in 1947. They lived among other Jews searching for the Promised Land, and believed they had found it.

In the early days of Israel's existence, Amos was in the IDF himself. He had fought in Israel's wars in 1949, 1967 and 1973.As the family spread its wings in the Promised Land, they went their own ways. While Amos was alive, he kept them close, but when he died, they drifted apart. Over the past several years Eli and Aaron had only gotten together for weddings, Bar Mitzvahs and to sit Shiva as the older generation, died off.

When they did get together, they always spent hours talking and laughing by themselves in one corner or another. Even though Eli had long since left the IDF, ending his career as a full Colonel, he and Aaron, now a Major General, and a member of the Prime Minister's personal staff, always had much to talk about.

Their conversations usually followed the same script. Eli would try to talk Aaron into retiring and joining him in his investment banking business, and Aaron would always offer Eli a new position on his staff, even if it were only as a reservist. Then both would laugh and toast to Israel, the country that had saved their family from the uncertainty and chaos of post war Europe under the Soviets.

Now here they were, together in a small office down the hall from Eli's spacious office, speaking in serious and subdued tones. The first thing Eli noticed was how simple the office was. The room was sparsely decorated and not particularly well lit. There was a desk and some folding chairs, a wall covered with maps, a computer and a telephone.

The serious look on Aaron's face caught Eli by surprise and his mind raced.

"Who died? It could only be his mother, but why should I be called here personally to hear about his mother's death? Oh my God, it's one of his kids!"

To break the tension of the strange meeting, Eli jokingly asked where the mops and brooms were. Aaron smiled broadly, but could not keep the seriousness of the moment from beaming out through his dull brown eyes.

"Meeting here has its purpose, believe me," Aaron said as he warmly embraced his cousin, and patted his shoulders.

Before closing the thick old door to his temporary office, Aaron gave the hallway a quick once over. When he did pull the door into place, he locked it and stuffed a piece chewing gum in the keyhole.

Aaron looked directly into Eli's eyes and spoke in Hebrew using three simple words, *Dom lated shlano.*

"Blood for Our Future," Eli thought.

He knew what the words meant and what the phrase meant. It might as well be the Stegman family motto. What he did not know was why he was hearing these words now, in this place, in such secrecy.

Aaron spoke in a firm and official sounding tone, "Israel needs you. We can no longer wait for the Arabs and their terrorist bastards to bleed us to death in a slow and steady crush. We have not fought so hard and so long to die watching from hiding places while the terrorists kill every last Jew in Israel. That Iranian mad man wants to show the world that he really does have nuclear bombs. He thinks we will sit here and be his demonstration targets, but we can't let that happen now or ever. That can't be allowed to happen and won't be allowed to happen. We have developed a plan that is dangerous for both us and our allies, but is necessary to the survival of our country."

"I like the idea of saving Israel, but why do you call me in to speak of these things? Shouldn't you be busy working out the details? Haven't you noticed that I'm not in the Army anymore?" Eli asked, using the classic form of Jewish conversation: saying things by asking questions.

"America is with us," Aaron said.

"Well, of course. Why would they not be with us? Are you asking me to take that staff spot you have always hocked me about? Is this what this is all about? Why the super secrecy, the James Bond shit? Couldn't you just have called me or sent me a letter? What's this really about?"

"The Americans and the P.M. have worked on several ideas. We have decided what we need to do. It is an awful and sickening plan, but we have concluded, very sadly concluded, it is the only way we can continue to live as a nation. The Americans want us to send someone to speak to their man personally about this. The plan is so dangerous and radical, that it can never be allowed to reach the Western media, let alone Al Jazeera. It would mean the end of Israel overnight. What few friends we still have would have to disavow us, maybe including America." Aaron answered.

"How can I help?" Eli asked.

"I have been assigned the duty of finding a very special man to send to the Americans to negotiate the final details of our plan. I had to find a man of integrity and intelligence who would strictly follow instructions. This man had to be someone completely unknown to any Arab intelligence service. He also had to have a soldier's understanding of the necessity of sacrificing a few for the good of many."

"You think I'm that man?" Eli asked.

"You fit the requirements better than anyone I could think of. You have military experience, intelligence and you are unknown because you have been in the private sector for so long. But most importantly you understand 'Dom lated shlano.' You sat with me at our grandfather's knee listening to the Stegman family story. You know the meaning of 'blood for our future' at the deepest, most personal level. You are the one Israel has to send to make certain every detail is worked through.

"Our plan is to sacrifice a few Israelis for the future of all of Israel. Not many people could comprehend how dire our situation is, and few could support what we have to do. Our representative cannot allow himself to be talked into an alternate plan, one that will 'work just as well, without sacrificing innocent lives.' Thoughts like that are American thoughts. They have never lived with the threat of death facing them morning to night. They live half a world away. They are interested in this plan only to avoid joining us as continual victims. They think they understand what we are going through, but..."

"I know these people are crazy and dangerous...is there anything else we can..." Eli asked.

Before he could complete his thought, Aaron asked: "Are you familiar with how these lunatics celebrate their holiday called Ashura?" Eli could not answer. All of the information he was being bombarded with was stunning him to his core.

Let me explain Aaron said: "Ashura is a very important Shia holiday. It commemorates the martyrdom of one of Mohammed's grandsons. It actually was the start of trouble between the Shia and the Sunnis. To prove their devotion to Shia Muslimism, these fools cut themselves on their foreheads and keep blood flowing from the wounds by slapping themselves with swords over and over. They still do this in Lebanon at a town called Nabatieth. They band together and march through the streets bleeding and chanting at the top of their lungs. They get young boys to join in and even cut babies and old people not strong enough to cut their own heads. They all have a wonderfully sick time."

Aaron continued, "If their own blood means so little, the blood of Jews is totally meaningless. People who do things like this can not be bargained with. You can't talk to them and solve differences. You can't say, 'You take this and I'll take that.' They want blood to flow. They want our blood to flow. They want us dead, every Jew on earth: dead. They have no culture. There is no civilization or refinement to these beasts. They choose to live in tents like livestock rather than settle and build a life like a person should. They're creatures from the dark part of man's soul who want only death.

"Human rights, self-determination, freedom and justice ... none of these will survive if they take over the world, which is exactly what they want. They hate peace. They hate anyone who is not an Islamist terrorist. These barbaric morons hate even other Muslims – they would execute three quarters of their own people for the love of Allah!"

Aaron handed Eli an envelope. "Open it now so there will be no misunderstanding about what we want to achieve by this operation, the Americans call it Operation Sucker Punch, ours is called Operation Purim Party."

The Israeli concept of how Operation Purim Party would work was very simple. It was no more than four pages. Its simplicity actually chilled Eli. "*This is it? A plan like this should be longer, more elaborate. People are going to be slaughtered for God's sake.*"

When Eli heard himself think the phrase *for God's sake* he was stopped in his mental tracks. "Yes, I guess they will die, for God's sake, that's for sure."

"Of course I accept. What do I do now?" Eli asked. Aaron handed him another envelope.

"Here are your travel orders and documents. Your cover story will be that you are traveling to Florida to visit your grandchildren. Once you get settled, contact this man...

"You will meet with him; here's his picture ... he will take you to a safe place to talk."

They embraced and Aaron whispered, "Go with God Eli. Israel and the free world are depending on you. Dom lated shlano."

"Dom lated shlano," Eli said as he kissed Aaron's cheek.

CHAPTER 3

MEETING HIS CONTACT

ELI SCHULMAN WAS TENSE AND EDGY all the way from Israel to Fort Lauderdale Hollywood International Airport in South Florida. His El Al flight was smooth enough and his seat was first class, but the trip reminded Eli that he was no longer a soldier. He prayed he was up to the mission he was about to attempt.

Waiting for his luggage was just as nerve racking.

"Was I made? Will they kill me here in front of my family? Oh thank God, there's my bag... and oh, there's my son."

"Ronald. I'm here! Ronald!"

"Finally he sees me."

Eli's grandchildren ran to him and jumped up and down with excitement at his presence. Seeing the youngest generation in his family steeled his resolve to complete his mission.

"Thank God they're here and safe instead of there."

The orders Schulman received instructed him to go to a local Borders bookstore at 11:30 the next morning. He was to bring the pile of documents he was given. They were phony personal tax return documents. As per his orders, Eli sat at the coffee bar reading a USA Today with the sports section draped over his left knee.

A few minutes after Eli sat down, a light skinned Black man wearing a cheap suit and well-worn shoes, joined him.

Following instructions, Eli said: "Taxes! I guess they have to be paid."

The man across the table answered; "Yes, taxes are the price we pay to live in this country." With this exchange, the second test of authenticity could be made. Eli was to use a party trick taught to him by a Mossad agent who was preparing him for his mission.

"This trick is easy unless you don't know how to do it," the agent had said with a wry smile. "There is no chance you can spring this on a fake agent and have him figure this out in ten seconds. This will assure you he is your contact. Now practice over and over because he is doing the same, and you will have to recognize not only that he knows the answer, but also that he knows our answer. There are two ways to do this. We want only our way."

Eli took four small pencils from his pocket and arranged them in a pitch fork shape. The figure formed a handle, the top of a fork and two prongs. He placed a penny in the middle of the two prongs, and challenged his companion:

"Take the penny out without touching it by moving just two of the pencils. You have ten seconds."

In two skillful moves the American finished the trick then quickly scooped up the pencils and handed them to Eli. Each man nodded his approval and the meeting began.

Eli's counterpart was Sam Carson an America Army major. Like Schulman, Carson had been selected by the highest levels of his government because he had a background that fit the mission's requirements very well. Carson also had a personal connection to the principle of sacrificing a few for the good of many.

Sam Carson

Sam Carson was the grandson of Lizzie Barth, an English woman who grew up in Coventry and married a Black American Army truck driver stationed in Britain during World War II. Carson was well aware of the November 14-15, 1940 bombing of Coventry by the German Luftwaffe. The Barth family, along with five other families on their street, was burned out of their home that night. Two of Lizzie's sisters and an aunt were killed by Nazi bombs in the raid.

History has accused Winston Churchill of letting Coventry be destroyed that night. As the story goes, he decided that saving the city, and giving its people time to evacuate, would jeopardize the intelligence sources that told him the attack was coming.

There were stories that Churchill himself had family in Coventry, but they were never verified. Just as Schulman had heard his family's story many times over the years Sam Carson's family had often repeated their Coventry story. Now as a soldier, Sam knew it was the best military strategy. He knew Churchill was right. Being three generations removed from those who died made it still easier to understand Churchill's position in 1940. The Prime Minister knew Britain was deeply in trouble in November 1940. The Germans had charged through Europe all the way to the Atlantic coast of France. In the fall of 1940, just 20 miles of the English Channel stood between Britain and the Nazi Army.

There were very difficult choices that had to be made to save the British nation, and now some very difficult choices had to be made to save Israel and the rest of the free world. Carson was not about to try to talk Schulman out of his nation's plan. He understood Israel's situation was just as dire as the one England found herself in during the dark early days of World War II, before America entered the war.

While pretending to read over the phony tax papers on the table between them, Schulman and Carson discussed Israel's "Blood for our future" plan and Operation Purim Party.

Eli spoke first: "Vengeance. It's a part of the Jewish psyche. All through our history, Jews have been conscious of *Yom Ha Din*. It means 'doomsday.' Jews are not afraid of Doomsday. We believe it will be a day of reckoning when God will destroy our enemies and we will return to His side ever after. "In our view, scum like the Muslims will be condemned to eternal separation from God and by the way, not with 72 virgins either. We know that not all of us were meant to live to see Doomsday. We know that some of us will die as slaughtered innocents for the good of those who come after us. But we also know that we are called to live in hopes that every innocent Jew, who dies to bring about Doomsday, will be rewarded by God and that this is the way God has arranged our lives."

Eli sipped his coffee then continued: "Over the centuries, Jews have been the target of Crusades, Inquisitions, Jihads and Pogroms. Whatever our enemies called them, they added up to the same thing: Kill Jews! While the rest of the world fought against each other in one century, then with each other in the next, Jews have always remained the central target." Carson said little but his eyes told Eli he was making note of everything he was hearing.

"Time has taught us the difference between Jews and Christians; it has to do with the Christian call to prayer for their enemies and the Jewish call for revenge instead. Revenge in the eye for an eye Old Testament sense... but in today's 'modern, clean fingernails' world revenge is not a very politically correct way to think. The Islamists have used the Western media as useful idiots to convince the Christians of the West that Israel is the aggressor in the Middle East. That damned Al-Jazeera is particularly dangerous. I've watched the English version of it and believe me it's no pile of 'home movie' shit. The programming is slick and every bit as professional as anything you could see in Israel or even here. They are manipulating world opinion with their bullshit and nobody is challenging a thing they say. Since most of the world—well most of the world that counts anyway, is connected, this electronic attack is very serious."

Carson responded with his concurrence, "Yes, it's the same here. The people of this country are being fed a steady diet of lies and half-truths about our situation. Some of these bastards actually come out and say we are not in any danger from terror, that the Generals and the White House just made it all up to get elected. Sad enough many Americans are buying that line."

"And the bureaucrats of your government do not seem to recognize the danger from this ongoing Psy-op attack, let alone have the will to do something about it." Eli said.

"I wouldn't bet on that Mr. Schulman," Sam said without looking up from Carson's coffee. His tone told Eli he had wandered onto grounds he should back away from.

"Let me smooth this over", Schulman thought, *"This confused public perception about what we are facing is not an accident. It is another front on which we*

must join together and fight. This is why we, Israel and America, must take this terrible step.

"Our goal is to provide ample grounds for those who want to believe that Israel is the aggrieved side in this ongoing dance with these Arab bastards while we crush them."

Schulman hoped he had gotten the conversation back on track with this comment, but had no indication from Carson if his 'olive branch' had been well received.

He continued, "We realize that as a Christian country, revenge doesn't sit well with you Americans. Even today you argue about whether or not you should have dropped Atomic bombs on the Japanese, a race that brought you Pearl Harbor and tortured your soldiers when they captured them. The British are just as squeamish about revenge, they fired Harris over their own guilt at the job the man did. To us, you are both naïve."

"Keep talking," Carson said.

"Jews and the Muslims share a similar fatalistic view of how the world ends. They think that some long gone Imam will come back to earth and bring about the end of the world in a vengeful and violent sweep across the face of the earth, with Muslims being saved of course.

"Jews believe in the blood and destruction part too; not from a made up Imam, but from God Himself. So you see my friend, true Jews have nothing to fear from this operation. If it brings on the end of the world, we are ready. We know we are God's Chosen People. We really don't worry that God will let us fall into the hands of swine like these people." Eli added.

Carson said, "And I guess you don't think too much of our chances, Christians that is?"

"Well, not religiously speaking, we don't. But we are in the same boat now. Even Marx, who was the grandson of a Rabbi, predicted as much back in the 1840's. He said America would become a Jewish State which in, at least, a quasi sense it is. The Jewish texture in America's public life would not allow you to refuse to join us in this operation. Israelis have a sense that your 9/11 was our 9/11. Given our current situation we see our only option, as taking this opportunity to set this trap and wait for our chance to destroy every last

Muslim on earth."

The starkness of Schulman's honesty hit the center of Carson's brain with a thud. It chilled him and demanded he rethink what was happening. Conflicted feelings flooded his thoughts. His soldier's mind told him he had no choice even as his heart shuddered at the destruction of innocents that Schulman was so casually laying out before him. That this truly was a religious war had not fully presented itself to Carson before.

"We don't fight wars because of religion. Any American war that had a religious tone, got it from our enemies. We don't saddle up and go to war to make people go to church on Sunday mornings. It's just not in our national make up," Sam Carson thought.

"We even have a day for vengeance. It's called Purim. The Book of Ester tells us of the Jews slaughtering thousands of our enemies and celebrating. Although few American Jews, and certainly no American Christians, understand this, Purim is a celebration of vengeance and slaughtering your enemies. And over the years, Purim has been used as a day of vengeance. In the past when people actually understood the significance of vengeful acts on Purim we had some great days. Did you know we got you Americans to execute some top Nazis at Nuremberg on Purim?" Schulman said.

Without being conscious of his actions, Carson bounced his head and pursed his lips.

"We would actually have liked to have run this operation on Purim, but we can't wait that long. We had to settle for calling it Operation Purim Party instead."

The smile growing across Carson's face told Eli he was on a roll so he continued, "It was no accident that thousands of Iraqis were killed in the first Gulf War, in a bombing raid by the American Air Force on Purim in 1991."

"So revenge is something that has always been part of Israel?" Sam asked.

"Yes, my friend, we call it *peulot tagmul* - acts of revenge in English. Think about how our military actions are always described in your media. Don't they always refer to anything Israel does as 'retribution' or 'retaliation'?"

"Well that's us. Fuck with us and we will fuck you back, fast and hard.

When we say, 'Never again' we mean it. 'Never ever again!' We needed the world's help to escape the Nazi death machine the last time, but this time we just need a few willing partners like America and Britain to crush these vicious bastards and do the world a favor."

Schulman realized it was time for specifics. "*It's not really important whether or not this guy understands the reasons why this is so Jewish. The history lesson is over, time to lay this out.*"

"Look, the plan is laid out here," Eli said, patting a second large envelope on the table between them.

"We are willing to use our own people as bait. We want these terrorists to charge into Israel to kill our own people. Yes of course this is a sickening thought, but once they do this, we'll have the grounds to nuke them to hell and bring this terrorist threat to an end. Fighting for survival is not for those with weak stomachs."

"In return, America has only to agree to join with us in what amounts to a pre-emptive war. We are well aware that you guys aren't comfortable with a pre-emptive war. We know this...but we're both at a point where we either act or all of our people will be murdered by lunatics who want to end the world in a second Holocaust, only this time, they want to torch the whole world. How will it unfold? It would be us first, the little Satan, then they would come after the Great Satan in an all out war; a bloody and totally destructive war. This is not a very complicated plan. It doesn't go on and on. There will be an End-game. Others will work out the details but the important thing is to get on the same page now. Details will come later as this agreement works its way up our respective 'food chain.' We are in agreement? Are we not Mr. American?"

Sam nodded and extended his hand. "We have a deal, sir."

"May God help us if this leaks out before we are ready to move." Eli said

"Amen," Sam answered.

"May I ask you a question?" Sam said looking into Eli's eyes.

"Of course."

"I have tried to understand why the Palestinians don't have a state and where it should be if they did have one. What's the Palestinian's claim? Is Israel sitting on their land? Please don't be insulted by my question. I just need to know."

"I'm glad you asked. Everyone should ask. Of course you are asking the wrong party, but I will give you the answer anyway," Eli said with a wry smile.

"In 1922 the Ottoman Turk Empire collapsed when they and Germany were humiliated in the First World War. Because they were the victors and could do such things, France and Britain divided large portions of the Turkish Empire and gave it away. They created three separate districts, two to be controlled by the Brits and one by the French. The area was cut up into an 80% portion given to the Arabs and a 20% portion given to Jews for a future state. Jordan is the original Palestinian State. The simple answer was they already had a state, but it was not enough. They wanted more.

"So even though they offered a state in 1922, again in 1948 right after the war, the United Nations tried to head off trouble by giving them again a state cut from half of Israel. The Jews, accepted it, and made a wonderful modern country out of arid desert land. The Palestinians were lied to then as they have always been. They were told Israel was historically their land when the truth was just the opposite. We got some help from the UN and from Jews around the world and we made a country for ourselves.

"You might remember the 'Plant a tree in Israel' drives in America when you were a kid? That raised millions for us, and we will always be grateful to our Uncle Sam for that help. We know not everybody who bought us a tree was a Jew."

"Yes, as a matter of fact I do remember those drives. Our neighbors were Holocaust survivors who ran a bakery on my street and I do remember those collection jars. My family bought a few trees." Sam answered.

Eli continued, "But to this day, the Palestinians live like drifting hobos in tents for four generations and Israelis live in the style of Americans. The Arabs would rather sit on their asses and hate Jews than try to make a real country for themselves. Their leaders steal every penny they are given and they are constantly told they could stop living like farm animals if only Israel would allow itself to be pushed into the sea. Even the name, Palestinian Liberation Army is a lie. The liberation part is to fool the compliant Western media. Who is being liberated and from whom? The Western media never ask such questions; they just know that any group with the word liberation in its name they believe.

"Even if only one fifth of one percent of all the people in the Middle East are Jews that would be too many Jews for these people. I have fought these people. I know them. Arab men are not warriors. They prefer to be able to overwhelm and decapitate people while acting in mobs. This is why they have turned to stealthy 'hit and run' terrorism. This is why they send children out to be homicide bombers to kill Jews in movie houses and busses while we go to work and they sit home drinking tea. They have to fill these kids with hate, drugs and lies to get them to kill themselves. These bastards even get little girls to blow themselves up."

"Why don't the people rise up?" Sam asked.

"The Islamists could never allow any progress for these people because they have to be kept angry and willing to murder people, Jews and Christians. There are over a million Arabs living in Israel in peace and prosperity. I'll bet most Americans don't know that."

"No, I'm sure you're right about that."

"Mohammed Waleed, that pig knows peaceful Muslims means no new troops to fight the West. He keeps telling his agents to agitate for the death of Israel, but you know what? If he killed us, he would come right after you guys. Remember, it was just in 2000 that yet another Palestinian State plan was offered. Their answer was to take down your buildings and kill thousands of Americans. Hezbollah wants to finish off Israel, then murder the descendants of pigs and goats, as they call Americans.

"Remember, these are the grandsons of the same Arabs that actively helped the Nazis trying to beat the Americans and Brits so they could themselves kill more Jews. One of their top leaders personally met with Hitler to work out the plans – the Mufti of Jerusalem. Many do not know the Bosnian Muslim (Nazi) Divisions as part of the Wehrmacht…recruited by the Mufti. Yes, a friend of Hitler."

"More people should know these things," Sam said.

"Yes, my friend that is very true, but right now it is very beside the point. They have to be stopped before they are totally portrayed as civilized people."

CHAPTER 4

In the Basement of the Whitehouse

THE BLACK SUV that picked Sam Carson up was new enough to still have a new car smell. Highly polished and richly appointed, it said FBI all over, although there were no actual letters on its doors. The two young men who came for Carson, one White, one Asian, were ordered not to engage him in any unnecessary conversation. He was not even to be answered if he asked a question about where he was going or whom he would be meeting. Carson didn't have to ask where they were taking him, and the soldier in him recognized his obligation not to question what was happening.

Sam was brought onto the grounds of the White House and directed to walk through a non-descript door. Once inside, he was strip searched and given two hospital gowns to wear, one opening to the front; one to the back. A pair of hospital like soft slippers completed his assigned clothing. He was then directed to walk down a short hallway to a small pantry.

The second door opened slowly to reveal two armed men. They striped searched him again, and then disappeared out the door. At least ten minutes passed before Harlan Andrews, the President of the United States, stepped into the small room and offered his hand. Carson snapped to attention and saluted.

"Sam I'm awful glad you're here. I've heard a lot about you. We have ourselves one hell of a mess on our hands, don't we?"

"Yes, Mr. President, we sure do."

"You've spoken to Israel's man?"

"Yes, Mr. President, I have."

"Son, you were there, I wasn't. What's your take on him and your general impression of their plan?"

"Well sir, I thought he was sincere and very scared of what he believes the Islamists want to do. Israel's plan is a serious step. It really isn't up to me to decide whether it's right or wrong for the world. That's way over my pay grade sir, and way over my head."

"Okay, Sam. We have to talk very honestly and openly about this. I appreciate your input. Tell me about their plan. If you get into your own opinion that's okay, just tell me when you switch to your opinion. We're considering a very serious step and we need to go slow and be sure of ourselves at every turn."

"As I said, 'It's over my head', but here goes. They have a plan they call 'Operation Purim Party.' It calls for baiting the Islamists into attacking a small Israeli town. Once that happens they believe it will give them the grounds to pulverize the terrorist all over the Middle East. They fully understand that hundreds of their own people will likely get killed and the survivors will be burned out, but they are willing to suck it up and make the sacrifice. I can't imagine having to make a decision like this Sir; not at all," Sam searched the president's face for any signs of reaction. There were none. Andrews' well known poker face made that impossible.

Carson continued, "They think Purim Party will give us a jump start in an all out war with Mohammed Waleed's Islamists. The Jews think the Islamists aim to retake all of the territory they once controlled."

"OK, what do they plan to do and how do we get into it?"

"Well, as I said, they plan to use one of their own towns as bait for the Islamic crazies. The Israelis have proof positive that Iran and probably Syria have fully lethal nuclear weapons aimed at Tel Aviv and they're going to take the fight to the terrorists by beating them to the punch. The plan comes from Israel's top man Prime Minister Ethan Gross. He and his staff believe this is the only way they can secure their future."

"Go on."

"As a way of assuring you that this message comes from Mister Gross himself, the man I met with in Florida told me to use a certain phrase. He said Gross knows you will understand the phrase and why using it would assure you this message is coming directly from him, personally. He wanted me to say to you, 'Don't be a *tutser.*' Does that mean anything to you, sir? Did I say it correctly?"

Andrews smiled and nodded his head. "Yes Sam, you said it correctly. I understand it alright and it does assure me this message is coming directly from Ethan Gross."

"Good. This is too important for mistakes of any kind." Sam said, forgetting he was talking to the president, a man who needed no reminders of the seriousness and importance of what was being discussed. Sam explained the Israeli's plan in a whisper.

"Their plan is to infiltrate Bint Jubayl, a Sunni controlled Lebanese town only two miles from a small Israeli settlement, Qiryat Shamona. Once their agents are in place on the ground and operational, the Israeli Defense Force will appear to be leaving their town unguarded. There will be some kind of a can't miss signal, which they would not tell even us. The signal will bring about a coordinated starting time. The agents will ferment a violent rally in the streets of Bint Jubayl and when the crowd is whipped into a frenzy they'll call for charging into Israel and killing every Jew in sight. They don't anticipate this being hard because the Islamic airwaves have been filled with calls for killing Jews, Americans and anybody else who's not a Muslim.

"Once there's been enough killing to justify a response, the IDF will pour back into the town and kill as many invaders as they can. Each body will be searched. Those that can be identified as coming from a particular enemy country will be photographed and fingerprinted. This is where we come in. They want you, Mr. President to get us to declare war on each of these countries, then call their chiefs of state and give them a quick, firm ultimatum to either surrender and disavow their people, the dead soldiers, killed while invading Israel, or get out of the way because their capital city will be flattened by America, Israeli, and our allies. When we do this, formally declare war that is, after they surrender even if it's an hour later, under international law we can legally go in and clean out the terrorists camps they have on their soil.

As Gross sees it, the countries that have legitimately been unable to clear them out themselves for whatever reason, will quickly surrender and tell us where to find the camps. The countries that declare war back instead of surrendering will be admitting they have been our enemies all along. Either way, knowing who is who will give us a big advantage. We can't ever allow this plan to get out. This means, Mr. President, we have to keep the Brits, the Australians and a few other friends out of the loop on this until the balloon goes up."

"It sure does, Sam, and I can guess that last part was your opinion." Andrews said with smile as he patted Carson's shoulder. "Go on."

"Gross and his people believe that an ultimatum like this will put these terrorist supporting phonies in a bind. If they disavow their own Islamic crazies, they could be overrun and murdered. If they sneak out of town, they might never be able to return because the Islamist world will know they acted like the cowards we know they are. That will be their problem. Of course we hope they will surrender so we can get into their territory and smash the camps ourselves. This is why Gross is asking us to formally declare war on as many countries as we jointly decide we need to."

Carson continued, "The Israelis are betting most of these countries will not have the guts to fight, that they will roll over and allow us and our allies to walk in after they formally surrender. Frankly, I believe they're right. I believe the guys running those countries are cowards, and once the ultimatums go out and the Israelis carry out pre-emptive strikes on the nuclear weapons depots they have identified, we can isolate Waleed and whoever stands with him and crush them. Gross and his people plan to ride out the expected nuclear counter attacks in a specialized bunker in the hills somewhere near Jerusalem. They have quietly constructed a honeycomb of tunnels that go deep into the ground."

"What's their time frame? When do they expect to be ready to go?" Andrews asked.

"Well that's the most important part of this whole plan. The Mossad thinks the Iranians will be fully loaded and ready to strike within a matter of months. They anticipate a nuclear attack two minutes after the Iranians feel they are ready to go."

Andrews replied, "Yes and now even Jordan who's supposed to be a friend of ours has a bomb. They did not build it to throw at another Arab country. I'd be surprised if they roll over, but we'll have to see."

"The Israelis have that covered too. They will hit Iran first and keep a satellite eye on Jordan and Syria. If the 'Little King' in Jordan gets rambunctious and decides he's more of a Muslim than a friend of the West, Gross will flatten him too. If the Syrians start thinking along the same lines, Gross promises they have enough muscle to blow them up too. The Jews want to settle a bunch of old scores and finally bomb their way to peace, all in one fell swoop."

"This is dangerous business, Sam. Makes me wish I was still just a country lawyer and ignorant as a bag of rocks, but I'm the President, and damn it to hell, I will not go down in history as the man who lost America to a bunch of murderin' bastards like these people," Andrews said as he lit a cigar. "Did Gross say anything about how much support he has, among his own people, for this fight?"

"The man I spoke with said their sense of it is that they have about two thirds of their people ready for what's coming. Imagine that." *About one in three, even in Israel doesn't get it?* Andrews thought.

"Gross thinks he can talk to these people and get them to see things his way, but he's not going to worry about them. He's not taking a poll about what to do, he's just gonna do it." Carson said.

Andrews sighed and waited a few seconds before he spoke. "Sam it's worse here. I'd be happy if we had one third with us. Personally I think we've got about 25% on board. The media has poisoned the waters so much that the average American doesn't know what to believe. When people don't know what to believe Sam, they will believe what makes them happy. What makes them feel happy, safe and least threatened is doing nothing and hiding if they have to. Believing the government has made this all up, for some damned stupid reason or another fills the bill. For too many people it certainly beats worrying. If we don't pull this off in a week, two at worst, if this drags on even for a month, I think this country won't have the stomach for this fight.

"But you know what? I don't give a damn about that either because they're wrong, dead wrong. We'll just have to fight and win with the ones that do get it and worry about the New York Times and the others later."

They stared at the floor briefly. Each thought about the seriousness of the dangers America and the free world faced.

"Was there anything else Sam?"

"No sir, but I do have one question, if you will."

"Sure, Sam."

"Sir, what does the 'tutser' message mean?"

Andrews smiled as he spoke: "Well Sam, as you might know, Ethan Gross is originally from New York. Brooklyn, I think. Anyway, a few years back when he was here with the Prime Minister before him, he and I had a chance to talk privately for a few hours. He taught me a lot about Israel and the situation in the Middle East. During the conversation, he said something like, 'Please don't be a tutser.'

"Then he explained his meaning. He told me that in Yiddish, a 'tutser' is a person who stands and watches someone's misery instead of either helping or moving on. As he explained, in the early nineteen hundreds, Jews from Eastern Europe worked in sweatshops making clothing and getting paid by the piece. They would work long hours without a day off for months. Every so often, some of these poor people would collapse and fall right out of their chair. When this happened there were three responses: First, there were the good people who stopped their own work and tried to help. Next, there were the ones who didn't even look up. They just kept working. That was most of the others. But nobody blamed them. Everyone knew the rules; if they didn't produce, they weren't paid. Everybody understood the situation, because they were all in the same boat. But then there was the last group.

"They were the worst people, the ones the others all hated. Those people actually did stop, but not to try to help. They stopped only to look at the guy on the floor and gawk. They'd suck their teeth making a 'tut tut' sound. So, for people like Gross's grandparents who worked in a sweatshop, 'tutser' was the worst thing you could call someone."

"So, if we just standby and watch Israel swinging in the wind, we're 'tutsers,' Sir?"

"Yes, Sam, and America's 'tutser' days are over. As far as I'm concerned Israel and America are both parts of God's plan. I'd no sooner let them go down than I would see us go down. We're in this together to the end and we win or lose together." Andrews said.

CHAPTER 5

LIVING AMONGST THE ENEMY

SCHMULIE RABINOWITZ and Joshua Geller were life long friends. They lived next door to each other as children and were classmates in high school and university. It was not surprising to anyone that they died together when Schmulie's fishing boat capsized in a storm and they were both lost at sea. To make things even worse, their bodies were never found. Hardship and death are not unknown experiences to Israelis. They face death and injury everyday just going out of their homes on their way to work in the morning. Vicious extremists are always trying to kill them. Just going to a market for a loaf of bread can be the last thing a young healthy Israeli does. Life in the Promised Land is dangerous. For the Rabinowitz and Geller families, the hardest things about these deaths was not having a body to bury and not getting any help from the government in their efforts to find their sons. There was a very good reason for both of these problems. Neither of these young men was dead. The Mossad faked the deaths of Schmulie Rabinowitz and Joshua Geller. The two young friends had been recruited during their first year at the University of Jerusalem and sworn to strict secrecy about their decision to become deep cover agents. As young students they burned with love for their country and wanted to do whatever they could to help Israel survive.

Their appearance made both boys perfect for the mission they were asked to go on. Neither cut of a very imposing figure. Both boys were small and very forgettable. Because of their Sephardic roots, they both had a dark Arab like complexion. More than this, as all good covert operatives, they were very intelligent, and very cunning. On a day in mid April when Jacob, their Mossad handler, thought conditions were right, the deaths were staged. The friends, by then known as *team nine*, were told to tell friends and family they would be out fishing in the Mediterranean Sea in Schmulie's small boat. Jacob had information that a quickly forming storm would strike the coast where the boys would be fishing. That provided a perfect rationale for their bodies being lost with no chance of being found. Jacob instructed them to wait until dark, then rendezvous with an Israeli special operations boat. Once they were aboard, they were dead.

From there they were taken to a secret safe house for intensive training. Their mission was simple: learn to live, think, and be a radical Islamist. Following Islamic law, the team regularly shaved their pubic hair, grew and regularly trimmed a moustache, shaved their armpits and kept their nails closely trimmed. These steps of Muslim cleanliness were required as was their circumcision. As Jews, they were already circumcised and that became a source of uneasy giddiness for the young students. Jacob explained that the Mossad assumed they were both circumcised, but if somehow they were not, he would have forced them to undergo the operation before they could complete their training.

"Your cock would feel like a burning torch was in your pants, but that would be alright. You won't be going to Lebanon to screw Muslims, just get them killed." Jacob told them at the end of their first day of good Islamists training came to a close. For Schmulie speaking various Arab dialects was easy. He had a natural knack for languages and acting. Joshua was mechanical and halting in his Arab impersonations. He had to work very hard to get his persona down. Learning to pray like a Muslim, using the proper voice intonations and body movements, was an easier task.

Seven months later team nine was ready for its mission. One night shortly after 3 AM, Jacob woke them. It was time to move. They weren't completely ready, but that made no difference, their country needed them now and that was all there was to it. They were blindfolded and walked out to the Land Rover. Jacob drove them to a point on the nearby road, said a prayer, kissed each of them and left. Ten minutes later while still blindfolded, they were handcuffed and roughly slammed into the back of a police van. They knew they were still in Israel because they trusted Jacob, but they had no idea of their actual location. The van rumbled and bounced along the way to a prison about twenty miles away.

They were brought to a small prison building with a holding pen for Arab prisoners awaiting release at the end of short sentences.

The prison guards were not involved in the scheme. They threw the boys head first into a large crowed and dimly lit room full of chattering Arabs from all over the Middle East. The dirty foul smelling and illiterate Arab men hardly noticed them. Most of them were petty criminals convicted of small crimes or guilty of things like working without proper authorization papers. Since many Arabs in Israel get into trouble because opportunities to work honestly can be limited; Jacob reasoned that the team should become "just another couple of Arabs tossed into prison for working without proper documents." Jacob's approach to creating a cover story for the boys was: the simpler the better. He believed the explanation for team nine's imprisonment should be easy to keep straight, because the kind of small time criminals they would encounter would not be the kind of men that cared about the team's cover story, let alone make any effort to unravel it. Most, but not all were harmless nobodies. There was one Arab of some importance in the pen that night. He was not placed there by happenstance.

The timing of the Israeli operation was impeccable. It was not an accident that team nine was put into the holding pen in time for Fajr, the Muslim predawn prayer to start each day giving praise and worship to Allah.

Only three prisoners dropped to their knees, faced Mecca and prayed as the sun's rays started to creep through the pen's only window: Schmulie Rabinowitz, now known as Abdul Awad, Joshua Geller, now known as Aziz Hussein and Abu Talib, a local organizer for the Muslim Brotherhood.

The team's prayers were perfect. They sounded sincere and reverent. They even inspired two more prisoners to join them. When Fajr was finished, all of the prayerful Muslims embraced, patted each other on the back and kissed each other's cheeks.

"Brothers, you must come with me. I will get us food and shelter," Talib whispered as they were put on a prison bus and driven to the Lebanon border. When the bus stopped at the Lebanon frontier, Talib warned the team to jump out and run for safety across the border.

"They will shoot you in the ass with rock salt just for the fun of it," Talib said churning his legs toward freedom. When they got into Lebanon, Talib brought the team into his world. For the first three days, he let them live with him in a small house he shared with his elderly father. By day four he had found them work with a friend on a fishing boat. This was perfect for them. They were easily able to carry off the part of fishermen with out being discovered.

As soon as they got their first pay they moved out saying they could no longer impose on Talib's hospitality. When they arrived at the flat they rented, they found a radio that was left for them by another operative they never saw; never could identify. When they ended their first report to Jacob, the team went to Talib's house to continue working him so he would help them penetrate the local Islamic community. Talib was a dull, unorganized man. Reading his secrets was as easy as looking at his face. He had no particular skills for the job of "angry Islamist" he was trying to fill. The team made it their business to end each day eating and talking with Talib; pumping him for information about the Islamists's plans.

The more they talked to Talib, the scarier he became, not for the threat he actually represented, but for the matter-of-fact way he spoke about the destruction of Israel. They came to see Talib's robotic adherence to Isamist hatred for the West in general and Israel in particular, as totally typical of the man in the "Arab street."

Both operatives had the same chilling thought, "These people think slaughtering every Jew in the world is as normal as peeling an orange."

One day Schmulie and Joshua got a break in their problem of how to handle the information the hapless Talib was unknowingly giving them. As had become their habit, day after day, they traveled through side streets to meet and dine with their target. On that day, they approached Talib's place from an alley to its rear. Something caught Joshua's attention as he peeked in on Talib through a small window. When it became clear what Talib was doing Joshua motioned to Schmulie to silently move forward. For a few seconds they stared in amazement as they watched Talib. He was masturbating with his gaze fixed on a glossy color picture of a nude blond in a cowgirl hat. Joshua motioned to Schmulie and both of them crouched and duck- walked back into the shadows.

"Give me the camera." Joshua whispered. "Stay back and keep watch."

He would capture the moment with the state of the art low light camera they had been supplied with by another operative. It was perfectly suited for the situation. Joshua crept as close to the window as he dared to, then shot 10 pictures in a matter of seconds. He then carefully folded up the camera and waved Schmulie to sit and wait.

"We'll have to wait a bit before we knock on his door. We caught him jerking off. That's a big thing to these people. We don't want to let on that we know what he was just doing," Joshua said.

"Good thing these people don't shake hands," Schmulie said only half joking.

"Yes, but he will take your ears in his hands as he kisses our cheeks."

"We should get extra pay for this."

"We can use these to persuade him to help us get in deeper when the time is right. But now is not the time. We'll know when things are right." Geller whispered.

Ten minutes later they were sharing tea with their friend Abu. It was obvious that he did not know they were looking in his window. Their instructions were to go as slowly as they needed to, but above all to make no mistakes.

They had no idea that Operation Purim Party rested squarely on the success of their mission. Neither could know how important this simple little set of pictures would become.

CHAPTER 6

MIND WAR
DESTROYING THEIR MORALE AND THE WILL TO FIGHT

BOTH PRESIDENT ANDREWS and Prime Minister Gross had copies of the psychological report on the best way to keep the average Muslim out of the war. They were the *fence sitters* the Islamists would need to wage a victorious world war and bring the world under Islamist rule. Andrews passed out copies to every man around the table.

The report was titled: "Keeping Muslim non combatants out of the war." A joint team of Israeli and American psychologists had written it 18 months earlier. Ethan Gross had commissioned the report, which was funded by the Israeli government and the American Jewish Foundation. American money also came from a group of retired military men and a few wealthy Jewish Americans who had become anxious about the rise of militant Islam. These Americans approached Israel because they could foresee the likelihood of both America and Israel engaging in a final *win and live or lose and die* shooting war with Mohammed Waleed's Islamists in the Middle East and around the world.

The psychologists did extensive research into what was written in the Qur'an about killing. They examined Haditha commentary on why some of the Qur'an seemed to contradict other parts of the Qur'an. They studied the *Verses of the Sword,* which are the suras or chapters of the Muslim holy book that seem to command Muslims to violently force their religion on infidels around the world. They concluded that adherent Muslims believe they are reading the literal word of God when they read the Qur'an. They came to the understanding that no adherent Muslim could deny the commands of the

Verses.

Consequently, the team came to the realization that it would be easy for the Islamists to convince non-religious Muslims that being a good Muslim meant being willing to kill and be killed in the name of Allah. They noted that while this situation was highly volatile, it was also filled with opportunities to use the Qur'an to the advantage of Israel and her Allies.

The executive summary of the report read as follows:

> The researchers looked at the psychological make up the Islamist and the non Islamist in both the Muslim controlled world and the non Muslim world. The similarities and differences were juxtaposed to get a 'work up' on which Muslims were likely to be, or likely to become, Islamist fanatics and which were not likely to take up a sword to force the world to yield to the virtues of Islam.
>
> The similarities between the average person in the Muslim world and the average non Muslim were examined. The study concluded the average Muslim who follows the Verses of the Sword, does so primarily out of fear of retaliation from Islamists who demand he do so.
>
> This is not to say or even imply that all or even most Muslims who become Islamists do so under duress. To the contrary, most are willing converts, though comparatively few in numbers.
>
> The point of this observation is that notwithstanding the small number of true Islamists in proportional terms to the larger worldwide Muslim population, their raw numbers are still very high. Extrapolation of available data suggests as many as 750 million Muslims may have emotional allegiances to the Islamist view of what is and is not true Islam.
>
> The research determined that the keys to keeping non combatant Muslims out of an all out war against Israel and her allies are: 1) to somehow show them what such a war would be like and 2) make them more afraid of the allies than of the Islamists. Neither of these choices would appear to be easy.

Two pronged approach

The approach to achieving these goals has to be two pronged. There should be an effort from a religious point of view and an equally powerful push from a secular view.

Religious approach

Popular media and penetrating radio waves must be used to undermine Muslim beliefs among those who are not religious, and merely nominally Muslim. Research shows that hundreds of millions of people who self identify, as Muslims, do not own a Qur'an and have never read the Qur'an.

Counterfeit Qur'ans

Counterfeit Qur'ans that do not include the dangerous Verses of the Sword chapters should be mass-produced and distributed worldwide. This would both frustrate recruitment into Islamist fighting units and busy our Islamist enemies with the work of countering the effects of these books. More than this, the very objections raised over these books would, by necessity, have to include a public acknowledgment of the missing chapters and force so called moderates to defend these violent chapters or remain silent. The Western media could be baited into asking questions about the missing verses that the Islamists have so far been able to keep a virtual secret

Mind War

This would force a worldwide discussion of the nature of the commandments in the Qur'an. The sunlight generated by such a controversy would greatly benefit our efforts at waging an effective *Mind War* against our enemies. At least some portion of the media might feel foolish at having been betrayed by their Muslim contacts who they would then see for the liars they have always been. While the vast number of media would still soldier on as *de facto* apologists for the enemy, their efforts might very well crumble under the weight of the public opinion tidal wave that could be generated by the remaining friends we have in the media both here and in Europe.

This table turning *Mind War* gambit would back the so called moderate Muslim community into a corner not even their media friends would be able to get them out of. It would force them to deal with a dilemma, which for them would be fraught with danger. Their hobson's choice would bring about their either having to protest that bogus counterfeit Qur'ans were being distributed, with all of the problems of 'sunlight' that would create for our enemies, or remain silent. Their silence on this issue could then be skillfully used as proof that the Qur'an does not in fact, require Muslims to murder non-Muslims in order to do Allah's will. It could be seen as a rejection of the Verses of the Sword interpretation of *Qur'anic* writings and make Islamists appear to be evil deceivers in the eyes of fence sitting non religious Muslims. Those neutral Muslims would then present a very real problem to our enemies.

If we can use this ploy to turn the, as of yet not 'Islamized' Muslims in America and Europe, and elsewhere against our enemies, such a development could become a tipping point in our eventual war with the Islamists. This could force Imams and other Muslim clerics in western countries to speak out against the murderous interpretations of the Verses or risk being identified as Islamists themselves. Following this course could force responsibility for terrorism on comfortable western Muslims who do not want to see themselves as supporting a terrorist religion. Once we can arrange this discomfort we can manipulate western Muslims to our advantage."

Inmates Sue After Prisons Ban Religious Books

America's implementation of the report's recommendations started with a bogus lawsuit brought by an FBI agent posing as a federal prison inmate. As the operation to distribute phony Qur'ans unfolded, it became clear that the best place to start would be in America's federal and state prisons. The plan called for a new heavy-handed policy on reading material in prisons, especially federal prisons. The FBI first ordered the Federal Bureau of Prisons (BOP) to order the removal of all Qur'ans from all prison libraries. The idea was to invite a civil liberties lawsuit, which would compel the United States government to immediately return the Qur'an to the prison bookshelves.

Within a month, the case of *El Mohammed vs. Federal Bureau of Prisons* was brought in a San Francesco Federal Court. The case was such a blatant violation El Mohammed's rights to the free practice of his religion that it was difficult for the United States Attorney's office to defend the action. For security purposes none of the U.S. Attorneys were told about the plan. The operation's planners made sure the case would be instituted in the United States Ninth Circuit Court of Appeals courthouse in San Francesco. That made secrecy even more important. Homeland Security had learned hard lessons about trusting the United States Attorney's Office in San Francesco in the past.

Within a few days after the trial started, everything was going as planned. Preliminary negotiations between the sides seemed to be moving in a predictable direction. The judge was about to order the government to restore the Qur'ans to federal prison libraries when there was an unexpected turn in the process. Just before the deal was finalized, the Attorneys General from California, Illinois, New York and Maryland submitted an *amicus curiae* brief to the court.

An *amicus curiae* brief is an application to a court asking it to consider the interests of a third party that will be influenced by the court's pending decision. In an overplay of their hand, America's civil libertarians demanded that the court hand down a sweepingly broad order instead of the narrow ruling that appeared to be coming. These guardians of civil rights demanded the Court compel the United

States government not only supply new Qur'ans to BOP prison libraries, but to every state prison across the country as well. The Attorney General and right wing talk shows complained loudly for a few days then the story went black.

The civil libertarians had helped the United States government switch the Qur'ans. The new Qur'ans were distributed by the Bridges of Peace Islamic Council (BOPIC) the government's front group established to carry out Mind War operations against the Islamists. The new "Qur'an" contained none of the Verses of the Sword that exhorted Islamists to commit violent acts of murder against the non-Islamist world.

Overnight the dynamic of having Qur'ans in prison libraries changed. It shifted from a terrorist recruitment tool for al Qaeda to a problem for every insincere effort to radicalize America's prisoners. The new converts to Islam knew nothing about the missing Verses of the Sword. The new holy books often confused them about Islam's true purposes and core beliefs when they read one thing and heard another from their Imams. Finding new terrorist zealots in America's prisons became increasingly more difficult.

It is widely recognized that the efforts of Radio Free Europe were a devastating weapon in America's ongoing efforts to end the psychological and physical enslavement of millions of people living in the Soviet Union behind the Iron Curtain.

For a relative pittance, America and her allies were able to capture the minds and hearts of the USSR's captives. This success can be duplicated by an aggressive program of attacking the comfortable detachment many western Muslims enjoy. We can use the airwaves to continually drive home our message.

Questions and doubts must be planted in the minds of the average European and American Muslim who has not yet been radicalized and is still living a secular lifestyle. Using popular media, purchased by our government if necessary, we must force these people to start thinking about how their world is not built on an existence of fighting and dying. We must clearly describe the reality of joining radical Islamists organizations.

The message must be very stark and totally accurate. We must talk about the problems of everyday life that will follow their entry into terrorist cells. We must talk about living on the run, having to always look over a shoulder before a simple meal even in a fast food restaurant. Our message must be aimed at Muslim mothers. They must be compelled to consider having their children live in travelling SUVs for the rest of their lives. We must ask these mothers what they will do when their children are sick while they are on the run. We must force them to envision what they will say and do as they strap a bomb onto their 12-year-old daughters and sons and send them off to die.

Each and every terrible choice that will be forced on those who try to bring down America, with Islamist terror, must be laid out and made easy to see. Conversely, the benefits of living in non-Islamist controlled countries must be clearly brought home to those who are potentially radicalized Islamists. The contrast between the two types of societies must be clearly highlighted.

The opportunities for advanced education and seeing their children maximize their potential must be enumerated and stressed. Asking the average American Muslim to remember why he/she came to America can be effective in warding off temptations to become members of Islamist terror groups. The basic goodness of the American people has to be outlined again and again.

The disadvantages of being forcibly dragged back to the seventh century have to be shown to those fence sitters who have not yet committed to life in a tent. Westernized Muslim women must be asked if they want to be forced to wear a hijab, the veil used to cover the face and body of Muslim women. We must explain to the women in *fence sitter* families that there is more to live for than to die for. We must point out to them the material benefits enjoyed by peaceful Muslims as opposed to the misery of living in an Islamist controlled village in the third world. We must ask these women to ponder what life is like in a patriarchal society. Western Muslim women must be reminded that in Islamist controlled countries, they are property and treated no differently than cows. In Islamist dominated countries women have no rights and their husbands have total life and death control of them. Western Muslim women must be reminded of these facts.

The truth about a Muslim husband's *right* to beat his wife, as well as arrange his children's marriages, must be explained. The horrors of honor killings have to be graphically depicted in our media campaign. *Fence sitting* Muslim women in western countries have to be made to ask themselves hard and brutally frank questions. Such as: Do they accept the possibility that if their teenage or college aged daughters are found to be having sexual relations outside of marriage, they could be murdered by a male family member? Do they realize that these killings are not even punishable offenses in many parts of the Islamist world?

These questions must be deeply planted into the Muslim psyche. As most people, Muslims living in the West are materialistic. If the differences between existing in the seventh century and living in a bountiful non-Muslim country are properly presented, great benefits can be derived from this campaign.

They can be swayed away from the hard and the short religious lives the Verses of the Sword offer. We must urge the average Muslim to ask why it is always his children being asked to *die for Allah* in suicidal plots, but the top leaders and their children are never suicide bombers. We must plant seeds of doubt about who really benefits from these deaths. We must make the average Muslim want to ask how a truly loving God could possibly order some of his children to murder other of children. We must hammer home that death is not a religious principle, but rather a sinister political and demonic plan.

USING MILITARY COURTS

In just the past three months, we have suffered eight car bombings in America. We have recently intercepted a shipment of parts meant to be used to build a tactical nuclear weapon. The FBI has arrested more high value targets in New York and Miami then ever before. While it is, of course, very important that we stop these attacks, we now need to maximize the benefits of these captures. To achieve this aim, we must immediately begin executing these conspirators. This is absolutely necessary to drive home the message of fear we want to project to the Muslim non-combatants living here already.

We have to keep them on the sidelines to minimize or avoid witnessing the appearance of violent fifth column of saboteurs attacking us on our own soil, while we are fighting Islamists around the world. Consequently, we must accelerate trials of terrorists in military courts that will not fall prey to the political pressures the Islamists, the media and the American left could put on civilian courts. In short we must fight terror with terror and make the *fence sitters* much more afraid of us than they are of the Islamists.

WORKING THE COUNTERFEIT QUR'AN PLOY

The counterfeit Qur'an ploy had already been put into operation by the time the battle of Qiryat Shemona was fought and Bridges of Peace Islamic Committee (BOPIC) went into action. In a finely coordinated effort, BOPIC mailed the American media the counterfeit Qur'ans. The media was vulnerable to this ploy because of its willful blindness to the dangers that an Islamist American population presented. Within days, the mass mailing of thousands of fake Qur'ans was complete and started to show results. They caused a great deal of disruption for those who wanted to bring down America and Israel.

Once the books were out and circulating, real Imams working for BOPIC, made phone calls to every possible media office demanding to be interviewed because they were so outraged by the phony Muslim holy books. The Imams said they wanted to challenge what they described as a foul and evil plot to disseminate false Qur'ans because the phony ones did no include certain verses and were, therefore an obscenity of the worst order most likely carried out by the

Jews. These Imams all had bona fide congregations and real credentials that could be verified.

Since they spoke like they were willing to go on camera and attack the distribution of the bogus Qur'ans as a Zionist American fascist scheme, none of their credentials were verified anyway.

The media swallowed every bit of the Imams stories, and helped them publish their complainants. The American media loved everything about the situation. To them, the Imams were another way to embarrass a president they were trying to destroy.

End of Report

President Andrews commented further on the report saying, "Of course the public knows about the car bombs, dozens of people have been killed by these sons-of-bitches, but they don't know about the nuclear weapon. Hell! We don't know about the damned nuclear weapons. We don't know if we got all of the parts, if they slipped any others in, we don't know if one of these could be detonated while we're here talking today. We've already had American blood running in our streets, they've hurt us and smacked us down on our asses. I don't think these people are just kidding with us. But it seems like some people, especially in the media and in Congress, think this is some kind of *Mouse That Roared* situation.

"I'll tell you boys this: I don't want to do any of this. This wasn't my plan, but I'll be damned if it isn't the dead on right thing to do now. Our friends in Israel have been fightin' this fight since 1948. Up to 9/11 it was easy for us to sit around and debate all of this. It wasn't our asses being blown up everyday. But all of that is in the past now. They are the experts in stayin' alive and they think this has to be done. I agree. I'd rather take this lesson from our friends in Israel than keep getting our noses rubbed in a lesson from these Islamists bastards. It's time for some violent confrontation. We're not waitin' for these bastards to finish off Israel. First that's not how the finest country God ever put on earth operates, but then, when they finish with Israel, we're next!"

Slamming his palm on the table, Andrews continued, "If we don't do this, there will come a day - maybe a long time from now, maybe next week, who knows - but that day is coming, when these people will be here chasing us through our own streets. Yes! This can happen. That's why we will join with the Israelis in this operation.

"One and only one actual operational plan will be put into work. All of us here in this room today, will refer to this plan among ourselves as Operation Sucker Punch. This will be just like a bar fight. I hope most of y'all, hell all of y'all, have been in a bar fight at least once in your life because we are about to get into the biggest damned bar fight you can imagine.

"For way too long we have been in something like a baseball game that we can't lose but somehow we are losin.' anyway. It's like we are the professional, world's best players. We have the best equipment, and the most experience; but just can't win this damn game! We aren't winning because these sons-a-bitches are playin' seventh century rules!

"They are threatening the umpires so's even when their pitcher throws one over the backstop, it's a strike. They run to first base with a sword swinging in front of them. They've threatened the scorekeeper so's he puts up our runs for their side. All the while the idiots on our left and our media are sittin' in the stands saying 'Wow these terrorist sure can play this game.'

"Well this losin' stops, now, here, today! From now on we're playing by their rules. We can't play them with 21st century rules and win, but we sure as hell can kick their asses back to their seventh century tents where they want to be. We can win and will win with the players we've got. And gentlemen, that's just what we're fixin' to do!"

CHAPTER 7

GETTING INVITED TO A HEZBOLLAH MEETING

THE MISSION TAKES SHAPE

WHEN THE TIME SEEMED RIGHT, Schmulie and Joshua asked Talib to take them to a Hezbollah meeting. "Brother, we burn with love for Allah and our sacred cause. We desire to join ourselves to those we know will strike at the Satan worshipping Jews. Won't you please take Abdul and me to meet the brothers who fight these filthy infidel dogs?" Geller asked Talib, over sips of tea in an open-air shop. Rabinowitz sat quietly, looking unconcerned according to their plans. "My brothers, how I wish I could bring you, this very moment, to those you speak of. All of us want the same things, but each of us has a job and not many of us are put here by Allah to be soldiers, in the real sense of what a soldier is." Talib answered. Seeing the puzzled expression on Geller's face, he continued.

"Yes, yes, yes," he said smiling, his eyes darting around the area. "Yes, we know the Holy Qur'an calls us all to be warriors for Allah, but brothers, we all know there is a big difference between 'wanting to be a soldier, with the full recognition that eventual death comes to those who follow a soldier's path,' and the rest of us," Talib said.

"But brother Abu, so many times you have spoken of your close relationship with those who we know want so dearly to die for Islam and live forever in paradise with Allah." Schmulie said, sensing he needed to get involved and pick up where Joshua seemed to be failing. This was no time to worry about hurt feelings. If one team member could not get the job done, the other had to pick up the fight.

Abu began to sweat and he fidgeted in his seat. He leaned forward and spoke very softly, "Of course I can be counted among our fighting brothers in Hezbollah, but I myself have no desire to die for Allah or anyone else."

"But why would you join those brave brothers if you feel this way? Is this not the cowardice we have been warned of? Is this not the conduct found only among the infidel?" Schmulie demanded.

"It is never hard to die, my young friends. People do so every day. The key to life is to make ones death such that it becomes an important contribution to our cause, to the love and worship of Allah. Praise be to His holy name."

Now all three were scanning the immediate area for prying eyes and ears; they all knew being discovered having such a conversation could mean certain death.

"I am not ready to die but you might be. Perhaps some day soon you will be judged worthy of dying a martyr's death for Allah. But now you are just two brothers in the streets. Hezbollah needs thinking men who can wage war ruthlessly but intelligently. You must wait your turn. You must study the sacred Qur'an and find the purpose Allah has for your existence before you can sit at table with the leaders of our sacred Jihad. I say this, because I believe that both of you have the intelligence for the tasks that must be done, but are lacking a certain maturity."

"Then why brother Abu, did you join Hezbollah if you feel these things and think these thoughts?" Geller asked.

"My brothers, this is a Hezbollah town. I pay my dues and attend just enough meetings to keep them from becoming suspicious of me, but not enough to lead them to want to send me on a mission. That way I can go about my business with no concerns for politics. For me to bring you to Hezbollah would send them a signal that I want to be an active player myself, which of course..." Abu answered dropping his eyes to the floor.

The team was stunned. Abu had just slammed the door on them and he was their only chance at being brought into Hezbollah by anyone. Over the following months, Team Nine settled into a routine mundane life as simple manual laborers. Changing occupations was Jacob's idea. In his plan, they could do the work without drawing attention to themselves or having to speak to too many people. It was a simple and effective cover. When they could, they spied on Hezbollah, but otherwise they lived a simple life of praying in the local mosque every Friday and going about their daily chores. While their stories were well constructed, they weren't really necessary. They soon realized they would have no trouble gathering information about what was going on inside Hezbollah. All the information they needed was easily available by hanging around the local Mosque and sipping tea in the shops in the town's marketplace. They made note of who the radicals were, while keeping a very low profile. Since their papers were expertly forged and well beyond detectable by anyone they could reasonably expect might challenge them, they easily moved through town without causing a ripple.

Rabinowitz and Geller's existence became: work, mosque, eat, sleep, then start over again the next day. They settled in, burrowing deeper and deeper into life as a Muslim man in the street. No one thought of them as anything but pious Muslims willing to do the things their religious convictions required. The reports they radioed back to Jacob were often bland, but that did not concern him. For months, neither the team nor Jacob knew the real purpose of their mission in Lebanon. He dutifully sent the reports up the chain of command and forced himself not to get too emotionally attached to Horowitz and Geller because, as all three of them understood, this was likely a suicide mission. For an old pro like Jacob, emotions were a luxury he knew he could not afford. He never allowed himself to give into the temptation to think of the team almost like sons.

On a Thursday morning Geller stopped at a dead drop before reporting for work. Under a stone marked with a scratch mark, Jacob had left them two envelopes. One contained a re-supply of cash, which was very much more than they had been receiving up to that point. The other held detailed instructions for their mission. Their orders could not have been clearer or any more important. Their mission was so sensitive, they were ordered to read the message then eat the paper it was written on.

THE MISSION TAKES SHAPE

The message started with a firm announcement, "The go signal is coming very soon. There must be no unnecessary communications." The instructions were to evaluate their progress toward fitting into everyday life. They were to consider whether or not anyone could be watching them or was in any way suspicious of them. They had to be sure they were properly embedded into life as average Muslim men in their new hometown, Bint Jubayl in Hezbollah controlled Lebanon. They also had to be sure they had blended into Friday afternoon worship services in the town's mosque and that they were no longer seen as strangers or newcomers in the Muslim house of worship. Jacob instructed them to contact him only if they were not sure of their acceptance into the local society or suspected that they were under surveillance.

"The go signal is coming very soon. There must be no unnecessary communications." Jacob's message repeated at its conclusion. He warned Geller and Rabinowitz to be ready to act immediately after Salatu-z-Zuhr, the Muslim mid-day prayers."

Without hesitation they agreed they were both properly embedded in the town and the mosque's congregation. They were certain they were now seen as pious Muslims who faithfully responded to each Friday's call to prayer. Since the only requirement to be a Muslim is to pledge faith in Allah and pray weekly in a mosque on Friday afternoons, Jacob had taught them the prayers they would need to know. Being accepted in the town mosque was up to them. Fitting in well was not difficult.

That Friday they were ready to go into action. Jacob's instructions told them to be alert for something they would easily recognize as their *go* sign. "What I am speaking about will enrage Muslims all over the world, so it will be the trigger for your mission. You are to attend services at the local mosque as you normally do. Once the moment is right, you will seize the opportunity to put our plan into action. May God help you and guide you as you follow your instructions and lead the Islamists in an attack on Qiryat Shemona."

The closing words of Jacob's message kept echoing in Geller's thoughts. "You are reminded to take no unnecessary chances with your lives, but frankly, as we have agreed, your grateful nation does not expect you to survive. I can give you only my prayers and a promise to honor your name for the rest of my life. I swear to you that when the time is right, I will speak to your families and tell them of your heroic sacrifice for Israel's freedom and safety. May God bless you and watch over you as you fulfill your mission. I know you understand the danger you are facing and you are driven by your love for our mother Israel."

At mid-day prayers, everyone in Bint Jubayl was talking about the reports of a video tape showing Israel's Prime Minister Ethan Gross, slandering the Holy Prophet Mohammed. The television and radio stations were running the reports, non-stop all morning. Even the Internet brought opportunities to see and hear this scandalous attack.

The story circulating throughout the Muslim world was that Gross made the offending statements in a private meeting that was secretly recorded by an Islamist spy working for the glory of Allah. The sound quality was very poor, but all indications were that it was authentic. The Muslim world believed it and that was all that counted. Of course it was authentic. Why should it not be? The Mossad produced the tape from an actual recording of Prime Minister Gross making the insulting slanders. Using the original video, Mossad technicians stepped on it and stressed its quality to a point at which those who wanted to believe it was genuine could easily do so, and those who wanted to argue it was a fake had ample room to argue in support of their point as well. The final package struck a perfect balance. It gave the Islamist zealots the spark the Mossad wanted them to get, yet still left much to dispute for the rest of the world. It gave Israel perfect *plausible deniability.*

It also gave Israel a chance to smoke out her enemies and test her friends. The world would not be able to hide its true feelings. Those who quickly joined in the condemnation would not be forgotten or forgiven. Forgetting and forgiving such slights is not in Jewish tradition. Gross was banking on Israel's friends standing by him and the rest acting as they always have at such times. It was all in the plan. Rabinowitz and Geller immediately recognized the importance of these reports. "That's it." Rabinowitz whispered as they walked to mid-day prayers.

"Yasher Koach" Geller whispered.

"Yes, may you have strength as well." Rabinowitz answered.

All over the world Muslim clergymen pounded their fists and shook with rage and disgust at the insults: "The filthy Jew, Gross and his defiling infidel band of Satan's helpers." The men in the congregations repeatedly smacked their own foreheads and chanted praises to Allah with tears running down their cheeks. The mosque where Team Nine was praying was no different. Rhythmic chants crackled throughout the assembled collection of Islamists and potential Islamists. Moans and cries of deep pain filled the room. For two hours they chanted without stop. The men worked themselves into a trance like state that slurred their speech and glazed their eyes. Even after months as Muslims, when the loudspeakers shook with the mournful whining call to prayer from the mosque's muezzin, or crier, it sent chills down the team's back.

Danger in the air tightened their stomachs. It took extreme concentration from the team to keep their composure and stay in the character of their cover story. They well understood that making even the smallest mistake in the recitation of their Friday afternoon prayers could lead to disaster and death. Ordinarily such a mistake is a deeply shameful action that would compel a Muslim to immediately leave his mosque in shame. But both operatives knew this was not an ordinary time. Both knew a mistake in their prayers today could lead to instant death and the failure of their mission.

The commotion would draw attention and cause a problem they could not easily explain away. Within minutes they would be literally ripped apart by a frenzied mob of radical Islamists looking to visit their vengeance upon anything or anyone within reach.

The team had all they could do to keep their waking state and maintain their self-control. They had a mission and they would not be deterred. Finally the frenzy reached a point of boil over. Without prompting from anyone, the throng spilled out to the streets of Bint Jubayl. Now was the time to test the Mossad's choice of Bint Jubayl. The value of this little town would have to show through or the Mossad's plan would fall apart. Months of planning had brought about its selection when Bint Jubayl's two main attributes were isolated: it was full of Sunni Muslims who would be prone to join the Islamists if properly agitated, and it is very near the Lebanon/Israeli border being just two miles from the Jewish settlement of Qiryat Shemona. The team's instructions were to join in any protest demonstrations over the insults against Islam. They were to get control of the biggest and most angry mob they could find, and urge it to charge into Israel to kill the people of Qiryat Shemona, which would be the closest Jews they could find.

Stirring up the men of Bint Jubayl was not a problem. Even as they walked to the mosque, the team had heard constant talk about the serious insults Israel's Prime Minister had spoken about the Prophet Mohammed in a supposedly secret meeting. That this was the signal was very clear. It was time to act. The team was to go into action. They both knew what was required of them. They knew their task was to ferment a killing frenzy among the Muslims in this small border town. They were intelligent young men who knew their actions would provide their country with a pretext for a retaliatory strike, but they did not yet know how big that strike would be. During prayer services in the mosque, they were secretly praying for the success of their mission and for their fellow Israelis who would soon be dead because of their mission. After mid-day prayers, the mosque was filled with tension and emotion.

Geller started a chant of *death to Israel, death to America!* The cries became rhythmic and intoxicating. Rabinowitz found it harder to yell *death* to his country and her strongest ally. It took him a moment to actually get the words out of his mouth. When the time seemed right, Geller carefully placed the pictures of Abu Talib masturbating on the floor and backed away. Less than one minute later someone picked them up and recognized Abu as a defiler. For the team it seemed like an hour.

The Imam found the pictures. "You swine!" he said pointing at a totally puzzled Abu Talib. Chants filled the air, "He must pay with his life for doing such a thing and bringing such pictures into this holy place."

"He must be killed to avenge this insult to Allah."

"Only blood can cleanse this stain."

"Grab him so we may rip his filthy body to pieces and cleanse the world of his memory."

"We must rip him to pieces with our own hands if we have to!" Geller yelled as he punched the hapless Talib's nose. The rest of the men set upon Talib and pulled his arms off his body.

The sudden brutality shocked the two agents. It brought home how dangerous their mission was. They watched in horror as Abu was dragged to the street still alive, kicking and screaming. In moments he was dead. Rabinowitz seized the moment. He climbed onto a car and started to chant "Death to Israel, death to America!" He did this for ten minutes hoping it would be someone else's idea to charge into Israel and kill the people of Qiryat Shemona just two miles away. He wanted this to come from someone other than himself. It was the last chance he would have to perfect a lie he could tell himself about his part in this terrible mission in his old age.

Finally the voice they were waiting for could be heard above the frenzied crowd. "We must go to the pig sty were the Jew infidel lives and kill him and all his live stock."

"That's close enough," Rabinowitz thought.

"Yes, that is the only way we can avenge the Holy Prophet's honor. We must bring jihad to those who would insult and defile Islam," someone screamed.

The team recognized the speaker. He was a member of the town's Hezbollah cell.

Having the responsibility of actually leading the charge to kill their own people weighed heavily on two Israeli college kids turned secret agents for love of country and her people. Nevertheless, they had a job to do and their mission came before their personal feelings. They joined in the screaming frenzy smacking their foreheads and screeching with savage rage. The Hezbollah then went into action. They started to hand out loaded AK 47s and amphetamines, a lethal combination from which there could be no safe return. Ten minutes later the mob was slipping on Talib's blood as it charged toward its revenge in Qiryat Shemona.

CHAPTER 8

MUSLIMS, THE WORLD OVER, EXPLODE WITH RAGE

MUSLIMS RIOTED ALL OVER THE WORLD. They burned cars and threw rocks at anything that even vaguely reminded them of the western world. In Rome, specially trained Italian Army units had to be air lifted, via helicopters, into the Vatican to protect the Pope and Catholic Church officials living and working with the Holy Father. Machine gun rounds rained down from the upper floors of buildings across the street from the tiny Catholic nation. In Paris, synagogues were firebombed. Throughout France, Jews were pulled from their cars, beaten to death and their bodies were either hacked to pieces or burned. The Louvre and Notre Dame Cathedral were ransacked. Crazed Islamists drove flaming cars into them and set fire to each. Before the French military could respond, thousands of French women, men and children were executed by shots to their heads. In many cases, the very young and the very old were dragged from their homes, screaming for their lives, and decapitated on French street corners.

In London, the railway stations became spontaneous slaughter pens. The Labour government had willfully blinded itself to the real dangers it faced from Islamists living among their own people. It had allowed itself to be cowered into political correctness. Consequently, there were no MI5 undercover officers in any of England's mosques or Muslim cultural centers.

The British had only a vague idea of how many dangerous Islamists were living in the United Kingdom or where they were concentrated. Their intelligence services had badly underestimated the number of Muslim Islamists they considered dangerous. Unarmed Bobbies were overwhelmed and beheaded in Muslin parts of London and all of England's cities and towns. Order was finally restored only after the British Army was brought in to patrol England's largest cities.

Israel was a different story. All over the country, IDF troops were on alert before the attack on Qiryat Shemona. With the world in turmoil, no one noticed how well Israel was able to handle the dozens of flare ups of Muslims living in Israel and the numerous attacks on its borders with Lebanon, Syria and Jordan. As far as the Mossad was concerned, it was actually *the more the better*. With more attacks to deal with, they reasoned, being unable to stop a human wave attack on one little town would draw no suspicion. With a large number of attacks from different angles, Israel would easily be able to plausibly say she was caught off guard at Qiryat Shemona.

The official story became: "We got to Qiryat Shemona as quickly as we could. We regret not being able to save all of our people, but we are proud of the swift retaliation we brought to bare upon the invaders."

CHAPTER 9

EARLY FRIDAY MORNING IN QIRYAT SHEMONA

AS THE SUN ROSE over Israel's frontier with Lebanon, Sergei Illnikov got out of bed gripped with feelings of fear and frustration. He had not slept well in two nights and the chances of his being able to sleep by staying in bed seemed remote at best. Illnikov was an immigrant to Israel. He had come from Minsk in Belarus, but years in his new country had done nothing to quell his constant suspicion of government. Over the past four days, he had watched in amazement as the IDF slowly withdrew its troops from the area around his little border town. In all his years in Israel, he had never seen this type of maneuver. By Thursday afternoon, he left his small bakery in his wife's hands, and walked around the town to see for himself and decide what was going on. Gnawing uneasiness filled his thoughts. They made his mind tingle with a mixture of fear and frustration.

By Thursday night, he had settled on his course of action. He would pack up his family and drive as far away as he could before stopping to consider his next move, "Something is wrong. They just don't pull out like this." Sergei told his wife. "Be ready to move out when I tell you to get the kids. I'll wait until after we get the orders finished ... then I'll take our money out of the bank. I hope I'm wrong. If I am, we can put the money back on Sunday and we'll have our Shabbat's orders done early. Let's see... but let's be ready."

By mid-day the radio and television shows were filled with reports about Prime Minister Gross and the secret recording. "This is not good. Their leaving and this happening didn't happen by coincidence. Nothing in government happens by coincidence." Sergei told his wife. "Be ready. I'm going to the bank now."

As Sergei waited in line he was stunned to see what looked to him like a swarm of ants moving a dust cloud toward the town. Just as he got to a teller's window, a town police officer threw open the door and yelled, "The Sunnis are coming, run for safety!"

The teller, a young man of about twenty, started toward the door when Sergei jumped over the counter and grabbed him. "Give me my money before you go! Or are you part of this coincidence too?"

The teller was totally dumbfound by the question, but he was smart enough to recognize that a threat from a crazy man, holding his arm, was more important than a threat from a crazy man still a mile away. He opened his draw and said: "Here take it all. Just don't hurt me?"

"Hurt you? I won't hurt you! I just want my money!"

"There it is. Take it," the young teller said over his shoulder as he broke free and ran for the door. Sergei stuffed his pockets full of bills, then had a better idea. He used his shirt as a sack and emptied all the draws. In thirty seconds he cleaned out the bank and had enough money to start over in a safer part of Israel or anywhere else, if suddenly, there was no Israel.

The swarm was at the edge of town when he saw it next. He had all he could do to get to his van and start for his bakery. Even before he got closer than a few blocks away from his store, Sergei realized what was happening. A crazed horde of Islamist fanatics was burning it and dragging his wife and three small children out into the street.

His oldest son was being strangled. An Islamist warrior had stuffed the boy's yarmulke into his mouth and was gouging his eyes out with one hand while choking him with the other. Sergei looked to the right of that scene and saw his wife being repeatedly punched in her face until only blood was visible and her features were gone. For a few seconds he was left stunned and frozen. Everything slowed down and he could no longer hear what was happening. It was not until he saw an attacker jumping up and down on his two year old daughter's head that Sergei was shocked into action. He grabbed a pistol from his glove compartment and killed the jumper with three shots to his head.

In the savage din of slaughter, no one recognized that he was firing back. Not even the attackers he was shooting seemed to notice they were being shot until they were dead. Sergei hit one in the chest three times before he realized his bullets were doing nothing to stop the man. Finally he had to put a shot into the wild man's head to finish him off. In just ninety seconds, his family and his way of life had been destroyed before his eyes. He sprung into action. Years of living in the Soviet Union had hardened and toughened him. Sergei went on the attack.

"If they would kill my family, I would kill each of them. As long as I have life I will fight and kill these bastards," Sergei screamed at the top of his lungs.

A small band of men from the town waved to him. "Come here. We will fight them together!"

Sergei ran to the group bellowing: "Gross! Gross, you bastard! You dirty bastard! You did this, Gross! You did this! Yes you did! Yes! Gross and his government lackeys left us unprotected! They wanted us to be the bait to fight these Arab bastards."

He turned to the crowd and yelled, "Please listen to me, I saw shit like this in Minsk!" When he turned back to confront the attackers Sergei Illnikov was shot in the forehead by Geller.

"*Talk like that can not be allowed. We can not let people realize this is a set up. He was right, but we, I* ...," Geller thought as he ran from the townsmen. Rabinowitz started to fire over the townsmen's heads and both of them chased the Israelis down an ally to safety. None of the town's people recognized they were being protected, but with no firearms and Sergei gone, they ran as fast as they could.

The carnage continued for fifteen minutes before the Israeli Defense Forces and Air Force swept in to the rescue. Helicopter gun ships carrying Special Forces troopers, hovered over the town. They were armed with Israel's latest urban combat assault rifle, the Tabor, as they repelled down to the streets to fight the Islamists attackers.

The IDF counter attack was a classic pincher maneuver with troops landing from the west and the south while gun ships hovered at the northern edge of town waiting for anyone trying to escape back into Lebanon. Moments after the helicopters were in place, three black SUVs burst through the dust and confusion heading for the safety of the Lebanon border. They were the Hezbollah leaders and had to be destroyed. They were the most important targets. If they escaped or were captured, they might be able to tell the real story of Qiryat Shemona and put an end to Operation Purim Party. The Mossad ordered that no prisoners be taken and the Air Marshall knew that was especially true for the leaders. Dead Hezbollah leaders could not contradict Israel's version of events; live ones could. The Air Force used its best air to surface missiles to achieve the most certain kill. There could be nothing left to chance. It was over in 45 seconds. All three vehicles were blown up and burned beyond any chance of anyone in them surviving. Again the ever-careful Mossad took no chances. A special kill squad was ordered to the burning wreckage and instructed to throw hand grenades at anyone who moved. No one did, but the hand grenades were thrown anyway.

The IDF instructed the surviving town's people to run to the South for protection and medical care. That cleared the streets of potential witnesses. The carnage and sheer brutality of the Islamists had their effect on the IDF's soldiers as they began to take in all that was happening. They went into their own killing frenzy. A nineteen-year-old private saw a crazed Islamist throw a little girl of about seven to the ground and with his foot on the child's chest, rip her left arm out of its socket. He saw the man laughing and screaming like a creature from hell as the child's blood spurted from the hole in her body. The young soldier fired ten rounds into the drug fortified madman before he could stop him. As the savagery of the battle swirled around him, the young soldier could hear nothing but the sound of the child's mother crying and asking "Why?"

The scene transfixed the young soldier. Soon he began to shake with rage. Before he realized what he was doing, he was smashing the attacker's face with the butt of his rifle. His rage locked him into a dangerous tunnel vision that kept him from seeing an Islamist attacker charging him from his right rear. With a single swing of a huge broad sword, the Muslim took the young soldiers head off. Almost instantly, he was then cut in half with fire from a hovering helicopter's fifty-caliber machine gun. Another IDF squad engaged a team of drug fueled Islamists in hand to hand fighting near City Hall. In a single action, five IDF soldiers and nine attacking Islamists were killed when one of the Muslims pulled the pin on a grenade that he picked off the dead body of a Special Forces Sergeant.

Three attackers staggered around dazed and bleeding after the explosion. They put their hands up and tried to surrender. Immediately, their bodies were pounded with .50 caliber machine gun fire.

They were slaughtered making their way toward a group of IDF soldiers. No one could say for sure that they were murdered. It was just the fog of war that killed them and orders from Mossad that no prisoners be taken.

There was no battle pulse. The Israelis were staggered and surprised by both the ferociousness and sharp intensity of the battle. Israel's toughest, most war-hardened veterans thought they knew what war was supposed to be like, but this was very different. They knew combat was an on-and-off process. Both sides fire; then duck for cover. Each side takes stock of its position; then resumes fighting based on regular evaluations of causalities, strength of numbers, available reinforcements, geographic position, supplies remaining and a variety of other factors. In conventional war neither side wants to lose more troops than necessary, but this battle was totally different. There was no battle pulse. Instead of an alternating cycle of engagement and disengagement, there was only engagement; non-stop, seemingly never-ending engagement. Everything was upside down. Engaging waves of enemy soldiers who were unafraid of death, and actually hoping to die, was not historically unknown, but the Israelis were not familiar with such warfare. Only in Mogadishu and a few other times since America's war with Japan had the world seen such die for your religion suicidal charges. In this fight, there were no stops. The Islamists kept charging machine gunners with antiquated AK47s, swords or their bare hands. The only pauses in the fighting came when every Islamist in a particular group had been cut down and left dead or dying on the town's dusty streets.

The actual combat was non-stop. There was no concern for survival among the Islamists. Fallen comrades on either side meant nothing to these men. Killing them demanded the full attention of the Israeli fighters. The Islamists' rage and drug induced frenzy blinded and deafened them to the realities around them. They came to die and did not want to fight according to western rules of war. They welcomed death. They wanted the death for themselves and the Israelis. In fact, they wanted the whole world to die. When the action began to slow down, the IDF realized it was losing people to a sniper pouring fire on them from a nearby rooftop. A Four-man squad was ordered to find the shooter. He was on a nearby roof popping in and out from behind a sign. The squad found a way up to the roof at the rear of the building opposite the shooter's line of sight. In perfect precision, they devised a plan then quickly climbed up after him. First they called for suppressing fire onto the sniper's position. That gave them the opening they needed to get close to him. He was hunkered down, waiting out the barrage, when they moved on him.

Carefully and quietly, they crept up to him ready to pounce. When he saw them, he immediately put his rifle down. Without being told to, he knitted his fingers together behind his head, and kicked his rifle away, again without being ordered to do so. The leader of the snatch team ordered him to put his hands down and stand at attention. It was obvious that the Israelis had arrested the man previously. He thought all he needed to do was follow their instructions to survive. In seconds, they had him in plastic handcuffs. It was a quick and bloodless snatch. When the sniper was in position, the leader took his picture.

It made the shooter start to laugh. He cursed them as weak cowards and spat at them. Seeing this, the leader checked the image of the picture, nodded and motioned the captive's soldiers into action.

An IDF soldier on the ground radioed them to say his position was taking heavy fire from another shooter who was positioned directly below them at a corner of the building. The snatch team pulled the sniper to the edge of the building and peeked down. Just as reported, there was a busy shooter firing away. The commander quickly ripped his captive's shirt pocket off, squeezed it into a ball and stuffed it into his mouth. He used two more plastic handcuffs and cinched the gag in the man's mouth. Two squad members then picked him up, pulled the pin on a grenade, stuffed it down his pants and threw him down on top of the street level shooter's head. Both of them were blown to a gooey mass of red jelly.

The battle raged for another forty minutes. The IDF's vice closed slowly, and methodically. As it got tighter, it got more deadly. The dead Muslims came in all sizes and skin colors. The Mossad agents running the operation were surprised and very pleased at the variety of groups the dead Islamists represented. Among the dead bodies, they found at least six with blue eyes and light brown hair.

The fighting was fierce, house-to-house and even room-to-room. Every effort was made to produce as many dead, but whole, bodies as they could gather up. The rules of engagement put Israel's soldiers in great danger because they could not simply blow up buildings from which they were receiving fire. The orders were, "No prisoners. Kill them all, but we want whole bodies. Whenever you can, bring whole bodies back to the command post." The fog of savage, non-stop battle raged through the streets of Qiryat Shemona. Muslims charged at the IDF troopers in waves screaming "Allahu Akbar!" (*God is greater than everything*). At one IDF machine gun position, the bodies piled up high enough to partially block off the gunner, but he kept firing and the Muslims kept coming and dying.

Schmulie Rabinowitz was killed first. An IDF sniper sent a round through his back slamming him face down onto a dusty street. He felt no pain. He never knew what hit him. He never knew a countryman shot him.

Joshua Geller tried to surrender. He had no idea about the rules of battle the IDF were fighting under. His Hebrew pleas for mercy only made him seem like a sneaky clever Muslim to the jittery IDF troops. He was burned to death with a Molotov cocktail thrown by a young soldier who found it and threw it at Geller, to see if one of these really works, which it did. Geller died in flaming agony.

Blood was everywhere. Body parts were everywhere. As their traditions demanded, the attackers had chopped off hands and feet, as well as heads. They had trapped families in vehicles and burned them to a crisp. Dead Jews jammed the doorways of the public buildings they tried to use as shelters. The Islamists hacked them to pieces with the large flat swords they swung with joy and excitement.

Killing infidels from a distance with AK 47s was not satisfying enough. They wanted to see the blood. They wanted to smell the fear and smell the death. They wanted to hear the crackle of children's bones as their swords crashed through frail little bodies. They wanted to jump up and down on the chests of their victims.

It was actually the attacker's preoccupation with inflicting painful death that saved many of the civilians who did survive. Torturing their victims, as they died, took time. Shooting them from a distance and moving on would have been much more efficient, but the Islamists were not looking for efficiency. They were looking for painful deaths because they believed Allah wanted them to not only kill infidels, but to punish them as they died.

Many of the first attackers killed by IDF sharpshooters, firing from arriving helicopters, were cut down as they went about gutting their prey. It was these first shots that told the IDF it had to switch to head shots to kill the Islamists because their targets were loaded up with amphetamines. At the onset of the battle, the IDF were putting round after round into the chest and center mass area of the attackers. In spite of these telling blows, they could not bring the Islamists down. Each shooter was placing what they call *keyholes* or tight patterns of round holes, no bigger than a quarter, into the bodies of their targets without any immediate tangible effect.

"This is not working. Use head shots on the ones that are immediately active. We have orders to try to preserve as much of their bodies as we can, but we can not watch while babies are being chopped to pieces." The operation's commander shouted over his radio, struggling to be heard above the confusing roar of battle.

The next voice heard over the IDF's radio was calm and firm. "This is the Mossad operations officer. I command you to keep shooting center mass and preserve the face of your target no matter what he is doing as you aim! Is that clear?" He could not hear the replies, even if we wanted to. The soldiers would do what soldiers in battle always do—they would kill their enemies. None of them would worry about preserving whole bodies of madmen who were slaughtering women and babies.

The Mossad man knew that, but he wanted to get his voice recorded giving that order so he could be cleared if anything went wrong. He understood Operation Purim Party down to the last detail.

As the attackers were repelled and slaughtered, the flow of action began to move at a more normal speed. Where adrenaline had slowed everything down to a surreal slowness during the height of the fighting and danger, the situation at last began to provide for normalized perceptions. Things began to move at normal speed and necessary numbness set into the minds of those who had to search the town and finish the job. The average human psyche is not designed to easily absorb scenes of dead and dying men and women let alone disemboweled children. For the IDF troopers, this mop up phase was a terrible part of their job. Although each man in the mop up squad was specially trained and selected for his strong psychological make up, many of them wept as they went about their business. Each could be counted on to do the jobs that had to be done, but each man was still a human being.

In this case, the job also included murdering Islamists who tried to surrender. Even the ones found wounded and helpless on the battlefield were shot.

The special unit knew the drill: no prisoners, just dead bodies and all kills made with body shots to preserve the faces for the Mossad team in which to work. As quickly as they could, teams of interrogators and photographers waded through the battlefield to question survivors and record the carnage. The variety of special weapons brought in by the IDF had done their job. Among them was the new Viper, a battle equipped robot that can fire a machine pistol and launch grenades. The useful little weapon can easily travel over stairs and slip smoothly into narrow alleys. There were at least seven Islamist gunmen killed by Vipers.

Vipers can also sniff out and defuse bombs and anti-troop traps as well. Their onboard television broadcasting capabilities made them excellent for the house-to-house fighting needed to secure the town. Once the shooting stopped, the IDF troops got back on their helicopters and left as fast as they could. Only the special Mossad officers and secret police personnel were allowed to remain for the after action's methodical search of the dead or dying. Body after body, of the attacking force, was dragged into the town's bank, which had been converted to serve as a Mossad headquarters. As the agents went about their business, single shots rang out from different directions. All of them knew what those single shots meant. They knew prisoners were being executed. But no one cared.

The Mossad agents busied themselves with finding documents on the attackers to prove that they were from a number of different targeted countries. The bodies were tied onto folding chairs and broomsticks were strapped to the torsos to make them stay upright. Then, using a new plastic surgery technique to open the eyes of the dead so they appear life like, each of the relatively intact bodies was photographed and then fingerprinted. The photographs and fingerprints were then expertly used to forge papers connecting the corpses to various Muslim countries on the Mossad's list. In cases where no actual bodies, with papers from targeted countries were found, these fake papers would serve the purpose of the mission. To the amazement and delight of the Mossad, the bodies included almost all of the countries on the must connect list anyway. That made the after action report easier to believe. The corpses were arranged in English alphabetic order by country name on the floor of the bank's basement. When the counts and recounts were finished, there were only three countries not represented among the corpses. The Mossad could not legitimately find corpses to connect to Libya, Iran or Sudan. Since these countries were the no-brainers as far as having connections to Hezbollah and world Islamist terror, manufacturing papers to prove a connection was a labor of love for the agents. They were able to choose from about ten fairly well preserved corpses, searching for unblemished faces of various shades with at least one hand from which to get fingerprints. The papers were ready for public release within two hours.

At every step of the way, Prime Minister Gross was kept closely informed. Almost immediately after Qiryat Shemona was secured, he was told there would be no problem tying at least one corpse to each of the targeted countries. The escaping SUVs may or may not have had Hezbollah organizers driving them, but there were certainly enough Islamists from all over the world to satisfy the needs of the operation. Most of the world skeptically cried foul, but that was to be expected. It was actually factored into the plan. The countries that attacked Israel for everything and anything had long since met the crying wolf saturation point. This time, they would be right to challenge Israeli's story, but, as planned, no one would listen anyway.

THE MOSSAD REPORTS

The message from the Mossad field office was simple. They sent their headquarters just a series of numbers from 1 to 27. To indicate which countries needed help in being represented, a # sign appeared instead of the number pre-assigned to mean a country. For instance, Somalia was assigned number 2, but since Somalia needed help the message read 1# 3-4-5 and so on. It was a simple but very effective way to transmit the information Ethan Gross would need to forward to Harlan Andrews. It said all countries on the mission's list were accounted for and the operation was a total success.

Gross could now call his friend and ally President Harlan Andrews. Andrews could now carry out the American part of the plan. The countries on the list had been selected because they were harboring terrorist training camps either with or without the permission and agreement of their governments. Over the years these countries had been repeatedly requested to do something about the camps. Each request fell flat. They were answered with claims that they were too weak militarily or flat denials that the camps even existed. Declaring war on these nations because their citizens "had taken part in an organized attack into Israel in which thousands of people had been killed," was the wedge that would compel them to respond to America's demands to clean out the camps.

After Washington's formal declaration of war had been made, each of them would be given an ultimatum. They could surrender immediately, which would then provide grounds under the international rules of war for the victorious Allies to legally enter upon their sovereign territory to search out and destroy the camps, or they could choose to stand and fight.

The genuine purpose of the declarations of war would be evident to the whole world. They would clearly say: "The camps will no longer be tolerated."

The countries on America's Operation Sucker Punch list included the following; Saudi Arabia, Bangladesh, Somalia, Afghanistan, Yemen, Oman,

Turkey, Morocco, Iran, Tunisia, Iraq, Libya, Jordan, Egypt, Indonesia, Nigeria, Sudan, United Arab Emirate, Albania, Croatia, Serbia, Slovenia, Syria, Lebanon, The Philippines, Ethiopia and Algeria.

Every nation that had sided with the *Verses of the Sword*, (the verses of the Qur'an that are used by Islamists as their grounds to murder non Islamists) and helped or harbored radical Islamists was represented among the dead bodies of those who had attacked and slaughtered the people of Qiryat Shemona. The most important exceptions to this rule were Saudi Arabia and the Philippines, both for different reasons.

The Philippines is a largely Roman Catholic country that was deemed to legitimately need help fighting the Abu Sayyaf, a group of Islamists operating on its southern islands. Abu Sayyaf means *bearer of the sword* and these terrorists lived up to their name. More than this, since the Philippines had cut her economic ties to the United States several years before, she had not fared well. A declaration of war would provide America the grounds to help out an old friend with rebuilding grants.

Saudi Arabia had always been an on again, off again friend to America and was therefore considered a special case but more an enemy than a friend in the final analysis. There would be more countries that time would prove should have been treated as special cases from the start, but that would have to wait for the moment.

The list of countries having soldiers killed in the attack on Qiryat Shemona was forwarded by Israel's Prime Minister Ethan Gross to American President Harlan Andrews.

PART TWO
READYING FOR WAR

CHAPTER 10

OPERATION SUCKER PUNCH
AMERICA'S RESPONSE

"I didn't come up here to be the president who was in office the day America died." -Harlan Andrews

SEVERAL MONTHS BEFORE QIRYAT SHEMONA there was a top-secret meeting held in an office in the White House. A small group of America's top military leaders met in the President's private residence to iron out the details of a serious special operation. There would be no Oval Office discussion of this plan. No one could be sure if all of the bugs placed in the Presidential Office by the former Chief Executive had been found and removed, so Harlan Andrews wanted to take no chances. Each man at the table knew he would be creating the details of the most secret, and potentially dangerous, operation ever carried out by the United States of America. President Harlan "Bud" Andrews knew he would have a better chance of getting his military advisors on board for this bold plan if he gave them everything he had in a face- to- face meeting. He had to level with them about the seriousness of the threat from the world's Islamists.

Andrews had to give them a way to see the grave nature of America's situation. They might have thought they knew, but Andrews realized they did not understand it as he did. In spite of his thirty-five years in public life, Bud Andrews was still a bit nervous. No president had ever been forced into taking the actions he was about to discuss with his top leaders. Before he could address them, he had to collect himself. He fumbled with his glasses and took a sip of water as he read over his notes. "Fellas, this is the real deal. We aren't just blowin' smoke to kick up the Defense budget. We got ourselves one hell of a tough and determined enemy in these Al Qaeda bastards. They seem to be everywhere and like some kinda fungus they keep growing."

"Oh they haven't been able to attack us again here on our own soil since September 11th, but it's just a matter of time before they break through our defenses and kill more of us. We can't let that happen, and as long as I'm in charge that's not going to happen. I didn't come up here to be the president who was in office the day America died. I'll be damned if I let that happen and I'm sure we're all on the same page on this so far."

The military advisors looked at each other in a combination of confusion and anticipation. "He couldn't have called us here to tell us we are in danger," each thought.

"I have no intention of being 'the first frog in the hot water,'" Andrews continued. "We're not gonna sit here and die from a million little paper cuts. These psychotic sons of bitches think they can just wait us out. Well they've got another thing coming, because our waiting and fretting is now over." The soldiers at the table perked up.

Harlan "Bud" Andrews

Harlan "Bud" Andrews was a small town lawyer from North Carolina when he was first elected to Congress where he spent years honing his political skills. Unlike his much younger original boss, President Peter Brownell, Andrews had served in the military. Although he never saw combat, he was a captain in an Army Intelligence Unit. He had been selected as a compromise from among a large group of contenders for Vice President four and a half years before. His main attribute was that nobody really knew him, even after all his years in Washington. The fact that the young, handsome Brownell would be elected was a foregone conclusion. Yet the pressure on him to select a running mate from among three men who represented the strongest factions of his party was so great that opting for someone not in any of these factions became the only sensible choice. Andrews was in The Oval Office for just the eight months since President Peter Brownell died from a heart attack on a suburban Washington gulf course, shortly after starting his second term.

"Bud" as he preferred being called, had been a virtual mystery man when he was selected. His low key, 'speak only when you have to' demeanor brought the Vice Presidency back to the days when the average American had no idea who the Vice President was, let alone where he came from. From the beginning of the first Brownell administration, Andrews spoke publicly only when he had to. After a year or so of this, the media stopped chasing him for quotes because getting anything useful out of him was too much trouble. They privately called him *Buttoned up Bud,* which he loved. He believed being known for being tight lipped in a place like Washington was a very valuable asset.

What he did not like being called, however, was *Bible Bud* which he knew was intended as a smug dismissal of his religious character. Harlan Andrews was known for taking out a bible during committee meetings. He never tried to force his beliefs on anyone, but he did enjoy watching some of his rabidly atheistic colleagues squirm when he quoted Scripture and suggested a Biblical solution to questions being considered by his committees. He learned to be weary of those who called him *Bible Bud* publicly, but never trusted those who called him that behind his back.

"Gentlemen what I'm handing you now is the most super-secret plan conceived by our nation since the Manhattan Project. It is a two-pronged plan of action. I want you to read this half of it first. You will have to crowd around it and look on because this document will never be copied and will be destroyed by me in front of you before we part company this morning," Andrews said, as he took the Israeli's plan from a locked diplomatic pouch. The top page read: "Warning! If you are not in the company of P.O.T.U.S. (The President of the United States) right now, you are not authorized to read this document. If this is the case, you are to immediately return this document to where you took possession of it and report this breach of security to your commanding officer forthwith."

The inside page started with an equally strong admonishment, "The contents of this document include instructions to perform certain actions that might violate your personal code of conduct. Your compliance with the plan described herein will require you to carry out duties and give orders not all of you will be ready to follow. Once you understand what you will be asked to do, if this is the case, stand down immediately and be recognized.

"You will be given ample opportunity to resign your position and retire from active military service immediately. Should you elect to stay no further options to divest yourself from these duties will be proffered. Your failure to follow these instructions in every way or your release of any information you are about to be given, will result in your summary execution by order of POTUS. If you have elected to stay in this room, you must place your initials on this page within 3 minutes. Now raise your hand to start the time clock.

A dead silence came over the room. The only sound was the *tick-tock* of a grandfather clock once owned by Teddy Roosevelt. Even the toughest men around the table had to think carefully about whether they wanted to turn the page. Slowly one after the other raised his hand until just one remained. At two minuets and fifty seconds the final hand went up. Now they were all *in*. They had all just given their futures and lives to this average looking country lawyer from little Pastureville, North Carolina.

The title page of the Israeli plan read "Operation Purim Party." As they read the details of this operation, the collective reaction was something between shock and admiration. Their eyes darted from side to side to gauge the reaction of those sitting to their left and right. It took a bit longer to cover the simple double spaced plan than it might have if they had been reading an order calling for a change of vendors for paper goods for the Pentagon. What they saw chilled them.

Finally an Air Force general stood up. "I can't go along with this. This isn't what being a soldier is about. Killing without just cause... No, I'm sorry. I know I should have backed out, but I'm backing out now. Let me off this train."

The president nodded and said, "I understand." He pressed a button. Seconds later two men dressed in dark business suits walked in. Their bearing was stiff, formal and obviously military. Each took one of the protesting general's arms, and they firmly guided him toward the door. It slammed with a thud that snapped the group into wrapped attention. The sound of the commotion from the next room told them the dissenter was not being handled gently. Andrews stared at the group with expressionless eyes.

"Good! They think I'm crazy and they're a little scared of me. Now I'll have to keep them more scared of me, then they are of Al Qaeda." Andrews thought.

Then he motioned them to look at him and not the door. "All of you come from families that are among the most wealthy and prominent in America. You joined the military service out of a sense of duty, duty to your country and duty to your families. I did as well.

"My family came to America in 1754. We were indentured servants. My people worked for people like yours. Both my mother and father's family fought in the Revolutionary War. In the War Between the States my father's great grandfather was with Lee at Gettysburg. My mother's brothers fought in the Ardennes Forest."

"And where is this leading us sir?" asked one of his generals as he stood up.

"Sit down general and let me finish!" Andrews snapped."My Uncle Evans wasn't but nineteen when he was killed at Iwo Jima and my older brother fought in Korea. This country has always treated my family very well.

"Over the years we have worked our way up the ladder and now here I am the President of the 'U-nited' States of America! I am the most powerful man on earth. And now the hopes and dreams of generations of my family and your families, in fact all American families, rest on what we do here today. I don't know about you, but I'm sick of the spineless cowards that seem to be swaying this country's mind away from believing we are the toughest damned fightin' force in the world, because we most certainly are! It's time for somebody to ram a broom stick up America's ass and get us standin' tall again," Andrews said sipping from a glass of Jack Daniels.

Immediately an Army General and a Marine Air Commander jumped to their feet in excitement.

"I understand. But this...this is beyond anything we have ever done," a voice protested.

"And your alternative is?" No one broke the silence.

"Just what I thought!" Andrews sniffed in contempt before he spoke.

"This thing has been building for fourteen hundred years. But it really got rolling when Isabella and Phillip kicked the Moors out of Spain in 1492. Spain was the last foothold the Islamists had in Europe. Let's look at the history. The Crusades that we, the white Christian Europeans fought were not expeditions of conquest. There only purpose was to push back the hordes of

Muslims who were killing Christians, and Jews for that matter, and taking over their countries. They were forcing Islam on Christians at the point of a sword. When the medieval knights went out to do battle with them it was to keep the hordes from overrunning Europe and killing every Christian they could find. As western technology advanced and with it, our ability to defend ourselves and kill invaders, the idea of charging into Christian infidel countries and converting them by the sword did not look so appealing.

"It has taken these bastards hundreds of years to get up the balls to come back after us, but they are ready now. Oh they're feelin' tough and strong now, but half of that is because we haven't whupped their asses for a while. Now they think they can come into western countries and start chopping off heads again just as they did before.

"They have wanted to do this for hundreds of years now. This has been their plan for seven hundred years gentlemen. I'm sure they think they are ready to take over the world, even us, but they aren't nearly tough enough. We constantly hear stupid talk from our enemies in the media that we have to learn to understand the Islamist Muslims so we can live in peace with them. These assholes don't have the slightest notion about what true Islamist theory is and always has been. To the Islamist Muslims it makes no difference if we send them Care packages or bomb them. They want to kill us anyway, not because of anything we have done or failed to do, but because of who we are and how we live our lives.

"They don't want to kill us because we are friends with Israel. It's more than that; way more. They don't really care who we are, or are not, friends with. They want to kill us because they believe God has told them to kill anybody who is not a Muslim. I'm personally sick to death of listenin' to jackasses sayin' otherwise. I'm sick of this bullshit about Islam being totally a religion of peace. The Islamists are a bunch of Muslims who mean us harm, period. They're not every Muslim, of course. But they are a segment of the Muslim world and denying that is a ticket to destruction. I know Christians don't convert by the sword. I know Jews don't and neither do any other religions convert by the sword. No, it's just these crazy bastards and I'm sick of their shit. I'm sick too of hearing 'Well if we kill the militant Islamists, that will turn the rest of the Muslim world against us and we can't kill them all.' My answer to that is: 'Well let's give that a try before we decide we can't do it,' because they sure as hell will be tryin' to kill us. I believe, if we do this right and make it quick and brutal we won't have to kill many of the fence sitters that aren't out there plottin' against us already.

"If we start by killing their fighters, you know, their tough guys, the ones that chop helpless people's heads off when the victim is tied up and caint move, we can get their attention. We can make them more scared of us than the guy next to 'em down at the town mosque.

"I believe when we run up the kill numbers into the hundreds of thousands or even millions, we'll begin to make progress and make our point about not even dreamin' about comin' after America. These people are cowards and we have to use that weakness against them."

A General asked, "How do we make progress by killing people even we know are not combatants?"

A voice said, "I'll take that one if it's okay with you Mr. President." Andrews nodded.

"We have been bombing and purposely killing so called non-combatants since the early days of World War II. We leveled city after city in Germany and Japan and..."

Another voice interrupted, "Yeah and we bombed some sense into their heads. Now they're on our side." A lusty laughter erupted. It was the kind of laughter that men who are in control and aware that they are about to do something great and important allow themselves.

"You bet your ass. Now as I was saying, we bombed the shit out of probably millions of civilians. Soft headed historians have always said those civilian bombings did nothing to end the war and in fact stiffened the resolve of the German and Japanese civilians to keep up the war. I say bullshit! I have never bought that line of crap. I just can't picture some guy named Hans Fuckin Shicklegrubber calling his job in Berlin and saying 'I'll be a little late this morning, the Americans bombed my house to rubble and killed my family, but as soon as I get the parts buried I'll be at my work station, whatever is left of it. Hail Hitler!'

"No, somehow I can't picture a conversation like that in Germany or Japan during the war. People don't get burned out and blown up then keep on working as usual. But if they do go into work they might make just a little mistake here or there, don't ya think?"

"That's all well and good but it still doesn't tell me how we decide where and whom to bomb now," the doubting voice said.

Andrews answered, "Okay, it's like this. Imagine you are the new principal at a really wild high school. Nobody has been able to get control of the place and most of the teachers have quit. You with me? Now imagine walking down the halls and stopping at a particularly crazy and out of control classroom.

"You look in and sure enough there is no teacher there, 'no controlling legal authority,' as that idiot Gore said. Now you walk in, grab the biggest boy and wail the tar out of him. When you're finished you say 'Okay partner you are now in charge of keeping these people quiet. If I have to come back here again, it'll be your ass I'll be kickin' to make my point. Do you understand?'

"We've got to grab these Islamist Muslim countries by the neck and let them know that from now on they will either cooperate with us and control their own people, or we will control 'em ourselves! It'll be kinda like the old song about, 'If ya can't be with the one ya love, love the one ya with.' Well this'll be 'If ya can't kick the ass of the one ya want, kick the ass of the one ya can.' What do y'all think will happen? The new principal will get control, that's what." Andrews said.

A doubtful voice said, "Congress will never give us permission to fight like that, and never let us place blame on countries we say are supporting ..."

"And what, general? And what? We can't fight a war the way it's supposed ta be fought because a bunch of cowards on the Hill won't let us? Well, you let me worry about Congress," Andrews shot back.

"But sir, how can we justify attacking these nations since none of them have actually attacked us?" asked another voice at the table.

"Part of the reason we're in this situation has been our concern for not taking innocent lives. I don't want to see innocent people killed anywhere, least of all innocent Americans. Gentlemen, we find ourselves down to an either or choice: Either some innocents in these countries get killed or some innocents in America will get killed. So if grabbing the leaders of these Muslim countries, shakin' 'em by the neck and makin' 'em help us stop these attacks gets us where we need to be...that's what I'll do. Let me tell y'all a little story," Andrews said.

"When I was a boy I lived in a small town. Everybody knew everybody. Well, at one point there was a series of vandalism incidents that had all the adults in town concerned. One Sunday mornin' somebody threw a lit pack of firecrackers in the Baptist Church we attended during services. Now we all had a good idea who did this, but we couldn't prove anything. My father and some other men went to the police, but they said they couldn't do anything because they couldn't prove anything.

"Then they went to the local middle school and had the principle hold an assembly to explain why these acts were wrong. That did nothing and the vandalism got worse. Somebody pulled the fire alarm in the old folk's home. An old man died from a heart attack during the confusion.

"After that, my father (and some other men) asked our local minister to preach a sermon on Sunday about responsibility. That did nothing. In fact somebody flattened the tires on the town's fire truck during the service. Everyone expected as much since the boys we all suspected, didn't come from a church goin' family. They came from families that lived in mobile homes on the edge of town.

"The dads in these families were drunken brothers who never harmed anybody but themselves. But they never amounted to much either and they were piss-poor fathers. Finally my dad and a few others went to the mobile homes to talk with the families. They got nowhere. 'We can't do anything with 'em either,' the families said. One of the drunks said he wasn't even involved since it was his step-son they were asking about. Dad thought he had delivered a message when he left. He was wrong. The next night the church was put on fire and burned to the ground. Again the police couldn't charge anybody because there were no witnesses and no evidence to use to arrest the boys. Finally my dad and my uncle went to the two houses and pummeled the fathers, whipped 'em good. They told them there would be more where that came from every time their sons did anything else out of line.

"My Dad told both of the fathers he would personally come back and whip the ass off both boys, then beat them up, too, if anything else happened. For good measure he walloped both of the fathers anyway before he left.

"I still remember my dad's words. He grabbed 'em by the neck and said, 'If you don't take care of them, I will; and when I finish with them I'm comin' after y'all again.' The two boys came to school the next day with black eyes and soon after that the families moved away. There were no more incidents after that. Do you get my meaning here?

"If we can't get our hands directly on these terrorist sons a bitches, we'll just have to say to the countries we know what they are up to. We'll have to tell them, 'You control 'em or we will, but you're not going to like the way we go about fixin' this problem.'

"We know many countries are harboring terrorist's camps. They are all over Lebanon. They are in Iran, Iraq, Sudan and Syria. They are recruiting the young from the mosques, from the slums and schools and street corners. They get their soldiers from wherever they can, even the universities, the madrassas...

"We know that Osama bin Ladin and Khalid Shaikh Mohammed have worked the poorest segments of the Arab world for bodies. They even have camps in England and the United States. They are in Southeast Asia and Saudi Arabia, all over...

"There is nothing good to come for the world in leaving these people alone. We have to go in and clean these rats' nests out because no one else will. They run Lebanon. The way they have run Lebanon into knots, the head of the country's Internal Security can not go after them in his own country. And the so-called Palestinian refugee camps in Lebanon are in fact terrorist training camps. We all know that. The guy actually needs permission from other Arab countries to go fix a problem on his own national soil!

"They draw their troops from the losers of the Muslim world. In their world, one that hasn't much going for it, they get the least of the least. Since Lebanon is so beat up, it is a perfect breeding ground for growing the type of fanatics that will blow themselves up for their cause.

"The Islamists have convinced themselves that their Qur'an allows blowing up innocent children and women. They believe God tells them to kill people before He'll be satisfied with them. They think the writings of seventh century Islamic scholars tells them to kill in God's name.. Our Intel folks tell me Hamas is all over the region. They are concentrated in out of the way camps training their fighters. They are in desert camps in Iran, and all over North Africa training with some very modern weaponry. I'm not interested in playing 'whack a mole' with them. I'm interested in killing them.

"I want them dead. Their weapons include katusa rockets like the ones they shoot into Israel when they can get away with it. That bastard Mohammed Waleed over in Iran is behind all of this. He wants to destroy Israel once and for all, and then come after us. I can't let that happen and I won't," Andrews paused to let his words sink in.

"I'd rather apologize later when we are free and safe, then ask permission now from people who 1) will leak our plan to the New York Times and the terrorists 2) demand hearings first and 3) not give us permission to go on offense away.

"No sir, I won't go to those pointy headed cowards in congress and ask for permission to save our country from the most dangerous enemy we have ever faced, no sir!"

Andrews set his reading glasses on the bridge of his small owl- like nose then placed a yellow legal pad on the table in front of him. His eyes swept the gathering. In his blunt plain speaking style he made eye contact with each man and said, "Standing by silently is no longer an option. We have to save America and the world and we can't wait much longer."

The Secretary of the Navy asked a question that had occurred to all of them. "Sir your list of countries makes perfect sense. But I have to ask you why we have not included Pakistan or Chechnya in the list of countries we will declare war on, even if just to use it as a pretense to enter their territory to hunt for the Islamists. Wouldn't Pakistan be a prime location for searching for Al Qaeda?"

"Of course the Vice President and I considered the Pakistan situation. We thought about it a lot before we arrived at our position. We decided to take a wait and see attitude on Pakistan. They have been helpful to us behind the scenes so far and we think they should be given an opportunity to jump one way or the other once we get rollin'. The Pakis will be too busy waitin' for India to attack them at first. Then when that doesn't happen its craziest bastards will identify themselves by running to the fight like all the rest of'em, only they'll have to travel through Afghanistan. We can catch up to them as they travel toward the fight. We don't want to really mess with the Pakis, they have their own bombs you know."

"Well then what about Chechnya? Why not declare war on Chechnya?"

Harlan Andrews smiled broadly before he spoke. "Well fellas, Chechnya is our little gift to the Russians. Once this war gets going, the Chechnyans, being the Islamists lunatics they are - well, they'll be itchin' to get into it. The closest target they will be able to find is Russia. The Chechynans hate the Russians to begin with so they will want to join the world wide Islamists in their attacks by going after them. So then what are the Russian bastards going to do? They will have to fight their own Islamists and in doing so they will have to take a side: our side. They won't be able to stand on the sidelines and watch.

"Leaving Chechnya off the list will actually insult them and *they* will nail Moscow onto our side whether those Commie bastards want to be with us or not! Besides, if we declared war against Chechnya, the Russians would be crying for us to come in and help them as they fought the Chechnyans. Well boys, the Russkees can fight their own battles and come on over to our side when they finish with the Chechynans. We'll be rootin' for 'em, of course."

"But sir that's a big risk, isn't it?" a general asked.

"Hell's fire, man! This whole bail ah hay is a risk. We cain't be worried about a little more risk here or there, now can we?"

When the question of the legality of wholesale round ups of citizens of the countries America would be at war with, was raised during the meeting, President Andrews had his aide pass out copies of a determination on the matter he had received from the Attorney General. Next he provided the council with copies of an order he had drawn up based on the determination.

> The Enemy Alien Act of 1798 is the foundation for the following Executive Order herein signed and promulgated by me on the

date so noted.

When war is declared or invasion threatened, all citizens of hostile, enemy combatant nations who are males at least ten years of age living in America whether legally or illegally, and not naturalized citizens, shall forthwith be liable to be apprehended, imprisoned and deported as may suit the exigencies for the United States Government in its ongoing efforts to protect America from such alien enemies.

Any alien citizen of the various nations we are now at war with, who is physically situated within the sovereign territory of the United States of America, is hereby immediately liable to be brought before any federal state or local court for examination and hearing. Upon a finding that said person is in fact a danger to public safety and peace, such declared enemy alien shall be restrained and imprisoned.

Upon orders from any duly authorized court, United States Marshals are hereby ordered to carry out any orders requiring the restraining and deportation of said enemy aliens, personally or through deputies. All able bodied federal employees are hereby ordered to report for service in the United States Marshal Service until further orders are issued to the contrary.

President John Adams signed this act on July 6, 1798. It is still in effect and has the same weight in law today as it did then. There was no further need to discuss the matter or worry about legalities.

FATHER TOM WESTOVER

After a short break, Andrews asked for an Air Force Lieutenant Colonel to come into the meeting room. He was Father Thomas Westover a Catholic Chaplin. "Father Tom" and Harlan Andrews had known each other for many years going back to the days when Westover was a young pastor in the first Catholic Parish in Andrews' hometown. As an elder of his own church, Bud Andrews was the first to welcome Father Westover and they became close friends.

"Father Westover has a brief historical overview to offer for your consideration. I think you'll find his words very enlightening." Andrews said as he offered the priest a warm welcoming handshake.

Father Westover got straight to his point. "For fourteen hundred years there has been a sub-division of Muslimism called the Islamist. Muslimism has some similarities to other religions in that its followers take and leave its menu of rules and regulations. Just as we in the Catholic Church have what we call 'Cafeteria Catholics': those who follow only the parts of Church law that they like and disregard the rest, the Muslims have 'Cafeteria Muslims.' Most Muslims are 'Cafeteria Muslims' who would not think of grabbing a sword and trying to kill us for being Christians or Jews or anything else.

"The Islamists have been trying to take over the world through conversion by the sword from their very earliest days. They are a patient people. They have little regard for the deaths and destruction they cause in order to get their way. What we are seeing today has happened before. 'We' of the western world have always been able to come out on top in our tangles with the Islamist world, but they will keep coming. They have used the same type of suicidal attacks, the kind that show no regard for human life, many times before.

"They have long memories and are always looking to avenge their defeats. Let me tell you about one of the Islamists' defeats and I'm sure you will recognize the parallels to our current situation. In 1565, the Knights of St. John won a big victory over the Islamists Turks at the siege of Malta. It was not the first time Islamists had tangled with Christians and come out on the short end. By that time the Islamists had been attempting to take over the Christian world for hundreds of years. They first spread out over the Holy Lands at the beginning of the 11th century. By 1095 the Pope, who was the leader of the Christian World in those days, put out a call to Christian knights throughout Europe. He commanded that all wars among European Christian countries stop. He ordered the knights of Europe to saddle up and do battle with the Islamists who had invaded the Holy Lands. The Crusades were a series of wars to recover the Holy Lands, and kick the Islamists out of them. The Holy Father also wanted to answer a plea for help from the Eastern Orthodox Church in her battle to stop the Islamist onslaught.

"When Pope Urban ordered these moves, Christendom was weak because of more than three hundred years of fighting the Islamists. So by no means was a Christian European victory a sure thing. Urban reasoned that attacking the Islamists was better than waiting for their next attack on Christian Europe. Even then he knew that taking the initiative was the best course of action when you are facing these beasts of hell.

"While Urban's move itself was not a success, it ultimately set the stage for a later very important victory. In response to the collapse of that Crusade, the Knights of St. John stepped forward at the battle of Malta. The way this battle unfolded is quite instructive for our purposes today.

"Those Knights fought their way into outposts in the Holy Lands and became a standing garrison to keep the Islamists in check. They were strong and skilled fighters who carried lethal weapons, effective armor and their own strong religious fervor. That made them tough guys who were feared and hated by the Islamists. Finally because of the sheer number of enemies and their own supply problems, the Knights were driven away from the Holy Lands. They then took up camp on the island of Rhodes and continued to fight them by sea.

"The Knights were so successful that in a very unusual concession, Sulieman the great Islamist warrior chief agreed to spare their lives if they would just leave Rhodes and get out of the way. That got them to move again. This time they ended up on Malta. It wasn't long before Sulieman came to regret having spared the Knights. In order to take Rome, he first had to conquer Malta. It was only a short sail to nearby Sicily and would serve well as a staging point to attack Europe. When the battle for Malta took shape in May of 1565, there were only about five hundred Knights to fight off Sulieman's forty thousand troops.

"The Knights commander was a man named Jean La Valette, who was seventy years old. He had not liked surrendering at Rhodes and as a former slave of the Islamists he was determined to fight to the death rather than become a slave again. He knew Europe had no inclination to come to his aid."

"Sounds familiar, doesn't it? Well, as the Islamist sharks circled, he called his men to pray with him and he declared they would be victorious because God would protect them.

"The Islamists approached the Knight's fort from the South and used Janissaries, men who had started life as Christians but were being forced to fight for Sulieman and his Islamists Turks. On that day Sulieman's army was the most powerful in the world. The Knights braced for the fight and sent civilians to every hiding place they could find.

"For almost four months, the battle raged. At one point, the Islamists were pounced on by a small group of Knights on horseback. This was a big win for us. We killed hundreds of them in a short bloody fight."

The Commandant of the Marine Corps said what others were thinking. "Father this is a great history lesson, but how does it connect to where we are today?"

"Well when the Islamist Turks finally shattered the fort's gates and charged in for the kill, they realized they made a big mistake. The Knights had allowed them into a trap. They ambushed them from above and slaughter them. After taking a terrific beating the Islamists began to pull back. Finally Sulieman decided that it was not 'Allah's will' that they win the battle. After four months they gave up. A small number of tough and determined Christian Knights had denied the Islamists a foothold on Malta.

"The valor and fighting skills of the Knights of St. John saved Christian Europe and kept the Islamists at bay for about a hundred years. Had they not won the battle of Malta, the history of the western world would look nothing like it does today. Yet it was only after the danger was past that the Europeans sent reinforcements to Malta.

"Doesn't this all sound so familiar? Aren't we living this all over again today? To the Islamists this might just as well be 1565 or sometime in the seventh century. They won't stop. They believe that dying in an effort to murder us will get them into heaven. Please act and act soon. The whole world needs America. You are today's Knights of St. John and Israel is our Malta."

When father Westover finished, there was little left to say. The room was now unified in its support for Operation Sucker Punch.

"Thank you Father, you have given us a clearer picture of who our enemy is and how to approach a battle with him. I will have to ask you to stay until after the completion of our meeting. You understand." Andrews said as he clasped his old friend's hand.

DR. AWAD KHAN

Andrews pushed a button on his desk and a few seconds later a dark skinned man of about thirty-five walked into the room.

"This is Dr. Awad Khan. Father Westover has given us an historic overview of the Islamist's view of the world now Dr. Khan will pick up where he left off with a description of life in Islamist controlled countries today. He has some chilling information to give us. Dr. Khan is a convert from Islam to Christianity. He grew up in the culture we are going to have to fight and defeat. He knows our enemies because he was one of them. He and his family fled Egypt because they were marked for death after they left Islam."

"Dr. Khan please tell us what you know of the people we have to defeat." Khan was obviously the genuine article. Even with a Brooks Brother's suit and wingtips he looked like he should be selling baskets on a Cairo street. His deeply copper complexion and chiseled features made him look as foreign to the American eye as he really was. Khan nodded a greeting to each man at the table and in surprisingly easy to understand British sounding English, started his report.

"Today my name is Awad Khan. It is not the name I was born with, but it the name I will use for the rest of my life. Let me explain. I am here today to warn you, warn the whole world about what the evil Islamists are planning for you.

"Make no mistake about the Islamist brand of Islam. It is not a religion of peace. The only peace they wish for is the peace they dream of having when the whole world recognizes their's as the one true religion, or those who refuse to submit to them are dead or their slaves. Let me say this very clearly: The Islamists want you dead. They want to convert you, enslave you or kill you. Their drive to kill all those who do not believe in their version of God as Allah comes directly out of their interpretation of their bible the Qur'an.

"I know this because I was indoctrinated into the Society of 'The Muslim Brotherhood' as a very young child in my native Egypt. I was a 'baby soldier' in their 'Army of God.'

"They pumped me full of hatred for Israel, American and anything western, and when they thought I needed it, they drugged me. This started when I was five years old, because my parents believed in their vicious hateful doctrines. By the time I was twelve the Brotherhood had begun to sense that I was fervent enough to train me as a suicide martyr.

"When I was thirteen I was deemed ready to become one of their holy martyrs. On the day I was to blow myself up on a bus loaded with Christian tourists in Cairo, I was discovered and arrested. Because I was so young the court took pity on me after I lied and told them I had just been recruited to do this act, the week before. They sent me to a prison block that housed foreigners charged with 'plotting to disrupt the peace of Egypt,' or some such other rubbish. It was their way of detaining foreigners they did not like for a while until they agreed to leave the country upon their release. The fact that they would be able to eventually leave alive took most of the heat away from the matter. The foreigner's country would not push too hard because they could claim credit for saving his life when in fact he was never actually marked for death, just deportation. That way everyone was happy. There were very few Egyptians or other Arabs in my cell block. I was initially sentenced to two years when they slammed the door behind me. When my family protested my innocence, the prison authorities laughed at their lies and gave me an extra year.

"I was in a cell with an American Christian missionary. He had been sent to prison for being a 'trouble making hooligan,' a phrase the authorities borrowed from the Soviets during the days when they were trying to bring Egypt under their control. The man's name was Reverend Wayne Thompson. He was from Lexington Kentucky. During my first night alone in a cell with him, I tried to smother him with a pillow. The American fighting men at the table tensed at his admission. He was a big powerful man and easily stopped me. Then he demanded to know why I would try such a thing.

"In my childish mind I believed that since I could not blow myself up and kill infidels, and I was not yet physically strong enough to kill him, I would follow the Qur'an's teaching for such a situation and make him believe I would not try to kill him again. Of course I intended to kill Reverend Thompson, as soon I was strong enough. Nevertheless, being a good Islamist, I decided to try to convert him to Islam to follow the Qur'an and be fair to him.

Father Westover smiled at that part of Khan's story.

Continuing, Khan said, "I started our conversation that night, sure that the power of Islam was stronger than anything a foreign infidel could counter my words with because I had the truth with me and he didn't.

"Over the course of that night and the many days and nights we spent alone talking about our religions Reverend Thompson opened my eyes to Jesus Christ. He showed me that the demands for murder and torture and enslavement found in the Islamist interpretation of the Qur'an could never be the commands of a just and truly loving God.

"At the end of my imprisonment I was sure I could no longer be a Muslim, let alone an Islamist. I was grateful for my ability to speak English so I could hear the Good News of our Lord and Savior Jesus Christ. I was also sure that I had a big problem because when it comes to getting out, Islamist cells are like a gang rather than a religion. You do not become a former Islamist and live. Because you are seen as someone who was presented with the truth and threw it aside, you are seen as the worst kind of traitor to God, your faith, family and community. Anyone who kills a convert from Islam is a hero in the Islamist world.

"When I was released, I was stunned to be told that my entire family had been killed when my sister had tried on her explosive martyr's vest and accidentally set it off. It was a clean sweep. Every close relative I had was gathered in our house on Faransa Street to celebrate my sister's coming martyrdom and entry into heaven. I didn't even have a place to sleep. After the explosion the government went nuts. They flattened every house on my street trying to contain the Brotherhood, whom they knew was involved in what happened.

"After a week without being contacted by anyone from the Brotherhood, I began to piece together why they were not trying to find me. They had recently lost their own top commanders and the new guys thought the party was for me to celebrate my release. They thought I was dead. With that turn of luck, I changed my name and stayed away from the radical mosques I knew they went to. I went through the motions of practicing Islam, but by then I was a Christian in my heart.

"The winds of change blew against the Brotherhood and their power was checked by succeeding Egyptian governments. Awad Khan is the name of a schoolmate whom I knew had died when we were around ten, so I knew it was safe to call myself by that name. I first used it officially when I entered university. I worked very hard and kept working very hard until I was finally awarded a PH.D in Engineering. I married a Lebanese classmate, who was also a secret Christian and when a job opened in England we jumped at it. One night, before we left for London, as I was leaving a Christian Church meeting at a friend's home, I was stopped and challenged by a Brotherhood thug who remembered me. I protested that I was not the teenager he once knew to be an Islamists, but I realized he did not believe me when I observed him following me. I did not go home, but rather I doubled back behind him through a small ally way I was familiar with from my boyhood. He became the one and only person I have ever killed. After that I could not take a chance with the lives of my wife and children. The next week after hiding the whole time, we slipped out of the country and landed in London."

Someone asked the question on everyone's mind: "How did you get here?"

"That is a very highly classified secret and in anticipation of your question, President Andrews instructed me to point out that the answer can come only on a 'need to know' basis and leave it at that. I will therefore leave it at that," Khan answered with a nervous smile. Please if there are no more questions, let me now continue."

Motioning with his hands, Andrews said, "Please continue."

"The Islamist version of the Qur'an is very clear about its commands to murder those who do not believe in Islam. They believe in the validity of the ninth chapter of the Qur'an, known as *Verses of the Sword.*

"Chapter nine verse twenty-nine commands 'Fight against those who are not Muslims.' To them, this verse is to be understood as '... kill every non believer you can lay hands upon.' To the true peaceful Muslim this verse is to be understood as a command to stand up for Islam when it is under critical attack. The Isamist mindset is very clear. They believe in 'Mushrikun' as the

Qur'an's command that infidels must either convert die or become slaves to the Muslims. Chapter five verse thirty-three commands Muslims are commanded: '...those who do mischief – cut off their hands and feet and crucify them.' Mischief, by Islamist definition is resisting the political and religious will of Islam. And make no mistake about Islam it is a political, as well as a religious, system of world government under their domination. The vast majority of Muslims believe 'mischief' is standard criminal activity.

"Please let me remind you gentlemen, I am not saying that all Muslims want to kill all non Muslims. I am saying that while the Qur'an can be interpreted as commanding this unrelenting violence, just a small but very dangerous minority of Muslims who call themselves Islamists, see it that way.

"Most Muslims do not follow such interpretations of their religion. Just as the Christian religions have those who pick and choose the rules they want to follow, Islam has 'pickers and choosers' as well."

When Dr. Khan said this everyone in the room smiled and looked at Father Westover.

"Dr. Khan they are smiling because I covered the same area using the same analogy about 'Cafeteria Catholics.'"

"Great minds think alike, as they say, Father," Dr. Khan said with a widening smile. "Let me continue. The vast majority of Muslims are not Islamists. But with a billion and a half Muslims world wide, if only 5% are Islamists, we could be facing 750 million crazed people who would do anything to kill one of us.

"Force-feeding Muslims with the hateful interpretations of the Qur'an is how they can get their believers to commit suicide, which is forbidden by the Qur'an. They tell these deluded fools that their mission is killing infidels and that their own death is accidental or incidental to the accomplishment of their goal of murder. As long as they die while trying to spread Islam's message of peace they will be welcomed into Paradise."

"In the Hadiths, which are commentaries on the meaning of the Qur'an, Jihad's traditional meaning is a military effort. This much is true. The more common meaning to non- religious Muslims is a struggle for personal achievement. But the Islamists are always talking about war when they say 'jihad.'

They are never talking about touchy feeling pop culture stuff. To the Islamists, jihad still has the thousand-year-old meaning; it is never a struggle for personal fulfillment as the useful idiots in the western media and the willfully blind Left in your country and mine want us to believe.

"The confusion about the meaning of the word has been almost wholly manufactured by the Western media. 'Jihad' is most frequently used as a term of personal struggle by all but the Islamists. When they talk about 'jihad' they mean war. This is no different from Hitler's Mein Kampf, except that he and *his* thugs made no pretense about their intentions. Right now, it is my understanding that there are more suicide bombers than there are bombs to put on their bodies. This is a double edge sword that offers some good news. Yes, there is now a dangerous number of these people out there who are willing to kill themselves to kill us, but it is also true that we must be doing something right to keep the number of their attacks down as we have.

"This condition also offers a solid point of evidence that if we can find the bomb makers and there laboratories we can enjoy still greater success against these attacks."

A gravel voiced general said: "They recruit in our prisons. They get criminals who see themselves as useless and unimportant to begin with."

Khan responded, "Believe me this is not so unusual elsewhere. Remember the shoe bomber was recruited in a UK prison. The Qur'an does not promote a genuine sense of morality that we of the west can relate to. Chapter nine verse twenty commands '...fight against Jews and Christians until you win and subdue them.' While the vast majority of Muslims interpret this to mean a struggle of economic proportions, the Islamists seize this language as support for the plans to murder people.

"Consider: our Old Testament calls for the stoning of adulterers, but we do not follow that rule and have not for centuries. In verse five of Chapter nine which remember; are the Verses of the Sword. It says '... kill non believers wherever you find them, ambush them, lay siege to them especially converts from Islam...' To the average Muslim that commandment is a relic of centuries past, but to the Islamist, that's means me. It is like your Mafia criminal mob. Once you are in you can never get out," Khan said with a slight smile and a nod.

"The Islamists believe they are extending a privilege to non believers when they force them to convert to Islam. To them, there are only Islamists and those condemned to hell. They believe that, as persons who had the truth and have thrown it away, non-observant Muslims will be sent to a special place in hell.

"Your western media and intelligentsia, as well as your liberal, socialist politicians, are seen as useful idiots by the Islamists. To them, these people are easy to lie to and use as shields when those who do understand the truth shine a light on them. Indeed as you will recall, there was even a group of deluded fools who went to Iraq to actually act as human shields for the Islamists who are in reality their mortal enemies. There must have been some hardy laughs in the teahouses of Baghdad over that display of Western foolishness. All of this is amusing to our enemies, but it is merely a sideshow.

"Understand this, nothing matters to these people but getting back the lands that they took by force and were eventually forced off of themselves. If for one moment you doubt that this current situation is a continuation of a never-ending movement to retake the old Islamist Empire consider this. As recently as the second half of the 17th century they pretty much had their way as they surged across Europe on their way to world domination.

"Then as now, with a largely secular Europe, it took the Christians years to gather themselves for a counter attack. It was only when the Islamists brought a siege to Vienna, that a Christian army under the command of the King of Poland, gathered the strength to kick them out and drive them back to the Middle East. The date of that battle was September 11, 1683. Yes September 11th! Bin Ladin picked September 11, 2001, as a rallying point to move Islamist jihadis to a frenzy of hate and a thirst for revenge over the massive defeat they suffered centuries ago.That defeat led to hundreds of years of their subjugation by the West. So they most certainly can be pushed back down their holes and kept there for hundreds of years at a time. But doing so is never easy.

"They have laid low for three hundred years after the last beating they took. We can beat them back down a hole again if you just have the will to get the job done. To the Islamists, this is all about getting their empire back and history is just like yesterday to them. When you hear about the Palestinians wanting to kill Jews and take their land, you can now understand that they will never, ever agree to accept some portion of the old 'Trans Jordan' which was the land originally marked out for them. To do so would be to abandon the Jihad to recover the part of the old Islamist Empire that is now Israel.

"So yes they want Jews dead because they are Jews, but even more so they want Jews dead to get their land. This is why there have not been an inordinate number of attacks on Jewish organizations in Europe where it would be very easy to carry out an attack. They would not want to, as they see it, 'waste an effort on European Jews.'

"You can not negotiate with the Islamist. They lie as well and as frequently as the Communists because they have the same goals of world domination. So anyone who says we can talk away our differences with the Islamist world is either ignorant or a liar.

"This is another bit of good news. As I said, not every Muslim believes he is commanded to kill people in the name of Allah. If somehow the average non-militant Muslim can be shown the true nature of what the Islamists stands for we may be able to peel him away or at least keep him on the fence.

"We may be able to convince him to stay out of the coming fight. We can not waste time arguing with idiots who see no threat of violence from the Islamists. We can never have anything but war with these Islamists. They do not want peace."

Almost all of the members of the gathering thought similar thoughts. "We? Coming to fight? Who is this guy? How much has Andrews told him?"

"In stark terms, to the Islamist a truce is a way of fooling an enemy. It is a sucker's play. Their word 'Hudna' which means, 'truce' is always merely a ploy. Imagine being in a boxing match and after five rounds your opponent calls for a 'truce' not surrender, but a 'truce.' You are clearly beating him, but now he calls for a 'truce' and the idiot referee, who is like the Western media says, 'Yes we will now stop for a half hour.' When the fight starts again both of you are equally rested and your opponent now knows what works against you and knocks you out. That is the situation the Islamists try to bring about by a truce. It is only when they are losing that they want a truce.

"Truce! What a joke!" Khan said in a firm determined voice. "They are also smart enough to know when to stop pressing. If they had not stopped during the 19th century they would have been destroyed. Before the days of political correctness and cable television and with nothing to restrain them, the British and the French would have killed most of the worlds Islamists and no one in the West would have even known it. Gentlemen, the Islamist culture is a coiled snake. It is ready to strike. Standing by and waiting for its bite is not an option. Doing nothing is not an option. Hoping for peace is not a strategy. America has an important advantage of distance and power. But even here the Islamists are busy working against you. They have taken over certain areas using politics and your media to pound their opposition into submission. Many Muslim organizations across America have been completely subverted by Islamists and they are gaining strength and support from the useful idiot core.

"But to America's advantage, Europe will be the first to fall. For the most part, the lights have gone out in Western Europe and it is five minutes before midnight. And be very well assured gentlemen, Europe will fall and America will stand alone. There is no unity to the European Union. They have sold out on religion and sovereignty. There is no central core of values those snobbish fools can gather around and defend, and they will suffer greatly because of it. When the snake strikes Europe, he will hit squarely in her heart and all but kill her. Let me close with this quote from Winston Churchill on the Islamists although he uses a different term. Way back in 1899, the very wise Mr. Churchill wrote this in his book 'The River War.'

"'How dreadful are the curses which Mohammedanism lays on its votaries! Besides the fanatical frenzy, which is as dangerous in a man as hydrophobia (rabies) in a dog, there is this fearful fatalistic apathy. The effects are apparent in many countries. Improvident habits, slovenly systems of agriculture, sluggish methods of commerce, and insecurity of property exist wherever the followers of the Prophet rule or live.

"'A degraded sensualism deprives this life of its grace and refinement;

the next of its dignity and sanctity. The fact that in Mohammedan law every woman must belong to some man as his absolute property - either as a child, a wife, or a concubine - must delay the final extinction of slavery until the faith of Islam has ceased to be a great power among men... Individual Moslems may show splendid qualities. Thousands become the brave and loyal soldiers of the Queen; all know how to die; but the influence of the religion paralyses the social development of those who follow it. No stronger retrograde force exists in the world. Far from being moribund, Mohammedanism is a militant and proselytizing faith.

"'It has already spread throughout Central Africa, raising fearless warriors at every step; and were it not that Christianity is sheltered in the strong arms of science - the science against which it had vainly struggled - the civilization of modern Europe might fall, as fell the civilization of ancient Rome.'"

"Sir Winston was right a hundred years ago about the nature of Islamist practice. He said it well, the Islamists produce nothing. You can not go to a shop and pick up an item made in some Islamist controlled country. Their only product is hate avarice and violence against people whose only offense is that they do not believe in the same God they believe in.

"Yes the vast majority of Muslims wish to live in peace, but these people and their numbers are not really the issue. The issue is that we hear very little about Islamists Muslims and very much about the vast majority of non Islamist Muslims. This is a clever trap they have used to employ the western media's help to ensnare us in a web of lies. They want you to be fooled into thinking that we should treat all Muslims, Islamist and non Islamist alike. The differences between the two peoples are the issue, very much the issue. It's the Islamist that we must fear and we must fight. It is the Islamists who love to hear this foolish obfuscating talk about the 'peaceful Muslim.' The so-called 'peaceful Muslim' is no more germane to this problem than the sands of the deserts are to America's cities. The so-called peaceful Muslims are a big part of America's problem with the Islamists. Their refusal to speak out, whether from fear or from secret approval of the Islamists, is the only important thing in this question.

"When this 'peaceful majority' of Muslims allows the Islamists to attach themselves to them and enjoy the protective covering of being among them, they must be called just as guilty as the Islamists they are helping to protect. No, they don't actively murder and terrorize innocent people, but certainly they add to the problems of the freedom-loving world. Every so-called 'peaceful Muslim' is a potential Islamist. Every one of them who is silent out of fear can be made more fearful but of us instead of the thugs like Mohammed Waleed. If they can be threatened or cajoled into siding with our enemies, they can be threatened into supporting us.

"So sadly, every Muslim must be suspect and should be considered an enemy until proven otherwise. This is why threatening them out of action before the Islamists can threaten them into action must be an essential part of your plan. Do not be swayed by talk of the 'peaceful Muslim' gentlemen, they are a genuine part of the part."

The Commandant of the Marine Corps asked, "Are you saying we have to watch our back with every single Muslim living in American? That seems like what you're saying and I just wonder how that position can help us navigate through this situation."

Dr. Khan answered, "Let me try explaining it this way: while it is true that there are not many Islamists in the Muslim world, it is also true that many Muslims who otherwise have no stomach for following the edicts of the Verses of the Sword, draw a vicarious thrill from hearing about Islamists attacks on the West."

In a significant, but subtle move, Khan stood up and began to pace around the room as he continued. He subconsciously projected an air of power to himself and a subordinate posture to his listeners. "Here in America, you have a similar condition in the support enjoyed by the Irish Republican Army in certain Irish American quarters. Irish Americans, who even work as law enforcement officials, will sometimes knowingly and gladly help the IRA raise money they know will go to buying weapons for killing British soldiers. Very few of these people would even consider leaving their comfortable homes in Rockland County New York to join the IRA as a soldier. No, that goes beyond their fantasies. To the contrary raising money and secretly cheering on the IRA murderers is enough for them.

"This is not, of course, to say that every Irish American who contributes to a charity putatively dedicated to helping violence orphaned children in Belfast knowingly supports terrorists. I say this to point out that the common thread of cheering on those willing to carry out one's secretly held beliefs is a function of human nature and we must not blind ourselves to the larger picture. We must remain cognizant of the fact that we are fighting a tough enemy, but also that his followers do not include every single person whose life is guided by the principles of the Holy Qur'an."

"Gentlemen I sincerely hope my presentation today has been enlightening. I gave it in hopes that it will help move America to the kind of action that needs to be taken. Thank you." The question had hit a deeply seated nerve in Khan's psyche. It had forced him to once again confront the question of whose side he was on. He had assumed that being introduced to the counsel, as the personal guest of President Andrews would have been enough to answer questions of his loyalty before they were asked. A man like Dr. Awad Khan does not feel sorry for himself, nor does he let bruised sensibilities stop him from completing a mission. He had come too far for that.

Andrews thanked him and showed him and Father Westover to the door. A voice asked President Andrews, "Have you formulated a battle plan yet sir?"

"Not down to the last detail, but I do think we ought to use the fact that the media traitors have convinced these stupid bastards that we won't fight because we can't fight. That bunch has these fellas convinced that we can't take it and all they really need is transportation to come here to make us their slaves after killing most of us. Operation Sucker Punch will set these people straight. I believe God has called this great country of our's to save the world from these savages. The Jews as the original Chosen People and America as His strongest Christian country, have to get this done.

"Christians and Jews having their heads cut off by wild eyed devils from the desert can't be God's plan and it isn't."

The gravel voiced general said, "Sir you have no idea how we have waited for a Commander In Chief who wanted to fight an all out war to win. You're damned right we can win and we will win. They want to live in a tent in the

Seventh century? I say fine let's help them."

Another general spoke, "I'm sick of hearing the word 'jihad.' They want a fuckin' 'Jihad?' They have no idea of the American Jihad we'll give 'em. When we get finished with these people they'll wish they never heard the word Jihad! Jihad, my ass! I'll push some buttons myself!"

"My thoughts about this plan exactly sir."

Another voice said, "The big bad terrorists actually believe they can wait until they are ready to attack us. Well that's not happening. We're going to slam this whole situation into 'fast forward.' They won't be expecting us to even fight, let alone sucker punch them. The Western media has them totally full of themselves. Now we use that against them," Andrews said, now more of a cheerleader at a pep rally than a commanding officer at a White House top-level conference. "We'll need a statement to keep the media chasing the wrong hound," Andrews said. "We'll need to say something like: 'we will be calling for an emergency session of the United Nations Security Council.'

"That will buy us enough time to get things ready when the time comes and gentlemen it is coming soon. We will also arrest and detain anybody we think is acting like an enemy or actin' for our enemies. FDR's internment camps will look like Boy Scout cook outs when we get rolling, I'll tell y'all that! Yes the New York media and the television people should absolutely be kept "in the loop" so we can use them to pump out the disinformation we'll need."

"That bunch up in New York is so smug they will actually believe we are being stupid enough to tell them our plans so they can turn right around and tell Osama what we're up to. When we finish with these bastards we should finally start prosecuting some of the media for the leaks they have used against us all these years," a gravel voice said.

Andrews added: "Yes and we'll use one of them, that Congressman from Michigan, as a 'diplomatic conduit.' You know the one I'm talkin' about. We'll just make believe we don't know he's been giving them our secrets. That way we can always know exactly where he is. When the time is right we'll arrest him and throw his ass in tent city too."

A voice said, "Keep your enemies close..."

"... but your friends closer," another finished.

"Right!" another general added.

Are You A Terrorist?

Andrews continued: "And one other thing, for the past two years, in anticipation of the situation we are in today, our Intel people have been posing as pollsters and talking to suspected Islamists here in America. I'm happy to report the project, code-named: 'Tell us who you are' but called 'Are you a terrorist?' around here has helped us compile an accurate list of thousands of young men who have Islamist leanings. Getting them to talk to us was easy. We had agents posing as pollsters working for Bridges of Peace, our front group. They just knocked on their doors and asked them questions. The idiots told us what we needed to know.

"In some cases just the thought of a group like Bridges of Peace made them so angry they were easily manipulated into truthfully telling us who they were and what they would be willing to do to destroy America. They actually believe that Americans are not smart enough to pull a trick like this. Some of them said things like 'You're not from the FBI are you?' while they laughed and said things like 'If you turn me in I'll have to get one of the Jew ACLU lawyers to defend me.'

"So we know at least some of the potential Islamist out there and we'll snatch them up when we need to. I'm sure glad those boys believe in America's system of justice and freedom of speech." After he spoke, Andrews recognized a general that had not yet spoken. "General it looks like you have something to add. Take the floor, please."

The quiet general stood and spoke, "I have studied these Islamists. I know something about what they think the Qur'an tells them to do and think, so I can add something on them. They are a very deceitful people and they are this way because they believe their bible tells them to be this way. Ironically they have instructions for the very situation we find ourselves in right now. They call being forced to do either of two evils, and selecting the lesser, 'wajib.'

"While lying is supposed to be a grave sin in Islam, they believe it is permitted under the Qur'an to lie to infidels. We will not be able to rely on anything we hear from these people. Once we start hunting them down they will lie as a weapon against us. They consider any Muslim who kills infidels as innocent of any crime, so lying to us to protect these murderers is a normal natural thing for these people. They make Gypsies look like Mother Teresa. I'm not saying that every Muslim buys into this "lie and protect murderers" theory, but the ones who do will be dangerous enemies.

"The Islamists fancy themselves as being 'lovers of justice and moderation.' Like the Jews, however, their idea of justice is 'an eye for an eye.' The Jews say, 'If you are kind to the cruel, you are cruel to the kind.' The Islamists say something like 'Tears for the opposed bring swords for the oppressors.'

"To them, love of fellow 'believers' automatically means hatred of infidel non believers because they are enemies of Allah. Their religious beliefs compel them to action. When they come across non-believers, they consider them enemies of God and they therefore feel compelled to kill us. To them, there is no such thing as escaping punishment for violation of Islamic law."

"So you agree with Dr. Khan pretty much straight down the line?" The Air Force General asked.

"Yes. I am saying he is right about everything he said and we really needed to hear what he just told us. But I'll add this: Once we start down this path there will be no turning back. We'll have to sit on their heads and be ready to start killing them again on short notice from now until we either kill them all or they kill us all. We have to make sure they finally get the message that we're not going to sit around and wait to be beheaded."

CHAPTER 11

PLANNING A PURIM PARTY

ONE SATURDAY AFTERNOON as Ethan Gross was considering the operation that would become "Operation Purim Party" he watched a televised speech by Mohammed Waleed. He was restating his wish for the end of Israel followed by the forced resettlement of Jews back to Europe or even *Alaska, if the Great Satan would have them.* For Israel's Prime Minister, Ethan Gross these words were a final confirmation of Waleed's real intentions. They also changed his assessment of Waleed's religious fervor. Early on Gross had considered Waleed a captive of his nation's radical clerics. He thought they were pushing him to his end-of-the-world war with Israel, America and the whole world. That speech changed the Israeli leader's opinion of which side was pushing and which was being pushed in Iran. At that moment, Gross suddenly drew a different meaning from Waleed's words.

"He is pushing the Imams! He is the crazy one over there! It's him. The son of a bitch! It's him!" came to his mind as he watched the speech with Hebrew subtitles. He had not actually watched Waleed perform before. He had always read the Iranian's speeches or had someone tell him what was said. Now looking at Waleed's eyes as he spoke convinced Gross that his words had to be taken very seriously. When he railed against the 'Zionist pigs and the evil Andrews,' it was time to move to the highest level of alert for Washington and Jerusalem. The Iranian madman's words were still more chilling because he used radio and short-wave channels to make the address instead of only television. That told Gross his enemy's words were not just bluster to get a response from the

West. It said he was being sincere in his threats.

Eighteen months before the first nuclear missiles struck, the Israelis met to plan a party for their good friend Mohammed Waleed

"Fast forwarding, that's what we are actually doing. The Mossad has done its job well." These were the only thoughts that came to Prime Minister Ethan Gross as he paged through the thick folder on his desk.

Smoke from his cigarette slowly rose to the ceiling of the deep underground bunker Gross and three of his closest aides used to insure complete secrecy as they went about planning Operation Purim Party. Retreating to the depths of the bunker for the planning sessions was his idea. Aside from the security it would offer, he thought it would help impress upon all concerned the seriousness of what they had to plan.

They all realized that moving to the bunker when the operation had been launched would serve other purposes as well. More than safeguarding Israel's top leaders from physical attack, the insolated location would also keep Gross and his staff from having to see and deal with ordinary Israelis. Since the decision to use Israeli citizens, as bait to start a war Gross hoped would annihilate the Islamists, was irreversible, nothing positive for the nation could come from Israel's command high coming face to face with the bait. Gross knew that having to order the certain death of some of his own countrymen would be a lot easier if he could avoid meeting them.

Making eye-to-eye contact with them and their children was something Gross dreaded. As the plan took shape something deep within his soul wished he would never have to leave the bunker, or that this would all go away. Looking at the grim faces of his inner circle, and their somber silence, brought Gross a deeper dread and sadness. It took all of the concentration he could muster to do his duty. The plan, however ugly, was the only way to protect his country's future generations. It was Operation Purim Party or the destruction of the Jewish race as he saw it.

WHEN THE AWFUL DAY FINALLY CAME

For eighteen months the weight of the terrible consequences of Operation Purim Party had pressed down on Gross and his advisors. Now it was time to explain their plan to his entire governing council. Ethan Gross had assembled them so they would know what was coming before the rest of the nation. He did not convene them to ask for their approval or permission. He wanted to prepare them for the truth he fully expected to have to face one day. He was going to give the *go* sign first and worry about his cabinet later.

The room was uncomfortably warm, even by Israeli standards. Although everyone wore casual clothes, all of them were sweating. No one wore the type of dress high officials in America would wear to a meeting with the president. The burden of dealing with the issue for discussion pushed down on Gross almost like G force would. As an old Fighter pilot he thought of the *G force,* he dreaded during his training. His thoughts seemed to actually compress him as he started to speak. Time had run out. Before Gross spoke, the grumbling of the hot and puzzled collection of politicians filled the room. They demanded to know why they had been summoned to this 'dungeon,' as they called the bunker.

As Gross rose to speak, his normally strong baritone voice was grainy and uneven.

"My friends as Jews we have always had to struggle for our very survival. This is a part of being who we are. Centuries of being the targets wherever we lived, has honed our sense of danger and survival skills. To shrink away from the plan I am about to outline would be to deny the five thousand years of history we have as a people. Each Jew knows this, but not all of us have had the courage to come to Israel or stay here in the conditions of our world today.

"Because of our courage and our willingness to step forward, we are the keepers of the Jewish flame. The heart and soul of the Jewish people has been entrusted to us. We hold millennia of Jewish tradition in our hands. Jews around the world know what we are facing.

"Of course some Jews are not with us. To those Jews I should like to say: make no mistake about our situation and our resolve. If we fail, if we are destroyed here in Israel, our enemies will not be satisfied until every Jew in the world is dead. Should we fail; every Jew in the world is next and instinctively all Jews should know this."

"What plan are you talking about?"

"Why have I not heard of this so called plan of yours before?"

"Who made this plan with you? Anyone?"

"Please, quiet! Let him speak already?"

"We have to act."

Gross took control, "Please let me speak and please listen before you speak. No one in Israel's history has ever had to carry out a plan such as the one I will be talking about, but we have to act. Mohammed Waleed has just issued us his warning. According to their logic and tradition they need only to warn us before they come to kill so they can act with moral decency. I believe he is deadly serious about his intentions. I have received a communiqué passed along by the Swiss in which he warns us and references our past military actions against his people. The fact that this note was not made public makes it clear this bastard is serious and has now locked himself into the Islamist proscribed preparations for war. He has morally cleared his soul to commit murder for his God.

"What these Islamic monsters want is to kill us all. What Waleed lives for is to carry out and finish what Hitler started. He and his people think that this time they can get it right and really kill every last Jew. Well I can tell you, there will not be another Holocaust. There will be no new gas chambers, no Jews heads chopped off, no trains to death camps.

"But each of you knows this. What you don't know is how we are planning to stop them." As he spoke his voice got stronger and louder. Gross dropped the Mossad report on the table and spoke in a stronger, more deliberate voice.

"I have here a very sobering report from the Mossad. It tells us the Iranians have just about figured out the final steps to putting together their nuclear bomb. That bomb ladies and gentlemen has always been intended for use against Israel. They think we will stand by trying to set up 'peace talks' while they ready themselves for the attack, but they are very mistaken.

"Thanks to the wise leadership of my predecessor, we have not waited for America or anyone else to come to our defense. We are coming to our own defense. The time for talk is gone. It is only action that will save us now. We can no longer do our silly little dance with the Americans over what we should do, what we would like to do or what they will allow us to do. We have our own plan."

"The current President of the United States Mr. Harlan Andrews is the first American president with balls since Ronald Reagan. We could not let this chance go by even if we did not have the proof on the Iranians."

Gross was talking about America's maddening habit of supporting his nation one day, than turning cool towards Israel the next. It had frustrated Israel's efforts to preemptively strike her enemies for decades. Now there were no more tomorrows left. America and the West and Israel were in the Mohammed Waleed's cross hairs. Now Israel's Mossad, the best intelligence service in the world, had put the last feather on the scale and proved the Iranians were looking for a chance to wipe Israel out.

This time things would finally be different. Where Israel's biggest worries always were about America's reaction to any move they made, now America was a full partner in Israel's plans. Both nations would act together in the boldest military plan in modern times.

Gross explained Operation Purim Party to his cabinet. They were shocked into total silence as he told them what it entailed, what he expected to be the immediate results and where it would take Israel. The numbers of dead he told them he anticipated were lower than he actually believed.

Nevertheless, he was brutally truthful about every other detail including that he fully expected that Operation Purim Party would bring about a nuclear attack that he was confident the IAF could stop. He was careful not to mention the name of the town.

Many of his cabinet members got up and started to leave. They were forcibly returned to their seats by beefy Mossad agents on hand for just such a possibility. Gross continued, "The so called international community can kiss my *tuches* if they do not like Purim Party and so can any of you who want to join them! There is no way we can sustain ourselves in a war of attrition. We are only a handful compared to the millions of Arabs and Billions of Muslims. Surprise is our most powerful weapon. We fought reactive wars up to now, but we can not win without surprise this time." When he finished speaking he could sense he was beginning to win some of them over, but getting a roomful of Jews to agree on anything, let alone something like starting a war was not easy. He wanted their support. He did not need their support, but it would go better for everyone if they were all behind the operation. Gross took a letter from his breast pocket and set his reading glasses on his nose.

"A Chief Rabbi sent me his thoughts. Let me read you a bit of it.

> "Everyday we are being bombed from the Arab's Kassam rockets on our small towns on the border with the Palestinians. Our people children, women old people are dying and being maimed by these creatures of darkness. We can not worry any longer from the fear of killing Arabs who would be living near the sites from where they are sending these rockets to kill Jews. We have the weapons to make them stop. I urge that you now to act. It is the moral thing to do to save your own people from unjust attacks. You must not be kind to the cruel. You must, this day, be a moral man and be kind to the innocent. Never again my dear Gross, never again!"

"He went on to plead with me to destroy these sites with everything we have, even nuclear weapons. What this tells me is that the religious community is with us and since they are so influential we can count on the rest to back us too."

The men and women sitting around the table knew they had to use the threat of a new Holocaust to move their people to accepting a preemptive war. In Israel, mentioning the Holocaust is the emotional electric charge that moves people. For modern day Jews, it embodies and evokes emotions many of them never experience under any other circumstances. Even ordinarily 'live and let live' Jews find themselves moved to fury at the thought of grandparents shoved into ovens and burned alive. Using the ultimate Jewish emotional "hot button" could not be done lightly. The group debated it back and forth in the type of give and take largely unknown to non-Jews. The language got hot. Voices ranged up to threatening tones and fists slammed on the table. Gross could only watch. He could only hope that his side, the one in favor of using the Holocaust to illustrate the urgent nature of their situation, would win out.

Of course the final decision would be his, but having everyone else on board would make selling the idea very much easier.

When the arguing dwindled down and the combatants seemed spent enough, Gross spoke: "The characterization of the present threat as a new Holocaust is not an exaggeration. These bastards will throw us in an oven unless we kill them first."

"We will use the image of the Holocaust and dissenters be damned. That's it. This discussion is closed. I appreciate everyone's thoughts, but if you felt 'no' you have now been over ruled. Now, I expect you will do your duty to Israel and the world. Is that clear?" Gross asked rhetorically then spoke in rapid fire fashion.

"The Iranians have said they will never bend to the world's demands to end their nuclear development. UN sanctions have led nowhere and will lead nowhere. The UN hates us as much as Waleed does. At least he is honest about it."

"The UN would be just as glad to see Iran nuke us with their first bomb. They think we should sit and watch the Iranians enrich uranium and smile when they tell us it is for making electricity to run their televisions."

"Let the rest of the world believe them, they are not living next door to the enemy. The rest of the world is not close enough to these animals to smell them. I think Iran is lying. It is in their Qur'an to lie to non-Muslims. As my mother in law always says 'An honest Islamist is like a unicorn, both are just figments of the imagination.' They speak blasphemies. Their clergy use their weekly sermons to lie to the world and scream kill the Jews." Everyone at the table nodded in agreement. As Jews they loved a good argument, but as leaders and protectors of the world's Jews they understood that the issue had been settled. Gross had won them over.

The Defense Minister spoke next.

"Yes, we all now understand we will be starting a preemptive war against the Iranians, but let us consider what else will happen once we push our button."

Gross replied, "Once we push our button we will probably have to be at war with maybe as many as two dozen Muslim countries. Remember there will be no subterfuge about why we are acting and whom we are acting against."

Gross asked his Defense Minister to further explain the plan from his viewpoint. "We will be making war against people because they are either Islamists – and we will have no trouble picking them out because they will go crazy ... or they will be potential Islamists we will not be able recognize right away, and that will be the hard part. I know we will be killing hundreds of thousands maybe millions of innocent people without any mans of knowing one from the other, simple Muslim from Islamist bastard. I know that when we kill our way through the pile, we will finally get to a point where we will be killing just the bad ones, the ones with their stupid jihad shit. Eventually at some point things will level out and we will be killing almost exclusively the right ones. Finding them will require us to wade through a sea of innocent blood, but it will be blood for our future. And it will not be Jewish blood."

"What else do we think will happen besides this?" Gross asked.

"Well, any peace treaties we have with any Muslim country, the Arabs... will be lost. Of course those 'treaties' are not even good enough to use to wipe your ass with, so that will be no big loss. Because of this I think we have to flatten every terror camp we know of from day one regardless of what country it may be in. That will include the ones in Egypt they do not think we know about. The monsters from those camps will be their shock troops unless we kill them first."

"Those are the guys who will be coming at us on the ground so we might as well kill them before they can even get out of their holes," another voice added.

The Finance Minister added his thoughts, "Foreign investors will run away as fast as they can. That will hurt us for years to come unless we can get a quick victory and the world sees us as the winners. You know the American media will savage us the instant this starts. The Jerusalem Post might even jump on us as well, but we can shut them up at least."

Another voice added, "We will get a flood of refugees and half of them will be enemy infiltrators."

"We will have to anticipate that and slam our borders shut immediately, using Uzis can not be ruled out, not once we start down this path," a voice said.

"That will swing both ways." Gross said. "We will have people *running out* as fast as they can. The young secular Jews, you know the ones I mean, the ones from Philadelphia who think being Jewish means living on a kibbutz, growing pears and marijuana. They will jump up and run for safety instead of helping. I hope I am wrong. I hope they will join in the fight, but I do not think they will. When things get started, I do not think being a Jew will be so attractive to them."

A female army general asked to be recognized, "Mr. Prime Minister this is micro managing no? I mean these details will be important, yes, but so important that we must stop developing the big picture to address them? I do not think so. I..."

"General, you are right, of course. Let us continue working on the overall strategy," Gross said, puffing his cigarette. "The way we are boxed in puts us in a kind of leg trap. We are like a small animal whose only means of escape is to chew off his own foot. My friends we are going to have to sacrifice some of our own people to save the Jewish people here and around the world. I would rather have my own eyes pulled out of my head then do what we have to do, but our options are very limited.

"I will give the order and we will use as bait a small town to bring about an attack from the Islamists. Then we will have a clear cut and defendable reason to destroy them. This will be bloody, very bloody. Many, many people will die but..."

His voice and his eyes dropped as he trailed off. He had to bring them back to the real issue. The 'nibbling around the edges,' would have to stop. It was time to get them to swallow the whole awful truth.

"Which town is it again? I was in so much shock when you said it, I missed it."

"When will this happen? Where?"

"I can not tell you which town or when this will happen. The essence of this plan is secrecy. If one of you leaked this plan we would be in grave danger overnight. No, I can not/will not say which town, nor will I even hint at it. Anyone who leaks this plan will be executed. Do I make myself clear enough?" The words Gross used were very sobering. They both stung and reassured his aides. The rest of the group felt uneasy that he so clearly did not trust them, but they felt reassured that their leader and his small circle of confidants were keeping the plan in the strictest secrecy.

A Minister asked, "How can we kill them all? I mean even if we do decide this is the only way we can survive, how can we kill all these evil monsters?"

Gross snapped back, "Minister, it is decided! We will do this because we can not survive otherwise! Do you doubt this?"

"Why can we not talk to others in the region? Why not try to use diplomacy to settle this question?" another voice asked.

Gross replied, "Settle this question? There is NO question here! They want all Jews dead. What do we discuss with them? Do we say 'okay will you let us live if we give you more land'? Do we beg them to please not kill all of us, just some, maybe the old people? How old is your mother sir? Maybe we can offer these bastards some old Jews; they are not doing anything but taking up space anyway right?"

"Things are not just black and white. You have to ..." the minister said.

"No they are not. And ordinarily you would be right, but not now. Now things *are* black white and *red* with the blood of our people!

"You are a young man. Yet you have never known a second of secure peace in your life. Do you think that negotiating with lunatics over who will be killed now and who will be killed later will bring you peace? I certainly hope not!" Gross said as he stood up and leaned his face closer to the young minister.

He continued, "In Europe in the 40's stupid Jews tried to reason with the psychopathic Nazis. Only those who ran are here to tell us what happened to those people. They are dead. Well this time, we cannot run. There is no place to run. Israel is our final destination. Either we live and thrive in this God forsaken desert or die here by the hands of today's Nazis. Can you understand this?"

The blank expression of the minister told Gross he had more work to do. "Look, the only time these animals want a truce is to steal time to regroup for the next battle. That way they, get to pick the time and place of the next battle. It's their way. They keep doing this until they wear their enemies down. They lie in negotiations hoping stupid people will believe they are sincerely searching for a way to peacefully coexist with us. But this time their 'lie and stall for time' tactic will work to our advantage. We will use their smug attitude of thinking they are smarter than us and turn it against them. Sure we are talking to them now. But the difference is that we have turned the tables. We have them convinced we do not have a clue that they have almost solved all of their nuclear bomb making problems, They have no idea we know they are almost ready to make their play and try to kill us all," Gross added.

"Okay but there are so many of them. How do we kill enough of them to get peace?" the still skeptical minister asked.

"Imagine this" Ethan Gross answered. "Imagine you are standing in the middle of a room that has no furniture in it. You have a jar with hundreds of cockroaches in it. Now you turn it upside down and shake them out. They start running in every direction. You start stomping your foot and killing them. You can not come near killing all of them, but you kill a lot of them. Next you round the survivors up and put them back in the jar and try again. What will happen?"

"You will still not be able to kill them all but..." the minister said. "But you will be able to kill more of the remaining roaches and each successive time you try this you will kill more. At sometime you we run out of roaches."

Gross smiled weakly and continued. "Well if we keep killing these roaches efficiently and quickly, at some point we will either turn the corner and get control of the situation, or die trying. It is my decision and I say, if need be, we die trying to kill them before they kill us. It is the only hope we have to survive. We are after all long past worrying about winning the hearts and minds of the world. The world my dear young friend hates us. They will hate us whether we are alive or dead, so I say let us keep our heads on our shoulders and hit them first, and not worry about who hates us as we continue to live our lives."

After a few seconds of silence, a deputy who is an open lesbian spoke her mind, "The United Nations estimates that these seventh century fundamentalists commit about 5,000 honor killings every year. Any unmarried woman they suspect of having sex is fair game to be murdered to save the honor of her family. Her own father or brother will come and slit her throat. Every lesbian and gay man will be killed under their Shia Law. They are lunatics that must be crushed and beaten into the dirt of their filthy countries."

Gross spoke: "I did not want to have to mention this, but I have also consulted Professor Avi Ben David of the Hebrew University. Professor Ben David is an expert on The Bible Code. He had some interesting comments when I asked him to look for any references to our situation in the Torah. He found many. "He found the phrases: Purim Party victory, Plan of fools, Punch, Fire rods, smash the crescent. Save the world, and the most chilling: 'False profits burn. Peace will again end.'" Gross briefly stared at the ceiling, pursed his lips, the asked in a slow and deliberate voice, "Anyone else have anything to offer?"

"Yes, sir. I think you should know that the Mossad has arrested a Jordanian doctor who was in our northern settlements under cover as a member of a humanitarian medical group. He and three nurses were plotting to kill you when you toured their facility, which had been scheduled for later this week. He was easy to break. He told us he was trained in *Krav Maga* so he could kill with just his hands and get by security checks with no problems. He was taught at a camp in Gaza run by the Front for the Liberation of Palestine. Now they teach their assassins to use even our methods! Palestinians teaching their killers our *Krav Maga*, what's next?" the Chief of *Shin Bet* asked slowly shaking his head.

As Israel's top security agency, Gross knew *Shin Bet* got its facts straight.

He went pale and could only say, "Thank you." There were no other questions about why Israel should be putting Operation Purim Party into motion. Ethan Gross was not as worried about his own safety as he was disturbed about the porous nature of Israeli security.

"What we do is always in public. We are always in the fish bowl. We develop something; anything and these bastards steal it two minutes later. Today it is *Krav Maga*, (the Hebrew words for *contact combat*) they would bring to kill Israel's leadership; what else will these people come after us with that we ourselves invented?" All questions about why Israel should be putting Operation Purim Party into motion had been settled. It was time to go into action. Unfortunately, it was time to spill blood, *blood for our future*, as Ethan Gross put it.

CHAPTER 12

IRAN READY TO ATTACK
PEEKING INTO THE MIND OF A MADMAN

THE MOSSAD'S REPORT was filled with details of the nuclear bomb building capabilities of Mohammed Waleed and his Iranian military machine. The executive summary narrative of the report read like the ravings of a rabid Nazi's fondest dream. The data and information it presented was the product of old fashioned on-the-ground human spying that was supported by Israel's early May 2007, launch of a spy satellite able to see everything happening on the ground anywhere in the Middle East. The Ofek 7 spy hardware was put into orbit with a powerful Shavit rocket fired from Israel's Air Force base at Palmahim, a few miles from Tel Aviv, on the Mediterranean Ocean. The Israeli manufactured Ofek 7, which orbits approximately 375 miles above the earth, collects its data while flying opposite the earth's rotation. The Ofek series satellites are radar equipped and able to penetrate clouds and the dark of night.

IRAQ'S NUCLEAR PROGRAM

"There is now a 99% chance that Iran's nuclear program is up and fully ready to deliver a lethal nuclear weapon within a radius that includes every corner of Israel. Our sources have followed the Iranian program for the last fifty-eight months. Our operatives have been embedded within the highest levels of their government for more than four years. We can say with a great deal of certainty what the Iranians intend. Their plan is to proclaim the coming of the twelfth Imam, a figure of traditional Islam whose appearance is believed, by Islamists to signify the beginning of the violent and catastrophic end of the world.

"Iran's leader Mohammad Waleed is planning to claim world wide leadership of Islam after wiping out Israel and taking on America. He and his people believe once they can claim credit for exterminating every Jew in Israel, they will immediately become the leaders of what is left of the world's Muslims. Thereafter they will seize the military assets of every other Arab country including their bomber planes which they will then use to fly to America and bomb America into submitting to a Muslim theocracy. They plan to kill as many Americans as they can, then make slaves of the survivors if the twelfth Imam does not appear. They have no plans for Israelis slaves. Their plan for us is to kill every single Jew in public beheading festivals to entertain their people."

A panel of psychiatrists had constructed a profile of Waleed and found him to be a dangerous paranoid schizophrenic. Their findings were next.

> He calls himself the elected president of Iran but he has never stood for election. He was put in office by a violent coup after which anyone that opposed him and his regime was beheaded in the nearest football stadium with all of the local people being forced to watch. This is how we can be certain he means what he says about public beheading festivals for the remaining Jews they find after nuking us into submission.
>
> Waleed worships Adolph Hitler. He often forces his inner circle to sit with him for hours watching the work of Leni Riefenstahl, Hitler's chief propaganda filmmaker. He especially loves *Triumph of the Will* because he knows it was Hitler's favourite. Waleed may have fathered as many as 106 children. He and his top lieutenants have set up 'baby farms' in several locations throughout Iran. These camps are modeled after the Nazi's Lebensborn programme. They find and kidnap girls between fifteen and twenty who have been deemed 'Perfect Daughters of Mohammed' by an Imam on Waleed's payroll.
>
> The girls' only job is to be impregnated by men who have been identified as 'Perfect Sons of Mohammed.' Of course that includes Waleed and his top lackeys. Waleed himself has a schedule that

includes having sex with five different Perfect Daughters each day. His schedule is built around impregnating these girls with sessions at 10 AM, Noon, 2PM, 7Pm and 10 PM. The final girl is always the one he beds for pleasure instead of out of a sense of duty. Each girl gets three months in which to get pregnant or lose her head, presumably as a reward so she can go straight to heaven for having given her virginity for Allah. It is unclear whether Allah gives them their virginity back so they can join with seventy one other virgins to serve as sex slaves for male 'Soldiers of Allah' who lose their lives fighting for the glory of Islam. The children of these unions never see their parents or any other family. They are trained like animals to be suicide bombers, executioners or breeders depending on how they have been assigned.

Waleed has no concept of time. He relies on aides to tell him when he must be somewhere and why. They tell him when to eat and try to get him to sleep at sometime during his day. Because he is so psychotic he can go two days without sleeping.

This of course makes him even crazier and more prone to do insane things. A tired paranoid schizophrenic can be extremely dangerous. They have learned that during such periods he can order the execution of even his closest lackeys.

The Mossad's report continued:

Since the Saudi's have started cutting the price of crude oil, Waleed's economy has been staggering around like a punch drunk boxer. Iran has no way to refine the oil it has for sale. Because Iran has been in the hands of one madman after another for forty years, the country's infrastructure is dilapidated. As one comes to power, he usually kills all of the ministers who served the previous dictator. Tasks like rebuilding old refineries, or opening new ones, do not make it to the top of the new leader's list of things to do.

They have just one antiquated refinery with only enough capacity to meet their own refinement needs. Because of the high sulfur content of their crude oil, the Iranians are a net importer of petrol. People in Iran's streets are growing restless, so the possibility of an internal revolt is very genuine, though not really likely.

Waleed deals very harshly with his internal dissidents. Nevertheless, with his regime in danger from both internal and external forces, Waleed seems to have decided his only option is to attack Israel with nuclear weapons.

Like his hero Adolph Hitler, Waleed is deeply into mysticism. He believes that if he can bring about the end of the world in the Muslim model, Allah will reward him with eternity in heaven enjoying his seventy-two virgins everyday. He believes in the Muslim tradition of the return of Mahdi, the twelfth Imam, whose return from hiding will be the beginning of the end of the world.

The Islamic tradition holds that a holy man born around 868, who was able to perform miracles, has been hiding from persecutors who have been trying to find him and kill him. Muslims believe this man has never died, but around 941 he was assumed directly into heaven, bodily without his physical death. This man, named Mahdi is said to have the power to return to earth to establish a new world. Waleed has used the bombing of the Golden Mosque, which was built in Mahdi's honor, as his platform to push his plans. He preaches that this represents an attack on all of Islam.

The summary concluded as follows:

Our intelligence has developed strong evidence that the bombing of the Golden Mosque was carried out by Waleed's men in order to create the opportunity he now believes he has. He apparently took a page from Hitler's *Krystal Nocht* sham.

The seriousness of this situation can not be over estimated. Waleed loves death and psychotic fantasies. He has always had the prerequisite lunatic's state of mind to try to bring about the Islamic version of doomsday. Now he seems to have the military capability to try to make his maniacal dreams come about. He firmly believes that a nuclear war will have the power to unlock the chains that have kept the Imam Mahdi in hiding all these centuries.

It is the firm belief of this agency that a preemptive strike, designed to knock out Waleed's nuclear arsenal, be very seriously considered. Such a strike appears to be the only available useful option for saving Israel from total annihilation at this point.

CHAPTER 13

MR. PRESIDENT, WHAT ABOUT EUROPE?

IN THE FINAL DAYS leading up to the launch of Operation Sucker Punch final details and questions had to be worked out.

"Mr. President what about Europe?" the Secretary of Defense asked, his voice intruding on the deep thoughts of President Harlan Andrews.

"Mr. President, we have to consider what to do with Europe once the war starts?"

"Mr. Secretary, most American families came from European stock. Over the years, we've grown from being Europe's child to where we are now Europe's parent. We poured out the best of our young men and our treasure to protect our ancestral homelands for almost a century and what has it gotten them or us? Because we've always been there to save Europe from itself or any other enemies, we have completely wrung out any ambition to stand and fight for their own self preservation the Europeans once had. They have been living artificially well for the past fifty years because they never had to put up two cents to support their own defense. Now they have wine cellars and villas on their coasts, but no defenses. They have danced away the night, night after night, and now here they are with the wolf not at their doors but in their damned living rooms. This time, we can not help them. This time we have to allow them to stew in their own 'anything goes' juices. As my grandma used to say: 'You made your bed, now you gotta sleep in it.'

"I'm really very sorry to say this, but in this one, Europe is on her own.

Andrews paused to let his words sink into his staff, and then continued.

"Maybe we can do something for them once we achieve tactical control, maybe we can, but I'm not losing any sleep over what happens to the Europeans right now. I've got America to defend and protect, as my oath says."

"I agree sir. I only raised the issue because it had to be raised," an aide said.

"The Europeans can go pound sand this time. Let's see if they can use their superior attitudes to keep their heads connected to their necks when ole Abdul comes ah knockin'." The Secretary of the Navy said, once again using his Mississippi accent as a weapon when he was dealing with "cowardly Yankees."

"I have no intention of doing anything to help them until we're in the clear. This time we're doin' this right. America comes first and that's that. This time they are beyond help. Take a look at these excerpts from the latest report on Europe's situation," Andrews said.

TOP SECRET

"It has gotten too late very early for our European friends."

"It will not be long before Europe is engulfed by its own Muslim citizens. The continent has opened its borders in a headlong charge to out do each other to have the most lax and porous borders. The Muslims have flooded Europe's public schools and turned them into madrashs right under their noses. They have used Europe's money to educate Muslim kids and teach them to hate Christian, Jewish and secular Europe. The latest estimates say that by the end of the next school year, all of the French public school system will be controlled by Muslims through the local PTAs.

"For a while, there was some slim hope that Europe would pacify the Muslims and forestall their movement to join the ranks of the Islamists. That hope is now gone. The recently concluded *Muslim re-settlement* program carried out by several European countries was a disastrous mistake. Our incountry agents have reported that in most cases the Muslim families who presented themselves for voluntary deportation were actually Islamist agents posing as families in order to receive the deportation bounty payments. Those payments were immediately used to purchase weapons and military supplies for their planed attack.

"Our estimate is that the European Union countries that participated in the "re-settlement" programs were duped into paying for the ropes that will be used to hang them. The sharp increase in the price of crude oil which has given America $4.25 a gallon gasoline, has sent European gasoline prices to the equivalent of over $10.00 on the continent and $9.25 in the United Kingdom. The advantages of small cars, good public transportation and short trips have disappeared. The Islamist plan has always been to crush Europe first. It is softer and closer to their North African base while still able to offer great tactical advantages as they prepare for the final all out war against America. Our economic experts believe it is for these reasons that the Islamists have forced the OPEC nations to re-set the standard of acceptable currency for crude oil purchases back to the American dollar.

"Our estimate is that they have calculated the risks and would rather have a very much weakened Europe, even if that means a short term boost to our economy, than have an E.U. with a strong economy when they make their move. Consequently, the Euro's recent sharp drop against the American Dollar and the Japanese Yen is a clear sign that we have in fact stepped on the Islamist's plans exactly at the right time. The Israeli Mossad's reports appear to be very accurate as to the urgent nature of our need to prepare for war with the Islamists. The number of Islamists in Europe is growing geometrically as are their demands on Europe's social service systems. This too is part of the Islamist plan to take Europe. It makes unrest among Europe's Muslim communities a virtual certainty while continually draining their treasuries.

"Stirred up and turbulent communities are easy to incite to the kind of useful riots they will need to divert attention from their attacks in the opening hours. While the Muslims that the Islamists actually hate almost as much as they hate Americans are keeping the civil authorities in Europe busy with their street riots, the real action will start.

"The current outlook for European Jews is as bad today as it was in 1939. They are not being rounded up for extermination yet, but such things may not be far off. Christian Europe has lost its will to coalesce around anything. There is no Christian Church of any size or power in Europe today. Consequently, there is no unifying force or belief system that can rouse Europe from its self delusional slumber.

"While it is true that Europe enjoys a standard of living that mimics America's, it is also true that the European standard of living is an illusion built on unpaid defense bills and smaller families made so by its self genocide. Europe has been aborting its citizens at an alarming rate for two generations. With few exceptions there is not a single country in Europe that can boast of a birth rate that can even begin to replenish its native citizens. For twenty-five years the Europeans have laughed at America's disapproval of abortion, while they have cynically used it as a form of birth control.

"Football is our favorite outdoors sport, sex is our favorite indoor sport and you American fools can keep your stupid bourgeois attitudes about such things to yourselves." The European love of abortion and smaller families has now caught up to them.

"It has gotten too late very early for our European friends."

"This has left Europe in a position similar to what the Roman Empire faced during its final days. There are now fewer and fewer traditional Christian Europeans who feel that saving their own culture is worth fighting for. Sadly, they have deluded themselves into believing that actual fighting can be avoided and the threat from the Islamists can be met with concessions and 'gifts.' Our estimate is that the Europeans are about to realize concessions and gifts will not work. It is estimated that the European population is approximately 925 million. Nevertheless, for some very clear reasons, no more than 35,000 citizen militiamen will step forward to defend the continent against an Islamist invasion. Moreover, it is doubtful that these volunteers will be immediately useful to the European Union's regular military forces. When the fact that these citizen troops will be spread out across all of Europe, and many would bring with them language and communications difficulties, it is not at all clear that they will be helpful. It is expected that many more will come forward to enlist, but because of Europe's thirty years of de-emphasizing its military power, even most of those willing to try to help, will be of no use.

"Because the European Union has had practically no military, it has practically no military trained citizens. When compared to Europe, the relative number of available militia troops in America, is another area where we have a clear advantage. Our estimate is that there are approximately 3 million Americans with military training, who own a firearm, and are in good enough physical shape to immediately step forward in response to a general call for volunteers. Europe is leaning toward a negotiated surrender. It is our estimate that the reported willingness of the Europeans to consider surrendering and attempting to negotiate with the Islamists is misplaced confidence and a foolhardy disregard for reality. The European position on negotiations is dangerous beyond their apparent understanding. The fact that trying to deal politely with the Islamists will set off a terrible chain of events has apparently been lost on the European Union. They appear to understand nothing about the laws of unintended consequences. They will learn that words and political correctness will not keep them safe from the Islamist's sword. In the cold war we were able to prevail because the Soviets finally came to realize they would die just as certainly as we would die if they started a nuclear war.

Today's enemies are 180 degrees away from recognizing that our enemies want to die and kill all of us as they do. They believe God will welcome them as His instruments for ending the world in a final showdown between good and evil on the world's final day.

Circumstances have now clearly shown that Israel and America must fight the Islamists and defeat them or the world will be plunged into a medieval darkness for centuries to come.

THE IRAN QUESTION

Those who would argue that the way to avoid war would have been to work toward undermining the regime in Iran were only partially correct. If Waleed's regime was replaced, only the Islamist's timetable would be changed. At some point in the very near future another Islamist leader would ascend to power either in Iran or another Muslim country and he too would immediately plan to make the Qur'an's end of the world scenario a reality at the West's expense. Thinking that successful negotiations with Iran or any other Islamist nation could avoid a war is very wrong. This is a dangerously false notion.

Harlan Andrews addressed the idea of negotiating a lasting peace with

Waleed by remarking, "Given that the American public's will to fight for freedom is not likely to increase any time soon, waiting for a new Iranian regime is not an acceptable option for preserving our freedoms."

He continued, "Nevertheless, our situation is neither lost nor necessarily irretrievable. We have weapons that go beyond what our Islamist enemies can match, let alone actually counter if we use them properly. For one thing, we can use the airwaves throughout the Muslim world. We can constantly broadcast appeals to Muslims to remain Muslims and resist being forced to become Islamists. We can make comparisons between how the Islamists want them to live and how they can, and do, live under our system of government and way of life. Recent survey data shows that, while most American Muslims are not as likely to want to destroy America as European Muslims are to want the destruction of Europe, the number who do feel this way is still dangerously high. It showed that more than 7 of 10 American Muslims believe he or she can make a good life in America with just hard work. This is a very valuable advantage that must be exploited. We must use friendly media outlets to improve this ratio to still better numbers.

"We must make the prospect of fighting to destroy America such a terrible and frightening thought that they will not want to lift a hand to us." We must reward our Muslim friends and put the fear of God in those who identify themselves as our enemies. We must severely hurt those we are forced to fight. Ruthlessness in dealing with our enemies must be the order of the day everyday. We have to make a war with us both over seas and here in America, so violent that joining our side is the only option for any sane person of any background" he concluded.

Gauging His Advisers

After giving his staff a chance to read the report on the state of Europe, Andrews paused to look at their reactions. He looked in the eyes of each of his staff. He needed to know that each one of them understood why helping Europe, as America had always done before, could not be done this time. He was uneasy with the shedding of Europe's blood, but willing to allow it to insure America's future. Andrews needed everyone to be on board.

"The Europe that sent its warriors out to conquer the world no longer exists. The beings they have who are masquerading as men, you know, the boys with the earrings and polished fingernails, aren't going to lift a hand to fight anybody even as they are being murdered. These days the closest thing Europe has to real men are the drunks they call *Soccer Hooligans*. They run around beating up other drunks from rival countries and think that makes them tough guys. Shoot! All the real men in of European descent either came here or were killed in the last couple of wars.

"Because of the strict gun prohibitions the Europeans have put on themselves, the average *earring boy* couldn't fight back even if he wanted to. Their own governments have stripped them of any way to fight back. The only people in Europe's streets with guns will be the Islamists.

"We are a free and independent people because we won our freedom at the point of a gun. I'm confident we will be able to keep it at the point of a gun. But the average guy in Europe? We caint count on them for anything. Shoot! The Japanese will be more help and they don't even have a real military!

"It's up to us to provide the leadership." Harlan Andrews knew full well that once the war started, the Islamists would need a target near enough for them to attack in their blind rage. That target was not going to be America as long as he had anything to say about it and he did. The thought of what was going to happen to Europe made him think of a phrase Ethan Gross once used.

Blood for our future came to his mind.

CHAPTER 14

WALEED INFLUENCES THE MEDIA; USES IMMIGRATION LAWS AGAINST AMERICA

AS HE PREPARED FOR A SHOOTING WAR with America, it became clearer to Mohammed Waleed that he needed to use every available weapon for him to have a chance to win. He sent out his agents all over Europe and the United States and gave them instructions to meet with and sway newspaper publishers who would interview them.

They had to do whatever was necessary to persuade major European and American print outlets to conduct polls on the attitudes toward America's treatment of Muslims. He wanted these polls to show that Americans and Europeans saw the United States as a hated pariah in the world because it was treating the Muslim world so unfairly.

The effort was quite successful. His men got a popular German magazine to run a front page headline asking:

"Has America killed civilization?"

An Italian daily newspaper conducted a poll that found 81% of its respondents had agreed with the statement that, "America is the world's bully." And 52% agreed with the statement, "I have more to fear from the United States than the Islamists."

The major newspapers and media outlets across America published the findings of these polls without challenging a word of them. A major polling firm asked 896 "adults" and found that 43% agreed with the charge, "The United States is a country that bullies other countries and makes you ashamed to be an American." The results were reported on the editorial pages of dozens of America's largest newspapers.

Each recitation of the numbers was accompanied by the editorial staff's own take on how awful America had become since Harlan Andrews took office. Some papers got Hollywood stars to write their own attacks on America, complaining about how the country was so well loved and respected during the 1990s, but now is hated by the whole world. One starlet, a militant vegan, complained about Andrews being unfit for office because his family farm slaughtered animals when he was a boy. The pull quote read, "This murderous way of life taught Andrews that other life forms are a danger to him. How sad?"

The end results of these polls were predictable. The Islamist's resolve to fight on became stronger, just as the same type of campaigns had boosted the Viet Cong's resolve in the 1960's. The American people once again began to doubt that their military, the strongest fighting force in the world, could defeat a force of militiamen using antiquated weapons. The morale of the American war fighters was damaged as well.

The anti war forces in Congress used the polls for fund raisers and various front groups used them as recruitment tools on college campuses.

The effects of being in a high state of alert for so many years were beginning to chip away at the nation's will to fight. The average American was tired of living under constant threats of death.

One college student was over heard asking a friend, "Could living under the Islamists be worse than this?" while waiting on line at an airport. A concerned news crew, who got him to repeat his question, put him on camera. It was shown to millions that evening on a broadcast news show. The fact that just such talk had landed Tokyo Rose and Axis Sally in prison after World War II was lost on many Americans who sat and agreed with the young man.

The Islamists and their friends in the Western media did not understand the true feelings of Americans toward the then long smoldering war against the Islamists. They could not understand that Americans were not against fighting an all out conventional war for their lives. They were just tired of waiting for the war to get underway so they could win and get on with their lives. Waleed's ploy ended up steeling the resolve of the Americans who had not thought about fighting the war. When forced to make a choice, their automatic reaction was to want to win, which was not what Waleed was looking for.

Using Immigration Laws Against America

For several years before the 9-11 attacks on America, Mohammed Waleed, the President of Iran and self appointed Caliph, or supreme leader, of the worldwide Islamist movement, had made getting agents into the United States his top priority. He could see a showdown, winner take all war with America coming and he wanted every advantage possible before the balloon went up. Waleed had a group of specially trained spies and saboteurs he wanted to have on American soil when the fighting started. The Islamists are a very cunning enemy. They diligently study every facet of America. They continually probe for weaknesses, and jump on them when they are discovered. Their studies gave them an understanding of the immigration issues confronting America and how they could exploit the chaos caused by loose enforcement of convoluted laws. Europe's immigration laws had made infiltration onto the Continent simple. Waleed wanted to discover if it might be as simple to put his agents in America using American immigration laws.

When his men studied how best to get into America to carry out their attacks, one thing stood out, as a shinning diamond in a pile of foolish immigration laws: legal entry was far preferable to illegal entry. Getting onto American soil legally would ensure that an agent could proceed with his assignment without fear of being scooped up in a raid and sent back to his country. Among the many ways to gain legal entry was to marry an American. As simple as that sounds, finding and marrying a willing American citizen was an uphill task until an ingenious plan was developed. The ploy called for marrying people in America's prison system. These marriages could actually be completed and made legal by proxy marriages between America inmates and Islamist agents. The Islamists called their operation *Mission Proxy*. The whole idea was a joke to them.

The *Mission Proxy* scheme was developed when an Islamist analyst assigned to Al Qaeda's America desk read a story about a British citizen who had corresponded with a California inmate and eventually married him.

Since the inmate had less than three years on his sentence, the British woman was allowed to come to America and receive the same treatment as a spouse of any other imprisoned American citizen.

The analyst forwarded a recommendation that agents should work through Black Muslim converts in US prisons and find inmates who would be willing to go through this process for a fee to be paid to a trusted relative or friend on the outside. Since the Black Muslim movement is represented in almost every state prison system in America, there was no shortage of willing inmates male or female to choose from. The states that offered conjugal visitation for married inmates became the best targets.

The Islamists reasoned that having had conjugal visitations would add a great deal of strength to an agent's claims to a legitimate marriage and therefore a clean green card.

Not surprisingly the male inmates were extremely easy to find, but eager females were in no short supply either.

The going price for an inmate marriage was between $20,000 and $30,000. Some of al Qaeda's most valuable agents in America got in to the States using this ploy until it was blocked by an amendment in an Agriculture Appropriations bill. Thereafter marriages to inmates would by limited to only those prisoners serving less than one year and would have to undergo extreme scrutiny before being approved. That cut the number of applications for these marriages by 97% during the first six months after the changes went into effect. The remaining three percent were deemed to be legitimate and were allowed to proceed. That was just enough to keep American civil libertarian lawyers busy for a while.

CHAPTER 15

DEALING WITH THE AMERICAN MEDIA

THE NIGHT BEFORE Israel launched Operation Purim Party and America would have to follow suit with Operation Sucker Punch, Harlan Andrews and his Vice President Walter Hodges met in the Oval Office for a quiet contemplation of what was coming. Hodges and Andrews had not been particularly close before Andrews had assumed office. Given a choice, Harlan Andrews would not have selected Walter Hodges as his appointed Vice President. He had no particular brief for or against Hodges, but he felt he should have been able to pick a man he knew better. For Andrews it was a matter of having to yield to the operation of law as proscribed by the 25th Amendment to the Constitution: the Congress gave Hodges to him. Over the months, since law tied them together, the two veteran lawmakers, both products of Middle America, had become close friends. Circumstances and similarities had forged the bond between them. They were exactly the same age. They were devout Methodists. They were both fathers of three daughters and a son, and they both loved fly-fishing. More importantly they both loved America very dearly.

Andrews filled a couple of glasses with 'two fingers' of Jack Daniels and Hodges clipped the tips of the Coa cigars he brought for the occasions.

"You know, Walt, the shit will really hit the fan tomorrow. There'll be so many things to consider. The frustrating part now is that we can't do much more than guess what we'll be faced with. This won't be like a political campaign where you know you'll need staff, you'll need fund raisers and workers and buttons and signs and so on.

"We can actually sit down and plan out every last detail and know it will pretty much be that way. This won't be that simple. No, sir. We can guess, but we won't really know what we'll have to decide on until we're already hip deep in alligators."

"Well, we might be able to trim around the edges. We know we'll have to deal with the media for instance," Hodges added.

Andrews stoked up his cigar, took a sip of his bourbon, and thought through his response. He and Hodges had not discussed his feelings toward the media before. Andrews knew he had to have Hodges completely on the same page regarding the way they would be treating the Western media in general and the American media in particular.

"Walt, we've never had a chance to talk about this before and now time is short, so I'll be blunt. I hold the idea of a free American media as an article of faith. It is one of the greatest concepts of government ever devised, and it is the thing about America that separates us from the rest of the world. Now those things being said, I have to add that none of what we see from today's American media even vaguely resembles what our founding fathers wanted to create when they insisted on a freedom of the press.

"Jefferson would howl in disgust at the way our media has become out and out anti-American. He would bristle against the tyranny of scoundrels who hide behind the First Amendment while they do their best to destroy our country. For my money they are a bunch of fifth columnists working for our enemies. Why? I don't actually know, but as the expression goes, 'All I know is what I read in the papers.'"

"I flat out hate the sonsabitches myself. I've kept this piece on how the media used to be on America's side and how it is now so willing to work for our enemies today," Hodges said. Then he reached into his pocket and took out a newspaper column he had down loaded. He slid it to Andrews and said, "It was written about four years ago about Brownell, but it could have been written yesterday about you."

The article was titled: American media: from lap dog to opposition party. It was written by Nicole Wian the editor in chief of American Truths.

"Peter Brownell is nothing like the dimwitted buffoon, and war-monger he has been portrayed. As a matter of fact, the picture is so distorted that it says more about the media's willingness to lie to sneak across their points then it does about Mr. Brownell. I've met him and I know the difference."

Roger Mosher, Boston Times

"If you arranged today's American journalists according to their political leanings, almost every one would be on the hard far left. Where they once served as a vigorous 'loyal opposition' who kept government honest, it is now the media that is dishonest and in need of reigning in. The principled opposition they once represented has now changed into advocacy for America's enemy no matter whom that enemy is or what he intends to do to our country."

Frank H. Standish, Detroit Mail

The relationship between the media and past American presidents, during times of crisis and war, has not always been a daily adversarial exercise, as is the case in today's Washington. When word of the Japanese attack on Pearl Harbor swept across the country throughout Sunday December 7, 1941 Americans came together as a single nation. Any doubts we had about getting involved in 'Europe's war' faded by the hour. President Franklin Delano Roosevelt (FDR) was, as today's historians favor telling it, finally out of any real danger of the American people finding out anything about the litany of violations of law he had perpetrated. His media was finally able to change positions. Where they had been studies in willful ignorance at best and chronic liars by omission at worst, over night they became FDR's cheerleaders as they rightfully should have been.

In the years leading up to America's entry into World War II, Roosevelt made a series of bold and correct decisions in his effort to protect our country from an enemy he saw just over the horizon. He knew that if he failed to act with firm resolve and without hesitation, America and the whole free world, could find herself under the heels of dangerous and aggressive thugs. Everywhere, from every corner of the world, the news was bleak and ominous.

From Roosevelt's crows nest view of the world scene he determined that protecting America meant helping Great Britain fight the Nazi threat, even if that meant breaking American law. Among the assets Roosevelt could count on was the certain knowledge that the news media of the day was composed of compliant allies who were more interested in helping and protecting a president who was saving the free world, than honestly reporting what they saw and heard everyday in and around the White House.

FDR's daily labors were a laudable undertaking by a president honestly working everyday to guard and protect his country from great danger. For his efforts and the support it gave him in his efforts, both Franklin Roosevelt and America's media of the late 1930s and early 1940s deserve the highest praise. When the immanent and certain death of the nation is at hand there is no time for scornful 'gotcha' journalism from the nation's media. It is therefore, all the more distressing and confounding that the media of today has chosen its socialist ideology over the safety and well being of our nation. The dripping contempt with which the modern media approaches every story concerning Peter Brownell and his prosecution of the war on terrorism, borders on maniacal. It clearly underscores the shocking truth that the vast majority of our media would rather see America fail in its anti terror war, then see Mr. Brownell succeed because they hate him so much. Clearly they hate him more than they love our country.

A comparison of the media's treatment of Roosevelt in the handling of World War II and the media's treatment of Peter Brownell in his handling of the war on terror is instructive.

The first thing that strikes an observer of the media's treatment of both administrations, is that while Roosevelt committed federal crimes to do what was right and the media dutifully stood mute about the goings on, Brownell has scrupulously followed both the spirit and letter of every pertinent law, and nevertheless, is accused of every crime their imaginations could produce.

The manifest truth is that while the Islamists hatred for America and Peter Brownell glows brighter each day, the hatred much of the media has for the president is not far behind.

Why the media acts this way is one of the mysteries of our collective lives. What is sure is that today's media has very little connection to the population as a whole. In the 1930's and 40's, even well known media people in America made salaries that did not place them very far above those of the man on Main Street. They were members of the local church. They were veterans and they could often be seen shopping in the same stores as everyone else. They followed our troops to war not to find fault and embarrass our soldiers, but to tell their stories in a way that honored and supported our troops and our nation. Unlike today's generation of journalists few if any of them thought of themselves as 'citizens of the world' or 'reporters'; before they thought of themselves as Americans.

The media of Roosevelt's days helped him carry out the necessary subterfuge for preparing a reluctant nation for a war he knew was coming and had to be won. In contrast to today's media, there is little evidence that they conducted monthly polls to try and gin up resentment of FDR or his policies, despite sure and certain knowledge that he was guilty of violating federal laws and the expressed will of the people. The media of Roosevelt's days regularly lied by omission about their president and his ways in order to help America win out during the crisis they knew was real.

The media regularly lied for Roosevelt. They lied everyday when they failed to report that he had not in fact 'beaten' polio.

They lied each time they neglected to report that he was an invalid who was unable to walk. When juxtaposed with today's media's attempt to use demonstrably false documents to smear Brownell any way they could, the picture is shocking.

This requires restatement: The old media lied continually to keep America from knowing a president they liked was an invalid and today's media lies to try to make Peter Brownell a political invalid during a time of war and major crisis. Make no mistake: Keeping discouraging news from a people working to get out from underneath an economic depression and Japan's sneak attack was exactly the right thing to do. Today's media is doing exactly the wrong things, and doing so with its eyes wide open and in total disregard for the consequences.

In the years leading up to World War II, Roosevelt violated federal laws against sending Great Britain war materials because she was a nation at war. He arranged for U.S. Steel, yes a big corporation, to receive war materials that were falsely declared 'surplus' (under his orders), for the purpose of allowing U.S. Steel to then sell the 'surplus' supplies to England for her fight against the Nazis.

Those who would maintain that the pre-war media knew nothing about this transfer are looking at the facts through childlike naivety. In comparison today's media has never stopped trying to make a scandal of the fact that Vice President Andrews was once connected to Vosberg Suppliers an honorable company that does much of the work of supporting our troops in today's theaters of war.

The media knew Roosevelt sent fifty destroyers to the British Navy and only announced his move after the transfer was completed. They said not a word about it. Roosevelt had the media on his side. Yet when the Army and Marines went into war recently without telling the media first, the cries from the fourth estate did not stop for days.

When the famous Doolittle raiders stuck Tokyo itself in April of 1942, Roosevelt's media asked where they had taken off from.

In response he smiled and answered 'Shangri-La' then the media joined him in laughing at the impertinence of the question. There is no evidence that the question was pursued thereafter. The media was too busy celebrating our victory and writing good things about our military strength to make a point of the president's failure to fully reveal its every detail. Today's media by contrast, has been in a headlong race to be the first to reveal as many military secrets as it possibly can.

Unlike their ancestors, many in today's media care nothing about maintaining military secrets to protect our soldiers. One member of the fourth estate actually drew a map of the location of the unit he was embedded with in the furtherance of a televised story. While today's media has continually searched for ways to actually put President Brownell in prison for imagined violations of the law, FDR's media 'knew nothing' about the truly illegal wire taping of suspected Nazi spies.

When he personally directed the FBI to violate existing law, which said 'No' to *any wire taping*, FDR's media rightfully kept that secret under wraps. Yet almost daily we hear much of our media complaining about Brownell breaking laws that exist primarily in the minds of the media itself. They cry about how the Patriot Act violates the rights of everyone they can think of, while rarely reporting the safety net the Act has given us with a minimum of intrusion into the lives of honest Americans. In 1942 the FBI captured a handful of Nazi spies who had penetrated our borders. In the space of six months these men were captured, tried, convicted by a military tribunal and executed. There was no media out cry for them to be tried in civilian courts for violations of applicable state laws.

Roosevelt's sending this case to a military court was a death sentence for those men, as they all well knew, but the media chose patriotism over journalism and said nothing contrary to the decision. In their continual cynical efforts to discredit President Brownell and our American military personnel, today's media are listening to, and granting credence to, the complaints of the worst terrorists we have captured on our battlefields. They are beating a drum to try and have over five hundred of the worst of the worst terrorists tried in mainland American civilian courtrooms, without regard for the obvious consequences.

When Roosevelt interned Japanese, German and Italian American citizens who almost universally had done nothing to warrant such treatment, his media said hardly a word. Today's media writes hand wringing 'exposes' about torture by under panties on criminal detainee's heads. More than this, the media of today wants to impeach Peter Brownell for 'his shocking conduct.'

In an effort to 'help' the American people understand the impact of the war on terrorism, the media insists upon showing us pictures of coffins draped with American flags. The contrast of this point, the fact that there were no pictures of dead American soldiers run by the media until mid 1943, is breathtaking. Today's media continually run stories denigrating the efforts and quality of our military by pointing out that they are paid to fight unlike Roosevelt's military. They never mention the fact that fully 2/3 of the 14 million men and women in uniform to fight World War II, were draftees not volunteers.

They almost never mention the fact that today's American military, is composed totally of volunteers who are the best and smartest troops ever put on a battlefield by any country in history.

While Brownell is not a religious man, on the few occasions he has made even tangential references to the All Mighty the media calls for his impeachment for mixing Church and State. Yet on June 6, 1944 while announcing the D Day invasion of Europe, Roosevelt asked all Americans to pray with him and ask 'God to help America preserve... our religion and civilization,' with full enthusiastic coverage of his media.

Finally, one of the stock media templates of today is 'Brownell can't spread democracy at the point of a gun. It can't be done.' This syllogism, like all others, sounds good but it is no more than

> gibberish. Peter Brownell has carried democracy to millions of people in America's war on terrorists.

They very conveniently cover up the fact that "gun point Democracy" does in fact work. Franklin D. Roosevelt and his successor, Harry S. Truman, brought democracy to Japan, Italy and Germany at the point of a gun.

When he finished reading the article, Andrews nodded. "Thanks, Walt. That tells me all I have to know. We're on the same page about the media. I think we'll just refuse to give them anything until we're damned well ready.

"I'll talk to Bill Tong and his people in the Press Section. I believe shutting them out will help us more than anyone can imagine." They touched their glasses together and parted. They had some tough days ahead so it was time to get some rest.

CHAPTER 16

NEWS OF QIRYAT SHEMONA SPREADS AROUND THE WORLD

WHEN NEWS OF THE BATTLE of Qiryat Shemona spread around the world it put every country on high alert. "High alert" in decaying Western Europe, however, meant something less than it did in other parts of the world. The French newspapers carried below the fold stories about "trouble" on the border between Israel and Lebanon. Dutifully, all major news outlets across Europe advised their readers and listeners to "take extra precautions."

Of course there was no explanation of what "extra precautions" meant, but having said so allowed the Europeans to put the issue aside as another "silly fight" among the lower orders of Arabs and Jews. The talk in all the cafes became: "Who cares what they do in Africa?"

"Here we have Arabs who want no part of all of that foolishness. Our Muslims are the good ones. They're here precisely because they want no part of ancient squabbles over a piece of desert."

"Let them fight it out, or better yet maybe they should have a football game over their differences and the winner gets the pile of sand these idiots are fighting over."

"Of course the sneaky Jews will win. They have all the weapons they need from their American friends. Those pigs!"

"There ought to be some balance. Maybe we should send support to the poor Arabs who are fighting to recover the lands the Zionist stole from them."

The official reaction from the European Union was a strongly worded note to the United Nations condemning Israeli aggression. It demanded a United Nation's High Commission investigation to determine whether Israel's membership in the UN could be terminated for her 'shameless conduct.' It further demanded that the United States pay for the investigation,..." but not be part of it since America would probably take Israel's side as she always does."

The world community considered The Israeli Defense Force's actions within its own country a retaliation, just as the Israelis had predicted. The note fell exactly into Israel's Operation Purim Party trap. Mohammed Waleed, the leader of Iran saw the reaction from Europe and believed Israel would be "punished" by the United Nations.

He believed that, while the world was looking at Israel and pointing a wagging finger, he could finish the last steps to make his nuclear missiles ready for launching at Tel Aviv.

With his reaction, another element of Operation Purim Party fell into place.

Waleed's naive belief that Israel would waste time worrying about the world's condemnation was just what Prime Minister Ethan Gross was hoping for. Mossad agents in Iran reported that immediately after the battle in Qiryat Shemona they saw a sharp increase in activity at the missile silos which they had been monitoring for the past two years.

Gross added this information to his report to Andrews. Everything was now on track. Purim Party was rolling. Israel and America were moving toward a winner takes all show down with their enemies. Both sides would go "all in" and the world would soon be in a total life or death struggle whether it was ready or not.

CHAPTER 17

NO BESLANS IN AMERICA

ONE OF THE CONSIDERATIONS for selecting the day of the week to launch both Operation Purim Party and Operation Sucker Punch was the manner in which it would be accepted in America. For purposes of managing the expected reaction from the nation, President Andrews wanted to make his announcement on a Saturday. He reasoned this would give Homeland Security an opportunity to do what was necessary to enforce the anticipated orders of curfews as well as the school and workplace closings that might meet with some resistance from the American people.

The declarations of war against the countries harboring terrorist camps would have to be carefully and effectively explained and people worrying about getting children off to school or getting to work would not be in the best frame of mind to listen to such serious material. He had to be sure his actions were understood as steps that were insuring the safety of the American people. Andrews did not want the inevitable 'breaking in' period to take place on a workday. People had to realize they were being ordered off the streets for their own good. The streets had to be clear of civilians for the military and police units to function. The most important concern on the President's mind, as he insisted on a Saturday announcement, was that it would insure the schools would be closed. He had very good reason for his concern.

For months before Operation Sucker Punch, Homeland Security agents had been tracking a group of Chechnyans, first from Eastern Europe to Panama and then into Texas through a blind spot in the virtual fence designed to keep them out. The Russian Security police started the investigation when they forwarded a report on the group's movements indicating that it was coming to America. The dossier connected a team of five European looking Chechnyan men and women to the Beslan Russia school hostage attack in September 2004. The Russians had sad experience with Chechnyan terrorists and their report came with a recommendation that they be shot on sight. The report included details about the horrific events of the school hostage taking, not previously released by the Russians. At the time of the attack, the world was told the hostage takers had made demands for independence for Chechnya and the release of some of their people being held by the Russians.

The story that was released was that they were insisting on their demands and were willing to kill children and school teachers as collateral damage when they blew themselves up in frustration if they did not get what they wanted. This was not the whole truth. This was not even near the truth. Harlan Andrews and his staff were given the whole truth.

By continuing the investigation of the attack after the world's media went home, the Russians had developed the truth, the real ugly truth.

It was much more frightening then anyone could have imagined. The real story was that the hostage takers cared nothing about independence for Chechnya.

Their true mission was to test their theory that they could do things to Christian and Jewish children that would incite Americans to violently retaliate against all Muslims. They thought this would bring on the war they so longed for. They wanted to turn the whole Muslim world against the whole non Muslim world.

The attack was designed to infuriate non-Muslims and incite them to grab guns and bats to attack the closest innocent Muslims they could find. The attackers were fully aware they were on a suicide mission. They expected that once their mission became clear to the security forces, the Russians would charge in and kill them as well as some of the children and staff. They also expected that when the video of what they had done was aired on worldwide television, non-Muslims around the world would storm peaceful Muslims and kill them. They reasoned this would give the Islamists the propaganda material they needed to rally the world's Muslims to their side. To them it was: Blood for our future.

MY LORD!

The report described what the Chechnyans did. It told how the female terrorists held down little girls while the men systematically raped them and threw their dead bodies out a window. The negotiations over demands for Chechnya's independence were nothing more than a ruse to give the men's semen reservoirs a chance to refill. Even twenty-year-old terrorist rapists needed time to recover between attacks. When Vice President Walter Hodges read this he gasped and softly said, "My Lord!" Tears dripped down his cheeks.

The Chechnya freedom fighters used the same window so the media would keep their cameras on it and not miss an inch of video. The attack purposely targeted a middle school because the girls would be old enough to rape, but the boys would be neither old enough nor strong enough to fight back. Their plan might have worked in a free country. In a Western European country or in the United States there would have been no way to keep a lid on the truth.

But Russia is Russia. They still do not allow the media to do anything it wants to do. A quick conference with the media at the scene brought a classic Russia compromise. If the media would immediately surrender all of the film they had of dead little girls being thrown out a window, the security police would let them know when they were going to storm the build and would allow filming as they went about killing all the hostage takers. Each media member present had to agree, or there would be no deal. They all agreed. A few hours later the school was charged and the Chechnyans were all killed. The video was like nothing anyone had ever seen, but not the worst that was shot that day. That footage never surfaced, thanks to the KGB.

Because of a miscommunication, the FBI team that was following the Chechnyans in Texas lost them for about six hours.

It was only by a stroke of luck that it was able to reestablish the tail. Since there was no way of knowing whom they might have contacted and spoken with, they had to be captured for questioning. The terrorists choose to shoot it out and they were all killed.

The scariest thing about them, besides what they had come to do, was how much they looked like ordinary white Americans, maybe even Christians. They would have blended in to American society very well.

President Andrews would not allow the Islamists a chance to do a Beslan massacre in America. He ordered American schools closed until further notice. American schools at home and abroad would be secured and protected at all costs.

There would be no American Beslans on Harlan Andrews' watch.

Chapter 18

The President's Announcement

Unlike any other American war announcement from any other president, President Harlan "Bud" Andrews' announcement was a surprise to very few people. Americans had heard about the declarations on the Internet, twenty four hour cable broadcasts, talk radio and even newspapers and broadcast television. Ninety percent of the nation already knew what was happening. Now they needed to hear their president, their Commander in Chief, explain why The United States had taken furious and aggressive military action across the world in such a rapid fashion.

Andrews selected the Rose Garden to make his address. He wanted the unexpected location to make the point that our action was not just another presidential decision. To subliminally underline the seriousness of the moment, he wore a short sleeve shirt without a tie. He knew there would be only one chance to get this announcement out and get it right. There would be no press conference afterward. Any questions posed by a media that Andrews recognized as an enemy core, would only serve to confuse Americans and possibly weaken the nation's morale. He knew the media would try to embarrass him and paint him in the worse light it could. Andrews had no intention of giving them a chance to get what they wanted.

Off to his right, he heard a count down: "Mr. President we start in, five, four, three, two, and one. Go!" ....

"My fellow Americans, based on the events of these past several hours and the dangers our nation now faces, it is my sad duty to report to you that

America and a number of our closest allies are now in a state of war with several countries around the Middle East and other parts of the world.

"We are not at war with the Muslim world, the Muslim faith, or Muslim people. But we are at war with ruthless and vicious enemies who have used the Muslim religion as a basis to justify their evil intentions to force their religious beliefs on the world at the tip of a sword. So let me be very clear about this: we are fighting only the Islamists and not all Muslims."

In a conscious attempt to stress his point he repeated himself, "America and our allies are at war with the Islamist faction of the Muslim faith, not Muslims. The Islamists are not a peaceful group of people trying to gain the freedom to practice their religion. They are a splinter group of a great religion that believes God, Allah as the Muslim religion calls him, has commanded them to find ways to murder or enslave anyone whom they decide are infidels, or unbelievers of Muslim religious principles. Although I am not a Muslim, this is not my reading of the Muslim faith nor is it that of the many Muslim scholars I have consulted over recent months. The inescapable conclusion I have reached is that Islamists do not want to negotiate with us. They want to murder us. We have lost enough precious time refusing to identify our enemies.

"It is now time to name our enemy and attack him. The time for talk is over. It is now time to hit back and hit back hard.

"Let's review the recent history of our problems with the Islamists:

"Since September 11, 2001, we have tried sanctions against countries that harbor violent Islamists. We have tried using diplomatic channels to appeal to their humanity. We have tried fighting them in a limited and contained war. None of these steps have worked. Along the way, we have been talking to whomever we could in an effort to bring peace and understanding to our relationships with the Islamic world, and that has failed as well. At every opportunity we have gone the extra mile for the sake of peace for our citizens and those of the whole world. Each effort, each step, each gesture was met with scorn hate filled contempt and now car bombings on America's streets.

"Taking steps that will plunge the world into war was the last thing America and our allies wanted to do. But living in peace means just that:

living and striving for peace. Living in peace does not mean allowing ourselves to be murdered to obtain peace.

"As a free and freedom loving people, Americans simple can not sit cowering in the dark waiting for the murderer's sword. We have an absolute obligation to fight for our lives when we are threatened as the Islamists have threatened us. None of America's military might, the most powerful military ever assembled, can help us unless we summon the courage and resolve to use it to defend and protect our country and our peace loving friends around the world.

"In 2003, we undertook a limited military action against Saddam Hussein's murderous regime in Iraq. This was a mistake. Not in the goal, nor in the courageous efforts of our war fighters, but in the feckless and timid manner in which we prosecuted that war. We will not make that mistake again. We will not fight a half-hearted war against this most vicious and cunning enemy. I solemnly promise you that. This war is not something America wanted. It is not a war America has tried to engineer or bring about, but it is a war we will fight to its eventual victorious conclusion, because we have no other alternative.

"In the past several years and particularly in the past several days and hours, world-wide events, beyond the control or influence of America's best efforts, have forced us to take drastic and serious action. Late last evening I received an emergency call from Israel's Prime Minister Ethan Gross informing me that Israel's intelligence services had warned him that Iran had completed her nuclear weapons research and was now readying an unprovoked nuclear attack on Israel and her Western European allies. The warning included details of an impending terrorist attack on American facilities and installations in the Middle East. This was a deadly serious warning.

"According to the report, the Iranian president, Mohammed Waleed was targeting Tel Aviv. But he has also targeted Rome, London, and Paris. The purpose of these attacks is clear but hard for those of us who love freedom, to understand or justify. As we all now know, in spite the valiant efforts of the Israeli Air Force, it was not able to hit the Iranian launching pads before their Topol M Russian made nuclear tipped ICBMs reached lift off.

The carnage and death in Tel Aviv, London and Paris caused by these strikes was staggering. These cities have suffered enormous losses of innocent lives. At last report the death totals reported by these cities had reached into the hundreds of thousands and were still rising. I have personally spoken to the leaders of all of these devastated cities and pledged whatever humanitarian aid we can get to them under the circumstances.

"Innocent Iranian lives were also lost in the retaliatory strike on Tehran. They have been murdered by the mad aspirations of Iran's leader Mohammed Waleed as surely as if he had ordered his missiles to be aimed at his own capital city. The blame for these deaths and those that are sure to follow rests squarely on the shoulders the murderous regime of Mr. Waleed and his followers. They have brought war to the world. They have taken the first step and plunged the world into war, now they will taste war, as they never imagined it could be. This I promise.

"Mr. Waleed is an Islamists. He believes chapters of the Muslim holy book, the Qur'an are to be read and taken word for word as the expressed will of an Almighty God who orders him and his followers to kill people. He believes the literal word of God, or Allah is found in the Qur'an and he believes the one true religion is Islam. Let me once again describe the distinctions between Islamists and Muslims. Simply expressed, Islamists believe that only the exact literal words of a collection of the Qur'an's verses referred to as the Verses of the Sword are to be followed, and those verses command the death of non Islamists.

"Part and parcel of following the Verses of the Sword means killing those who do not believe in Islam. That includes men, women, children and babies. Yes, if we do not stop them, the Islamists will come here and kill even our babies. In the eyes of the Islamist, almost all Americans are infidels and therefore targets.

"Islamists are misguided fanatics. They are evil people who throughout the centuries have risen up and tried to kill non-believers in the tenets of Islam.

"The medieval Crusades were fought to free the Holy Lands from the grip of the Islamists. Europe's Christians had to rise up and fight back or be murdered to a man. It was belief in the Verses of the Sword that caused medieval Islamists to surge across the face of the known world killing or converting peaceful people wherever they found them. The Islamists will not stop. They can not be reasoned with because their only aim is to kill every American who will not convert to Islam and follow the Qur'an, as they believe it must be followed.

"Their attacks on America are nothing new. At the very beginning of our history, as a nation, Islamists pirates regularly murdered American seamen off the coast of North Africa. President Jefferson had to send United States Marines to conquer and control these enemies at that time, just as President Bush had to send our war fighters from all branches of our military services to fight Hussein and Al Qaeda in Iraq and Afghanistan.

"We have been attacked several times over the past thirty years. Evil men who follow the Verses of the Sword carried out each of these attacks. They have never changed their goals. They have never considered peaceful coexistence. The only peace they believe in is the peace they want when we are dead and in our graves.

"Here in our own nation, our Islamist enemies have found many well-meaning but very foolish allies. Every media story calling for America to withdraw from the battlefield is a source of great rejoicing and encouragement for our Islamist enemies because they believe in nothing less than final victory. In fact such stories make our enemies laugh at us. These stories have made America's fighting men and women the butt of Islamist jokes.

"We Americans have always treasured our rights of descent and freedom of speech, yet some of our college campus anti-war rallies have seriously damaged our efforts to keep ourselves free and secure. These rallies, based not on fact and genuine understanding of the grave nature of our situation, but on mere wishful thinking, hurt America and help our enemies. It is well past time that Americans young and old accept the truth: America is not the threat to world peace. America is the world's only hope for peace."

This brought a cheer from the President's advisers and a few others in attendance at his announcement.

"Neither America nor any of our allies has done anything to deserve or bring on these attacks. America and all other freedom loving countries are targets simply for living our lives and worshiping God as we believe in him without interference from anyone.

"We can not buy our safety and our future security by standing down from this fight. It is simply not true to say or think: 'If we leave them alone, they will leave us alone,' because they will never leave us alone. Those who understand the nature of our enemy know with certainty the world will never be safe again until the Islamists stop trying to kill us, and the only way to achieve that goal is to force them to stop at the point of a gun.

"To achieve the peace through security our nation and the whole free world yearns for, I have requested the Congress to return to me formal declarations of war against the nations who sent troops to the vicious attack on the Israeli town of Qiryat Shemona. These countries will receive formal declarations of war according to the Geneva conventions. I expect that in short order all but the countries that are now being run by governments that are little more than Islamist puppets, will quickly sue for peace and submit to our terms. These terms will be simple and generous. We will hold back any military strikes provided a country surrenders immediately and allows our war fighters to enter their territory to search for and destroy existing terrorist camps. Consequently, until further notice the United States of America will be in a state of war with the following nations.

"Saudi Arabia, Bangladesh, Somalia, Afghanistan, Yemen, Oman, Turkey, Morocco, Iran, Tunisia, Iraq, Libya, Jordan, Egypt, Indonesia, Nigeria, Sedan, The United Arab Emirate, Albania, Croatia, Serbia, Slovenia, Syria, Lebanon, The Philippines, Ethiopia and Algeria.

"Many of these nations have been our allies before and I expect they will be our friends and allies again very shortly. Nevertheless, they now serve as safe heavens for terrorists training camps whether willingly or unwillingly, and this must not be allowed to stand. Until the camps are destroyed either by them, or by us with their help, we must treat each of them as a hostile enemy. Being in a legal state of war with these countries will give America and our allies, who have also declared war on these nations, the legal right to enter upon the territory of these nations. Since we will, in effect be clearing out nests of terrorists who have set up camp within their borders, we expect full cooperation from each nation on this list.

"With full cooperation from the heads of state of these nations, there need not be a single drop of innocent blood shed during our search and destroy operations. The decision is of course in the hands of each leader, but preliminary indications are that we will be settling with most of these countries very shortly. At this hour American air, ground and naval forces as well as those of the United Kingdom, Australia, Canada, South Korea, Japan and several Caribbean basin nations are carrying out joint operations against the enemy.

"Winning this war will demand sacrifices from every American. In response to the requirements of our situation, I have issued orders that will temporarily suspend some of our civil rights. While this is very regrettable, it is a reality of being in a state of war. For purposes of national security, I have ordered the immediate federalization of all components of the National Guard of every state. This will include both Army and Air force National Guard commands as well as any existing Naval Militias belonging to National Guard Units. Further I have ordered the federalization of every employee of the United States Government who carries a firearm in the normal course of his or her duties. All such employees are to report to his or her workplace office and be prepared for conscription into active military service. There will be no exceptions to this order.

"I have also ordered that, starting at 6 AM tomorrow, Washington time, Eastern Standard Time, a total curfew will begin. This means that only those with good and sufficient reason to be outdoors will be allowed access to our streets. No one except military, civilian police and emergency personnel will be allowed on our streets under penalty of arrest and indefinite detention. I have ordered other steps as well. Starting immediately no travel visas will be issued to any country in the Middle Eastern region of the world, whether America is at war with that nation or not.

"I have ordered that all foreign nationals who are citizens of the nations we are now at war with are to immediately report to special field offices of the Immigration and Naturalization Service for questioning. If these foreign nationals from enemy combatant countries are deemed to be a danger to our security they will be deported. Those covered by this order will be captured and deported at the earliest possible moment after the current state of emergency is over.

"I have ordered our United States Marines to seize and close the embassy and consulate buildings of all nations we now at war with. I have further ordered that all property being held in American banks and financial institutions belonging to enemy nations, and certain identified individuals, be frozen until I approve of a resumption of normal banking commerce.

"I have also ordered that all funds, now invested with enemy combatant nations by private or public agencies be immediately withdrawn and no future investments be made until further notice. It is my understanding that most, if not all, of our state pension funds are invested in financial products that directly or indirectly help those who want our destruction. I have asked state officials to commence an immediate review of their holdings and report their findings to the Attorney General's office without delay.

"Finally, I have ordered the establishment of processing centers to receive and make good use of any American under the age of 45, with military experience, in good physical condition that wishes to volunteer in America's hour of need. I urge every veteran American who is physically able to volunteer, to come forward and lend a hand. Americans will teach our enemies a simple message: You don't find out that you have disturbed the hornets until you walk into their nest.

"As the Islamist wolves silently circle around us, we will not hide. I have sworn an oath to protect America from all enemies, foreign or domestic and I fully intend to follow my oath to the letter.

"Let all who would plot the destruction of America be on notice. America will not hide from you. If you come to kill American families we will slaughter you. Your plans to defeat America with your thousand little cuts, bleeding us to death, will not kill the home of freedom and democracy. We will soak the ground with your blood.

"America's days of negotiating with murderers are over. We can no longer pretend that we can reason with Islamists. Our days of trying to use sanctions are over. Our days of fighting a limited politically correct war in self defense are, from this moment, now over my fellow Americans. America is now on the offensive and it is full speed ahead. We are now at a kill or be killed point.

"The days of giving credence to the doomsayers who have cautioned against using all of America's full military might are also over. We can not and we will not lose this war. As the days and weeks before us unfold, we will hold back nothing from our arsenal as we hunt down and destroy any force that would dare to bring war to America.

"They will fight with fury and unflinching devotion. To beat them, we will have to fight with still more dedication to our mission of protecting freedom.

"This war can not be wished away. It can not be ignored away. Only facing it squarely and attacking our enemies will preserve our freedoms. I can not tell you how long this war will take. I can not say how many American lives will be lost in this war. I can only tell you that it will be fought on every emerging theater on our terms, not the enemy's.

"Our lives will not soon return to normal. For many Americans, including me, the chances are very great that this war will be the final chapter of our lives. Many Americans may never see a day free from war again. Yet it is for each and every American to join in this life or death struggle for the sake of our families, our children and generations of Americans yet to come.

"While life in America may never be the same, it need not be as deprived and diminished as our enemy would wish. We are a strong and resilient people. The superiority of our American character will allow us to endure the hardships to come. Of this I am certain.

"Our nation has been placed here by God to be the beacon of freedom for His world. I am confident that the strong arms of our Lord will be with us as we persecute this war. Our enemies will soon discover that the spirit of America is tougher, stronger, smarter, more determined and meaner than any other people on earth. Our allies are equally tough smart and up to this fight. But we will prevail with your help, your sacrifices, your prayers and we will continue to breathe free and enjoy peace and safety once again.

"My fellow Americans, we are in a fight for our very lives with a savage enemy whose murderous history goes back hundreds of years.

Our enemies will fight to win, but by their very nature they will fight to die for God, as they believe in him. Yet as it always has been, American courage and resolve to fight and live will win out over those who fight to die.

"I have one final request: Please pray for our nation. Now please join me in saying the Lord's Prayer.

"Our Father who art in heaven, hollowed be thy name. Thy kingdom come, Thy will be done, on earth as it is in heaven. Give us this day our daily bread and forgive us our trespasses as we forgive those who trespass against us. Lead us not into temptation but deliver us from evil for thine is the Kingdom and the power and the glory forever and ever. Amen.

"May God bless you all and may God continue to bless the United States of America!"

Ironically on that day a syndicated news column that appeared in newspapers all over the country had mocked the Andrews Administration for steadfastly maintaining that the nation was in grave danger from Islamist extremists. No one cared about what the print media had to say by that point. All over America cheers went up, car horns blew, church bells rang and people ran to the streets to celebrate. Americans were ready to fight back and now they had a leader to follow to victory.

CHAPTER 19

THE MISSILE SILOS AT JANDAQ

TWENTY-FOUR HOURS before President Andrews made his declarations of war, Prime Minister Ethan Gross broke the news to his top advisers. America's had launched Operation Sucker Punch and there was no turning back. They cheered at first, then the need to figure out an immediate next step gripped each of them. The bunker room went calm as they quietly contemplated Israel's next move. They were not perplexed as to what to do. That question had been settled in the details of Operation Purim Party. They were concerned about making sure that their timing was right and the two operations would hit Waleed in a one – two combination

The silence was shattered be a hotline call from the Mossad's Chief of Intelligence. As he listened to the caller, Gross nodded and blinked, but said nothing more than, "Thank you, amarta amarta," mixing English and Hebrew for, "You said it, that's good enough for me."

Gross started to speak even before he hung up. "The Iranians are queuing up their missiles. They are even now opening their silos. This is it. We have to launch now to stop them. They have ten missiles aimed at us and probably the largest cities in Europe." He pointed to the Air Force Chief of Operations and said, "Today is tomorrow. There are no more tomorrows. Send the fighters."

In the desert lands of central Iran, just outside of the town of Bafq, Waleed's missile silos sprang to life. But the activity was a ruse. The silos were dummies and the Mossad knew they were. The deep cover agents Israel had in place for many years had supplied the coordinates for the dangerous silos; the real silos. They were situated at Jandaq in the arid Dasht-e Kavir region 200 miles south east of Tehran. It was time for the world's guessing game about Israel's nuclear capabilities to end. Over the span of forty years and a succession of American administrations, the Western media had made it their top priority to discover and report Israel's nuclear capabilities.

Ethan Gross was about to answer the world's questions about Israel's nuclear power with Operation Purim Party. Now the world could only sit and watch, regardless of which side they were rooting for, as the Israelis went to work. Israel was about to rain her own fire down on those who would not let her live in peace. Gross launched two nuclear tipped *Arrow* interceptor missiles toward the dangerous silos and three nuclear missiles at Tehran. The Arrow, a weapon jointly developed by Israel and America, is one of the few reliable operational ballistic missile defense systems in use anywhere in the world.

Leon Hershcovitz, the head Israel's Missile Defense Ministry, Homa which means *Fortress Wall* in Hebrew, was confident his missiles could find and destroy Iran's missiles even up to 11 minutes after an enemy had launched his attack.

To Leon Hershcovitz the son of Holocaust survivors, and a man who had a picture of J. Robert Oppenheimer on his desk, the Islamists were his personal enemies. He openly enjoyed planning their destruction, which was the reason Ethan Gross selected him for his job.

Hershcovitz assured Gross the *Arrow* system would work when called upon. "It was very effective against the Katyusha rockets fired by Lebanon's Hezbollah guerillas into Northern Israel. It will work in this attack."

Gross managed a weak smile and said, "From you lips to God's ears." As an extra measure, they sent forty F-16 Falcons, recently purchased from America, to finish off any remaining strike capabilities Jandaq might have after the missile strike. Each of the specially chosen pilots understood his orders: "Leave nothing to chance, no prisoners. No survivors. Kill everything that moves. I repeat: No survivors. If you must, fly directly into a silo to stop a missile."

Other Falcons soared to engage the antiquated Iranian Air Force above Waleed's lone gasoline refinery. In a country sitting in the middle of the world's most oil rich region, Iran had never bothered to build more than a single oil refinery. For decades it seemed as if they never would have to build anymore either. But as he was in so many other facets of his insane plan to Islamize the world, Waleed was wrong. In a total miscalculation, both Syria and Iran had opted to put all of their money into missile development. Now at the moment of truth, Israel was going "all in" and chopping the Islamist's Air Forces to pieces. The Syrians could only watch and wait until it was their turn for an ass kicking from Israel. Their nukes were not quite operational, which was another important part of Operation Purim Party. Syrian nukes would not get off the ground.

Both Iran and Syria bought their war planes from North Korea. Both realized very much too late that believing communists is as foolish as believing Islamists. The snowmen had been snowed. Their planes were not up to fighting the Israelis Air Force. The fights turned into quick kills for Israel and that cleared the way for the Israeli Defense Force's heavy bombers to destroy Iran's refinery beyond recognition. In that single strike the Iranian military was choked and halted. All the oil under the ground was useless. There was now no way it could be turned into petroleum products to fuel and grease the wheels of war. Waleed's war machine would have to win quickly or not at all.

Syria's nukes were also purchased from North Korea. They were not even worth bombing. The Mossad had detailed information on what Damascus had been sold. They knew the North Korean communists had snuckered the naive Abdullah.

PART THREE
War in the Holy Lands and Europe

CHAPTER 20

Operation Sucker Punch Gets Going

THE PRESIDENT'S ORDER to go to war against the countries the whole world knew were guilty of helping terrorists caused an explosion of morale both home and abroad. Around the world military posts of every service snapped into action. The written orders started with the same opening sentence. "Preparation plus courage equals victory." It became the central theme of everything America's war fighters did in the first six hours of the operation.

All of the Navy's eighteen Ohio Class nuclear submarines were moved to the highest level of readiness. Each boat carried twenty-four nuclear missiles, each armed with eight independently targeted warheads. Like a gathering pack of angry wolves the submarines rendezvoused at points all over the world.

Each was assigned to monitor an area of the theater of war and stay ready to launch flaming scorching death on cities in countries that refused to surrender. The Marine Corps base in Kuwait was equally abuzz with the preparations of war. Since the securing of Iraq, as a major theater of war, most Marine and Army combat units had been re-deployed to the oil rich kingdom to stay close if needed and provide protection for petro-businesses throughout the region.

A special Air Wing of combined Air Force, Navy and Marine Corps fighter planes protected the Army and Marine Corps ground troops. The unit, designated as the 509th Composite Group, to send a clear message about its fighting capabilities, was built around one hundred and twenty F-22 war planes. These planes are among the finest aircraft any nation ever put in the air. They can seek and find targets in any weather flying more than 500 miles per hour. They are hard to shoot down and extremely durable.

The name of the unit directly addressed the need to impress the Islamists with the fact that America remembered her history as well as they remembered their history. It said America was not going to roll over and be enslaved. The 509th Composite Group was the name of the World War II special air wing that included such planes as Bok's Car and the Enola Gay.

Both planes dropped atomic bombs on Japan. Both bombs underscored American determination to never be dominated by anyone. Within three hours, the Joint Chiefs of Staff reported to Andrews that all services were in *Go* condition. One hour after the President's announcement and request for a declaration of war, combined regiments of Marine and Army combat troops were on their way toward the countries the Joint Chiefs determined were most likely to choose fighting rather than surrendering.

In rapid succession, America declared war on each of the countries President Andrews had named as the nation's enemies. Within twenty minutes after the announcement, Iran went into high alert. Having been flattened by an Israeli nuclear strike, Iran's capital Tehran was in shambles. The beautiful centuries old center of the ancient nation was a toxic wasteland. But Iran's Air Force had fared well in the Israeli's retaliatory strike. Most of its planes were parked at various bases awaiting orders when the Israelis turned the tables on Waleed's plans to nuke his enemies. The next move would be the Islamists.

Waleed's missile silos were now useless. Qiryat Shemona had destroyed his timetable for war. He was not quite ready to move when he was forced to do so. He was not able to threaten many of the countries he needed to join him to have a genuine chance to win a conventional war with America. Only Syria and Sudan had stood with Iran and the Islamists. The first objective of Purim Party/Sucker Punch had been reached: the war would be fought on America and Israeli time table, not Waleed's.

THE UNFOLDING BATTLE

The Syrian/Iranian attacking force could not have envisioned the events of the first day. Waleed's dreams of wave after human wave assaults that would over run and destroy Israel were built on the thoughts that came to him when he took too many of the pain killers he survived on each day.

When his multiple sex sessions with numerous young girls could no longer sufficiently distract him, Waleed tended to take too many 'happy pills.' When he was mellowed out from the pills, he would have hallucinations of great Islamist victories in battles against the infidels. During these "battles" he would speak to his heroes Saladin and Mohammed and ask for their advice. His hallucinations always told him human wave attacks were the best strategy in battles against infidels. Saladin and Mohammed would urge him to bring about the "mother of all battles" to end the world. They called him "Al Madhi" and told him he was the missing man of the Muslim Trinity.

Waleed's dreams never included the high altitude bombings the infidels would bring to his troops splattering them on the desert sands. Nor did they entail Jordan's refusal to join him which doomed his mission of destroying Israel. The modern firepower the Allies brought to defend Israel made things worse for him.

The Jordanians made their decision quickly. They did not want to self immolate along with Iran's madman because he now believed he was the returned Al Madhi. They knew Waleed's bragging about what he was going to do to "those infidel swine" and actually doing something were entirely separate matters. They knew that Waleed had no concept of reality.

Because Jordan was not on board, the attack could not be a complete envelopment of Israel. Jordan had opened her territory to Allied military units to help them get into fighting positions along her border with Syria. It was only after a shouting match, between Waleed and Abdullah Bey Jessin the president of Syria, that threatened to fracture their alliance, did Waleed agree to end his insistence upon opening an additional front against the Jordanians. He backed down only to keep the Syrians at his side. The news that the brothers from Sudan had been blown out of their boats as they tried to move up the Red Sea and join the Islamist forces was another crushing blow. He would deal with Jordan later, so he thought. The Islamists battle plan was to use the Golan Heights corridor to attack northern Israel. It would not be an easy assault. The path called for advancing around the natural obstacle of Lake Tiberias.

When Waleed's human waves started to cross the Golan Heights, Israeli and American F-17 and F-22s flying off of the carrier USS Boyington met their advance with lethal firepower. Waleed's dreams about hand- to-hand, seventh century style combat were not going to be accommodated by the United States and Israel.

While the Allied planes hammered away at the advancing ground troops Tehran was digging herself out of nuclear rubble. This created command and control problems that hampered the Islamists movements. In retaliation, the enraged Waleed diverted his warplanes to finish off what was left of Tel Aviv. Without enough air cover the Islamists ground forces had a still more difficult time making progress. During the first day of the battle, hundreds of thousands of civilians died by the hour in cities all over the Middle East.

RETALIATING WITH SUPER WEAPONS

In response to the continuing attacks on Tel Aviv, the Allies divided responsibilities for their air strikes. President Andrews suggested that, for post war political reasons, America would use its super weapons only against combatants on recognized battlefields.

The United States still had a stockpile of 15,000-pound *Daisy Cutter bombs* and their successor the 21,000-pound MOABs *Massive Ordinance Air Blast Bomb*. These monster bombs killed every living thing in a 600-yard radius. They terrorized troops on the battlefield. The deafening sound and ground shaking effect of Daisy Cutters made Saddam's troops openly weep and attempt to surrender to Western reporters covering the first Gulf War.

The Daisy Cutters arrived at the battle of the Golan Heights first. When they were dropped, it was in a deliberate pattern, which cut huge holes in the lines of the attacking forces. The enemy troops that survived these massive bombs were subject to follow up around the clock conventional bombing strikes.

IRANIAN NEUTRON BOMB SUICIDE ATTACKS

Even after these big bomb strikes, Waleed was far from done. He threw his first big punch at about 3 O'clock in the morning on the second day.

He had three old MiGs; loaded with Neutron bombs, fly directly into the Israeli Army headquarters just behind the front line of the battle. The Kamikaze like attacking planes caught the Allies off guard because they were in the air so briefly and flew at almost ground level to avoid radar detection.

Neutron bombs, more formally called *enhanced radiation weapons* (ERW) are designed as tactical nuclear bombs. Their killing power is about one-tenth of the intensity of the bomb dropped on Hiroshima.

The attack was a thorough success for Waleed. The bombers killed or wounded almost four thousand allied troops and destroyed millions of dollars in valuable equipment. The trade of three old MiGs for the damage those bombs caused was a huge boost to the sagging morale of the attacking Islamist forces who then immediately charged the impact area to kill the remaining troops. They had no fear of radiation because they had no fear of dying. The charge was beaten back with air strikes by American and British Air Force fighters. There were not enough troops left to do the job.

The affect of the raid cut both ways. While it boosted the morale of the Islamists, it also infuriated the Allied troops. The fighting spirit of Israel's defenders sprung back to life quickly after the initial shock of the devastation wore off. Within hours the necessary regrouping was completed and the Allied ground troops were ready to defend their territory again.

Trouble in the Enemy's Tent

There were very clear educational, social and cultural differences between the Syrian troops and Waleed's forces. This was especially evident in the officer corps each sent to the battle. Waleed's Iranians were mostly religious zealots who were obviously not concerned so much with actual victory as they were with bringing about the flaming end of the world.

Syria's higher ranking officers had been part of the world community's when it successfully fought against Saddam's heavy handed grab of Kuwait in the first Gulf War. They were proud of their nation's part in putting a thug in his place. Some of them believed that cooperation with the West, in this current war against another thug, would bring about the liberalization and modernization Syria needed to advance and become a leader along the lines of Turkey. Among themselves, the Syrians laughed at the backward Iranians and called them 'ignorant goat herders' behind their backs.

The Syrians Army officers were not happy about being ordered into battle against the United States. They knew America's capabilities to make the Golan Heights a 'meat grinder' that would chew them up. They had watched the Iraqis be slaughtered on the famous *Highway of death* during Gulf War I.

They saw the terrific beating Saddam got when his army, the one the naïve Western media kept calling his *Vaunted Republican Guard*, was pulverized in just days as recently as 2003. The Syrian Officers were not fooled by America's pull out of Iraq. They understood that America's ground troops were winning their war with Al Qaeda and Waleed's Islamists when they were taken off the battlefield by America's politicians. Many Syrian Army officers believed Syria should have followed Jordan and Egypt and taken American's offer of a quick *paper war* and surrender. They wanted their country to cooperate with the efforts to end the Islamist's perversion of their religion. Nevertheless, they were career military men, so their sense of duty pushed them forward in spite of their feelings of impending doom.

When the Syrians saw the Iranians taking drugs, it was clear that they were dangerous as allies. The Iranians carried swords and ceremonial scarves into battle along with their standard assault rifles. When the Syrians saw this, they were only too happy to put them in the front of their own mechanized troops. Waleed's men were seventh century warriors and proud of it. They were fiercely brave and not at all afraid of death, but troops bent on suicide do not win wars as the Syrians knew.

Waleed's men got high on brown-brown, a cocaine and gunpowder mixture and amphetamines, to prepare for their charges on the Allied lines. Tens of thousands of Islamist troops steeled themselves with drugs and hatred before they moved forward. As they would soon discover, widespread drug use is not an asset to any army.

SEVENTH CENTURY WARRIORS

Even on the most modern battlefield, victory still rests on the basic infantryman's shoulders. He is the one who feels the pain, sees the explosions.

He is the one who slips on the blood of the dead and dying and smell the death all around him. When that infantryman is a seventh century remnant the dynamics of warfare change. Modern well equipped troops can slow down seventh century warriors and always eventually stop them, but if there are enough of these ancient warriors charging a position, some of them will get through almost any wall of lethal fire aimed at them.

This is just what happened in the battle for northern Israel. In a quick and surprisingly coordinated attack, lead by the Iranians who had come to consider the Syrians cowards, Waleed's men ran and died and ran and died and ran and died again. They engulfed the forward Allied positions so quickly in some cases it was impossible to bomb the locations for fear of bombing Allied soldiers.

Whole units of Israeli combat troops were first cut off from their lines, then surrounded, then chopped to death with broad swords. During the fighting, first dozens, then hundreds, of Waleed's troops were mowed down. The deaths meant nothing to them. They stepped over their dead and dying as if they were floor mats and ran slipping and sliding in the freshly shed blood searching for someone to kill. Not a single wounded Islamist was cared for by his own troops. Neither side cared what happened to them.

Reaching Deeper and Deeper into Israel

In spite of the forty-five percent casualty rates Waleed's Islamist Militiamen were taking, they began to make progress. Before the Turks had a chance to shutdown the flow, forty-thousand fresh volunteer militiamen pour into Syria over her border with Turkey. These reinforcements were a much needed help to the Islamists efforts. Backed by artillery units of both the Iranian and Syrian Armies and the remnants of their combined Air Forces, the volunteers helped Waleed's troops to begin to move deeper and deeper into Israel.

For the time being, the Islamists started to win their ground war in northern Israel. As the Allies retreated, the Islamists rapidly took control of all of the small towns in a straight line moving west toward Haifa, Israel's major seaport and third largest city. To soften it up, the Islamist's had launched a huge surface to surface missile attack on Haifa's 270,000 residents.

Situated just 70 miles from Tel Aviv, Haifa presented a unique problem for the Allies and a genuine opportunity for the Islamists. It was a truly cosmopolitan city that saw both Jews and Arabs peacefully living side by side. Together they had succeeded in largely secularizing their town.

HAIFA

Haifa was so secular that it was the only major center in Israel that did business on Saturdays. Its modern world class city status had attracted many American companies including Microsoft and IBM.

After World War I the British and French forced the Ottoman Turks to give up Haifa at gunpoint. Because of its history as another city that had once been, conquered, owned and controlled by the Muslims, Haifa's status as a Jewish city infuriated the Islamists. In Israeli hands it served as another constant reminder of the basic impotence of the Islamist way of life. It reminded the world their 1400 year campaign to force Islam on the world was a failure.

As Islamist troops fought their way toward Haifa, they sustained a vicious pounding from Allied air power. To balance their attack and finish off Haifa, the Islamists used the Syrian Navy to try to catch the city in a pincher. The Syrian Navy was not up to the task. Their patrol ships were splintered to pieces as they approached Haifa Bay. The defenders of Israel drew a line and dug in at Haifa.

They would not yield another foot of their homeland to Waleed. They would not allow their country to be pushed into the Mediterranean Sea. Once the sea was swept clean of Syrian ships, Haifa's civilians came out of hiding and were transported to Tel Aviv. With the city cleared of non combatants, the Allies were free to let the Islamists take parts of Haifa.

When they did most of them were vaporized at will by the American and Israeli combined Air Forces. The skies had been cleaned of enemy planes in a series of spectacular dogfights in the opening hours of hostilities. The Arab pilots were flying better planes than they had been in earlier wars, but they were still not better pilots than the Americans, the Israelis or the British. Getting Syria to surrender was the next objective in the Allied plans.

LATAKIA: CONVINCING SYRIA TO SURRENDER

Syria was immediately identified as a soft spot in Waleed's coalition. It had been under the thumb of its tyrannical President Abdullah Yassin Bey whose father had been the nation's dictator before him. The Yassin Bey family ran Syria as their personal fiefdom for more than forty years. The son was a well educated petro-chemical engineer overseeing Syria's oil production operations when his father died suddenly of an unexplained illness. Young Abdullah was the classic *babe in the woods* when it came to being a dictator. He relied on the council and advice of his father's inner circle for his understanding of how to run a country.

Over the years since his assumption to power, Abdullah became very skilled at, and comfortable with, the methods of cruelty and murder needed to stay in power. Where his Western education seemed at first to offer a glimmer of hope for liberalization and modernization, he eventually became a worse tyrant than his father. When Syria opted to remain loyal to Iran she immediately became a Mind War target. Every back channel available to the Allies was used to discover and gauge the true level of support Abdullah had among his own people. The results were encouraging. The Intelligence reports on Syria's internal unrest told a story which was very different from the public face Abdullah put on for the Western media. In Syria's national elections held the previous May, Abdullah received 100% of the popular vote. The Western media hailed him as a beloved figure to his people. They praised him for allowing and even encouraging write-in candidates against him. But of course the truth was quite another story.

The French news service Agence France-Presse (AFP) giddily pointed out that even though, under Syrian election law when no opposition candidate comes forward no election is necessary, Abdullah the great democrat held the election anyway and had his men help write in candidates. One French newspaper gushed, "This is the type of democracy the French Republic was founded on, where is it now? Syria is the answer!"

Sober examination of the facts showed the Allied war planners they could split Syria away from Iran if they moved quickly and carefully.

The action would have to be stunning to the Syrians but not infuriating.

There could be no rallying cry material. Latakia, Syria's main seaport became the answer. The decision was made to bomb and destroy Latakia, a seaside town in northern Syria, that had been important and a point of battle during the 1973 Yom Kippur War. The town was attacked in a surgical strike designed to show the Syrians the awesome military power they were fighting.

Latakia is a thriving town of over 560,000, with ancient roots going back to the days of the Roman Empire. It had been a trading point used by the French until just before World War II. Its deep water harbor exports food stuffs, pottery and asphalt among other commodities. Losing Latakia would be a major but not fatal blow to the Syrians.

The high altitude bombing of Latakia started at 4:15 AM on the day after Syria rejected America's demand for her surrender. As expected, the humiliation of surrender without a fight was too much for Abdullah to accept. The bespectacled little man fancied himself as a 'tough guy' and to him, tough guys do not back down, even if others will do the actual fighting and dying to prove this point. There was no way 'tough guy' Abdullah would accept the temporary loss of Syria's sovereignty rights that would come with her capitulation to America.

The operation went smoother than the Americans and her British partners could have hoped for. With precision workman-like efficiency the F-22s and Harriers Tornado GR.4s, peeled the valuable portions of Latakia away from the rest of the town. The bombing was so effective that when the combined Israeli and American Naval Task Force started its bombardment there was very little of importance left to destroy. The damage to Latakia was extensive and gave the Allies good grounds to demand Syria's surrender. When the six hour deadline came and went without an answer, Halab, a northern city and the capital of the Province of Halab was next to be hit.

Halab was a major agricultural center situated between the Mediterranean Sea and the Euphrates River. As Syria's second largest city, Halab's destruction sent a clear message to Abdullah: Surrender or Damascus is next. With no Air Force left the Syrians could not put up protective umbrella to keep Damascus safe from attack. In a desperate attempt to save Damascus and keep Syria in the war, Waleed sent all of his best fighter planes to the rescue. His Air Force still had 15 Russian built Sukhoi-30 long range fighters. The Iranians soon found that the best planes can only perform as well as their pilots can fly them. Waleed's pilots were valiant and fought hard but they were no match for the Top Guns America sent up to meet them. The Sukhoi-30s held the Allied forces back for a few more hours before they were shot out of the skies above Damascus.

With air superiority achieved, Allied bombers could take all the time they needed to carefully break the old city into pieces no one would be able to put back together. Reports of the astounding destructive power of America's MOABs and Daisy Cutters had painted a terrifying picture of what life in Damascus would be like if the Americans brought them to the nation's capital. Islamist controlled media had accurately described what these monster bombs could do on a battlefield. Imagining their effect on city streets was horrifying for the people of Damascus.

The nub of the question for the Allied Commanders came down to allowing Abdullah to keep his power after the surrender.

How he handled the matter of losing face after yet another defeat by the West would be up to him. What the Allies could do and would do was rely on the media fashioned fiction that Abdullah was popularly elected by a people who loved him.

When Syria surrendered, the Allies made a statement to the effect that since Abdullah was one of the few democratically elected leaders in the Middle East he would not be removed from office. The western media howled with outrage, but the Allied military spokesman answered their demands for an explanation by citing the glowing editorial praise that had been lavishly heaped on Abdullah when we won his last election. The few remaining Syrian forces in the Golan Heights were withdrawn after a public statement made by Abdullah. The Allies demanded it before they would recall the bombers they had circling Damascus like hawks waiting to pounce on a helpless rabbit.

Chapter 21

Israel Trains Her Air Force to Crush Waleed

The David Team

ETHAN GROSS knew that preparing for the day Israel would launch "Operation Purim Party" meant training her pilots for the fight. Without being told exactly what they were training for, Israel's top pilots trained day and night, drilling in formation missions and practicing airborne refueling. In joint exercises with American pilots, Israel's best flyers traded tactics and ways of approaching Arab enemies. Although they never spoke indiscreetly about the purpose of their training, both groups of pilots knew the target would be Waleed's nuclear facilities.

The combined new informal Air Group of Israeli and American pilots named itself the *David Team*, after one of the most famous Israeli pilots in the Jewish State's history. It was a perfect name because when Captain Zevi David performed his most amazing flying feat he was in a Mc Donnell Douglas F-15, so both groups could rightly be proud. In May of 1983 while flying in a training exercise Captain David's F-15 Eagle collided with another plane and his Eagle's right wing was ripped off. Through a combination of superior flying skills and superior American design, David was able to safely land his aircraft, save his life, and what was left of his airplane. The Team had an autographed picture of David standing in front of his mangled F-15 on the wall of its headquarters. The inscription read "Building weapons like this is why America wins every time!"

Because the Iranians were clever enough to spread their nuclear striking capabilities throughout their desert, some locations being decoys and a few being the real thing, the American/Israeli Air Group had to train to hit various types of targets. They had to carefully study the intelligence reports to keep their focus on their mission. The best intelligence estimates about Waleed's progress toward constructing a nuclear bomb said he was almost there and just waiting for the optimum moment to attack Israel and the rest of the non Muslim world.

Unfortunately, as happens when two countries join together on a special mission, a major misunderstanding split the American/Israeli partnership. It happened when an over eager Israeli Air Force (IAF) commander thought he was given the green light to strike at Waleed's nuclear bases. He ordered his fighter-bombers to arm their own nuclear weapons and fly off on an attack from the Team's base at Hatzerim Air Base in Negev, approximately 75 kilometers south of Tel Aviv. The situation was only contained when a group of American F-15s raced out to intercept the attack.

A Team of Mossad and CIA analysts had studied Intelligence reports on Waleed's nuclear activities and determined the activity in and near his nuclear facilities was a faint designed to learn how closely he was being watched and what Israel's Air Force would be able to do in a real situation.

Mohammed Waleed was a sly fox. He remembered that in 1990, just after the conclusion of Desert Storm, Israel had launched an attack using nuclear armed fighter planes that had to be recalled. Americans had called the shots than and he wanted to know if the Americans would be calling the shots in his war.

Using specially manufactured transponders to discover if a fly over is *friend or foe* even if not seen; the Iranians turned the tables on the Israelis. They used the opportunity to unveil their new SA-18 Igla-S Russian mobile anti-aircraft batteries designed to defeat attacks from low-flying jets. The Iranians were able to defeat the *squawk codes* the Israeli Air Force used to confuse and uncover their anti-aircraft batteries. When the Israelis approached Iranian airspace they were the ones who were confused.

The counter measures employed by Waleed's men rendered the plane's radar systems useless and unable to guide them to their targets. At least that was what both sides initially thought. The 'problem' was not really a problem given the new ultra smart radar systems that were undergoing final testing over the deserts of Western Texas. The new systems could filter out radar disinformation and follow it back to its source thereby knocking it out as surely as the old systems did. As was the case during the 1980s Russian/Afghani war, America had once again used surrogates to demonstrate that her war fighting technology was superior to what the Russians could produce. With their own highly developed abilities to tweak and improve American technology, the Israelis enhanced the capabilities of the new American counter radar so they could reduce an F-16's radar signature to almost nothing. There was a major difference between the mindset of Israel's pilots and their American brothers. The Jews always take a longer view of their struggles for survival. Given the distance to their targets, which sat beyond the range of their American F-16s, the Israelis accepted their assignment as a suicide mission. There would be no way to land and refuel and there would be no practical way to complete an airborne refueling maneuver.

Once this reality was accepted, fighting off the Iranian's F-5 and MiG-29s was less daunting. The brave IAF pilots had pledged to ram their attackers after delivering their payloads. As part of their orders, they were authorized to hit targets of opportunity including Waleed's Tabriz Air Base and Hamadan training camp, where his Revolutionary Guard's storehouse of Weapons of Mass Destruction (WMD) was located.

Early in the IAF's reconnaissance program of Iran's nuclear facilities the Mossad targeted a plant at al-Jesira where Waleed's scientists produced hexafluoride, an ingredient necessary to produce highly enriched weapons grade uranium. Another special target was the Tehran laboratory that processed the dangerous biological weapons, Anthrax, botulism and various strains of the black plague, all gifts from the Shiite military officers in Saddam's army as his regime was falling. When Israel's Military Intelligence Chief Aharon Ben-Raave declared that the theoretical *red line* of Iran's nuclear progress had been passed, Ethan Gross had to take him on his word. He was then able to speak to Harlan Andrews with a great deal of authority.

The final inch of the progress was reached when Waleed's base at Dimona was deemed to be capable of launches that would incinerate Tel Aviv with nuclear tipped warheads. Gross had no intention of allowing his city to become another Hirosima. By his way of thinking, the only logical course for him and his nation was to target Tehran and try to kill Waleed.

CHAPTER 22

DEATH SLIPS THROUGH
WALEED SENDS HIS NUKES

FOR ALL ITS ATTENTION TO DETAIL, Israel was late with her response to the warning of Waleed's impending nuclear attack. By the time the IAF strike hit the Iranian silos, four of Iran's missiles were launched and away. The deadly payloads made their way toward: Tel Aviv, Rome, London and Paris. Waleed's missiles were single warhead Inter-continental ballistic missiles (ICBM) Topol M, Russian weapons produced in 1997 by the Moscow Institute of Thermal Technology. They were ordinarily very accurate and reliable, but on that day one failed.

The missiles aimed at London, Paris and Tel Aviv flew straight and true. But by some stroke of fortune, the missile sent to incinerate Rome malfunctioned and fell harmlessly into Mediterranean Sea. Waleed had carefully and secretly built up his nuclear weapons arsenal over a number of years. The missiles were purchased two or three at a time starting in 2004. Waleed also launched Shihabs, his long-range missiles developed by trial and error from the"scuds" of the early 1990s. His Shihabs were sent to various targets around the Middle East. He was settling all of his scores at one time. He wanted to not only destroy Israel and America, but flatten any countries he thought were not living up to his ideas of Islamic life as well. Waleed's over grown 'scuds' turned out to be more error and trial than reliable weapon. His Shihabs went everywhere but where they were aimed.

They failed in what Waleed tried to do, but they did send a message he was not trying to convey. Seeing the huge holes in their desert lands and a few small towns was enough for the Muslim leaders of many surrounding countries to conclude that Waleed was the dangerous radical they hoped he was not. They had to admit that Israel and America were right about Waleed. That point would become very important sooner than anyone could have anticipated. Waleed's wild shots around the desert pushed almost all of the countries on Harlan Andrews's list into the safety of a quick surrender.

If it had not been for the damage the Saudis had done to the Iranian economy when they lowered the price of a barrel of oil, to below their own cost of production, the Iranians would have purchased even more of their deadly toys from the Russians. They would have been better armed and anything could have happened. The Saudi's move caused Waleed's cash flow to dry up forcing the Russians to cut them off. The always cash poor Moscow, could no longer sell their weapons on credit. Since the fall of the Soviet Union, the Russians had learned a lesson about the differences between ideology and hard currency.

The Topol M, a three-stage rocket, had enough range to easily guide it to virtually any intended target. These deadly weapons typically can travel over 6,000 miles. They can put an explosive package with the same punch as almost 500 tons of TNT on its target and do so with remarkable accuracy.

Since Waleed's enemies were much closer than 6,000 miles away, the most attractive feature of the Topol M was that it could be used either as a mobile or silo based weapon.

With so much easily traveled open space, Waleed reasoned that he could keep his weapons moving during a war and be almost certain that at least some would be launched safely toward his targets. For the most part, however, the Iranians used silos to overcome the problems of traveling over sand bed roads that would crumble under such massive weight. The additional problem of having sirocco winds clog delicate mechanisms with swirling desert sands meant that in practical terms, all of Waleed's missiles were stationary. His men were too frightened about what would happen to them and their families if he found out that there were no mobile missiles in his arsenal, so they never told him his plan would not work.

Waleed's men did not realize the advantage their stationary missiles would give the Israeli Air Force. Although the silos were dug into mountain fortresses, they still had to be slowly and carefully unveiled to be fired. Nevertheless, because of the Topol M's powerful first stage boosters, its vulnerability to attack at its launch inception is only just a bit over sixty seconds. The IAF had to have split second timing to blow them up before they launched. A late hit would do little good. An early hit would be useless as well. The attack resistant silos, built to Russian specifications, were capable of defeating a direct hit by a nuclear tipped missile. The odds of stopping these missiles on the ground, in their silos or at the moment the silos opened, was not very good. Given the chaotic circumstances of the Iranian launching, it would have taken a perfect shot and lots of luck for Israel to destroy the Topol Ms before they were in flight. Neither the world nor the Israelis had the luck they needed to stop Iran's death cylinders before they fell on some of the largest cities in the western world.

CHAPTER 23

TEL AVIV IN FLAMES

THE NATURAL ISRAELI TARGET for one of Waleed's nuclear tipped missiles should have been Jerusalem. As the center of the Jewish state's government, Jerusalem seemed to be where he would hit first. Waleed knew Israel would probably hit his capital of Tehran, but for very important reasons Tel Aviv was selected as his first target.

Among those important reasons was the fact that although over 3 million people resided there, more Muslims lived in the Jewish capital than anywhere else that could be hit. Additionally, Tel Aviv became the target because Jerusalem is the location of the Al-Aqsa Mosque, one of the most important mosques in the world. The mosque is known as the Noble Sanctuary, and can accommodate as many as two hundred thousand worshippers. More than this, as the future location of the capital of the nation of Palestine, Waleed could not destroy the city. He was not yet ready to reveal his true plans for the world when the decision to target Tel Aviv or Jerusalem was made. He knew that if he chose Jerusalem and that information leaked out he would have trouble recruiting his Palestinian brothers to the fight. There was no way Waleed could surgically destroy the rest of Jerusalem and he knew it.

Tel Aviv is Israel's success showcase. It is a modern thriving metropolis which is home to almost 400,000 people. It serves as a hub for wealthy Israelis wishing to live a trendy upscale lifestyle. It is 92% Jewish and just 4% Arabs. They live in a very tight density of 7,500 people per square kilometer. Its people are primarily secular and well educated, by Middle Eastern standards. Where Jerusalem is the religious center of Israel, Tel Aviv is just the opposite.

Tel Aviv's Muslim population was expendable because they were willingly living among the Zionist enemies.

When Waleed's nuclear missile started toward Tel Aviv, just seconds before the Israeli Air Force preemptive strike, the doom of over 175,000 people was sealed. The blast occurred barely minutes after IAF frantically broadcast its warning to Israel that a missile was coming, although none of the pilots knew where it would hit. The streets of the city soon filled with the dead and dying struggling to put distance between themselves and the cascading buildings giving way to the shock waves of the powerful Topol M Russian missile. In the blink of an eye, the city was gone. Only the rubble and a deadly lingering cloud of radio active dust remained. A strange and misleading calm filled the air.

For a long while, the victims could not utter a word. There was nothing to say, even if they could speak or find someone to listen. The virtually simultaneous nature of the strikes on Tel Aviv and Tehran had robbed the victims of the hope and anticipation of retaliation. By the time the survivors processed what had happened, they had to rethink their feelings because the retaliation had already been made. The thirst for revenge that runs so deeply in the Jewish soul had been denied. There was nothing to do but live and remember those who had been incinerated in the attack.

The Western Christian powers could do nothing for the survivors in Tel Aviv. The British were reeling from the direct hit Waleed had delivered to London. The French were flat on their backs and soon to be in worse shape.

In addition to dealing with the destruction from the Gonesse strike, the French survivors would soon be fighting for their lives against healthy savage Islamists trying to murder them. The Americans were fighting the same enemies at home and they would not soon be coming to their rescue. With their country in a war whose outcome was not at all certain, the survivors of the Tel Aviv strike were in a hellish situation with no way out for the immediate future.

CHAPTER 24

NUKING TEHRAN

AT ALMOST THE SAME MINUTE Waleed sent his Topol Ms off to destroy Tel Aviv and other cities, the Israelis sent their missiles to Tehran. The real confirmation to the world that Israel had nuclear weapons and the political will to use them came with the strike on Tehran. Nevertheless, even at the final moment of truth, Prime Minister Ethan Gross still felt compelled to wait for confirmation that Waleed was readying his Topol M missiles for the destruction of Tel Aviv before he actually gave the order to launch his own weapons.

In the days leading up to "Operation Purim Party," Gross and his advisors had studied an intelligence dossier on the City of Tehran. It gave a clear picture of the importance of Tehran as the heart of Iran. The summary of the report read, in part as follows:

"Tehran is the political, social, cultural and military center of Muhammad Waleed's Iran. He runs the city with an iron fist and it is very much like a prison camp. In spite of Tehran's reputation as an open cosmopolitan city, just behind the facade is an ugly totalitarian theocracy based on Shia laws. Tehran is both the capital of the nation of Iran and the Province of Tehran. It is a 2500 year old center of Persian life. Its location at the foot of the Alborz mountain range gave the city its name which translates to "bottom of the mountain" in Old Persian.

"Tehran is 580 square miles and has 7.8 million residents. This makes it densely populated and an ideal target. The City produces cars, electronics, military weapons and chemical products. Iran's main oil refinery is nearby. The

City is the hub of all of Iran's railways and highways, and a center of culture and art dating back to well before Mohammed Waleed's ascension to power.

AZADI TOWER

"The city has a natural aiming point like the famous doomed building next to the 'Tee' shaped bridge in Hiroshima. That aiming point for Tehran should be the Azadi Tower at the city's cultural center. The sweet irony of hitting the Azadi Tower is that they call it Borj-e Azadi, a name in Persian, which means 'Freedom Tower' the same name as the Americans in New York City have given to the new World Trade Center complex they are building. It is 148 feet high and, if God is with us and, we are able to hit it anywhere near that height, the resultant shower of radio active particles will triple our killing power. It is truly a beautiful white marble structure that Waleed uses as the backdrop for his five and six hour Saturday afternoon speeches. Its lower decks contain a museum displaying seventh century items and a one thousand year old Qur'an. Because Tehran is composed of largely modern high-rise, high population density buildings, the chances of inflicting major damage with one missile are greatly enhanced. Sending more than one missile will guarantee big kill numbers.

DEMOGRAPHICS

"About 8 million people live in the immediate center of the city with maybe as many as 15 million living near enough to be sickened by radiation fallout provided it does not rain and the winds are favorable. While the largest majority of people speak different dialects of Persian, a number of other languages are very commonly spoken in Tehran. This fact should prove very valuable when our forces start to broadcast misinformation in several of these less well represented languages. We can send out false information that will cripple recovery efforts and tie Waleed's people in knots for the first critical hours after detonation. It is estimated that since Waleed is very chauvinistic about speaking only Persian and having only Persian speaking officials in his government, it will take a great deal of precious time and resources to straighten out the communications problem we will cause.

Religious Law Problems

"Shia Islam is followed by the majority of people, although many other religions are represented in tiny numbers. The added concerns for Shia Law will provide still more problems for Waleed, because it requires very specific rules for handling dead bodies. Sending false messages about when and how the dead can be handled could bring civil defense recovery efforts to a stand still.

"We will take over their civilian radio bands and send out messages as if they were coming from Waleed. These messages will order people to go out and perform the rituals required for attending to Muslim dead. Survivors would be reminded of *wajibun kifa'ie* the Muslim collective obligation to tend to the dead. They would be ordered to go out in the streets as soon as possible to carry out *ghusl* the cleansing of dead bodies in preparation for burial. The laws hold all Muslims whether Shia or Sunni responsible for the proper burial of the dead. In the Muslim tradition, martyrs must be honored and buried when possible before non martyrs. Since the question of whether or not the dead from our attack should be treated as martyrs would have to be settled first, things will get worse and worse as the first days go by. Because Waleed is such a tyrant, there will be a certain percentage of the lower classes, who are less educated who will be too scared to take the chance that the orders did not come from Waleed. They will be out in the radioactive dust, digging holes, washing body parts and dying as they do. That will put more dead bodies on his streets causing Waleed further sanitation problems.

"We will tie his religiosity around Waleed's neck. Even when he gets on to us, he will not be in a position to go on the air waves to order Muslims, especially Shia, to disregard the Muslim rites of burial for the faithful departed. The matter will also distract him at exactly the worst time for such a frivolous use of his time. There will be Muslims running around the streets of Tehran looking for dead bodies to tend to and arrange so they face toward Mecca. As they are doing so, they will be contracting radiation sickness and becoming a burden to Waleed. Getting them off the streets and off the highways will be an enormous task and still worse because of our disinformation broadcasts.

"What survivors there will be, will likely immediately jump into their cars because in spite of Waleed's efforts at establishing a viable public transit system, Tehran is more dependent on private cars than any other large city in the world. Azadi Tower is near the Mehrabad International Airport where the people attempting to tend to the dead will be ordered to bring the bodies. In normal times Tehran is usually choked by serious traffic jams. Our "messages" will make getting around after the attack, impossible.

"Tehran has extreme air pollution problems and is often blanketed by smog. Respiratory ailments, such as asthma, are very common. In a recent month more than 3600 people died from breathing disorders. The radiation dust from our blast will increase this problem ten fold. The Alborz Mountains makes the air in Tehran stale and polluted and significantly raises the level of the dangerous ozone. The smog in Tehran's air will cause the radioactive material to hang in the air and thus remain dangerous for an extended period of time. It is anticipated that "Beta burns" from shallow ionizing radiation would cause the skin of survivors to fall off, terrorizing them and making them useless as volunteers to fight against us"

When he got to the section on smog making Tehran a city where it is sometimes difficult to breath, Gross said in a deadpan manner, "We will clear the smog up for Waleed. It is the neighborly thing to do, no?"

DEVASTATING IRAN'S ECONOMY

"Tehran is Iran. Three in ten of Waleed's government workers are based there and 45% of the semi private firms in the country are located in Tehran. Large industrial firms are located in Tehran and almost half of these workers indirectly work for the government.

Smashing Tehran will smash Iran's economy and put Waleed back on his heels."

"It will help him get back to the seventh century where thinks he is anyway," a smiling Ethan Gross thought.

SECONDARY TARGETS

"Slamming Tehran with nuclear missiles will also smash Iran's Imam Ali Military Academy, and several religious schools and seminaries. All of these secondary targets make hitting Tehran a very logical target.

"Tehran's football stadium the *Azadi Sports Complex* holds 100,000 spectators. Its poor design makes evacuation so slow that FIFA was alarmed enough to order that international matches be limited to 70,000 for spectator's protection. All of this says it loud and clear: smash the Azadi Tower and you stop Waleed and keep him on the sidelines of the war long enough to subdue the rest and successfully refocus on Iran. If we get lucky and we can hit him when the stadium is full we will have a major bonus."

The report had been presented in a slide show and projected onto an overhead screen. Everyone saw it and read it together. When it ended, there was a short period of contemplative silence. Some in the room considered how best to use what the report said. Some prayed for themselves and their country.

The Defense Minister Leon Hershcovitzs spoke, "Given any kind of choice, no one here would follow this path, but we must act to save our nation. The Jewish people are at a crossroads. God is depending on us to save our people and save the whole world. I believe God wants us to once again become His Chosen Ones. I say a demonstration bombing as some have suggested, would be a foolish step away from what we now recognize as the truth. It implies that we can talk this threat away 'if we can only find the right words.' I know that, even at this late hour, there are still people in this room who want us to 'open a dialog with Waleed.' Trying to open a dialog with this rabid dog would get us wonderful coverage from the media. They would praise us even as we would be flat on our backs dying, but I say to hell with that! I want to fight. I want to live and see my grandchildren live. I want Jews to run the world and I want to kill every Islamist bastard on earth."

Seizing the moment, Gross bellowed: "Damn it that's the attitude we need! Let us start laying out our plans. What were those coordinates?"

Israeli Air Force Bombs Tehran

Once the green light to nuke Tehran was given to the Israeli Air Force, it set off a wave of joy and anticipation. As military people sometimes will, an enlisted Airman wrote a message on the missiles they were about to launch toward the Iranian capital. It read, "To Mohammed Waleed and the people of SHISHEHSTAN enjoy life while you can!"

The name Shishehstan was the Airman's way of saying the Israeli Air Force was about to turn the sands of Iran into sheets of glass. He could read and write Farsi, and he put that knowledge to use for the celebration of the moment. He explained it this way, "The suffix "Stan" means "place of, or home of" in Persian, and "Iran" in old Persian means "place of sand. Since "shisheh" means glass in Persian, "Shishehstan" would mean "Place of glass." When the extraordinary heat of a nuclear blast is applied to sand, it instantly turns it to glass. In just a few hours they would be turning Tehran into sheets of glass and make it the true capital of "Shishehstan."

The damage to Tehran was every bit of what Gross had anticipated and more.

CHAPTER 25

THE ISLAMIST'S WORLDWIDE CALL TO ARMS

WHEN THE IRANIANS joined the Syrians and followed up Waleed's nuclear strike with a massive ground attack, they found themselves standing virtually alone. They called out to Muslims around the world to join the jihad in any way possible. All over the world, Islamist run and controlled radio stations, broadcast calls for Muslims to report for their sacred duty. The appeal went to men who were told that the Holy Qur'an commanded them to fight and die in Waleed's all out war for world dominance. Imams who had no military training started to raise militia units and follow their own war plans. With so many different militia units pulling in so many different directions disaster was almost a certainty. Radio and television stations throughout North Africa carried a fiery diatribe calling Islamists to war.

One speaker was Imam Aziz Nahyan. "Brothers the moment of glory is upon us. Allah has called each of us to do His work on earth and clear away those who will not yield to his Holy Will."

The announcement started at 4:30 in the morning of day two. The bitter defeat of Qiryat Shemona and the declarations of war from the hated Israel, America and their allies had come as a complete shock to the Islamists. Now they had to shake off these major set backs and prepare to fight an enemy they were always told would run and hide from their *Sword of Allah.*

"Brothers, now that we have crushed the evil Jew and forced him from our holy grounds at Qiryat Shemona, the great Satan America and her putrid lackeys have dared to challenge the power of Allah's warriors. Now is the hour to come forward and be counted with those who will share Allah's eternal life with him and His seventy two sacred virgins."

"At this very moment brothers are streaming into holy mosques all over the world to pray for strength and guidance. Each of you is commanded to report to your local leaders to be formed into fighting units, which will drive the filthy Jew into the sea. Once we are finished with the Zionist dogs we will invade Europe and America, to place them under our feet as well. The fat lazy swine in these infidel lands have no stomach to fight and we will probably find them hiding in burkas on their streets. We will bring them to heal and convert them if we can. We are the just and peaceful instruments of Allah's holy will and our first concern will be for the souls of those trapped in the decadent infidel life which has been falsely taught to them as the way Allah wants them to live. Each militia unit will have an Imam serving as a holy converter. Your job will be to bring the infidel wretch to Allah's holy grace through conversion to the will of Allah, by your superiors. There will be much suffering in the days to come. Many of you will be called home to Allah's side, but we will prevail!

"No enemy no matter how powerful he may appear to be can long resist the power placed in our hands by the Great and Benevolent Ruler of the Universe. Those sinful mockeries of all that is holy, Israel and the United States of America will wilt under the power we will bring to our battles with them. These evil countries can not long endure. They must be crushed according to Allah's holy words.

"This struggle will not be easy and it will not be brief. Many of you hearing these words this very moment will not return from this holy jihad, but be carried into Allah's glorious arms to be rewarded forever. The weapons our hated enemies possess are lethal and able to strike many of us at one time, but we will win out because Allah will not let us lose this struggle. One day very soon my brothers the joys of holy victory will fill our hearts and our mosques. On that day we will stand with our feet on the throats of the evil United States of America and its sinful little child Israel. Then both of these stains on Allah's precious earth will be washed away.

"The cruel Jew oppressor will not prevail!

"The cruel Jew oppressor will not prevail!

"The cruel Jew oppressor will not prevail!

"The cruel Jew oppressor will not prevail!"

Those listening began to rhythmically repeat the phrase stopping just slightly between "oppressor" and "will," so it came out "The cruel Jew oppressor..... Will not prevail," and sounded like two short sentences.

All over the Middle East this phrase was chanted over and over until its quality and substance transcended words and became an intoxicating force that drove Islamists into a frenzy. They poured into the streets firing rifles in the air and smacking themselves in the forehead in frustration at not being able to attack Israel at that very moment.

When the chanting had gone on for at least five minutes, Imam Nahyan asked for calm from his live audience. "Brothers please let me continue, please brothers.

"Allah's world will never be peaceful as long as the Jew inhabits the earth! There will be no security for Muslims as long as the Zionist state looms over us everyday. As long as the Jew squats on Allah's holy land and we do nothing about his defiling presence Allah will refuse to find favor with us.

"So hold these words dear, my brothers: The destruction of Israel and the United States of America, its protector must be carried out by us. Just as past American presidents have done before him, this president of America is on a course to certain ruin as he dares to try to pervert the will of Allah. All of his soldiers will die and all of his fortune and wealth will be squandered in this foolish attempt to force Allah to change His holy will.

"To the Americans I say this warning: Make right your affairs, for your day of reckoning is fast approaching. Heed my words; throw off the blinders that have brought you to reject Islam and worship falsely. Allah loves you and wants you, as his children to submit to His holy will as He has spoken it only in the Holy Qur'an. End your infidel way of life and save yourselves from the 'Sword of Allah' while you still can. Peace be unto you!"

The fuses were lit all over the Islamic crescent. When the explosions came, not all of the victims were Jews, Americans and their allies. In Afghanistan centuries old hatreds burst into open fires wherever Taliban tribesmen intent upon continuing their poppy growing businesses were confronted by foreign fighters drawn to the country by the chance to fight America and her allies.

These Islamic zealots heard Nahyan's words as a call to cleanse the earth of drug dealers, even if they were Muslims. Committing the crime of dealing drugs revolted the Islamist fighters who gathered in the high mountains of Afghanistan. They had naively poured into the country to live the life of Spartan-like warriors, shunning the comforts of the modern world, fighting for Allah, dying young and ascending to paradise for eternity with their seventy-two virgins. These men were like Islamist monks with modern weapons. They were the most ardent followers of the Qur'an's every word. Each of them believed the Holy Qur'an required that Sharia Law be strictly observed which they understood as never taking innocent life. They spoke among themselves and quoted the Qur'anic Law on the subject: "Whosoever killeth a human being for other than manslaughter or corruption in the earth, it shall be as if he had killed all mankind, and whoso saveth the life of one, it shall be as if he had saved the life of all mankind." (The Qur'an 5:32)

The al Qaeda fighters interpreted the call to fight for Allah as a call to attack the Taliban drug thugs. The Taliban, they came to discover, had always been more of a criminal enterprise than a religious organization. They had only fought the Soviets in the 1980s because the CIA was paying them to. Each side claimed the support of true Islamic law in the intramural jihad as the Islamists in Pakistan watched and waited.

America did not have a very tough time getting the Taliban to step up. They recognized the Soviets as just another criminal gang who would take away their poppy monopoly if they were ever to get control of Afghanistan. The CIA supported the Taliban with millions of dollars in arms and outright payments. They used the Taliban-Soviet War as a proving ground for all of America's latest infantry weapons. The relationship worked perfectly for both sides. America got to test her weapons against the very military the weapons were designed to kill, and do so with no "fingerprints", and the Taliban got all the help it needed to kick a potential drug dealing rival "off their corner."

The fighting started in a small, but important poppy-growing center in Afghanistan's Helmand Province. After the Canadians and the British had pulled their troops out of Afghanistan, America had to redraw her plans for supporting the central government in Kabul.

The pullouts forced a change in the rules of war in Afghanistan. Small provincial towns were abandoned, and this led directly to the town of Musa Qala falling back into Taliban control. When it happened no one noticed. It was just another poppy town, after all.

The foreign fighters had watched Afghanistan's neighboring Muslim countries of Uzbekistan, Kazakhstan, Kyrgyzstan and Tajikistan being destroyed by AIDS caused by intravenous use of cheap heroin from the Taliban's drug dealing operations. They hated the Taliban for being 'blood suckers,' as they called them. The Taliban was well entrenched in the poppy growing areas of the country. They had been able to bounce back to being an effective fighting force, thanks to the money they had been given by the United Nations Food and Agriculture Organization. After their defeat at the hands of the combined forces of America, Britain and Canada, the delighted Taliban watched as the United Nations came into Afghanistan doling out wheelbarrows full of money. The UN was trying to pay the country's farmers to not grow poppies.

Whenever the UN moneyman came around, the Taliban was right there to pose as local farmers. Had it not been for the United Nation's money, much of which comes from American taxpayers, the Taliban would not have been able to get back to its pre-invasion military strength. The money the United Nations gave the Taliban went straight into the hands of the world's top arms dealers.

They were also able to sell their rifles to the Afghan government when silly politically correct policies were tried as a means to disarm the country. The Taliban had no second thoughts about selling their old rifles, because they were getting UN money to buy new rifles anyway. The old time Taliban thugs were very often more narco-mafiosi than Islamist holy warrior. When the money from the rejuvenated heroin trade began to roll in, along with the United Nations and World Bank money, the Islamists in Lebanon and Syria expected a percentage of it to come their way. Between the fall of Saddam, which took a large bite out of their budget, and the crushing effects of America's anti money laundering laws, funding for world wide terror operations had been severely reduced.

The whole al Qaeda/Taliban world knew that the Afghan Taliban was holding back. They had read the New York Times stories about the hundreds of millions pouring into the hands of the Taliban brothers.

What the Taliban narco gangsters lacked in actual numbers, it more than made up in advanced weapons and the ability to put those weapons in the hands of an army of mercenaries they were quickly able to raise to fight the 'true believers.' For all their burning Islamist zeal, the foreign fighters came to see they were never more than useful diversions to keep the Afghan government and the Americans busy while the Taliban drug dealers made millions in the shadows. Over the years the Taliban had always been supportive of the foreign fighters, but they always made certain their support would be just enough to keep them fighting, but never enough for them to succeed and be able to leave the country. The battles in the mountains went on for ten days before the foreign fighters were all killed or run off by either the Taliban's mercenaries or the Allies. Both armies had the same approach to taking prisoners: They did not believe in doing so.

CHAPTER 26

DAMAGE TO PARIS AND LONDON

AS MAD AS WALEED WAS, he was sometimes able to experience moments of brilliant clarity of purpose. When it was time to make targeting decisions and he had to designate exact coordinates to hit with his deadly Topol M missiles, Waleed had a moment of ironic genius. As a true man of the past, he studied every war the Islamists had ever fought against Christian Europe. He knew Muslim history as if he were present at each event. He talked to Saladin frequently. As the man who defeated the French King Philip II in the third Crusade in 1192, Saladin was the embodiment of the Islamist warrior Waleed longed to be. He worshipped Saladin even more than he worshipped Adolph Hitler.

As his tribute to the great Saladin, Waleed targeted Gonesse a small town about ten miles from Paris. It was Philip's birthplace. He thought long and carefully about hitting Paris, but rejected the idea for a number of reasons. Beyond the historical aspects of the targeting, Waleed knew he had to be sure to leave his modern day Islamist warriors something to conquer. He wanted to make Paris into Paristan and declare it the capital of Eurostan. Having it despoiled by radiation for the next fifty years could not work in his grand plan.

TAKING DOWN THE CONCORDE

During his studies of the third Crusade, he noticed that King Philip was born at Gonesse. For Waleed, targeting the birthplace of Philip was perfect. The more he studied its location and relationship to Paris, the more suitable Gonesse appeared. Sending a nuclear armed Topol M Inter Continental Ballistic

Missile (ICBM) was not Waleed's first attack on France. On July 14, 2000 Waleed's agents, working with agents of the Iraqi Intelligence Service the Mukhabarat, caused the crash of a Concorde flight from Charles de Gaulle International Airport in Paris. It had been scheduled to land at John F. Kennedy International Airport in New York City some five hours later, but it never got there. Concorde flight 590, as it was designated, carried exactly 100 passengers and 9 crew members. It had been chartered by a German company. Except for two passengers from Denmark, one from Austria and a single American, all of the passengers were Germans. All were flying to make a connection to a cruise ship docked at one of New York City's Hudson River piers.

Having so many Western Christian countries involved in that particular flight made it an irresistible target for Waleed and his partner in Iraq.

As they planned the attack, he and Saddam laughed at the naivety of the Western media experts who occasionally wrote about how Iran and Iraq could never work together long enough to coordinate any kind of a terror attack on the West. The attack on Concorde flight 590 was carried out by four Iranian agents who were given logistical support by their Iraqi counterparts.

The plan called for three of the agents to do whatever was necessary to get the fourth man close enough to fire a high powered round into one of the tires of the sleek airplane as it was rolling down its runway for takeoff. The operation allowed for ample time to get off at least three shots, but the second and third shots were hardly necessary. The shooter used a 7.62 caliber Russian Dragunov SVD rifle equipped with a PSO-1 scope. As soon as the round left his barrel, the Concorde was doomed. The shooting team was amazed at how quickly serious problems developed for the pilot. Almost immediately the plane was all but uncontrollable.

The plane's resultant unbalanced aerodynamics were made worse when a piece of the blown out tire's rim flew up into the plane's underside and punched a hole in the fuel tank. Thereafter the leaking fuel ignited, making things still worse. In spite of the rapidly mounting problems, the pilot was already too committed to the takeoff to abort the flight. He tried to get enough thrust to achieve lift off, but the plane hurtled through the air out of control. When it came down approximately ten miles away at the little town of Gonesse, the attack team was as surprised as anyone else. In a minor miracle there were no deaths on the ground. The people of Gonesse were spared. The attackers had calculated that the blow out might have caused the out of control Concorde to crash into one or two other planes. They had hoped those planes would also be filled with passengers waiting to takeoff. They prayed the death count would reach over five hundred. They were disappointed, but not for long. The shooter's back up team was recording the attack from a hiding place on the edge of the airport. The video is available and can still be seen on a terrorist website. Excited cheers are heard as a background to the death of the Concorde.

France's official explanation of the crash was that a piece of metal, mysteriously situated on the runway, flew up when it was run over. It then pierced the fuel tank and caused the plane to burst into flames. Thereafter a chain of events led to the crash. Official explanations aside, within forty-eight hours the truth of the incident was known to European Intelligence services. The French, the British, the leaders of the European Union and the United States knew the crash was the result of a terrorist having shot out a tire of the Concorde.

Because that truth was inconvenient, they agreed to deny the attack was a terrorist act. During their deliberations, the argument to deny the attack as a terrorist action was led by the United States. Washington did not want Americans thinking about terrorism going into a presidential election in the fall of that year. A cobbled together explanation of the event as a tragic accident was quickly fed to the compliant Western media. The major nations counted on the media not being curious enough to ask questions. They were not disappointed.

The strangely coincidental presence of a piece of scrap metal on a very busy runway was never questioned by the French press or anyone else. True to their nature, the French accident investigation bureau waited four years to release its final report.

Not even the intervening events on September 11, 2001, caused anyone in the media to raise an eyebrow or attempt to 'connect the dots.' Not one voice was raised in recognition of flight 590 as another in a long line of terror attacks on the West that started in earnest with the 1983 bombing of the United States Marine barracks in Lebanon.

For Waleed the flight 590 operation was the attack that kept on giving. The crash caused a sharp decline in Concorde ridership. Within three years the flying public had obviously put two and two together and realized France and England were hiding something by not releasing the results of the investigation. If governments wanted to play make-believe with the truth that was one thing, but those seeking to fly across the Atlantic were not going to bet their own lives they were being told the truth about flight 590. The numbers eventually grew so weak that by October 2003, the Concorde flights were quietly discontinued. Shortly afterward, in a pathetic attempt to add a sense of believability to their findings, the French initiated criminal investigations of airline executives and even the engineer who designed the plane. Not surprisingly neither went anywhere.

To Waleed, the fact that flight 590 was able to travel ten miles and crash into Philip's hometown of Gonesse on July 14, the exact date that Philip died, was a sign from Allah.

Hitting Gonesse with a Topol M ICBM made perfect sense to Waleed. He could kill many people, blow up the birthplace of an old enemy and preserve Paris as 'red meat' to feed his marauding hordes when he launched his invasion of Europe. He wanted to triumphantly stroll into Paris as his modern day hero Adolph Hitler had in 1940. He even wanted to go Hitler one better and plant a crescent flag on top of the Eiffel Tower. While the Topol M, that struck Gonesse, immediately killed all 25,000 people living in the little town, because it was ten miles away from the center of Paris the explosion was not strong enough to destroy much of the City of Lights. Few of the two million people living in Paris died from the initial blast. Nevertheless, the number of deaths grew alarmingly high by the day immediately after the detonation.

The deaths from radiation sickness grew exponentially. People living closer to Gonesse who were outdoors at the time of detonation began to literally fall apart. They walked the streets in a semi trance like state neither talking nor eating nor sleeping nor drinking. They were like windup dolls maintaining an upright posture until the windup energy finally failed and they fell dead face down into the ground. Their bodies would then decompose from the inside out. More than sixty thousand additional people died from radiation sickness. Moving people into the tunnels under Paris saved hundreds of thousands over the next several days until help could arrive.

LONDON

London was a different case. Because of its physical structure she was able to save many more of her people from radiation sickness than the French were able to save in Paris. The missile hit the London branch office of The Muslim World Congress, (MWC) a social and charitable organization established in 1996, to ease the transition of immigrating Muslims into British society. The MWC building was located at the intersection of Tottenham Court Road and Percival Lane in the Marylebone section, which had a sizable Muslim population. Those who were at MWC headquarters or the vicinity died quickly or within the following forty-eight hours, but London's tunnels saved hundreds of thousands of others. On hearing the exact location of the impact, Waleed was enraged. He immediately realized that the spy, he had placed at the MWC, had apparently provided his agents with the coordinates of the MWC headquarters where he was, instead of the coordinates for Buckingham Palace as he was instructed. That actually killed more Londoners than the originally targeted strike on the Palace would have achieved, but most of the dead were Muslims. Waleed's plans did include collateral Muslim death, but not flattening the MWC building. He knew he could not easily smooth over such a devastating blow to a Muslim population in London that he would need to rise up and help him take over the city. The missile attacks had started a world war that he was at the center of, so there was no time for conciliatory gestures to his victimized "brothers." There would be no easy recruitment of young Islamist fighters on what was left of London's streets.

London's public and private buildings burst into flames. Some melted in the thermonuclear blast of extreme heat. Prime Minister Mac Intosh called up every available reserve military unit. All of the United Kingdom's airports and seaports were shutdown and mass round ups of Muslim radicals were carried out. The reaction Mac Intosh got from President Andrews freed him from concerns about the political considerations of anything he had to do. Ordinarily in a dire emergency as this one, everything he did would have needed approval from Washington. With America's rejection of his pleas for help, he could now act freely knowing he was shielded from criticism from the British media and the Left. Anything that he did that worked, he could take credit for. Anything he did that did not work or worked but exposed him to attack in the press, could then be chalked up to, "I had to do this or that because the Americans abandoned us and left us to provide our own security. If I erred it was because I had to do something and not wait for help I was told would not be arriving."

As the days after the denotation passed, the United Kingdom fell under a marshal law system that came down very hard on England's Muslims. The M I-5 knew who the dangerous Imams were. They had a collection of secretly recorded audio tapes of many of the most inflammatory sermons from these men and used them to get arrest warrants from compliant judges all over the country.

CHAPTER 27

MR. PRESIDENT, EUROPE IS CALLING

PLEAS FOR AID START TO COME IN

AFTER WALEED'S NUCLEAR TIPPED Topol Ms struck Tel Aviv, London and Paris, Europe's leaders reflexively reached out to President Andrews. The devastation of the cities of London and Paris was so complete it took two days for the first guesses at the extent of the damage to reach the White House. President Andrews had been a military officer, so he thought he understood war, but he was shocked beyond belief at the reports.

The number of deaths and the amounts of property damage the British and French reported staggered him. They were heart breaking. Britain was able to gain a sense of control before France, but neither was in anywhere good shape.

The reports from around America left Andrews privately terror-stricken as well. The estimates he saw put the death totals at around 17,000 civilians including hundreds of local law enforcement personnel. The causality numbers for actual military personnel were not as grim. They were in the vicinity of 35 to 50, due mostly to the fact that in this war, the local police and innocent citizens were attacked first and America's war fighters came in afterward.

The British Prime Minister Roger Mac Intosh was the first to call President Andrews with a report and a plea for help.

"Mister President this is the worst disaster in the history of the British people." Mac Intosh said before he had to stop and compose himself.

"The miss-isle that hit London has apparently killed more than 80,000 people and injured an untold number beyond that. Our central communications systems have been severely damaged and our water supply is now poisoned. The scenes on our streets are impossible to describe. Neither of us has any point of reference in our own personal experience, that can serve as a useful gauge to comprehend what has occurred. These devils have dealt us a crippling blow. Were it not for the deeply set air raid tunnels we have from the German bombings in the 1940's, our people would have no escape from the radiation.

"I think we will be able to save thousands of people by keeping them down in those tunnels, but we need help sir. Anything you can send us will be very much appreciated."

Andrews paused before he spoke. He wanted there to be no misunderstanding of what he was about to say. "Mister Prime Minister at this time there is nothing I can send you. As you will recall, the European Union virtually forced us off the continent and the only bases we still have are the ones in the Baltic States where the locals refused to allow the E.U. to kick us out.

"You yourself told me you wanted American military installations in the United Kingdom closed within sixty days when you took office. Well sir, we *are* out and there is nothing we can do right now that will change that fact."

"But Mr. President certainly you have ships that you can send with supplies." Mac Intosh replied.

"Sir, I am not sending American military personnel anywhere near the radiation cloud you have hanging over your country."

"But our countries have always been shoulder to shoulder against common enemies..."

"I believe your public statements at the time were something along the lines of your wanting to insure the safety of the United Kingdom by clearly demonstrating to the Islamists that Britain had cut all her ties to the United States. You said Americans were the only real targets of Muslim extremists, and you were sure they would recognize your gesture of peace. I also seem to recall one of your ministers publicly calling me a son of a bitch who was 'more dangerous than any phony threat' I made up about the Islamists. Now I don't mind being called a son of a bitch, but saying the Islamist threat was something I made up, well..."

"But that was for domestic political consumption, Mr. President."

"I am not unsympathetic to you and your people, sir. We are a country built on European roots. As you well know many of us can trace our families to Europe and especially England, but as you know we are fighting a war, against a foreign power, on our own soil for the first time since 1812. We won then and we will win this time. It'll just take some time. When we do we probably will be able to help you, but right now I can not spare anything until I am sure the American people are safe. You have to understand that this is like the situation on an airplane. I mean you know when they give you the little talk about what to do if the masks drop down? They say if you are traveling with someone who will need help putting on the mask, make sure your's is on properly first before you try to help anyone else 'Cause if yours isn't working properly, both of you will be in trouble. Well when America is secure I'll see what help we can send you. We will incorporate your military forces situated outside of Europe into our command, but for now, that is all. Godspeed Mister Mac Intosh, my prayers are with you and your people."

Andrews pursed his lips as he hung up. Vice President Walter Hodges said "I know that wasn't easy Bud, but as you've said, 'this time around America comes first." An hour later, French President Jean Paul Leblanc was able to call. He had just been treated for a mild heart attack then released from a hospital in Nice. His voice betrayed his condition: weak and frightened.

"Mister President we need your help. The town of Gonesse, a small village about sixteen kilometers from Paris has been flattened by one of that madman Waleed's bomb. We have little idea of the total extent of the damage. I believe we have seen at least 27,000 or more killed but we really have no true idea. "We beg you sir, I beg you sir, please come to our aid as soon as you can. Today would not be too soon."

"We are also being over run by Islamist gangsters moving through the wreckage killing survivors. They are making their way to Paris as we speak. They are ani-mals these Islamists. They have no fear of themselves being killed by radiation. They are like demons. They have set fire to Norte Dame, the animals! I beg your help sir."

"Mister President I can only tell you the same things I have just told

Prime Minister Mac Intosh. It was the European Union that decided separating from America and insulting America was the way to appease the Islamists. You told your people you would actually cut diplomatic relations with us if you thought that would strengthen your point that France was not a friend of the United States. Just two months ago you personally described me as the biggest terrorist in the world. I can hardly present myself before the Congress asking for aid to you before America is secure, given these facts.'

"But Mister President .... LeBlanc stammered.

Before he could complete his thought Andrews continued, "Yes, I understand you are about to tell me what you said was for internal political reasons, but doesn't that beg the question of why America should help a nation of people that is so pleased to see us insulted? Since the early 1960s your country has gone out of her way to show contempt for America. You have stabbed us in the back at every turn, voting against us in the UN and siding against us in every major dispute. Now you ask us to risk our lives for you yet again. Your administration has been no different than all of your predecessors in spite of the encouraging language you used to praise America at the beginning of your term."

Andrews paused again. He wanted to give LeBlanc time to find some words, any words that would make helping France and all of Europe a sensible thing to do. LeBlanc had nothing to say.

In sad resignation, Andrews continued, "Just within the last year since you have assumed office, France has kicked us in the ass at least twice. That sir was because you thought you would never need us again. That sir was because you people in the European Union thought that damned tower Babel you created made you safe from each other. You thought you only had to worry about each other. You never thought your former colonies would nuke you. This is a different situation now sir. We will be taking care of ourselves first this time. Then maybe we will get to you at some point if we can, but for now we can not help you. I would like to, even in spite of yourselves, but well.... not now."

Hodges smiled and winked, "Well that one wasn't as hard."

"No Walt, not nearly as hard."

"Mister President the Prime Minister of Italy for you," an aide said.

"Yes, Carlo how are you holding up?" Andrews greeted his old friend Carlo Mazzetti the center right Christian Democratic Prime Minister of Italy.

"Bud, we have big problems. There is much unrest on our streets. So far our Muslims have not generally risen up, but there's trouble coming our way. I can feel it in the air. I think they are waiting for some kind of a signal from their leaders. Can you send us anything? I know sending us troops is out of the question, but maybe we could coordinate our efforts at least behind the scenes. Can you fly something into Aviano (US Air Base in Italy) We can use signal jamming equipment to break up their communications. The missile that failed tells you they want the Vatican..."

"Carlo I have no intention of letting these bastards take over Italy. And let me be frank about this, I feel this way primarily because I will never let them overrun the Vatican. I'm not a Catholic as you know, but the Catholic Church is the only rallying point left in Europe. Besides the Pope is a damned fine man. I'll have the Secretary of Defense contact your people. I will instruct him to do whatever is necessary. Now keep this in mind Mister Prime Minister, you have my support and best wishes but my policy in this war is America comes first. I am only deviating from it because of the Vatican. Things have changed. America will no longer be the automatic guarantor of Europe's safety. As long as I am president we will help you people on a case by case basis. In this case the answer is a qualified yes."

"Thank you, mister President. Italy will not forget this." Mazzetti responded.

"We'll help, but not beyond saving the Pope and securing Rome. After that if we think we can pull out without endangering the Holy Father we will."

"I understand Bud and I don't blame you. I have tried to tell my people we should stand with you, that we owed America a great deal of appreciation for all America has done for Italy. I only ask you to be fair with us as you carry out your new policy."

"Good luck and keep me informed of your situation Carlo. Give my best to the Pope."

When he put down the receiver, Andrews was speechless for several minutes. Walt Hodges poured them both a cup of black coffee and they discussed their next move.

"Get me the Vatican," Andrews said in a subdued voice. In the next ten minutes he explained to the Pope's staff how committed America was to saving the Vatican and above all the Holy Father.

"All I ask is your cooperation when we ask you to make public statements. We will ask you to say nothing at times and at other times we will give you prepared statements. I will send the 82nd Airborne Division to Rome to guard the Vatican.

"Understand that this is the only exception to my no American boots on European soil policy. Cardinal you can tell the Holy Father he has the personal guarantee of the President of the United States of America that his safety and the security of the Vatican and its personnel will be maintained. And please ask the Holy Father to pray for America and pray for my staff and me. If America goes under so will Europe."

"Thank you senior Andrews. I will explain your most generous offer to His Holiness. And of course we will keep you and America in our prayers."

CHAPTER 28

MONKEY BALLS ON SWAN LAKE

WHEN HE HAD TO DEAL WITH THE QUESTION of where to put the terrorists the U.K. had rounded up, Mac Intosh had a problem: where to put them so they could not cause anymore trouble. His solution was both simple and creative: The Falklands Islands. The United Kingdom had gone to war with Argentina to hold the miserable little piles of rocks in cold Atlantic waters off the tip of South America in 1982, and now they would finally be of some value. He knew if he was ever to get any aid from the United States he had to show Andrews that Britain was getting tough on the Islamists. He ordered them shipped to the Falkland Islands. Given the condition of London, he got no negative reaction from his media of any kind.

Mac Intosh's plan called for a quickly constructed prison camp to be placed on one of the Swan Islands that sits in the Falkland Sound between the two largest Islands of the Falkland chain, West and East Island. The island selected was well suited for use as a prison camp. Its center is a cleared, flat grassland next to a fresh water lake that can be used all year. Because it is between the two big Islands, it is protected from the harshest weather as well as any sneak attack the Islamists could mount, and, of course the prying eyes of an untrustworthy media. There was only one problem with the plan: after the crushing attack on its capital city nerve center, England had neither the resources to build it nor the personnel to staff a prison in a "God forsaken" island half a world away.

Mac Intosh had no choice but to again ask America for help.

When word of the Swan Island plan came to Andrews he saw it as an opportunity to help the Brits and solve one of his more nettlesome domestic problems at the same time. He called Mac Intosh and offered to have a US Navy Construction Battalion team build the facility and US Army Military Police personnel staff it.

When Mac Intosh accepted the offer Andrews was able to announce the closing of America's Interrogation and Detention Center at Guantanamo Bay in Cuba without worrying about losing control of any of the very dangerous terrorists it held. As soon as Swan Island was ready they would be sent to the Falkland Island facility which would remain the property of the United Kingdom.

This move immediately took pressure off both Mac Intosh and Andrews. The rabid British press could not attack Mac Intosh for shipping some of their country's worst and most dangerous terrorists off to the Falklands Islands hundreds of miles away. The rabid American left and its press core could say little about America helping an ally in such a dire situation. That it meant closing Guantanamo Bay added to their consternation. They had cried for the closing of Gitmo Bay for years. They had used lawyers, exaggerations and lies to try to get the detention facility closed, but their efforts always rang of insincerity. Most fair observers of the efforts to close Gitmo had concluded that they were mere smoke screens hiding the real aim of the left which was to actually free the detainees and send them home.

Now the American left had gotten its wish for an end to Gitmo but their lies were exposed and they were tongue tied. The Cuban Island prison would be closed but no terrorists would be going home. They could not complain about Swan Island because it did not even exist yet. They could suspect they had been out foxed, but that did not give them any plausible stories to write about a place that would be owned by another country but run by American military personnel. With the streets of America turned into battlefields, the nation's media was busy writing stories about how everything was Andrews fault so Swan Island stories would have to wait.

The Falkland Islands prison camp put Islamists captured by both the U.K. and America as far away from their own bases of operations as geographically possible. It, also, put them in a location out of the public eye and away from the Western media. Moreover, the new base in the Falklands gave the British an opportunity to remind the Argentines that they would not be getting them back anytime soon.

While it did not seem likely that Argentina would try to use the war as an opening to invade and repossess the islands, neither did it seem likely that the Iranians would hit London with a Topol M.

The environmental specifics of Swan Island were perfect for the Allies purposes. It is on the same latitude as London making climate adjustment for the prisoners and troops stationed there no problem. The range of average temperatures is roughly 26 degrees in July (the Southern Hemisphere has its summer in January) to about 58 degrees in January.

Swan Island has a twenty-four inch average yearly rainfall. Its almost constant eight-mile an hour wind, combined with the predictable rainfall, made the Island well suited for using temperature as an interrogation device. Water soaked prisoners were placed in the open air and allowed to turn blue before they were asked any questions. That helped many detainees decide to cooperate.

America's can-do attitude got the Swan Island facility built in an amazing seventeen days. Because it was opened so quickly there were weak spots in its ability to keep men safely confined. As a precaution, all detainees were delivered with black hoods over their heads. Because of this blinding, they had no idea of where they were when they were walked off the helicopters that brought them to their new homes. This led to a few escape attempts. Some terrorists saw only the opportunities to get past the fences, but not the fact that they had been effectively placed in the "middle of nowhere." To their surprise, they were still nowhere once they breached the fences.

Monkey Balls

Since Swan Island was being run with a skeleton crew, these attempts had to be controlled. Once again the American military was up to the challenge.

The thousands of interviews conducted by America's interrogators over the years had produced hundreds of valuable pieces of intelligence. These debriefings provided a window into the workings of the simple minds driving America's terrorist enemies around the world. Among the items of information developed by the Mind War team, which was assigned to do the interviews, was a description of the morbid fear of castration held by a significant number of detainees.

They reasoned that if they were castrated in this life, they would not be able to enjoy the sexual favors of the Seventy-Two virgins promised to those who die fighting for Allah against the evil infidels. Initially the item seemed trivial. It was treated as a joke and even became the punch line to a cartoon showing a beautiful harem girl stretched out on a heavenly cloud, who was laughing and pointing to the limp penis of a neutered Islamist warrior dressed only in a turban.

The value of the castration item went unrecognized for weeks, partly because the analysts were busy with other matters, but mostly because no one could figure out how to use it. The first idea backfired badly. It called for deliberately spreading the rumor that captives would be castrated. That turned out to be a serious mistake. It might have been a deep seated fear of life as a eunuch, or panic over not being unable to perform in their bordello-like version of heaven, but the immediate result was a marked increase in Islamist resistance and an upturn in the savagery of their fighting.

It soon began to cost American lives and victories. The idea of using the castration rumor was scrapped, but not forgotten. Before long, American cunning produced a better way to use the item. The staff at Swan Island thought they had a way to use the information. Their plan became known as the *Monkey Balls Plan.*

They reasoned that, while the threat made tougher fighters of Islamists on the battlefield, this new plan could become a potent device to scare detainees out of trying to escape. The childlike Islamist captives could easily be convinced that castration awaited those caught trying to escape. The best place to try out the new idea would be the isolated Swan Island.

Before long, however, even the *Monkey balls* plan began to unravel and it needed tweaking. The problem was that, since America was not actually castrating detainees caught trying to escape, the inmates started to believe they had been lied to about the serve punishment they would receive if they forced the hand of their captors.

A solution was quickly developed when an analyst discovered that large chimpanzees had testicles that are approximately the same size as those of an average man. A call was immediately put out to all military and civilian government controlled laboratories that used chimpanzees.

"Send monkey balls in formaldehyde jars," the order said. Eventually enough pairs of chimpanzee testicle, which had become commonly known as 'monkey balls' were collected so that every detainee facility had a jar prominently displayed for its detainees to see. As cover, those few who did try to run were transferred to a special island prison off the coast of Australia. Once they were gone, a new jar of monkey balls was displayed and word was leaked that they belonged to the recaptured brother who died as he was relieved of his manhood.

Monkey balls became an inside joke on the American left and the media. Although it was politically dangerous, it had to be done. If the Swan Island experiment worked it could be used world wide, but if it failed it would not easily come to the attention of the adversarial Western media. The New York Times put *Monkey Balls* on its front page above the fold. Showing a picture of a pair of Chimpanzee testicles in a formaldehyde filled jar sent the left into apoplexy. That it worked and it scared detainees out of trying to run would mean nothing to them. After a while nobody cared about what the media had to say. Within a few days escape attempts dropped off sharply and that was all that mattered.

CHAPTER 29

THE PRESIDENT REPORTS TO THE NATION

AS THE HOURS immediately after America declared war on more than two dozen countries past, President Andrews found himself dealing with serious domestic resistance. The Liberal establishment and the leftists in the media came out swinging at the first reports of what had happened. They immediately tried to paint reported events in the worst possible light.

Dealing with the media was a major distraction for Andrews and his inner circle. The western media was very skeptical about the motivation Andrews attributed to the Islamists. The American media was especially unable to accept that 'anyone could start a war over religion in this day and age.' At the end of the first day of Operation Sucker Punch, Harlan Andrews went on the offensive to further enlighten and educate Americans to the nature of the threat from the designs of the Islamists on the world.

"The President of the United States."........ A voice on FOX News channel intoned.

In an instant, America's television screens went from a static long shot picture of the White House, to President Harlan Andrews sitting at his desk in the Oval Office.

"Good evening fellow Americans. I am pleased to report to you that although we have suffered many causalities and deaths since the world awoke and found that Islamists soldiers of terror had invaded us, and viciously attacked our allies, Israel, the United Kingdom, France and Italy, and those nations are now valiantly fighting shoulder to shoulder with our armed forces to repel those who would destroy the our way of life.

"Here at home, I have received reports that we are already beginning to turn the corner and regain control of America's streets. I expect that peace and safety on our streets will soon return.

"On battlefields all over the world, our brave men and women are fighting side by side with our Allies in a show of courage and fighting ability that I am confident will lead us to victory. Our forces have joined with troops from the world's freedom loving nations in this struggle for the survival of civilization, as we know it. Those who would plunge the world into darkness will not prevail.

"Here in our own country the fighting has been hard and destructive to thousands of lives and millions of dollars of property, but we are protecting even our most vulnerable citizens.

"To assist our war fighters, I ask you all once again to please stay off our streets. I have instructed our civil authorities to respond only to urgent requests for food or medical assistance. Any other requests such as personalized status reports or requests for care for animals can not be honored. Our enemies are cruel and sadistic and we have little time or resources to direct toward any crisis not involving the preservation of human life.

"If you are in need of medical attention place your call and please wait inside your home. Do not leave your home. By doing so you will risk bringing attention to yourself as a person in a weak and vulnerable condition and this may invite the worst of consequences. These heartless and soulless marauders are well embedded in our nation's towns and cities, so be very slow to draw attention to your family's home for any reason.

"I know many Americans are confused about the rapidly unfolding events that we have witnessed over these past several hours. Many are demanding an explanation of why America has declared war on more than two dozen countries in spite of the fact none of these countries has attacked us or outwardly seems to have any plans to make war against us.

"My friends, each of these nations, have been a safe harbor for our terrorist enemies to train their troops and regroup. We have proof that the planning for some of their most successful operations against our nation and other freedom loving countries across the globe has been carried out in these camps.

"Over the past twenty-five years we have tried every diplomatic approach imaginable to try to force these countries to clean out the terrorist camps on their own soil, but sadly everything has failed. Now with nuclear weapons in the hands of Mohammed Waleed and his Islamists allies the time for talking is over. The threat is too great to trust the words of these men especially since time has proved they are liars who will say anything to gain the time they needed to build their nuclear weapons.

"They have used these weapons. There is no more time for conjecture about the seriousness of their intentions. Therefore in consultation with the Joint Chiefs of Staff and the leaders of the House and Senate, I have concluded that declaring war against these nations was our only option.

"This was not an easy decision but it was the right decision. By formally declaring war on these countries under the Rules of the Geneva Convention, as we have, and accepting their surrender as we have in many cases already, we can now legally enter upon their soil and occupy them. The countries that have repeatedly protested that they were not strong enough to clear out the terror camps have now been put to the test. Our only requirement for accepting their surrender has been that they point out the camps and stay out of our way. In return we have assured them that no harm will come to their citizens and we will pay for any property damages caused by our hunt and destroy missions.

"Many of these countries have been friends to America over the years, some better than others. It is not surprising then, that most have already surrendered and begun to help us in our necessary seek and destroy mission within their borders. The nations of Libya, Somalia, Algeria and Saudi Arabia requested time to meet in consultation with their councils of leadership and they were granted that necessary time. All have since willingly capitulated.

"After discussion with Prime Minister Ekin of Turkey our declaration of war against his nation was withdrawn and I am pleased to report that Turkey has agreed to become an active partner in our fight for world security.

"At this hour the nations of Iran, Sudan and Syria have refused to capitulate and are actively fighting against our Allies and us. We will bring war to these makers of war and bend them to their knees, this I promise you.

"Sadly, as you well know, we are also fighting a shooting war on our own streets. The reports of violent fighting against insidious well-embedded sleeper cell agents that have been in our midst for many years are pouring in. We must expect that these battles will be fought over a long and drawn out period and anticipate that we will not soon see peace and safety on our streets.

"Our civilian police forces and National Guardsmen and women are fighting hard to protect us and to that end I order every one of you who is not directly engaged in the homeland war effort to stay indoors until further notice.

"This war we are fighting on our streets will take time to win. Do not expect this crisis to end any time soon. And again I ask you to join me and my family in praying that, by the grace of God Almighty, we will win this war here and abroad.

"Many of you are asking why we would have to fight the world's Muslims. My friends we are not fighting the world's Muslims, we are fighting only the world's Islamists and there are great differences between the two.

"Throughout our history, our citizens of the Muslim faith have lived side by side with all Americans in peace and security. They have added to our country a rich element; one of the world's great religions. Muslim Americans have been good and productive citizens of our nation and fought and died for our freedoms. So, I say again: We do not make war today on Muslims. We make war on those who would twist the meaning of the words in the Muslim holy book, the sacred Qur'an and use them to justify their mad vision of how the world should be. We can not allow our enemies to separate us from one another with lies about our purposes and their.

"They seek to act as agents of evil and we seek to secure peace through victory and the end of their threats to destroy the world. It could not be clearer than that. Many in our country and indeed the whole western world have a grave misunderstanding about the nature of the driving force behind the Islamists desire to murder or enslave the whole world. To our way of thinking this concept is so foreign that we can not even attribute such motives to an enemy such as President Mohammed Waleed of Iran. My friends the truth is before us and we must force ourselves to see it and recognize how dangerous it is to our very existence. I have examined the words and writings of the Islamist aggressors who have brought war to the world. To help us all better understand the situation we are facing, let me review my findings with you. What I have found is chilling.

"The history of Iran since the late 1970's has moved it inexorably closer and closer toward the nightmare scenario of willful instigation of the end of days we are faced with at this hour. You see friends, the enemies we are fighting want to end the world with a killing of everyone on earth so we can all stand together on Judgment Day. They believe that God will save only Muslims who read their holy book, the Qur'an, as they do. They have no concept of religious freedom or tolerance of alternative religious doctrines.

"As soon as the Islamists took control of Iran they began plotting the ultimate end of the world through a nuclear war with Israel and America. The evil men who run Iran do not care about surviving the war they are trying to start. Their leader Mohammed Waleed has said this many times. In fact the Islamist fanatics want to die by starting the end of the world so they can be rewarded in heaven for doing what they mistakenly believe is God's will. They believe starting a nuclear war with the west is what God desires and they want to act as His soldiers and instruments of this war.

"The Iranian leadership believes they will miraculously bring about the reappearance of Mahdi, the twelfth or Hidden Imam who is a figure in traditional Islamic belief. In orthodox Islamist tradition the Hidden Imam's reappearance signals the immediate coming of the end of the world.

"Here at home we have been fighting an internal battle to educate ourselves to the truth of the Islamic plan. The western media, who mock this theory because they have no religious grounding themselves, has helped our Islamists enemies. Because they have no understanding of religion or the power of religious ideas, our media can not tell genuine religious faith from a fake religious scam. These men and women do not seem to understand that their naivety makes them part of a scheme and in some ways a danger to all of us.

"To many in our media, religion is only a superstition backwards people believe in. They smugly see themselves as being much too sophisticated to believe that the Iranians are anything but harmless religious crackpots, not dangerous zealots capable of destroying us all. As if their program of purposefully ignoring the threat of Islam has not been bad enough, has not done enough damage to America, some in our media and some in the western media, actually willingly serve as public relations agents to promote the Iranian/ Islamist version of any event. Sadly, some in America's media are helping the Islamists bring about the end of days, by disregarding the facts."

The President stopped speaking. He waited for total silence before he continued.

Restarting his announcement he said, "Like many who follow some western religions, the Islamists believe they have been made privy to God's plan for the end of days. They think God has revealed the means He intends to employ to end the world and it is just up to them to add the date.

"Let me also say that although the purpose of their attack on America and our Allies has been to murder Americans, our enemies know they can not achieve this goal. Their alternative is to put a gun in our faces and enslave anyone who survives and refuses to be converted to their religious beliefs. To achieve their goals, the criminal regime in Iran developed the nuclear tipped missiles that they used to viciously attack Israel, France and The United Kingdom.

"I am pleased to report that Israeli Air Force has joined Air components of the United Kingdom, Australia and our own Naval Air Force to destroy Iran's capacity to launch further nuclear tipped weapons. I have contacted the leaders of the European Union to assure them that we will be sending aid of whatever nature they can use as soon as it is feasible.

"Our experts have determined that the 2006, letter the Iranian Islamists sent which was addressed to 'The People of America' inviting us to convert to Islam was a Qur'anic proscribed prerequisite to attacking us. In the Islamist interpretation of the Qur'an, they are compelled to make this offer to non-Muslims before they can justifiably kill them if they refuse to be converted. Mr. Waleed, Americans have heard your invitation and politely declined. Now let me add this..."

Andrews leaned forward and looked directly in a camera before he continued.

"Mister Waleed, there will be no slaughtering of infidel Americans. America is a nation founded on religious freedom and tolerance. Since our Revolution of 1775, Americans have fought and died to worship Almighty God as we see fit. As always Americans stand ready to protect our religious rights at the point of a gun if need be. Those who would try to practice the evil of forced conversion to any religious doctrine on America's people had better keep that in mind as they prepare to try. You will not succeed. No matter who or what says you are justified in murdering Americans for rejecting your religious doctrine, you are very mistaken if you think that will happen. Do not even try it or the power of the United States of America will drop you where you stand. Your force will be met by superior American force and fighting courage.

"Do not tangle with America. We are a people slow to anger but mighty and efficient in our ability to destroy those who would try to kill or enslave us. If you would save yourselves, your children and the future of your way of life from certain destruction, surrender now. You will be treated fairly. You will not be taking your war to us. We will be taking our war to you, and our way of making war is more terrible than any nightmare scenario you have ever had."

"Friends, we face dangerous days ahead, but you can be confident in your government's ability to protect you.

"Today we stand at an historical crossroads. This is a moment of extraordinary clarity. We are fighting a nuclear war against enemies bent on killing everyone in the whole world, Muslim, Christian, Jew and all others. We can not lose. We will not lose.

"We have been left with no alternative but war with the Islamists."

Andrews paused briefly collecting himself for the next sentence. When he was ready his face turned slightly pale and his eyes turned to slits before he continued. "So now" Harlan Andrews came to a full halt before saying the most serious part of his announcement.

"So now that they have used nuclear weapons and reintroduced them to the ways of war, we have just one option: to decimate and eradicate our enemies from the face of the earth so they can never again even consider raising a hand to harm Americans. To this aim I have authorized the use for every weapon our military forces possess, and that will include nuclear devices.

"My friends, I understand many of you might be hearing my words and asking why America must take the lead in this world wide war. You might be asking why the United Nation does not handle this problem, let me address your concerns.

"I have made a formal requested to the United Nations asking that it send troops to the Middle East to augment our efforts. As I speak the United Nations Security Council is debating whether or not to send troops. I do hope that should they decide to send them, there is still a need for their presence on the front lines. Experience has shown us that trusting the United Nations to combat and stop aggressor nations has simply not worked. To meet this threat, America must stand and fight without concern for the United Nations approval or assistance. I will not trust the security of America to the United Nations.

"We do have allies, strong allies to be sure, but in these circumstances, we will primarily rely upon our own strength and fighting skills to win this war. As events unfold, I will be giving you frequent updates. But for now, let us resolve to stand together at this hour of America's need. If we do, America cannot be beaten.

"I ask every America to put aside petty differences for the good of our nation. Please pray for America. Pray for our brave men and women who are fighting and sometimes even dying for America. Pray too for our children and pray for our world. Finally, I ask you to pray for me and all of your leaders.

"As Second Timothy tells us, let us be found 'fighting the good fight, keeping the faith. Thank you and May God continue to bless the United States of America."

CHAPTER 30

KILLING AMERICAN TOURISTS

AS THE CURRENT of savage life or death combat came down upon the entire world, many Americans were caught on foreign soil. Less than three hours after the President's announcement of war, urgent messages from American Embassies and Consulates from all over the world began to pour into The State Department's office in Washington. In some cases American tourists were complaining about, "the nerve of that son of a bitch Andrews declaring war on the world." Others complained of not being able to secure refunds from the tour companies they were "planning to sue." On orders from the Secretary of State, such complaints were thrown in the garbage. A FLASH TOP SECRET! message was sent to all American Embassies and Conciliates. In part it read as follows:

"America is at war with several nations around the world. As a consequence of this reality, you are forthwith ordered to open and follow your standing orders for extreme emergencies. This current crisis is a war, not a drill. I repeat this is not a drill. America is at war and you are ordered to respond accordingly. You will forthwith cease and desist from forwarding any further complaints of any petty grievances made by ill informed American citizens coming to your attention. Further orders regarding your orderly evacuation will follow. Stand by and Godspeed."

In eastern Turkey teenaged boys who had only seen Westerners on television, stoned a group of American tourists injuring dozens of them and killing their guide. On Malta, the irony of seeing a group of 15 Franciscan Friars from Ohio visiting the old Muslim settlement of M'dina intrigued a local Islamist terror group. They saw the Catholic priests as the descendants of the Friars who had once embarrassed the great Sulieman. The gentle priests were beheaded in a wild orgy of blood and revenge.

In many countries stranded Americans were immediately taken into protective custody. This happened even in the countries that were technically at war with America and her allies. Most of these countries knew that Harlan Andrews meant it when he told them they would not be harmed if they cooperated with invading American and Allied troops. The last thing any of these countries wanted was a dead American grandmother on one of their streets. Once the shock of the declarations of war began to subside, only those countries that Americans could logically expect to be dangerous places actually turned out to be perilous.

In the Middle East, the Muslim dominated countries had not been safe places for Americans for years. Things only got worse when war came. Mexico and some of the Caribbean rim countries were a little different story. When President Andrews started to get reports of American citizens being tortured and killed in Mexico, Jamaica and Grenada he acted immediately.

His call to the president of Mexico was made separately. Andrews asked for the full cooperation of the Mexican government in protecting American citizens. Using his best diplomatic language, he explained that he was very busy and would not be able to say what he was saying again. When the President of Mexico hesitated to respond, then asked if the American government was threatening Mexican sovereignty, something deep inside the stressed out Harlan Andrews snapped.

In the midst of all he was dealing with, he was in no mood to hear whining from the President of Mexico, a man who had not called him to offer his country's support when blood started to run in the streets of America. Andrews held the phone closer to his mouth before he spoke. He then turned away from the few trusted staff members he was with and whispered, "Mister President I had hoped to hear from you with an offer of support in this current crisis. It is after all, you people who have that '*mi casa su casa*' saying. I guess that only means 'our house is your house' and only if America's fridge is full of cold beer, but not when America is in trouble.

I guess you see yourselves as America's children hiding in the root cellar waitin' for your Daddy to kill the bear at the front door. Well let me tell you this son. If I hear of any American tourists being hurt or God forbid murdered on your *sovereign* soil, the United States government will consider your country to be acting like an enemy. You will then be treated like an enemy. We will invade your country sir and treat you no differently than Iran. Is that clear senor? I do not speak your language but I'm sure you speak enough of mine to get my meaning."

To the stunned Mexican's surprise, Andrews hung up without waiting for an answer. He was a very busy man after all. When it came time to straighten out the few Caribbean countries that were failing to protect American citizens and tourists in their care, Andrews decided he had no time to talk to them individually. He ordered that a conference call be set up.

He gave those countries essentially the same ultimatum: Act like an enemy and be treated like an enemy. Act like a friend and be treated like a friend. It was their choice.

CHAPTER 31

HOW EUROPE PREPARED FOR THE WAR WITH THE ISLAMISTS

OVER THE YEARS, like all ungrateful children, Europe actually became militant in its demands on America. When America had the nerve to reduce her presence in Europe and demand that NATO shoulder more of the responsibility for Europe's defense, the Europeans howled. They demanded that America live up to her responsibilities to defend them. They reasoned that since America had saved them from themselves, America now owned Europe and had to perpetually protect her from every and any enemy. Over recent years, any news of even slight cuts in America's defense budget started spontaneous demonstrations in the streets of Europe's major cities. The sense of entitlement to America's military protection became as familiar as a Euro. Of course the old European powers had militaries. Every year they participated in joint mock battle exercises fighting themselves. Not surprisingly Europe never lost one of these battles.

Since the mid 1950's Europe's countries had taken on the persona of the *Three Little Pigs*. The first little pig who built his house with straw was the old Europe. They were the heavily socialist countries that would have been happy to live as Soviet slave states as long as they were fed and given jobs. Many of those Europeans resented America for bringing down the Soviet Empire. That resentment also bubbled over to strong anti-Christian feelings because of Pope John Paul II's part in ending the Soviet Union and as a result, Christianity fell further out of favor in many parts of Europe. Those countries recognized straw was cheaper than brick and anything stronger was unnecessary because America would always be there to keep the big bad wolf from their door. They decided to spend their Euros on social programs. The social programs in turn acted like the sheep that attract wolves. Some European countries saw the need to build their house from sticks. A few grudgingly spent a few extra Euros on their own defense. They knew these small steps did not actually protect them from any real danger, but they wanted to do something to show America they were trying to do something for themselves. They were the little pigs who built their house from sticks.

The last group of countries, or little piggies, took a much different position. They were primarily the countries that had once been prisoners of the Soviet Union. They understood they needed to keep as strong as they could. They knew America was there, but they also remembered America's shameful conduct during the 1956 Hungarian revolution. They remembered seeing a feckless America turning her back on them when Soviet tanks rolled in to crush the upraising.

Those countries built their houses with stone, as much stone as they could find. They believed Ronald Reagan's *trust but verify* cut both ways and America would have to be met more than halfway in order to protect their peace and safety. In the traditional version of the Three Pigs story these pigs are cunning. The wolf tries to talk them into voluntarily giving up the security they have in the brick house, but they do not fall for his tricks.

In the original story the wolf fails because his tricks are so transparent that the pigs could not miss them. In the modern version the Islamist wolf has had much success in luring Europe's little pigs out of the safety of their stable democracies because his tricks are subtle and not transparent.

The modern Islamist wolf used public opinion, socialism and political correctness to break down Europe's walls and pour his people into Europe's cities. Little piggies that were both gullible and willing victims gladly opened the doors that could not be blown down or kicked in, by the militarily weak Islamists. Europe's jealousy of America's historic ability to smoothly absorb immigrants burned brightly. The European socialists could not accept that a 'nation of cowboys' could take in the world's rejects and turn them into some of their most productive citizens.

"If America could do it, we certainly can!" they moaned and grumbled.

Europe convinced herself she could merely open her doors to whoever showed up and make them good citizens. They had little understanding of the dangers of an 'open borders' policy until it was too late. While America was preparing for war, Europe was setting records for the most people in a photo of nudes taken on a public street. Its core institutions were issuing resolutions declaring resistance to any governmental efforts to track the activities of Muslims living legally or illegally among them. When a college professor's union representative was asked why he would not report suspected radical Islamist students, he said universities should encourage students to 'think outside the box.' European countries passed special laws kowtowing to Muslims in ways unheard of before. Rome set aside a portion of its public beach for the exclusive use of Muslim women. The Parisians, a people largely void of moral concerns, passed a law forbidding women from appearing topless on public beaches. In Amsterdam the City Fathers closed almost half of its famous Red Light district upon the demands of its Muslim immigrant residents. Of its own volition the European Union incorporated parts of Muslim religious law into its civil codes.

In England for the past several years the most frequent name for a new born baby boy has been Mohammed. In British public grade schools children were encouraged to talk about their fears and anxieties over the looming threat from the Islamist. They were told to sing the old John Lennon song *"All we are saying is give peace a chance,"* until they achieved a trance like calm. They were not told the people that were scaring them had been welcomed into British society by their parents. The children in Britain's Islamic controlled schools also sang songs. Their favorite song was *"Death for the glory of Allah is my destiny"* which was at least more to the point. Like the children at Britain's public schools, they sang until they achieved their own trance like calm.

Every Saturday Europe's public squares were filled with socialists blaming the Islamists hatred of America and Europe on American Imperialism. These rallies always included the origami crane making and planting peace flowers. The people at these events were told their enemies would be impressed with their gentleness and decide not to attack them.

CHAPTER 32

WAR IN EUROPE
THE ISLAMISTS RISE AND ATTACK

EUROPE'S ISLAMISTS SAW THE BOMBINGS as the sign they had waited to see. The French Islamists were the most organized on the European continent. France had the highest percentage of Muslim immigrants who had come specifically to position themselves for the war they knew was coming. It was Waleed's first target. In late 2005 the Muslim quarters on the edges of Paris exploded in a series of riots that saw young Muslim men roam local streets overturning and burning cars. The riots went on for eleven nights before a show of police muscle and a promise of jobs brought them to an end.

These uprisings were a dry run ordered by al Qaeda leaders and designed to test the speed and strength of Western governmental response. The Muslim students were well coached. They knew their lines and positions. When interviewed by French television, the student leaders complained of a lack of concern for their welfare on the part of the French Government. They said they were forced to drop out of school because of discrimination, and of course they cried about unemployment.

Wherever poor uneducated Muslims lived the riots broke out. In the Paris suburb of Stains in the Seine-Saint Denis region an elderly Parisian was murdered by roving bands of Islamic young men. More than one thousand arrests were needed to regain control, but that effort took over 9,500 civil police to achieve. In all, over 4,300 cars were burned in close to 300 towns and villages all over the French countryside. Officially the French position was that 'criminal gangs of young men' were to blame for the riots.

French leaders repeatedly expressed sympathy for the goals of the rioters while insisting immigrant street gangs, not religious fanatics, were behind the violence. Not once did anyone in the French Central Government say that Islamists were orchestrating what was happening, in spite of the proof they had indicating exactly that. "They are delinquents. It is our duty to give them hope," became the standard parroted line.

The only steps taken by Paris were the predictable ones. Paris decreed that local cities be given the authority to declare curfews. That meant nothing because cities had held the right to declare curfews since 1955 and none of them had the political will or police manpower to enforce a curfew anyway. It also said children were given the option to quit school at the age of fourteen; and that an official 'struggle against discrimination' must be undertaken. The French Government's answer to the riots boiled down to a rehash of an old curfew law, a lower age to quit school and a vague promise to fight discrimination against Muslims. When the smoke cleared the only concrete proposal was to have fourteen year olds opt out of school. That put still more aimless dangerously undereducated teenagers on French streets.

France the nation that led the world in passing compulsory universal education laws had thrown those laws overboard to satisfy Islamists who were in many cases illegally in France and cared nothing about French society.

In a press conference proclaiming a conclusion of the riots, a French Official declared, "...from this day forward France would change and be more welcoming to new comers without regard for their immigration status. We will never again allow discrimination against Muslims or anyone else."

He had not meant his response, to a question about Muslim immigrants, to be a new invitation for anyone in the world to come to France, but that is exactly how everyone including the world's Islamists understood it. When he heard that remark, Waleed grabbed his favorite rifle and ran outside to fire off a clip of rounds to celebrate. He was delirious with glee. In retrospect many analysts came to believe that the perceived open door policy of France might have briefly forestalled an attempt to overthrow the Paris Government while the Islamist kept pouring into France. Waleed had considered launching his attempt to take over Paris at that time, but elected to hold off to see how many more troops he could get into Europe.

"Why would I want to stop sending our brothers into France when they will not stop them from getting in?" Waleed thought.

To press home his advantage and to gather still more intelligence about how Europe would react to a military coup, he ordered his people to start trouble in Germany and Belgium. These uprisings featured Islamists who were, for the first time, armed and acting in concert with other soldiers in military style assaults on police stations and Christian churches. The national press corps in each country withheld that information. The Islamist paramilitary troops carried shotguns with bird shot filled rounds. Once again their orders were to press as hard as they could, but avoid being arrested. Waleed did not want to loose his troops to prison sentences or get them police records that would make them easier to find and consequently rounded up. He knew that when the European authorities realized his men were armed only with birdshot, they would treat them as a nuisance instead of a threat. Mohammed Waleed watched and weighed every uprising. He had agents on the ground gathering data on every aspect of the responses he got from local and national forces. He found that the Germans moved much faster than any other country.

They were organized and seemed to actually be ready to repel armed efforts to overthrow their government and take control of their lives. Germany was the only country that fired live rounds back at Waleed's troops and killed some of them. The French and the Belgians were largely disorganized. That was something that interested Waleed and his planners.

The uprisings in France and Germany were diversions to cover the actual plan. Brussels was the real target.

The other countries were tested in a methodical scheme to make the European Christians believe that by the time Brussels, the military capital of Europe, exploded it was merely their turn to experience an uprising as the rest of Europe had. Over the centuries Belgium had always been a battleground for warring European factions, so it was not surprising that NATO, The North Atlantic Treaty Organization and the European Union were headquartered in Belgium's capital City.

Waleed's Brussels operation was planned and carried out by Hezbollah.

Their assignment was to inflame the streets of the city to a point that demanded action by NATO since it was happening in their own backyard. Initially it looked like the local police and the Belgium army would be able to put the uprising down. The half million Muslims living in Brussels and its suburbs had always been peaceful citizens and visitors who lived rather well in comparison to Muslims in other parts of the continent. For that fight Hezbollah had to bring in troops from all over Europe, and still they were seriously undermanned. To stretch the effectiveness of the troops they had to their maximum possible usefulness, the Hezbollah commanders gave them brown-brown a special mixture of granulated cocaine and finely powdered gunpowder. When inhaled, the mixture makes its users irritable and increases aggression. Hezbollah's campaigns in the Middle East had taught them that having their fighters snort brown-brown in preparation for battle made them angry and savage fighters. Brown-browned soldiers, however, are not methodical fighters.

On nights one and two of the Brussels operation, the Islamists were arrested or shot in larger numbers than it looked like they could sustain. The operation was only saved from failure by the heavy-handed actions of Belgian Military Police (BMP) who insisted upon enforcing a curfew aimed only at Muslim men up to the age of fifty. This made solid tactical sense, but no practical civil or political sense whatsoever.

By night three the Hezbollah organizers had no trouble recruiting local fighters angry with the BMP. This turn of events gave the Islamists the escalation they wanted. The local volunteers were sent to the 'hottest' sectors of the city with orders to continually engage the BMP and keep them busy. On night six, the BMP began to regain control and the fighting seemed be dying down. The Hezbollah knew it was time to use weapons that would bring the locals up short and force them to recognize they were fighting more than ticked off Muslims angry over being ordered to stay indoors at night. They used internationally known battlefield weapons designed to stampede NATO's leaders into action. On night seven they lured a BMP personnel carrier from Queen Elizabeth Barracks, into an ambush and killed its eight men with a Javelin Shoulder Launched Missile, stolen from an overrun

American Marine supply depot in Afghanistan.

The Javelin Shoulder Launched Missile system is so devastating that it is unmistakable for those who know and understand military weaponry. The damage the investigators cataloged the next morning was beyond anything the Brussels City Police and BMP had ever seen. They sent their reports directly to NATO. NATO's Military Intelligence analysts knew what they were looking at. They knew local Muslims did not kill that vehicle.

On night nine NATO put troops on the street and in doing so, revealed their local strength and emergency response plans. Hezbollah was not yet finished with NATO, however. They wanted to try out a few more weapons. The Hezbollah had always been leaders in development of improvised explosive devices (IEDs) and explosively formed penatrators (EFPs).

They hoped to try their latest EFP on a NATO armored vehicle and got more than they could have hoped for. In an attempt to use a show of force tactic to try to scare the rioting Islamists into giving up their nightly attacks, NATO rolled out their latest most sophisticated M-1 Abrams battle tanks. These massive killing machines are enough to scare anyone with their awesome and obvious capabilities. Being scared of an Abram did not require any military genius. As tough and scary as NATO's Abrams were, however, they were no match for Hezbollah's (Iran's) latest EFP's penetrating power.

Their latest EFPs were shaped in a new configuration designed to capture almost all of the explosive punch that would escape and dissipate in the action of the older models. The EFP used on the streets of Brussels penetrated the Abrams tank's armor killed its crew and destroyed its communications systems rendering it not even useful for salvage. It was a complete destruction. The new EFPs were no homemade Molotov cocktails made of gasoline soaked rags. The Islamist then knew they could kill Abrams M-1 tanks. Unfortunately NATO did not want to accept this fact.

Every European life that was lost was wasted. The NATO top command convinced themselves the personnel carrier was hit by a 'one time use shoulder held missile' that the Islamists would not be able to lay their hands on again, and that their Abrams had been hit and killed by a lucky shot. On the other hand, every Muslim death had added to Waleed's understanding of how

NATO would fight back when he made his move on Europe. The final body count was fifteen Brussels Police and BMP officers killed and thirty-seven 'civilians presumed to be Muslims' killed.

CHAPTER 33

EUROPE FIGHTS TO STAY ALIVE
STARTING FROM FLAT ON THEIR BACK

WHEN THE NUCLEAR DUST HAD SETTLED to reasonable levels at Gonesse, Waleed's shock troops begged him to travel to the newly renamed Paristan to officially open the newest city in the Islamist Caliphate. Even before the Northeastern half of France was fully in their control, the Islamists, who had taken over the French capital implored their now deified leader to make a personal appearance at the renaming ceremony.

Under extremely heavy guard, Waleed arrived just before 2 AM on the fourth day of the siege of Paris. There was nothing left for either side to do at that point. The French were drained of any will to fight their Muslim "countrymen" and the Islamists were eager to start publicly beheading random French citizens. They were promised the executions would start as soon as they took Paris, and they demanded what they came for.

Waleed's top Shura (commanders) set up headquarters in the finest hotel they could find, the five stars Hilton on de Suffren Avenue. The 460 room hotel would serve as a combination militia barracks and temporary headquarters for the new nation of Franistan. Waleed and his inner circle took the finest suites facing the Eiffel Tower. Even on the first night, they got right to work.

The plan was for an elaborate celebration. Waleed would walk to the base of the Tower and address his troops. When he had them whipped up into frenzy, he would personally climb to the highest point of the Tower and plant a Red Crescent flag, which would drive his followers completely wild. The loose barely scripted format was perfect for a consummate showman like Mohammed Waleed. His handlers were never sure of what he would do and this excited even the most veteran fighters among his inner circle.

At 10:30 AM Waleed and his lieutenants made their way through a crowd of approximately sixty-thousand cheering Islamist soldiers. They greeted him with joyous screams of, "Allahu Akbar!" (God is greater than everything!) and "Al Mahdi, Al Mahdi, Al Mahdi" in a rhythmic chant. They fired their rifles into the air and chanted, "Death to America." The few remaining cars in the area were turned over and burned. Men ran to Waleed and kissed his cheeks, his hands and his feet.

At a point halfway to the tower, the crowd picked him up and carried him to the base of the symbol of French pride. When the crowd was finally almost quieted by his handlers, Waleed raised his arms and ordered total silence. With tens of thousands of blood shot eyes following his every move he tore away the bed sheet he was wearing to reveal the *ihram* he had on under it.

His *ihram* was a brilliantly white seamless robe that carried enormous significance. The fact that Mohammed Waleed was wearing an *ihram* was a signal of his intention to consecrate Paristan as a Muslim holy place. This message was very clear. It signaled that he, Mohammed Waleed their leader, was proclaiming himself to be the long missing twelfth Imam Al-Mahdi ready to bring about the violent end of the world and the salvation of all faithful Muslims. The *ihram* could have no other meaning. The mob cheered and danced and cried with joy, excitement and anticipation. They chanted "Al Mahdi, Al Mahdi" for twelve minutes without stopping. At least six of the older "soldiers" died of heart failure from the excitement. Others died when they fell to the ground in a state of total spiritual bliss and were trampled by their wildly dancing comrades.

The crazed mob was stunned by what happened next. It confirmed the breathless expectations of the mob, but not in a way they expected. His men knew Waleed would have to deconsecrate himself in order to actively lead them into battle, but they could never have anticipated his method of deconsecrating himself.

Waleed lifted his *ihram* took out his penis and urinated on a French flag he had placed around a supporting pillar of the Tower.

At first the silence was eerie. Thousands of men could be heard breathing in unison. Others murmured prayers. Then hundreds of his followers pushed forward to do the same.

"If the returned 'Al Madhi' did something it had to be holy," they reasoned. The urinations went on for hours, but after ten minutes the foul disgusting odor was too much for Waleed to stand. He took an elevator to the highest point on the Tower, and then climbed the superstructure to a point near the top. He knew the risk but had no second thoughts. He wanted to use every asset he had to keep his troops at the highest level of alert possible. It was what the "Al Madhi" would do, he reasoned.

When he climbed as high as he could, he tied his Red Crescent flag to a strut painted in the French tri colors by a patriot French teenager before fleeing the city. That made its placement perfect.

Waleed was figuratively, physically and theologically at the top of his world. He had crushed the first Western Christian country he had faced; now he was reenacting his hero Adolph Hitler's triumphant entry into Paris. Once he declared himself the returned, "Al-Madhi," he really was the new Caliph of all of Islam.

Not even Hitler had the courage or the élan to pee on the Eiffel Tower and a French flag. When the rally was over, he ordered his troops to disperse and kill. "Make every infidel either dead or a slave...burn Franistan to the ground to purify it as the home of Paristan Islam's new Holy City."

Through all of his pomp and ceremony, Waleed was not aware of the spy satellites passing miles over his head. He did not know they were taking pictures of the crowd.

The images these satellites sent back gave NATO's commanders a very good estimate of the number of Islamists troops Waleed had in France. Their estimate, which later proved true, was that more than 95% of the fighting men the Islamists had in the country were at the Eiffel Tower that morning. The images were amazingly clear. They provided a clear likeness of the very top Shura of Waleed's forces. As the war in Europe progressed, these pictures would come back to bite them all.

Within minutes the NATO headquarters planners in Brussels were pouring over this treasure trove of hard intelligence. If Waleed had not pulled this stunt, accurately determining his troop strength would have been impossible. The satellites kept sending pictures that told NATO exactly where the murderous crowds were at all times.

The Capture of Charles De Gaulle Airport

Knowing where your enemy is and being able to stop him are, however, two different things. One of Waleed's first objectives in his taking of France was taking Charles De Gaulle Airport. Because of earlier ill-advised actions and failures to act by the French government, seizing control of the airport serving Paris was a relatively simple matter.

After the 2005 Muslim work riots in the suburbs of Paris, Muslim "community leaders negotiated an end to violence by extracting a promise of public sector jobs from the French government. Since both sides knew, if there is one thing the French government always has more of it's public sector jobs, the solution was a perfect fit. Soon the Islamists had the positions they wanted and the French government had the appearance of peace it wanted. The jobs the French gave the Muslim youths were mostly menial positions as maintenance men and porters at Charles De Gaulle International Airport outside of Paris.

For those applying for work at De Gaulle, being an alien Muslim went from a deal breaker to a deal maker. The situation progressed to a point where not being a Muslim meant one would be wasting time applying for a porter's position at France's leading air transportation hub.

When the signal to take the airport went out, the fighting was fast and ugly. Blood sprayed the walls of the terminals. As planned, the Islamist workers went directly to the weapons they had stashed in various hiding places around the grounds. They started shooting immediately and killed many of the Gendarmerie stationed at the terminal. The Gendarmes did not go quietly, however.

If the average Frenchmen looked at the Muslim employment agreement and got a vague feeling he had been sold out, the police officers at the airport, knew for certain that their country had been stabbed in the back by the central government. They smoldered with resentment and hatred for the Islamists who had muscled their way into sensitive positions all over the airport. When the shooting started, they were eager to train their weapons on the Islamists they saw everyday.

The sounds of shooting and passengers screaming in terror gave the police a sense of freedom to start killing people they knew were enemies. They took full advantage of their unexpected opportunity.

Crackling gunfire made the terminal buildings ring like slip notes on a piano. Once the ringing from shot one began to bounce around the inside of a building, it echoed and joined with the sound of the next shot and the next shot and so on, until all that filled the air was a jangling sound that made it impossible to tell where the sound of one shot ended and the next one started. Musicians call the sound Bent notes.

In fifteen minutes French Army troops arrived, but they were unable to turn the tide. By that point picking out the terrorists from thousands of screaming frantic passengers was all but impossible. The Islamists realized their advantage and blended in with civilians to fire at the troops. That made firing back very difficult. Soon the Islamists, who were eager to die in battle for Allah, charged the troops and police officers, swarming over them. Angry maniacal terrorists ran every which way firing and yelling Arabic phrases.

When the combined cadre of troops and police called in reinforcements it was a matter of too little too late. The Islamists had also called for reinforcements. They ran to the fight from every direction. Roads and fences meant nothing to them. They came from everywhere. They rammed holes in the fences surrounding the runways and cut miles off their trips by driving straight to the fighting. They came and came and kept coming.

While the fighting was progressing, those Islamists who had won their battles and were still looking for a fight, ran to the runways and fired at escaping jetliners. When they received the reports about the attack on the airport, the Air Traffic Controllers ordered all planes that could fly, up in the air and away from danger. The rules that created multiple levels of safety regulations before a plane can take off were put aside. Planes attempting to land were waved off and ordered to various nearby fields. Some of those planes came as close as several hundred feet above the ground before veering off and making their escape. Many were riddled with AK-47 rounds as they made for safety.

The army had about one thousand troops, but the Islamists kept charging them and trading lives for territory. In the mistaken belief that taking the airport was either a labor issue gone very badly, or just a flash point in the upraising and not tactically valuable, after two hours the French Army withdrew from the fight.

Six hours after securing the control of the De Gaulle, the first plane loads of Waleed's North African troops began to land. The landings did not stop for hours. By daybreak the next morning, the Islamists had poured in twenty-thousand additional fighters. Among Waleed's followers were air traffic controllers, qualified pilots and every manner of other worker required to operate De Gaulle as a military air base. For the following several days the Islamists supported their fighters with materials flowing in from Iran.

CHAPTER 34

MARSEILLISTAN

BRIGITTE BARDOT, FRENCH PATRIOT

MOHAMMED WALEED'S planned attack on France had both general and specific targets. As a general aim, he wanted to take military and political possession of the country so he could personally change its name to Francistan. His specific goals were to destroy the physical manifestations of French culture including its buildings and monuments. He had plans and directives to blow up Norte Dame Cathedral, and the Arc d'Triumph, but he also issued instructions to find the retired actress Brigitte Bardot. Bardot had written a book condemning the unchecked flow of immigrants, especially Muslim immigrants into France. She had written that Muslims seemed not to want to become French Muslims, but rather remain Muslims who are living in France. She also talked about Islam being a danger to France. Because of her ardent love for animals, Bardot also attacked the slaughter of sheep in a cruel ritual demanded by the customs of Eid a Muslim holiday.

For Waleed, these statements were simply intolerable, especially from a Christian woman who had bared herself in films. He demanded that Bardot be captured and taken to him so he could personally torture and murder her in the name of Allah. In a stroke of luck, when Waleed's troops came for Bardot, she and her husband were not in their Bay of Biscay villa. They had flown to Montreal for an international animal rights conference. All the surging horde could do was burn the beautiful building to the ground. They shot her house staff and all of the animals on the estate and then moved on to continue killing and destroying France.

BEING OF "FRENCH ROOT"

During the years leading up to the Islamist War, the French people had come to identifying themselves in a way they had never had to before. The native born white French had come to calling themselves *français de souche* or 'French root.' This was a deeply psychological response to the angst they felt at the bad choices they had made that brought them to their fast growing condition as merely sustenance providing guests in their own country.

The most recent census numbers had confirmed the worst fears of the français de souche. France had become more than fifteen percent Muslim immigrant.

Although it was an example of *too little, too late*, a recently installed conservative administration rammed through a change in the question structure of the French national census form. For the first time in more than one hundred years the French government officially asked questions of race and religion. The answers to these questions revealed that France was soaked with Muslim immigrants to a greater extent than any European country had been since the Moors were kicked out of Spain in 1492.

The most alarming population imbalance was in Marseille which had openly and defiantly been called Marseillestan by the Muslim immigrants who were called *beurs* and *beurettes*. This was white French slang for Arab. Its use signified that in spite of the fact that the beurs and beurettes were usually born in France, educated in the French school system, and spoke perfect French, they were not emotionally accepted by français de souche.

Marseille's Muslim immigrants totaled a full twenty-five percent. Two hundred thousand of the town's 800,000 residents were Muslims. At the onset of the war in Europe, Marseille exploded in a wild orgy of violence. The government estimate of individual adherence to Muslim religious practices was that roughly one in four Muslims were religious. Marseille's Muslims were no different.

Of the city's fifty-thousand active Muslims, there were approximately five percent, or twenty-five hundred avowed Islamists. This five percent of Muslims being avowed Islamists was a relative constant throughout the European

Muslim community.

A large number of the town's Islamists came from a north side low income housing complex called La Bricarde. Most of the very poorest Muslim immigrants lived there and this made it prime recruiting grounds for al Qaeda and the Muslim Brotherhood.

The *français de souche* had to fight for their lives when the streets of Marseille filled with irate young Islamist militiamen who had poured out of the stench filled La Bricarde. Many lost the fight. Within a few hours, more than 15,000 *français de souche* were dead or dying and most of the rest had fled or were in hiding.

During the opening hours of the war there was little or no coordination in the actions of Marseille's marauding Islamists. What could not be stolen was burned. Hundreds of homes, shops, public buildings, schools and churches were incinerated in a joyful orgy carried out by the local Islamists. When they were finished with Marseille they moved north. Their next target was Toulouse.

PAYING BACK TOULOUSE AND TOURS

Islam has a very long memory. Islamists are the keepers of these collective memories. They never forget their victories, but more importantly they never forget their defeats.

The Islamist murderers burned with a desire to avenge their 721 defeat at Toulouse by Duke Odo of Aquitaine. He broke the siege of Toulouse on June 9, 721, when he destroyed the army of Al-Samh bin Malik al-Khawlani, the wali (governor) of Al-Andalus, (the Moorish Muslim name Spain). That defeat stopped the movement of the Umayyad, the Muslim army that was forcibility taking over all of known Southern Europe.

Duke Odo, the Christian ruler of Toulouse, had escaped the Islamist siege just as they were consolidating their hold on the city in early March 721. In what was to become classic Islamic disdain for the courage and fighting spirit of the Christians of Europe, seeing Odo flee made the attacking Islamists overconfident. They convinced themselves that victory would be merely a matter of time. They were wrong. Odo did not run away. He went for reinforcements and brought back an overwhelming army of Christian warriors. When Odo returned, the Islamists were so surprised that the only troops that survived the counter attack were the ones that dropped their weapons and ran. Those that stayed to fight were slaughtered. The sting of that defeat has never left the soul of the true Islamists.

The modern day Islamists burned Toulouse and killed every non Muslim they could find. The only thing that stopped them was their desire to pick up more troops and make their way to Paris. There would be at least one more stop for revenge, however. They would have to burn Tours to the ground to settle another 1,400 year old score. The 721 defeat the Islamists suffered at the hands of Duke Odo was merely a hint of the worse defeat in store for them at Tours on October 10, 732.

Under the great Christian warrior leader Charles Martel, the advances that the Umayyad army of Islam had made during the preceding twenty years were washed away in the blood of dead Muslim invaders. Historians have estimated that as many as 375,000 Islamists were slaughtered in the battle that claimed as few as 1,500 Christian lives. These numbers make Martel's victory at Tours the most one sided military triumph in history. The victory was so complete that the Islamists of the day were never able to continue their conquests in Europe. After the victory, Martel was called *the hammer* which was an acknowledgment of the Latin root of his name: *martellus* meaning hammer.

Burning and destroying Tours was seen as a sacred duty for modern day Umayyad warriors. The destruction of Tours was complete and most of the city's 140,000 citizens were quickly overrun and murdered. That Tours was called *Le Jardin de la France* (The Garden of France) made its destruction even sweeter for the demons who had sprung from history and leapt across 1,400 years to avenge the terrible beating their grandfathers had suffered. There was not much of Tours left when they were finished with the *Le Jardin de la France.*

After the rapid destruction of Toulouse and Tours they marched toward Paris like a colony of fire ants destroying its way to a target. They longed to actually gaze upon Mohammed Waleed, the man they believed was Al Madhi, the returned twelfth Imam.

Each of them believed their days on earth were dwindling down to just a handful and that the fiery end of days was at hand. Men who hold these beliefs are dangerous opponents.

The Swarm Moves Toward Germany: A Major Mistake

Even before the Islamists could reach Tours, efforts to stop them were well under way. NATO F –19 fighter planes were sent to join the French Air Force in all out attacks on the columns of crazed fighters streaming toward Paris. The strafing was constant along every important roadway leading north, but men who are determined and not afraid to die are not easy to stop.

Twelve hours after the sack and destruction of Tours and Toulouse, the first Marseille brigades of French Islamists reached the edges of Paris. Initially, bombing and strafing the rampaging terrorists running through the streets of the French capital was something no one felt authorized to order. The French government is housed there. Neither NATO nor the European Union wanted any part of blowing up Paris. Blowing up De Gaulle airport was bad enough. The NATO commanders in Brussels and the leaders of the E.U. felt their grounds to level Paris were very shaky if the French were not at least approving it, let alone demanding it.

When Waleed, the newly proclaimed Al Mahdi, finished the consecration of Paristan and consolidated his military hold on the city, he was ready to march across Europe. He ordered the Iranian and Syrian Air Forces to send whatever fighters they could spare from their battles with the Allies. This turned out to be a dozen old MiG 17s. Waleed's Air Force did what it could to cover his ground troops but soon found that they were no match for the loaded F-19s NATO could send up after them.

Waleed's battle plan for conquering Christian Europe relied on popular Islamist uprisings across the continent. He knew he would not be able to overpower all of Europe and take it by force solely using troops brought in from the Middle East. The only hope he had was home grown and already in-4place personnel willing to step forward and fight in order to die quickly and go to Paradise. He hoped that would be a powerful enough recruiting agent to swell his ranks as he burned his way through Europe toward NATO's nuclear weapons dump near Brussels. After the returned, Al Mahdi finished blessing and purifying Paristan, he divided his troops and gave them orders to take and burn every city they could. The largest portion of his militia was sent toward Brussels. The remaining one-third was directed to start to take Germany. Its first objective was Stuttgart.

The Islamists sent to Stuttgart were somewhat protected by their route. They had excellent maps that brought them through the Black Forest. The heavily wooded area provided cover for camps, make shift hospital grounds and places to regroup. The advance on Stuttgart went very well for the initial twenty-four hours. The Islamist troops were able to get all of their units into the forest where they believed they would be safe from air attack.

They were correct about not being vulnerable to air raids, but not about being safe from attack.

Paratroop elements of the German Army were dropped into a wide circle around the largest camps. On signal they used flame throwers and set a blazing trap for the would-be new rulers of Germany. Soon the air was filled with the smell of cooking flesh and the horrible screams of tortured men finding out they had wasted their lives.

The French had been initially frozen by indecision and that had cost them lives and property beyond belief. The Germans had no such problems. The destruction of Waleed's German invasion force was almost total. The Germans had not been the first day target of the war so they were ready for their new masters as they made their way into Germany.

Davy Crockett to the Rescue

During the cold war the United States had supplied the West Germans with a variety of weapons. Perhaps the most useful of these was the Davy Crockett, recoilless gun, one of the smallest nuclear devices America ever produced. The Davy Crockett fired a tactical low yield nuclear warhead that weighed just 76 pounds but could deliver an explosive punch equal to 20 tons of TNT.

The Crockett fired a round that could bathe roughly a one quarter square mile area with a lethal radiation designed to kill or sicken every human in its path. Although the last Crocketts were produced and shipped to West Germany in the early 1970's the German Army still had over fifty of them left. After the Cold War, the Americans had ordered the Germans to destroy the Crocketts. They never did. As time went by, a succession of German government and military leaders had carefully hidden them and hoped the chance to destroy them could arise before their continued existence came to light.

When the German officials realized that they could serve two purposes with the Crockett's they still had, using them was too attractive to pass up. After they burned the Islamists alive they covered the area with the Crocketts and irradiated the forest with them. That way no one could search the battlefield and prove the Germans had burned men alive, even evil men like the Islamists.

After the Islamists were stopped, the German Intelligence Service (BND) immediately rounded up every Muslim they thought could be trouble. They merely imprisoned them and prepared to deport them because Germany's past had not completely faded. In an irony of war, the former land of Hitler, run by his actual heirs, wanted nothing to do with his legacy as they fought against a man who idolized the tyrannical murderer. After sixty years the Germans were still sensitive to being compared with Hitler. There were no Islamist prisoners shot or tortured by the Germans.

CHAPTER 35

STOPPING THEM IN ROME

A SURGICAL STRIKE TO SAVE THE HOLY FATHER

WHEN THE COUNTER ATTACKS actually got started, the airport's runways were among the first targets destroyed by NATO's F-18 Air Wing. The difficult part of taking the action was the requirement that NATO get clearance from the European Union before being allowed to destroy major targets belonging to 'important' people. Getting the green light to blow up Charles De Gaulle Airport took a full day instead of hours. The civilians running the E.U. insisted upon having the final say about targeting.

Waleed realized that European bureaucracy was keeping his airfield window of opportunity open. He wisely ordered that until he said otherwise, only planes carrying supplies could land. He knew he needed guns and rockets more than he needed troops. When the window finally did slam shut Waleed wanted any planes that might be shot down to be troop planes. To him troops were expendable, but weapons were essential. Not surprisingly, by the time the Europeans got their counter attack coordinated, virtually all of the material Waleed needed had already been delivered. Since the arriving Islamist troop planes were unarmed commercial airliners, shooting them down was not difficult.

Because of the delayed response to airport takeovers, around the continent, huge numbers of troops and munitions were at Waleed's command. In Italy the takeover of Leonardo Da Vinci Airport outside of Rome was an exception. The Italians exercised their option to ask for America's help in saving the Vatican and the Holy Father.

Italy's Intelligence and Security Services the (S.I.S.M.I.) had done its job well. When the fighting broke out across Europe, Italy was able to quickly go on the offensive against known Islamists living in and around Rome. Combined patrols of English speaking S.I.S.M.I. officers and 82nd Airborne Division troops augmented by special CIA kill squads, fanned out to bring war to the enemy before he could get an organized attack up and running against the Vatican.

During the first of these raids conducted in the heart of Rome, a patrol team knocked on a known terrorist's door. This created an opportunity for the man to escape down a rope and run to freedom through a back ally. After that failure a hasty meeting was called between the leaders of both elements of the kill teams.

When both sides talked things over, the Americans admitted they thought the Italians wanted to approach the capture of the terrorists as if they were civil authorities come to arrest a scofflaw who refused to pay a traffic ticket. The Italians, it seemed were also deferring to how they assumed the Americans wanted to proceed. Each was wrong.

When the misunderstandings were cleared up, all of the leaders of the teams were called to a meeting at the famed Spanish Steps. The respective leaders revealed their true feelings and thereafter there were no more polite knocks on terrorist's doors. Everyone got on the same page and the result was bad news for Rome's Islamists.

At all stops after that when the wanted men were found the Special Kill Squad summarily executed them. Their bodies were dragged out and loaded into the bed of an Italian Air Force truck. The process continued until every patrol team had exhausted its list of names and locations. When the search and kill mission was over, the bodies were delivered to Urbe, an Italian Air Force base. They were loaded onto a C –130 transport plane, flown out to sea and dumped. Although at least some terrorists escaped, once word of the operation spread, the kill numbers were very significant. The Islamists had few agents in Rome to start with. Losing any sizable number of them would present operational problems to local Islamist commanders. Neither the Americans, nor the Italians ever spoke about what happened officially or unofficially

There were no records of the mission.

Shortly after these visits were completed, an advance party from the 82nd Airborne Division retook Da Vinci Airport. The rest of the troopers were flown in via helicopter, from a small carrier off the Italian coast. The first component of the rescue team repelled from gunship helicopters in the middle of St. Peter's Square. They immediately came under harassing small arms fire from a rooftop overlooking the Square. To clear them out, three helicopter gun ships blasted away at the snipers.

The Islamists were armed with RPGs (rocket propelled grenades) and were able to bring down two gun ships that had closed to within one hundred feet of the building's roof so their fire would not hit any unintended civilian targets on the next street. Both crews were killed in fiery crashes. The third helicopter blew the attackers up by training its fire on the terrorist position and igniting their own rockets. In a few minutes the threat was neutralized.

Once the streets around St. Peter's were secured, the rest of 82nd's troopers repelled down between the famous Bernini columns onto St. Peter's Square. With crisp military precision, the Americans evacuated the Pope and his staff, and then pulled out leaving Italian police and Army personnel to guard the priceless treasures of the Roman Catholic Church. The Pope and his party were flown to the USS Iwo Jima, a United States Navy *Wasp* class amphibious assault ship at anchor off Civitavecchia about seventy miles from the Eternal City.

Getting the Pope and his aides out of danger was another dangerous and difficult mission completed with professionalism and precision by America's military. The rescue was accomplished in two hours. The Americans had quickly gone about their business and left before the European media could make a point of their presence on the continent. Nevertheless, if the European media was not impressed, the Islamists, especially Waleed were very impressed. He now knew America was not going to let him take Europe by merely walking across the continent. President Andrews had made good on at least one American promise: the Holy Father was now safe and under the protection of the United States military. Waleed had to wonder what else America would do. He contacted his agents in North America and demanded they turn up the heat on America in the mistaken belief that he could keep the United States pinned down and busy at home while he burned Europe to the ground. He would be proved wrong.

Because of the running start the Italians got in their fight against Waleed's terrorists, Italy was quickly able to become a leader and contributor in Europe's fight for survival. NATO did not have to worry about Italy or more enemy troops coming into Europe through the tip of the Italian 'boot.' More than this, NATO and the E.U. saw the whole operation as proof that the Americans really weren't coming to the rescue again. Ironically they were forced to believe Harlan Andrews although Waleed did not. The truth was that his warnings could not be ignored. Europe would have go it alone.

THE ITALIANS RESIST ISLAMIST TERROR

In terms of her willingness to resist efforts to be turned into an Islamic society by Muslim immigrants, Italy was uniquely successful.

The experience the S.I.S.M.I. had gained in simultaneously fighting the Mafia and the Red Brigade, over a number of years, had toughened and prepared the Italian government for the fight to survive. The Islamists were not only small in numbers in Italy they were also at a great operational disadvantage. The ruthless assassinations of Rome's known Islamists had eroded the strength of the Islamists. The Italian government's relentless attacks against al Qaeda type organizations through diligent hard work destroyed the appeal of Islamist romance for Italy's Muslim *fence sitters*. It short, when a threat was detected, Italy sent her best operatives after it with orders to attack until it was destroyed. By the time the war started, the al Qaeda in Italy more correctly resembled an ideology shared by young romanticized Muslims than an active paramilitary threat to the nation's survival.

Two years earlier, shortly after an Islamist poison gas attack in Vancouver Canada that killed three hundred people in their airport, the Italians arrested and deported more than 150 suspected Islamists.

Because of that action, the European Union received dozens of complaints of mistreatment of the prisoners, but when called upon to explain herself, Italy ignored the charges. Instead the Italian government passed new laws giving the S.I.S.M.I. even greater freedom to act in their efforts to protect Italians from terrorists. They were ordered to 'uproot terrorist activities' in known Islamist gathering places, internet cafes, financial institutions and even grocery stores. In a single sweep conducted in Sicily, over 700 people were summarily deported for violations of Italian immigration laws. Many were sent to countries they had not even come from, and again the Italians ignored the howls from civil libertarians.

CHAPTER 36

CRUISING TO WAR

TRULY A SHIP OF FOOLS

WHEN THE NEWS of Waleed's war and the Islamist's mission to kill all non Muslims rippled through the Middle East thousands of Islamists, who had never been part of a formal organization, yearned to join the cause and sacrifice their lives. With no particular leadership to follow, many traveled to rallying points across North Africa to sign on as militiamen for Waleed and become part of the Iranian Army.

In Egypt the Muslim Brotherhood boiled with rage at their government's kowtow to America and Israel. They ran through the streets in frustration and as they did they gained in strength and numbers. Young men in Egypt's capital city of Cairo dropped what they were doing and joined a mob moving through the city's streets toward the Egyptian Parliament. They intended to kill the Prime Minister and President then declare Egypt to be an Islamic Republic. The plan's ultimate goal was to have Egypt join Iran and Syria in their glorious jihad against the hated *Satan's America* and Israel. In anticipation of the reaction from the Muslim Brotherhood, the Egyptian government moved thousands of troops to Cairo with orders to form a protective ring around the center of the country's government. The troops dug in and barricaded themselves to wait for the explosion.

The showdown was very bloody. Wave after wave of infuriated Islamists ran headlong toward every entrance in the parliament's stately old building. They were cut down in swaths of forty and fifty at a time. Machine gun fire rained down on the mob like sheets of tropical rain. These deadly sheets killed and killed but more and more kept coming. The mobs were armed with AK 47s, handguns and shoulder held rocket launchers that had been hidden in various safe houses around the city.

The fight went on for hours until Egyptian Army helicopter gun ships came to the area and shot everything that took breath. At the end of one long day's fighting the peace was restored and Egypt held her position as a 'compelled neutral,' as President Andrews had described the status of Muslim countries that surrendered without a fight.

In Alexandria, the Brotherhood made a tactical decision. They realized that starting toward an attack on Israel from so far away would not work. It would mean traveling by truck and car on open and exposed roads for hundreds of miles. They knew the Americans and Israelis would destroy them as Saddam's men had been ground up and destroyed in their *road of death* retreat. They devised a unique plan. They would highjack the cruise ships at anchor in the city's harbor and sail to Europe to join their jihadist brothers in their conquest of Europe.

On that day, there were four Western cruise ships in Alexandria's harbor. In a superbly coordinated strike, the local cell of the Muslim Brotherhood led local Islamist volunteers on successful attacks on the ships.

The first ship, the Bright Star Line's *Bridget Marie* was just getting underway when the swarm came to take it over. The ship's captain was an old hand at Middle East upheavals. He knew what he was looking at when he saw the mobs forming several blocks from the waterfront. The gangplanks were drawn up and the crew was issued small arms within minutes. The Bright Star's ship got away clean that day. Others were not so fortunate.

The three other ships were taken over in short order. The crews were rounded up and passengers were picked up and thrown overboard by blood thirsty Islamists. The captains and the navigators found themselves forced at gunpoint to set sail for ports in Spain and France. The crews were ordered to cooperate or die, as the ships sailed west toward where their captures heard the fighting was. The Islamist Navy left with approximately three thousand jihadists on each ship. They were 140 miles out of Alexandria when trouble came to them.

The alarm describing the events of the docks at Alexandria went out immediately. The European forces had to weigh their reaction from every possible angle. No one could be certain of the fate of all of the passengers and crew members on the hi-jacked vessels. At that point the horror stories about what the Islamists were capable of were just beginning to circulate. As Western trained military leaders, their first reaction was to reject the reports as unbelievable. When actual real time video of passengers being thrown overboard was send back by a specially equipped E-3 Airborne Warning and Control System (AWACS) surveillance plane, the truth became apparent. The plane saw and recorded what was happening from miles away. The footage was reminiscent of the scenes of World Trade Center office workers jumping to their deaths from eighty floors above the streets of Manhattan.

After a hastily called conference, NATO's commanders requested the British Navy to sink the ships. The video was all the proof they needed that the passengers who were not yet dead would be killed anyway if the ships got to Spain. The hi-jackers assumed the passengers on the ships would guarantee they would not be attacked. They had no understanding that things and circumstances had changed. They had allowed themselves to believe that Waleed's nuclear attacks would cower the West and allow Islam to rule the world. They were very surprised when Cruise missiles blew them and their hostages to Paradise. The commander of the hi-jackers on the leading ship was on his cell phone making demands about what supplies the Europeans should have ready for them, when he was crushed by debris.

CHAPTER 37

THE LUXEMBOURG TRAP
A LAST ROUND UP FOR THE BAD GUYS

ALL ACROSS EUROPE nations faced with popular uprisings by their Islamist residents had to make decisions about how menacing the threat was and how best to neutralize it. With Germany and Italy setting the example of firm military response instead of talk, heavy fighting went on for about fifteen days. The fighting that occurred after that was largely a series of small and uncoordinated flare-ups. The major fighting came to an end after what became known as the *Luxembourg Trap* had been sprung.

Although President Andrews strictly held to his decision not to commit any American troops to the European theater, he also kept his word about "helping where and when he could, without sending troops." By that time the Europeans realized he was not breaking his word when he sent the 82nd Airborne into Rome on a brief rescue mission to secure the safety of the Pope. They all understood that an exception had been made which would not signal a change in American policy.

The *Luxembourg Trap* was a simple but effective method to break the fighting capabilities of Waleed's troops by tricking them with a false "broadcast" of him telling his men to start to gravitate towards the little and defenseless nation of Luxembourg. The CIA provided NATO with a voice synthesizer it had developed that would enable them trick Waleed's troops. They would use one of their agents, who was fluent in Farsi, to go on controlled airwaves and give very realistic sounding orders to the Islamists. By use of the machine, their man sounded exactly like Mohammed Waleed himself.

The plan rested on a few basic assumptions. The first was that Waleed spoke only Farsi so very few of his followers had ever heard him speak. Next those few men who had heard Waleed would have to be sold that it was Waleed and become salesman to sell it to the others. Finally, it had to sound unreasonable to Western Christians for it to sound reasonable to young uneducated Islamists.

When the *Luxembourg Trap* was sprung it involved little more than discovering which frequencies were being used by Waleed to speak to his men, and using them for NATO's disinformation mission.

The announcement, made in a perfect duplicate of Waleed's whinny nasally sounding voice, was as follows. "My brothers we have done many great things in our Holy Jihad. We have killed hundreds of thousands of infidels and burned thousands of their buildings. We have an opportunity to now strike a major blow directly into the heart of Christian Europe. We can draw the blood of the Christian infidel to cleanse the stain of our forefather's defeats and inability to capture this pig sty called Europe. We can avenge our losses in the past and build on our victories today. I am ordering you all to travel to the infidel nation of Luxembourg to destroy it."

"This Luxembourg is the Catholic heart of Europe. It is the only place besides Rome where Catholics control. You will go to the forest in Esch and wait for your orders to attack. The leaders we have chosen for you will give you further directions."

"MAY THE ALMIGHTY ALLAH GUIDE YOU IN BATTLE AND..."

The transmission was cut off to give it a more authentic appearance. The CIA reasoned that since his troops knew Waleed was fighting in the field with them, he could have been forced to stop and run in the middle of a transmission. The trap was set with the bait of hatred. It was irresistible. For the Islamist foot soldiers, challenging the wisdom of this order to put every one of them in a concentrated place, away from a populated area, even after the Black Forest defeat, would have been a treasonous act.

Waleed's men were a loose collection of militiamen who were largely untrained volunteers, but they did what they were told when they were told, without questions. Since Waleed had revealed himself to be the returned *Al Mahdi,* his every word was believed to be an echo of the tongue of Allah Himself. Within fifteen minutes Waleed broke radio silence and tried to countermand the bogus orders. When he did, his transmissions were jammed and the fake Waleed was put back on to warn the troops that the infidels were playing tricks and sending out false messages.

"Brothers, do not believe this blasphemous trick of the Zionist pigs and American goat fornicators. They are trying to stop our Holy Jihad. Do not let them brothers."

When Waleed's position was identified by triangulating his radio signal, he actually *had* to run for cover from incoming rockets. Two days later when another dozen attempts by Waleed to correct the misinformation had been drowned out, most of his troops were camped in the forest in Esch Luxembourg. A Srike Force of NATO Fighters swept in firing rockets and dropping five hundred pound bombs. They destroyed most of Waleed's remaining troops.

The terrorist troops had expected to be met by stiff ground resistance, and they welcomed such combat, but none came. They did not recognize they had not been strafed or even confronted as they traveled toward Esch. The least educated troops saw the lull in the fighting as a sign that they were winning and defeating the cowardly Christians. NATO covered their encampments with deadly cluster bombs and killed most of them in moments. The survivors were taken prisoner and housed in quickly constructed prison camps under German supervision. Luxembourg's European Union representative was furious when he learned his country had been used as bait for the terrorists.

His protests were turned aside by the French representative who said, "My friend each of us must give what he has so humanity can win this struggle. Yours was to sit still and you did that very well, now please continue that posture."

CHAPTER 38

INDIA AND PAKISTAN
DEALING WITH THE "STANS"

ALTHOUGH THE LARGEST PORTION of India's Muslim population was removed when the nation of Pakistan was established in 1947, the sheer numbers of Indians meant that if even a small percentage of them were Muslims there would be millions of Islam's followers in India. Islam is second only to Hinduism as the most prevalent religion of India. With more than 174 million Muslims, within its borders, India necessarily had approximately 20 million Islamists. That made dealing with her a thorny problem.

In spite of the large raw numbers, India is a nation of one billion Hindus. A group of 20 million Islamists surrounded by a billion people is very insignificant. Muslims in India have long been the victims of discrimination and treatment as second-class citizens. In view of that reality and the nuclear muscle of India, President Andrews and his advisors decided to leave India's Muslims to the whims of India's Hindus. Treating India the same as any other Muslim nation would have been foolish. Saying nothing and leaving India in the dark about Allied intentions would have been equally foolish. When President Andrews finished calling the smaller Muslim countries, to explain what America and her Allies were trying to do, he called India.

The relationship between America and India had been an up and down one starting with India's 1970s flirtations with Communism. During that period, the India shocked the world by successfully testing her first nuclear weapon. The Indians had a one million man army armed with modern weapons. They could put thirty- four divisions on a battlefield and not have to dip into their reserves.

Vice President Hodges summed up the India question best. "Mister President there just won't be anything good to come out of messing with the Indians. If we treat them as equals, maybe they'll join us and help keep an eye on Pakistan. Maybe they will remain neutrals, but either way we win since we won't turn them into an enemy and have to fight a million man army. So long as we don't stir up that hornet's nest we'll be better off."

Pakistan was treated in a special manner as well. Even though it had been a haven for Bin Laden and his troops it had also been a valuable back channel friend in the efforts to control Afghanistan and keep both the Taliban and al Qaeda bottled up in the mountains between the two countries.

Even after the assassination of Prime Minister Mansoor, following the bombing of the famous *Red Mosque*, the Pakistani government had stood with America and Britain in their counter pressures against al Qaeda.

"We really dodged a bullet when Bhutto was assassinated," Walter Hodges said as he stoked his chin and starred at nothing in particular.

"We sure did, Walt. Of course, if the Islamists had not believed her line about wanting to democratize Pakistan she won't have bought it." Andrews added.

"What does that mean?" Hodges asked wrinkling his brow.

"It means we had strong doubts about her. She was a crook the first two times she was in office and there was no reason to think she would have changed her stripes when she was trying to come back. We determined she was going to be a problem if she came back in and started her same old act. That would have given the Islamists the bad guy they needed to rally people to their side and take Pakistan along with its nuclear stockpile. Believe me we shed no particular tears over her assassination. When she came back and ran Brownell approved it, but it was show business to temporally get the media off his back. Remember he thought an awful lot of himself and he believed that bad things just didn't happen to him. He really believed he could put her in office and take credit for being the man who put a modern liberated woman in office in an Islamist country. Obviously he was very wrong. Nobody had read the script to the terrorists."

"It wasn't us was it?" Hodges asked.

"No Walt, Brownell was worried about her but not that worried. He didn't have the balls even if he thought it was the best answer. It was bin Laden and Waleed. They couldn't stand by and lose Pakistan at the ballot box and to a woman at that. The Pakistanis have been good friends behind the scenes, even going so far as to let us force them to give Bhutto a chance." Andrews said taking a long satisfying pull on his cigar.

Pakistan earned a pass and got one. As soon as the fighting started the Pakis came forward to ask what they could do. Their Intelligence services were very important to keeping a lid on the Indian sub continent.

The dead bodies collected and tagged after the battle to retake Qiryat Shemona included no fighters from the Muslim *Stan* countries.

After declaring a start to Operation Sucker Punch, America had to weigh how to deal with the *Stans* as the unofficial internal memos called the several nations whose names ended in the suffix *stan* which meant *home of* or *place of* in Persian. *Sucker Punch* had to address them as well. Each of the *Stans* that was a stand alone nation was heavily populated by pious Muslims who mentally lived in the seventh century.

To the *Stans*, people black was black and never white. Anyone who was not an Islamist was an untrustworthy pig. The body count from the battle of Qiryat Shemona only proved this to the average goat herding Islamist living in a *stan*. To him the defeat was a signal that he needed to join the fight to murder all Americans and Israelis. Harlan Andrews and Walter Hodges recognized that the *Stans* people could not have cared less about the niceties of the Geneva Convention. They would have to be handled according to street fighting, or sucker punch rules.

If their governments had been ordered to surrender by the *two-headed Evil Satan* of America and their *Zionist lackeys* that would be their business, but the stans true believers would never surrender. If allied troops came to their lands it would become the people's business. They would fight to their last ounce of blood against invading infidel troops.

The plan for the *Stans* became to treat them as islands. They would not be invaded, because the only way to subdue them would be to employ the type of massive death producing conflagrations that would have to be used sparingly. The United States and her allies had no intentions of fighting or nuking the whole Muslim world. That path would quickly degenerate into simple murder sprees and be totally counter productive. No one in authority in the allied powers wanted any part of trying to kill every single Muslim on earth, even if the true intent of the Islamists was to kill every living non-Muslim.

The *Stans* were quarantined. They were essentially treated the same way America had treated some of the inconsequential Japanese held islands in the Pacific during World War II. Nevertheless, those who tried to leave the "stans" were deemed to be doing so to join the worldwide fighting on Waleed's side. They would not be allowed to do so. Each of the larger *Stans* was subject to having Allied bombers create a ring around it that would extend up to ten miles inside of their border. Anyone in the ring was bombed until he turned back or was killed.

Those who escaped were strafed and sprayed with G Juice from helicopters to track them. The Allied fighters were ordered to use as little force as possible to stop *stans* fighters and turn them around. They were considered to be innocent dupes willing to give their lives for a religious/political system that offered them nothing but a quick death. They lived a painful dreary life that made them suicidal to begin with.

In one case where a large number of volunteers from Tajikistan on their way to fight in Europe, were taking shelter in a cave in the Gorno-Badakhshan Mountains, the strictures of a *no excessive force* policy presented a real challenge. The American Air Force had the firepower, but logistically it could not unleash its full might. A smart bomb would have killed the group by sealing the cave, but it might not have. Intelligence reports were unclear as to whether there was an alternate egress from the cave. Many caves in the region were known to have two or more passageways leading back out to open fields or wooded areas. This was another problem solved by good old Yankee ingenuity.

An untried secret weapon was flown into for this special situation. The United States Army had raised and maintained a troop of wolverines for just this type of mission. The wolverine is a small muscular carnivorous always hungry and angry four legged animal found in the cold country of America's upper Midwestern States.

The male wolverine is about the size of a large dog and looks like a miniature bear. It gives off a very offensive odor and has teeth and jaws designed to crush bones and rip frozen animal carcasses.

Wolverines are among the most ferocious small ground animals commonly found in North America. When agitated they have been known to kill a full-grown moose. They will fight a black bear if they have no escape route.

Using animal psychologists in a top secret laboratory, the American Army was able to train their wolverines to attack any manually when they had been purposely starved for four days. The tests showed that starvation for more than four days made the animals too fierce, unstable and ultimately uncontrollable. At three days without food, they could still be safely handled and small cameras could be attached to some of them without the others eating it off his back.

On the third day of waiting and appealing to the Tajiki fighters to surrender, a plan to bring in the wolverines was given the green light. There would be no nuclear like explosion that would come back to haunt the Allies after the war was over. A troop of forty wolverines who had not been fed in two days was brought in under cover of the cold dark skies of the Tajikistan countryside.

The animals were sprayed with G Juice re-sprayed and tested every four hours until the special chemical soaked through the thick fur of the fierce little animals.

The following morning ten of them were fitted with television cameras and, under heavy covering fire, the cages were brought to the mouth of the cave. Apache Attack helicopters hovered over head with G Juice signature receives at the ready. After a final demand for surrender was answered with a volley of small arms fire, the command to release the hungry wolverines was given. The hungry animals did their job. Screams of agony could be heard for hundreds of yards. Some of the terrorists ran out of the cave with wolverines still hanging, by a strong bite on their arms and legs.

In spite of the best efforts of the United States Government, a video of the bloodthirsty wolverine attack made its way onto the internet. The action and accompanying audio of the ravenous beasts attacking and eating the Tajikistanis was available the world over. The sound of cheering American war fighters that could clearly be heard along with the carnage was a stunning touch. No additional exits were available to the hundreds of fighters, as the G Juice soaked animals proved. The entire contingent of would-be Islamist warriors was devoured by the Army's animals. When the feeding frenzy was over, explosive charges strapped to a number of the animals were detonated and all of them were killed.

Many American newspapers ran furious front page editorials condemning the action. They said the use of wolverines was, "reminiscent of the things the Nazis might have done," and worse. There were calls for Harlan Andrews's impeachment. To his great credit the President ignored the complaints.

The Army promised a full investigation and the tactic was not used again. It did not have to be used again. The fact that the personal computer had penetrated to even the most backward seventh century countries had not been lost on the Army planners. The Western media uproar made the *Wolverine attack* the most watched Internet video in the world. The "stans" had enough computers to get the word of the ruthlessness of the Americans out to some of their smallest villages. The number of *Stan* men volunteering for service in Waleed's army was drastically reduced in a very short time.

CHAPTER 39

CHINA, COLUMBIA AND MEXICO

AFTER THE INITIAL WAVE of war news and the urgent matters of the first hours were digested and dealt with, Andrews and Hodges faced the question of which countries could be counted on to join the fight and which ones would beg off and stay neutral. Andrews had an advantage in this matter. As Vice President, he was a very active roving ambassador to many parts of the world. Since Peter Brownell wanted him to stay out of Washington as much as possible, Andrews traveled the world trying to make friends for America. Because of these trips, he had a personal relationship, if not a friendship, with most of the world's leaders. Still the question of loyalties had to be settled.

DEALING WITH CHINA

Starting in the mid 1990's China had become the manufacturing power of the world. America depended on the massive emerging Asian super power for everything from toothpicks to electronics. The yearly sales numbers involved in China's supplier/consumer relationship with America's discount stores alone were larger than the Gross Domestic Output of almost every country in the world. America was China's best customer. Without American orders, China would have to turn to the European Union to sell her goods. In spite of the hype surrounding the EU's purported prosperity, the Chinese knew they could not survive on what they sold to Europe. Simple demographics told them they could not sell many toys to countries that did not have children to buy them for. Europe's slow self imposed death from birth control and abortion had cut her number drastically. The Chinese also knew the Muslims flooding the continent were either too poor or too disinterested to buy western looking toys for their children. Moreover, the fact that Europe was herself involved in the war and not likely to come out of it in better shape than it went in was not lost on Beijing either.

To the Chinese the reasons for the war were somewhat of a mystery. They had little or no understanding of religion and its power to drive men to war. Officially they viewed religion as a form of superstition that should be practiced by old peasant women. This formal stance aside, they also recognized that the Islamists were deadly serious about wanting to convert the world and end it in a cataclysmic war. The Chinese wanted to stay out of the Islamist's way, but would destroy them if they somehow came out the winners. China saw herself as the coming master of the world and would not hesitate to nuke the Islamists if it looked like they might win this puzzling war with China's best customers.

The first response from the Chinese was a predictable public statement. They ordered their United Nations Ambassador to go through all of the motions necessary to make them look like calm peacemakers.

While they were doing this they called Harlan Andrews and Ethan Gross to assure them that China would not be involved in any unnecessary shooting, but would offer back channel help. The words *unnecessary shooting* was not a throw away line. In typical cryptic China-speak Beijing was assuring Andrews and Gross that if necessary China would lend a hand militarily to see to it that America and Israel won the war.

In an irony of the times, one of the first tangible bits of help China offered was missile technology. A junior assistant to Primer Liu Fong, who was not in office in the 1990's when China acquired the technology from America, made the offer of a guidance system America already had. Upon hearing this offer, Andrews and Hodges merely smiled and shook their heads.

Once the question of where China would stand was settled it was time to look around the globe and weigh the likely positions the South American countries would take.

"Get me the Vatican will you please?" Vice President Walter Hodges asked his aide, a young Marine Major.

"Yes, Cardinal, we are very aware of your situation. That is why I am calling you. Sir the United States of America is committed to protecting the Holy Father and his staff. You will very shortly begin to see American soldiers on your grounds. They will be bringing food and medical supplies. As soon as the situation is stabilized our commander will draw up evacuation plans to see that all of you folks are brought out safely and relocated."

"On behalf of the Holy Father and our entire staff I must extend my deepest gratitude to you and President Andrews for this most magnificent offer. What can the Church do in return, I mean aside from offering our prayers for the safety of all of the world's people?"

"Cardinal, as you may recall we said we would in fact be asking for the Church's help in winning the peace. We do have a specific request."

"Name it sir and if it is within the power of our Holy Mother Church we will of course comply and do so following your instructions."

"We are very worried that the Islamists may find some way to capture the South American countries. So many of them are rich in natural resources and they are so poor we fear anything could happen down there.

Given the alliance between Iran and Venezuela already, we have to be concerned about the Islamists spreading their influence throughout the region. Our CIA tells us that while you are not as strong as you once were down there, the Catholic Church may still have enough influence with the people of those countries to head off any coups that would put Waleed's people in power."

"Yes, my heart breaks for the Church of the Americas in general, but particularly for those long suffering people in South America. I will present your request to Holy Father. I am sure he will help."

"Sir I really hate to be so blunt, but this is not a negotiation. Having the Vatican make recordings, and let's call them what they are, propaganda recordings, for our war effort is the price of your physical salvation. America probably has more practicing Catholics than any country in the world, but we can't deal with anyone, I repeat anyone, who doesn't do what we say when we say to do it.

This is a matter of the survival of the world and..."

"Yes, Mister Vice President, the survival of the physical world. I will speak to the Holy Father immediately and call you back within an hour. Will that suffice?"

Deciding not to take this any further, Hodges replied: "Very well sir I will await the Holy Father's reply."

Twenty minutes later the Cardinal called to say the Holy Father would make a recorded appeal to the people of South America not to allow their countries to be forced into an alliance with the Islamists. He would speak in Portuguese to the Brazilians and Spanish to the rest of the continent. More than this, he would order the Bishops of South America to hide, destroy or do whatever would be necessary to keep valuables from the local government officials. He would order all Catholics in Europe, the Americas and around the world to practice passive resistance if their governments did fall to Waleed.

The Pope's order was almost medieval in its scope and spirit. He ordered able bodied Catholic men between the ages of fourteen and sixty to actively take up arms against any efforts to forcibly convert them to Islam. Vice President Hodges display of patience and diplomacy had secured much more than he had hoped for and had given America and her allies a clear picture of what could be expected from the Vatican in the future.

COLUMBIA

The Pope's order would go a long way toward alleviating concerns about how South America would react, but before they could consider the question settled, Andrews and Hodges had to think about using every advantage America had in the region. One such advantage that came to mind had to do with the ongoing war being fought by Columbia against the FARC revolutionaries and the narco gangs. Both groups had been trying to overthrow the Columbian government for years. Throughout most of their struggles to suppress these threats, the United States had been a very supportive partner. Aside from a few rough spots in the relationship over the years, the two nations were friends. Columbia had emerged as America's best friend in the region once Harlan Andrews became President.

As Peter Brownell's Vice President he had traveled to Bogotá to personally discuss the ways the United States could help the Columbians win these duel wars. In the give and take of American politics, many of his recommendations were acted upon, but many more were killed in committee.

Now as President he was able to do much more for his friend Jose Hernandez the President of Columbia whom Andrews knew personally and called "Joe."

"Walt we've done a lot for Joe Hernandez. Let's think about what he can do for us."

Hodges replied, "Hernandez has a tough bunch of men in his army. Our Green Berets have trained them and they have been runnin' up some big victories against the insurgents and the drug dealers. I'm sure we can get them to at least have a call up of their reservist. We can tell them we'll pay for it later."

"We can tell Hernandez he doesn't have to do anything but make the public call up and keep his troops at the ready. That will get Rios and Waleed's attention and keep them thinking for a while until we figure out what we have to do. Personally, I'm leaning toward having the Air Force level their base, how about you?" Andrews asked.

"That sounds about right. They do owe us for helping them all these years and it would be pretty bad for them to have Waleed move in next door.. yes it sounds right. Shall I get Joe on the phone?" Andrews nodded and made some notes on a yellow pad.

WAR BRINGS THE MEXICO QUESTION TO A HEAD

Given the nearness of both Mexico and Canada the question of their loyalties was among the last to be weighed. Canada had recently elected a Conservative government for the first time in many years and relations with America's northern neighbors had been improving. Canadian cooperation in the ongoing war in Afghanistan and the Middle Eastern theater had always been strong and important, so there was no real concern with the way Canada would go. Canada was just as much a target as the United States. The Canadians had nothing to gain but everything to lose in this war. If America fell Canada fell. Mexico, however, presented a different set of facts.

The massive grassroots push back by America, against the constant flow of illegal aliens pouring into the United States over the Southern border, had changed the relationship with Mexico. It slammed the door on almost all Mexicans and others seeking to enter the United States from the south.

This put a tremendous strain on the weak and stagnant Mexican economy which had been predicated upon dumping its poorest least educated people on the United States. Relations with many Central American countries and Mexico had been sour at best and hostile at worst.

Mexico was in a constant state of civil unrest. There was always a threat that just the slightest incident could cause the country to explode in a simultaneous combination revolution and civil war. The president and his cabinet lived under a twenty-four hour armed guard and could never be seen in public for fear of being murdered in a revolution that might have sprung to life that very day.

During the years leading up to the war, the Mexican government began to sell high quality cheap crude oil to Iran and establish favorable trading partnerships with the Waleed regime. They were drilling in Gulf of Mexico waters claimed by the United States, but America seemed to have no will to do anything about it. The Congress was on record as having prohibited Americans from drilling in the disputed waters. With that in mind, Mexico never had to look over her shoulder while it stole America's oil from waters less than seventy-five miles off the coast of Texas.

Claiming a need for national security, the Mexicans purchased over four-dozen short-range ballistic missiles from Iran and followed Venezuela into an agreement to allow Waleed to build a military base on the Yucatan Peninsula. As he did for the Rios government in Venezuela, Waleed shipped tens of thousands of AK 47s to Mexico City to help the Pablo Sanchez administration in its program of confiscating privately owned guns.

Mexico Makes Herself a Special Case

"Walter what are we going to do about that gang down in Mexico?" President Andrews asked.

"We have a few options. First, I think we should use the Pope's recording asking Catholics to resist any efforts of an alliance with the Islamists and to take up arms against them if need be. Of course that will be easier said then done now that Sanchez has confiscated all the guns he could find down there," Hodges answered.

"We've got to support anything that looks like a counter insurgency by Mexicans trying to keep their country from going Islamist. Instruct the CIA to closely monitor everything that is happening down there. And one other thing, I've been thinking about that air base Rios gave Waleed at Punto Fijo and the one he is building in the Yucatan. I've decided we can't let either one of them go unchecked. Order the Air Force to 'MOAB' the two of them pronto."

"*Yes* sir, Mister President!" Water Hodges said as he reached for his phone.

The letters MOAB stand for Mother of All Bombs. By passing along that order, Hodges would be unleashing the most powerful non-nuclear bomb ever built. MOAB, of course was the affectionate nickname given to the United States Air Force's Sensor Fused Weapon (SFW), a super cluster bomb that has killing power beyond the imagination of war fighters of past generations. The SFW is a thirty foot 21,000 pound bomb that has the capability to cover an area the size of sixteen football fields with guided death dealing projectiles called *skeets*. Each of the skeets is a separate mini bomb with a built-in heat seeking guidance system that either brings it to a target as big as a tank or detonates above the ground to cover huge areas with deadly shrapnel.

When the skeets explode they turn to scolding hot molten copper that can punch through the toughest known armor. Once the liquefied copper sprays the inside compartments of a tank, it turns it into an oven and renders its appliances useless. The MOAB is not only a deadly physical weapon, but a devastating psychological weapon as well. No army could sustain its morale and fighting spirit after being hit with a MOAB.

On the morning of day two of the war, American bombers and fighter planes poured fire on Waleed's bases in Venezuela and Mexico. The Punto Fijo base had been able to send up a dozen Russian made MiGs in an attempt to fight back and protect themselves from the American F 17 warplanes. The Mexican base was still under construction and not yet operational when the

F 17s swarmed over its skies.

Because of the very heavy weight of the MOABs, they were flown to their targets in two huge specially modified C 130 transport planes. Each of the C 130s was sent to their mission from Carswell Air Force base in Texas near Fort Worth. The bombs were actually housed in Eglin AFB in the Florida panhandle, but were flown to Carswell for the sake of the symbolism of having the bombs launched from a Texas AFB. Texas had been most at risk from the Mexican missiles and because of its size and importance it was given the launching as a special morale booster.

The first MOAB to find its mark was the one sent to the Yucatan to obliterate Mexico's ability to join Waleed's war effort against America. It made a huge hole in the center of the would-be base, and killed hundreds of Iranian and Mexican construction workers working on the grounds. The shock waves were felt thirty miles away and the fires it started burned for hours. When the smoke cleared the Iranian Air Force base in Mexico was no more. Mexico declared itself a neutral country that evening. Pablo Sanchez called President Andrews to offer any help he could provide.

Solving Another Problem

Mexico's willingness to become a *compelled neutral* presented an opportunity the Andrews administration could not pass up. Initial reports from the southern border told of unusually high number of illegals pouring into the southwestern states. The Mexican intruders understood nothing about the war Waleed was making on America. All they knew was that it presented a great chance to sneak over the border while Uncle Sam was busy with *The Arabs.* Andrews saw it as an opportunity to slam the door shut and force Mexico to snap the lock. He told Sanchez to move armed soldiers to the Mexican American border and have them aim inward. The Mexican government understood that the days of their helping people to sneak into America would have to end.

Caribbean Countries

The relationship between America and the countries in and around the Caribbean Sea had always been a peculiar one.

On the one hand there was no need to be concerned about the dozen or so nations in the Caribbean community because they are mostly small and populated by people who meant no harm to America. On the other hand because they are populated by racial and ethnic minorities' internal politics demanded that they be treated with more concern than their size would ordinarily command.

Over the years, the relationship could best be described as being parent/child like. Before the war, the alliance between Venezuela and Iran would have been a bump in the road and not much more. When the war started, the President's attentions turned to questions of how best to explain to the Caribbean community what would be expected of it. He called Sir Randolph Spencer the Prime Minister of St. Lucia and chairman of The Caribbean Community Countries (CARICOM) and asked for his help.

They had a frank conversation about the problems CARICOM's overly friendly relationship with Venezuela and Cuba could potentially cause for the United States and CARICOM. Andrews was pressed for time, so there was little opportunity for subtle niceties. He told Spencer that America fully anticipated a fairly short and victorious war, and he had to insist that CARICOM suspend its relationships with both Venezuela and Cuba.

There was no need to talk to Venezuela after they were hit with a MOAB. The only question left was how to deal with Cuba as the remaining diplomatic concern in the Americas. Both Harlan Andrews and Walter Hodges had long political histories of antagonism toward Communism. That ruled them out. Hodges had an idea.

"I'll ask our friend Bill Stephenson at the Canadian International Development Agency (CIDA), to help us. CIDA still has plenty of sway with the Cubans and I'm sure they'll listen to Bill, especially after word of the MOABs reaches Havana."

"Well, we'll have to go with that. He won't take a call from us, thou I doubt Fidel is dumb enough to dance with Waleed. If there's anything he hates more than capitalism it's religion, ours or theirs. We'll have somebody monitor the situation but that's all we can do for now," said Andrews.

PART FOUR
WAR IN AMERICA'S STREETS

CHAPTER 40

ISLAMBERG

LONG BEFORE THE WAR the Islamists had been preparing for their attack on America. For a number of years they had been training their fighters to become the soldiers they would need in a camp they called Islamberg. Because of a string of court decisions won for them by volunteer civil liberties lawyers, the Islamist movement became a protected group in America's courts.

First the lawyers won them tax exemptions as a religious organization. Next they won a major case in which a court ordered the American government to stay clear of any of the Islamist's installations anywhere in the country. The order was modeled after what an abused wife might get from a local Domestic Relations Court judge. Under the order, any governmental agent found to be within one half mile of any of a list of locations owned by the Islamists who sued under the name "Muslim People's Committee" (MPC) would be personally liable to be sued for harassment. The list went on for three pages, but the Islamists had overreached and over-played their hand. When government lawyers turned the order over to Homeland Security agents, they were amazed. More than half of the list had been previously unknown to any of America's Intelligence agencies.

The list became an inside joke to the Intelligence community. In the type of humor law enforcement people share among themselves, it became known as "The Guide to bin Ladin's Secret hiding places." The "set back" America's intelligence agencies received by that decision was turned into a huge plus in less than two weeks. In cooperation with Canada's newly elected conservative Prime Minister, dozens of Canada's famous Royal Canadian Mounted Police (Mounties) were re-assigned to duty in the states. They were paired with American agents who traveled with them just up to the half-mile radius around MPC installations.

That way not only did the surveillances continue virtually without missing a beat, but if by some chance an agent was discovered, he or she would be lawsuit proof since the order was very specifically aimed at "American government agents." Canadians could not be held liable under the order. As a result of "The Guide," the FBI, which became the lead agency in the ongoing investigation, was able to amass complete dossiers including photos on almost every important Islamist leader operating on American soil. One of the most productive surveillance operations conducted at a location listed on "The Guide" was at a camp the Islamists had tauntingly named Islamberg. It was located in rural upstate New York.

The FBI knew about Islamberg but because of its name, the Bureau's analysts had discounted its importance. They reasoned that a name like Islamberg was so blatant; such a taunt was probably nothing more than a hoax.

It was only after a thorough review of the evidence that the Intelligence Community concluded Islamberg was indeed just what it appeared to be: a jihadist's terror training camp. Islamberg was another example of the unintended damage the Islamists' useful idiot pro bono lawyers had done to their clients.

They had given the Islamists a false sense of what America is about. The "Guide" decision they had secured for the MPC reinforced the smug superiority the terrorists felt toward America. It fed their belief that the New York Times and the courts ran America. They believed Americans were too weak to violate court orders, even to save their own lives. When the war started, these misconceptions worked out better than anyone could have imagined.

Cracking their way into Islamberg became a top priority when it appeared on "The Guide" restraining order. It was listed with other locations that had to be given the half mile 'no – surveillance' radius, which the FBI knew were dangerous places. That indicated it was not a hoax and would have to be surveilled. The Mounties did a great job. They were skilled partners in the war on terror and brought with them a few tricks the FBI had not seen before. One of those tricks became crucial in breaking into Islamberg.

Let's Fight Hunger

The Islamists public relations efforts played the MPC's Let's Fight Hunger program for what it really was: a perfect way to collect money and materials for the coming war. The fact that they would be doing it with the help of the American media, and thereby thumbing their noses at America's Counter terrorism forces, made the whole thing even sweeter. The MPC put out a call for canned foods and other nonperishable items, to "help the needy among us."

To tug at American Muslim heartstrings, they announced that some of the money would buy religiously sacrificed meats for pious old Muslims who had fallen on hard times. They showed pictures of children hobbled by missing legs, blown off by American and allied bombs. They also used the program to help them find potential recruits as future Islamist soldiers, by asking people to recommend collection points. The MPC realized that any place that would collect money and food for them might be fertile grounds for recruiting new members. The program's real purpose was obvious to everyone but the sycophantic American media, who insisted it was a benign effort at self-help by a struggling minority.

To feed the media the red meat it longed for, the MPC said they would forward at least 10% of the donations it received to victims of natural disasters all over the United States. On its face, the program looked perfect. None of the media ever asked tough questions. They just wrote whatever the MPC – America's enemies – fed them.

Terrorists Court Victories

Once the civil rights lawyers started to win their cases against the government on behalf of their terrorist clients, the court victories began to come so quickly the Islamists could hardly keep up with their good fortune. All over America, the left was celebrating the advancements in personal freedom they were winning for their brothers and sisters in the struggle.

The Muslim People Committee's probono lawyers won the right to have all terror related cases tried in civilian courts with public funds paying their fees. The terrorists won the right to be released on bail in almost every case as the courts rolled further to the left. Many of the released terrorists immediately fled the country to continue fighting against America in the Middle East and elsewhere. In a few cases, the courts ordered the government to transport leased terrorists whose rights had been violated back to specially selected neutral air fields in the Middle East. In at least one case a bail jumper was recaptured in an Egyptian bomb making safe house.

When a captured terrorist actually did stand trial, the Islamists would flood the courtroom with menacing looking thugs. Often they were able to intimidate the jurors into acquittals. Although trials were unheard of in the countries they came from, the terrorists apparently got the idea of intimidating witnesses and jurors from a PBS documentary on the Mafia.

Every new acquittal and every hung jury led to a major propaganda press conference in front of a courthouse. The Islamists and their lawyers attended each one. They were non-stop diatribes demanding the American government stop its persecution of the peaceful Muslim people of America and the whole Muslim world. These press conferences were scripted and always went the same way. In every one the American government was accused of waging a war of extermination against Muslims instead of war against the Islamists

During these events the Islamists would station their own photographers around the edge of the crowd. They knew FBI agents would be taking pictures and they wanted to get pictures of the agents so they could target them for death. Soon the terrorists had pictures of dozens of agents and the agents had pictures of dozens of them. The Islamists drew a false sense of security from the pictures they took. The FBI got onto the picture taking stunts very quickly. As a counter, they assigned older analysts and office workers - who never went into the field - to take their pictures. This rendered the MPC's pictures largely useless. When the Mounties showed up for surveillance operations, they were total unknowns to the MPC. The hubris of the Islamists would not allow them to believe their photographers had missed any agents, so they ruled out the Mounties they photographed at their compounds as people to be concerned about.

Consequently, the Mounties were able to get very close to the Islamist compounds. Some of the Black Mounties were eventually able to infiltrate some of the camps.

Nevertheless, at a certain point the FBI recognized it was not getting very much new information about what was going on inside Islamberg and similar training camps across the country. For weeks the investigations of the *Islambergs* went nowhere.

Using G Juice Against the Let's Fight Hunger Program

On a Saturday morning two months after the investigations started, the FBI got several routine field intelligence reports saying the same thing. The Islamists were now so sure of themselves that they had announced a charitable program they called *Let's Fight Hunger* (LFH). They made announcements at all of the Islamist controlled mosques as well as on Arabic radio and television shows. The LFH program was dutifully picked up by the Islamists friends in the New York and Los Angeles print media. Most cable television news shows did fawning segments on how the MPC was'doing for their own'just as earlier immigrants had.

The operation reminded older agents of the way Joe Columbo had tried to make the Mafia seem legitimate through his Italian American Civil Rights League. When the analysts put all of the reports together, they had a golden nugget for the Bureau's Operations Section.

The Operations Section ran with the opportunity in a creative and effective way that became known as *Operation G Juice*. When the FBI and the Canadian Mounties joined forces, the Mounties brought with them a number of spying devices they had gotten from the British MI-5 agents they were working with in a Toronto-to-London bombing plot. One of the devices was called G Juice, an odorless, colorless, tasteless liquid that could be used to track the movements of people who had it on their person. The compound was known to make some people experience low-level headaches and coughing, but it was otherwise undetectable. Trial uses indicated that most people infected with G Juice interpreted their symptoms as a common cold or allergies depending upon the season. As a tracking device, G Juice worked because it emitted a signature that could be picked up by a specially designed device. A G Juice signal could be detected up to five miles away in a line of sight. The effectiveness of G Juice was limited only by the imagination of the agents using it.

At a joint Task Force meeting of Homeland Security agents, FBI agents, National Security Agency (NSA) agents, CIA and Military Intelligence agents, an idea to tie the Islamist's *Let's Fight Hunger* ploy to the newly available G Juice began to develop. Someone pointed out that recent FBI laboratory tests on G Juice showed that the signature it gave off could be enhanced by increased exposure. The distance at which the substance could be detected could be increased to about eight miles before it ultimately trailed off. While eight miles was an improvement, it was not enough to appreciably add to its usefulness because of the line-of-sight limitation.

This complicated the question of how to use the substance. Line-of-sight observations would be a tall order. The signal would pass through heavy foliage, and one or two layers of metal such as a car door, but not much else could be overcome. Having a requirement for such a clear view would be too hard to work with in actual field conditions.

Because of its limitations, G Juice was almost ruled out as a tool that could be helpful as a tracking agent. Most agents thought of it as more of a toy than a serious investigative tool. One Army Intelligence Officer an idea that could make G Juice work.

"We need to know who their leaders are, but we have no practical way to find out. Now they are running this *Let's Fight Hunger* bullshit. Of course we know it's nothing more than a money laundering scam they put together, to raise the money they'll need to make their play. Now what happens to the money? I mean in the short run when it is first collected?"

Another agent said, "The top guys gather it up to funnel to the right channels and clean it up."

"Right! And how many of their lower level guys get to handle the money?"

"Not many if any at all."

"Riiiight," the agent said dragging out the word. Then he continued, "because they won't trust lower level guys with the information about where and how the money gets cleaned up."

The Army agent continued: "It's my guess that they will give a small portion of the money away as they advertised and give a small amount to the lower guys to run their operations and feed themselves in these camps. Now, when the hundred dollar bills come in, we can guess that the big guys, the leaders, will handle those. And that's how we find them! We soak, re-soak then soak the hundreds and the fifties again until they practically glow."

"But our tests say we need practically complete line of sight, how will even that help?" someone asked.

An FBI agent joined in: "I see where this might be going. While the increased signal still needs basically line of sight... we can get line of sight from one angle; straight above."

"The Army agent smiled and said, "Bingo! We can reprogram a bunch of low flying spy satellites to pick up the G Juice signature. Since it will be straight overhead there will be almost total line of sight access to the movement of their top people because they will be the only ones with the large denomination G Juice soaked bills on their person."

"Yes and when they make the play we know is coming, we can use the G Juice signature from the big bills to catch the top leaders in their vehicles and slam them into road kill. Hey, and they'd never know how we knew which vehicles carried the top men," the CIA representative added.

When the top leaders of the Islamists brought their war to America's home soil they would have a surprise.

CHAPTER 41

FIGHTING IN THE STREETS OF AMERICA

WHEN WORD SPREAD about Qiryat Shemona, the Islamist world burst into flames immediately. To these seventh century zealots, the time had come for the world, as they knew it, to come to the violent end their Imams had predicted. Islamists saw the battle as the flash point they had been waiting for in order to bring the chaos and slaughter necessary to cause the return of Al Madhi, the long hidden miraculous twelfth Imam. They believed he would deliver the world to them and all of mankind would be judged by Allah. To them it was a signal to start their all out, fight to the finish, attack on the *infidel* world. Everywhere that Islamists lived battles broke out, in the streets, in the malls, in public places of all description. America was no exception.

In America Islamists exploded with maniacal rage. Gangs of crazed Islamists ran amok in Brooklyn's Atlantic Avenue section. They killed anyone they could find that even looked like an infidel. Their furious surge immediately sent terror flowing through the streets of New York City not felt since the hours after the World Trade Center attack. The wild mob's first target was the neighborhood's only major medical facility, Long Island Jewish Hospital.

Furious Islamists jumped head first through the ground floor windows to get to those who were cowering and trying to stay alive. The attackers didn't even want to "waste" the extra few seconds to enter through the revolving doors. Dripping with blood from dozens of cuts, the marauders immediately set about killing even Muslim doctors. To these wild attackers, Muslim doctors who would work at a hospital run by the'dirty Jew infidel' deserved special and serve punishment.

A Condition Misjudged

In a huge blunder, the New York City Police Department was quickly restrained on orders from the city's mayor. That would have helped the Islamists if they recognized what was happening and stayed away from the police. But events did not unfold that way. Fortunately the rage of the Islamists would not allow them a clear and calculated thought, so they foolishly did not stay away from confrontations with the city's police.

Like all super charged groups running wild over their supposed grievances, the Islamists attacked the police as quickly as they attacked anyone else. Many of them soon learned something about life in America's liberal big cities: Yes the politicians had made it safe for them to attack and murder non Muslims by forbidding their victims from arming themselves, but the police in these cities still had firearms. They learned New York was not at all the unarmed city they wished it to be. Because of their self-imposed separation from the rest of the world, the Islamists knew nothing about the culture of America.

They never cared to learn about America either. They had come to America for only one purpose: to wait for the signal to burn America to the ground.

The Islamists totally underestimated the amount of resistance they would face as they attempted to kill Americans on American streets. To them: Infidels are infidels all are the same as the soft and willing victims they had been bullying in Europe for many years.

The police in Brooklyn and throughout the big cities of America responded with their own savage force. Street cops are the smartest and toughest people on America's streets. Many are military veterans who understand the Islamist threat. They may have to smile and put up with abuse from the generally liberal political leaders in their towns, but they would never allow themselves to be murdered to satisfy politically correct ideas about how to deal with Islamists. America's cops well understood the difference between the Muslims they dealt with regularly and the Islamists. They knew which ones meant them harm even if the politicians could not quite make out the differences between the two. The police work in the heart of the communities that are most likely to be violent breeding grounds for trouble and they have instincts that keep them alive in tight situations.

America's cops sized up what was happening and recognized the high stakes of the battles raging in their streets. Collectively, they knew they were the final line between the Islamists and the destruction of most of America. They recognized that they needed to hold on until America's military could organize itself for war at home as well as abroad.

They understood there was no way the liberals running America's big cities would be up to fighting this war. Experience told them America's city halls would try to characterize what was happening as 'civil unrest,' denying the reality of the war in their streets. They were not about to trust their safety and the security of their families to the city hall liberal class.

Across the country the same scenario played out. Feckless and totally panicky city officials tried to reach out to the Muslim community through their Imams. In many places they were naive enough to give these community leaders radio and television airtime to talk to and calm their communities. The airtime was used to send battle plans to their troops. In almost every city, the Imams selected to speak a 'calming message of peace' were covert leaders of the Islamists.

The mayor of New York was dumb enough to try to walk the streets to restore calm. He attempted to walk along Atlantic Avenue with a Black AME minister, a Catholic priest, a Black Muslim Imam and the head rabbi of the most important synagogue in Manhattan. In minutes a mob of at least two thousand Islamists charged at them seemingly from nowhere.

The attackers did what they always do. The first thirty Islamists gave their lives and were killed by the bodyguards with the *peace walkers,* so the mob could reach the *peace walkers* and kill them. They were ripped to pieces by bare hands. The priest and the rabbi were carried away still alive. They were never found.

As the 'worst kind of traitor,' the Black Muslim Imam was tortured then literally flogged to death by three men swinging a home made cat and nine tails fashioned from lengths of small link chains with screw gun nails attached to their tips. Imam Hakem Jabbar a man who was born Arthur Mason in a rural Alabama shack and grew up to spend ten years in the Mississippi State prison system was flayed like a fish on a Brooklyn street corner. A local cable station broadcast some of his beating death, thinking it would horrify the attackers into calming down. Those who saw it cheered. The broadcast stopped when one of their producers finally realized the crowd was using Imam Jabbar's head as a soccer ball.

The attack was so furious that several Islamists were actually killed by wildly swinging machetes. One hundred and seven attackers and nineteen police officers and *peace walkers* were killed in less than eight minutes. The attack was like a piranha feeding frenzy. Body parts flew in the air.

Street battles flared up all over the country. In each case the police shot and killed as many attackers as they saw. They did not wait to be pounced on or told to use restraint. Word spread throughout the police ranks that this was a fight to the finish. The street cops were quickly transformed from protectors of the citizens of their city to men and women fighting for their own lives.

When a police officer driving an extra large emergency service truck found himself surrounded and likely to be overwhelmed, he mashed his accelerator and ran over dozens in the menacing crowd before the dead bodies stopped him and he was pulled from the cab and murdered.

America's police soon saw the Islamists as a horde of maniacal rats that had to be killed on sight. The Islamists fought from a similar point of view. They wanted death and would do what was called for to kill their police enemies and themselves. The police fired first most the time. They followed the old police adage, "It is better to be judged by twelve than carried by six." Civilized conduct was the first casualty on America's streets that day.

Police officers who had served in Iraq and Afghanistan took control of fire fights as they developed. They knew first hand how tenacious drug crazed Islamists could be. They knew exterminating these fanatical warriors, was the only way to insure America's safety now that the war had come to their streets.

Mobs of Islamist longing to die for Allah ran through America's big cities fighting those they found, smashing heads, smashing windows, shooting infidels, chopping heads hands and feet off. Many of them were high on drugs of one kind or another, an inconvenient fact always left out of Western media reports on the threat the Islamists posed to civilization. Stopping people running on "tanks" filled with half religious fervor and half amphetamines was not easy. Killing them required extreme bravery and careful shooting.

All over the country, local police had little more than courage and, side arms to fight the mobs. Nothing in the average American police officer's training adequately prepared him or her for what was happening.

The first day of Islamist attacks ended with tens of thousand of deaths all over the country. The spontaneity of the early violence brought mostly hardcore but unorganized Islamist zealots into the streets to battle anyone they could find. That made killing them by the bushel full fairly easy. From then on it would get tougher before it got easier.

DAY TWO BROUGHT VERY DIFFERENT BATTLES

The battles of day two and thereafter were characterized by the emergence of well-organized, sometimes well armed, semi military Islamists gangs. In Buffalo New York, large bands of attackers overwhelmed the outgoing day shift platoon at the city's largest police station and took it over. This gave them a cache of handguns, bulletproof vests, Thompson machine guns and Billie clubs. They also took a number of radios and at least fifteen patrol cars.

Armed with these weapons of urban combat they were able to roam upstate New York's largest city, shooting and killing people on sight.

Children were especially vulnerable. Frightened ten year olds were cut down running toward patrol cars they thought were manned by friendly police officers. The loudspeaker systems of the cars were used to lure people out of churches and synagogues so they could be murdered with machine gun fire.

By mid afternoon the Governor of New York was forced to order the state's Air National Guard to patrol the skies of Buffalo, and its surrounding areas, with attack helicopters. All actual police officers were ordered off the streets and the remaining patrol cars were rocketed into piles of rubble by air to surface missiles. Before evening came in Buffalo, all of its mosques were burned down by mobs of civilians taking their safety into their own hands. At least ten thousand people, mostly non-Muslim women and children were killed in the Buffalo area. Such attacks were exactly what the Islamists wanted. They believed the killing of innocent praying Muslim *fence sitters* would swell their ranks with *Islamized* men and women looking to get their *revenge*.

The number of dead Islamists was too high to immediately count because body counts were now well beside the point. The hospitals were guarded by local hunters and in many instances men and even women who appeared to be Muslims, were shot and killed as they came in for treatment of wounds. All over the country, the Islamists attacked any groups of Americans appearing to be helpless and vulnerable.

In Omaha a home for retired Catholic Nuns was surrounded by a squad of home grown American Black Muslims and set ablaze. When the aged sisters staggered out of the one hundred year old building, they were hacked to death by strong young men using timber axes. A group of armed town's people attempted to save the nuns. At first they were able to save a few, but eventually they are also annihilated by much better armed attackers, who were using Tec 9 machine pistols. The counter attack was quickly turned aside. Each of them was beheaded along with the surviving nuns, according to the Islamist understanding of Qur'anic law.

Wherever these attacks took place, the problems and suffering of ordinary Americans was compounded by career criminals who took advantage of the chaos. In the large cities, where strict gun control laws kept guns of all kinds out of the hands of honest citizens, the situation was especially dangerous.

Completely oblivious to what was happening, but recognizing an opportunity to steal, bans of young drug addicts prowled the streets in packs like wolves in search of prey. In a few instances Islamists who hated them on sight just because they were Americans summarily annihilated them. That these drug addicted enemies of American society did not see themselves as Americans or anything else, made no difference to the Islamists. They were shot, stabbed and beheaded as quickly as anyone else.

All stores containing anything useful to those battling up and down the streets were broken into and looted. Citizens ran off with foodstuffs and combatants on both sides ran off with anything that could be used as a weapon. The same things happened all throughout every city with a sizable Islamist population. In some places where the Islamists were well entrenched, Americans were forced to make their way in caravans to public buildings to try and wait out the attacks in relative safety.

ROCHESTER, MINNESOTA

Rochester Minnesota is the home to the famous Mayo Clinic, one of the finest hospitals in the world. Because of its reputation, the Mayo Clinic's doctors and staff are among the top professionals in the healing arts. They represent every developed country in the world's community. That array of personnel also included a number of doctors who were Muslims.

The number of Arab speaking Muslims attached to the Mayo Clinic, in one way or another was so numerous that there were three full time television stations broadcasting exclusively in Arabic in the Rochester market. This turned out to actually be a blessing in disguise for America's intelligence services.

All three stations were constantly monitored after the September 11th attacks and many important bits of information had been gathered from this program, until the New York Times found out about the project and wrote a full page article condemning the practice as 'un-American.'

Fortunately by the time the piece was written, the Intelligence services had anticipated its exposure. The monitoring project was pushed deeply under cover and both the Islamists and the media naively accepted the story that it had been discontinued. In reality Homeland Security never stopped watching the 'children's hour' which was being used to send instructions to the soldiers of Islam.

Among Intelligence professionals the whole matter was an inside joke. Their laugh was on the Islamists who, in their smug haughtiness believed they understood America.

The nation's dangerous guests actually thought the monitoring stopped after it was featured on Nightline in a segment that complained about the 'violation of Arab' American rights. The Intelligence services often let minor operations go forward in order to maintain the charade that they had been scared off.

When Operation Sucker Punch got started, highly trained American agents with full knowledge of Islam and Arabic, were able to seize control of the Arab Cartoon channel and send false messages and disinformation out to the "soldiers" they knew where out there waiting for instructions. Rochester has a population of about 100,000 making it the third largest city in Minnesota. It's over 80% white 10% Black and a mixture of what the Census people call 'others.' Besides the Mayo Clinic complex the most prominent building in town is the Federal Medical Center which is a federal prison hospital that was once the campus of a failed state hospital. The Islamic Center of Rochester is on South Broadway in the middle of the heart of the city very near the Mayo Clinic. When the attacks started all of American Rochester was shocked to see Muslim doctors from the Clinic whom they had considered to be their friends, joining in the carnage. The wave of action quickly spread.

To the surprise of the Americans who were not too spooked to notice, the Muslim doctors turned all the televisions to the Arabic Cartoon channel. All of them stared, trance like at the flickering screens listening and mumbling Islamic prayers.

The knots of white jacketed men and women around the sets made for an eerie scene. They became like islands in the panic that was swirling around every public area in the building. The uproar had even taken the real broadcasters at the Arabic Cartoon channel off guard. For the first hour there were no orders being sent out to eager Islamists. After 87 minutes of just cartoons, the station went off the air for about 3 minutes. When it came back on the air, the covert Homeland Security take over had been achieved.

"Soldiers of Allah the merciful Lord of the Universe, the hour has come for you to step forward and fight the evil Jew and his Christian henchmen," the announcement began. It went on to describe the insults from the Israeli government and the 'false' reports of Islamic attacks on Qiryat Shemona, Tel Aviv, London and Paris. At the end of a 'boiler plate' litany of complaints about Israel and America, the "announcer" who was actually an American agent, instructed the Islamists to slowly make their way to the federal prison hospital.

The instructions urged the Islamists to arrive at the hospital via the front gate which would be opened in about one hour.

"Brothers, we have a group of brothers inside the facility. They are, even now, taking control of the infidel's prison hospital so we can use it as our Rochester headquarters. Each of you has been given a unit designation ranging from 1 to 8.

"If you are assigned to unit one, please wait 30 minutes and travel to the federal hospital as quickly as you can. Once you are at the gate, wait for the signal to enter." The announcer closed his instructions with: "You will recognize the signal."

WAITING FOR THE ROCHESTER MINNESOTA ISLAMISTS

When the Islamist doctors and staff from the Clinic arrived at the prison, they had a reception committee they did not expect.

Quietly and secretly members of the 334th Infantry Division Special Troops Battalion (334th ID STB) of the Minnesota Army National Guard were being helicoptered onto an open field near the hospital and walked into the hospital through the back gate away from the center city complex. The inmates were moved to the gymnasium and told to remain silent if they wanted to live through the day. Two tried to escape. They were shot dead with silencer equipped 9 MM handguns and left where they fell. The soldiers moved a twenty man special unit into position just inside the prison grounds without being noticed.

The 334th Infantry's Special Troops Battalion is a well trained and highly prepared unit of troops whose mission is to assist civil authorities during a disaster. The unit traced its roots directly back to a Union Army Civil War Regiment from Minnesota and Michigan known as the *Black Hats,* a nick name the unit still proudly used. Now the Black hats were moving into place to complete a very important mission to defend their country.

When the medical men who had become Islamist "Soldiers of Islam" began to arrive, they were waved through the front gate by a bearded Black man wearing a federal prison guard's uniform. Once they were let in, they were led to a small room and shot twice in the back of the head. The silencer equipped

Black hats did their job. There would be no medical units in the Islamist's Rochester area army. While the special troops were mopping up the Islamist lemmings pouring into the prison hospital, other members of the 334th battalion were moving in from the rear and destroying the rest of their "Islamic brothers" waiting to enter the grounds.

Carnage in the Clinic

The Americans who were trapped on the upper floors of the Mayo Clinic watched the action on the streets below with "slack jawed" wonder. In frustration, some of the Islamic attackers who had charged the building in an attempt to take it over, began to run throw the pediatric ward killing new born infants by smashing them into the walls. On seeing his baby daughter smashed open like a melon, a young father tackled the nearest attacker. The two wrestled in a furious fight to the finish. Finally when they stood up, the Islamist hugged the young father and pulled him along as he jumped through a huge plate glass window. This signaled a wild bloody hand to hand battle between the hostages and the attackers.

Two Americans picked up a waiting room couch and used it as a battering ram to push three attackers through the gapping hole left by the picture window and out into the air over the streets of town. In a surprising turn of the flow of the fight, when seven more attackers flew out the window, the remaining five ran off. In the other states with heavy concentrations of Arab immigrants, street fighting broke out as well.

California

In California the Islamic Center of Bakersfield was a staging area for Islamist fighters to gather and plan attacks on Santa Clarita a small town just to the south. The prize in Santa Clarita would not be clear in normal circumstances. It is a small city forty miles north of Los Angeles. By its outward appearances, there was not much importance to it. The Islamist soldiers know better. They knew Santa Clarita had something they needed. One of the largest motor home sales lots in Southern California was in Santa Clarita. The value of these motor homes was very clear to them; even if it was not immediately clear to others.

In a lightening fast raid on Santa Clarita Vacation Vehicles, the attackers took forty of the most well equipped and functional mobile homes to be found anywhere. These units gave the Islamists immediate mobility and army like striking abilities. The mobile homes would serve as rolling headquarters providing command and control capabilities vital to coordinated attacks on American targets. They also came equipped with generators that would provide power sources anywhere electricity was needed. They had dish satellite televisions that would provide access to intelligence on what the Americans would be doing to counter attack. The Islamists were counting on the American media to be eager to tell them what they should expect the American military was planning for them.

The Islamists also recognized the value of well appointed mobile homes as both troop transport vehicles and mobile surgical hospitals for treating their wounded. Those forty mobile homes served as command and control centers for urban combat attacks on cities all over the west coast from Los Angeles to Portland. They remained "in action" for all of the general fighting on American soil.

THE CLEVELAND TRICK

In the early hours of the war, local independent cells were caught without clear instructions as to what to do. There was no one to give them orders and no way for them to join with other Islamists since they did not know each other. The unexpected start of an all out war meant they had to take action on their own without waiting for instructions from their contacts. The contacts that would be coaching them through their destructive attacks were nowhere to be found. In some cases they were arrested because they were known to the FBI. In some cases they were too busy hiding or trying to connect with their own assigned command and control structures.

In Cleveland a group of very dedicated Islamists who were trained at Islamberg, the terrorist camp in upstate New York, quickly gathered together a number of brothers. While the moment of truth stopped a few in their tracks and they hid and refused the call, a group of about forty hard core America haters responded to their mobilization point. Once the men were gathered, the question of what to do with them had to be addressed.

A review of his troops told Abdul Rahman, a blond haired blue eyed Chechnyan that these men were not the best people for his plans. He wished he had been able to get to know them, to determine what they could reasonably be asked to do, but there was no time for wishing. At Islamberg he was taught to improvise. The phrase *adapt and overcome* was used for situations like the one he was facing. It had been taken from the American Marine and Army war fighters. Rahman knew this was an *adapt and overcome* moment. His playbook had a number of simple operations in it. Now his job was to fit the brothers he had into his plans.

Rahman and cell leaders all over the country knew the opportunities to kill large numbers of Americans would present themselves. It was capitalizing on them as they came along that was the trick. Years of the Western media's non stop shilling for the Islamist cause had paved the necessary ground work. Americans had been told for years that there really were no international terrorists and the very idea of violent Islamists was a fairy tale. They were also told that anyone who thought otherwise was a religious bigot.

Americans were initially told that what they were seeing was merely a repeat of the urban riots of the 1960s. Every time an American safely completed a short trip to a market, it fed his/her belief that there was actually nothing to fear in the first place.

The anchormen and women on America's top television network broadcasts all said the same thing, "The Muslims are just reacting to Israel's attack on them at Qiryat Shemona. They have no cause to attack us, just some of our public buildings."

Most Americans believed this line because they wanted to believe it. That made attacking them and killing them that much easier.

In what became known as *The Cleveland trick* Abdul Rahman and his troops were able to strike a vicious blow to Americans who would not accept that they were the real target of what was happening in their streets. Rahman ordered three of the oldest and least physically able of his men to shoot their way into an office building which was open in violation of Presidential orders.

They approached the lobby dressed as maintenance men. Their orders were to avoid a confrontation as long as they could and keep a low profile. It was not until they had all of the cleaning equipment dragged right up to the guard's desk that they were even challenged.

With no thought for their plan or coordinating their movements, all four pulled out guns and shot the two guards behind the black marble desk just in front of the elevators. They pushed the button and in seconds they were shooting their way into an insurance company's offices and toward a window facing the street. Immediately the first one jumped through it yelling "Allahu Akbar," which is Arabic for something like "God is greater than everything."

A woman who screamed was shot and killed. Those that did not try to stop the remaining two were not shot, immediately. One of the men then sat on the window ledge which severely lacerated his buttocks and the back of his thighs. Blood began dripping from his feet. The third man faced toward the office to make certain no one would interfere with their operation. When the man at the window and the remaining gunman were settled in, the gunman called Rahman to tell him they were in place and a good sized crowd was forming on the street below them. The local police had no choice but to respond and start trying to negotiate with 'window man' and his partner. Soon the phone rang and lines of communication were opened.

Much to window man's surprise, a news helicopter arrived, seemingly out of nowhere, and he was being waved to by the pilot who was using a loudspeaker to ask him why he was sitting on the bloody window sill. While this was happening, Rahman was readying his strike.

He drove five bomb vest wearing troops to within a few blocks of the scene. Like water slowly making its way down a gentle slope, they eased in among the crowd which had built to over five hundred onlookers. On Rahman's signal, three of the bombers detonated their payloads and the carnage began. Body parts were everywhere. Blood ran like sewer water along the edge of the sidewalk and into the gutter.

Stunned survivors begged for help, but the killing was just beginning. The next phase of Rahman's plan quickly followed. The remaining two bomb draped men mingled among the survivors and waited for the emergency services to arrive. The site was just four short blocks from a Fire and Ambulance Service station, a fact that had not been overlooked by Rahman and his top lieutenant. In less two minutes an ambulance, two fire rescue trucks and four police cars were on the scene. When they were totally integrated into the crowd of their dead and dying countrymen, the remaining two bombers blew themselves up and took most of the first responders with them. When "the window man" saw this, he looked down, and carefully aimed, then jumped and landed on two of the four remaining Emergency Medical personnel who were staggering around in a daze trying to regain their composure.

The gunman forced all of the remaining office workers into a corner and, using hand signals, ordered them to sit down. He knew it would be a long time before anyone thought to come up to look at the office since the police did not know he was with window man.

Twenty minutes later, his patience paid off. The news helicopter came back and was hovering at his eye level. At this point the office workers were both scared and happy. They were, of course, scared because what they had witnessed and the uncertainty of their own futures. They were, however, happy that the gun man did not seem to want to harm them as he assembled a rifle and fitted it with a launchable grenade. He took careful aim and fired the less than fifty yards his missile needed to travel to bring down the news helicopter. It broke into enough pieces to kill at least thirty more onlookers who just had to get a first hand look at what was happening after they had been shown the standoff on television. Once the grenade did its job, the gun man ordered the office workers to walk toward him. Almost all of them did.

A middle aged secretary who was looking to retire very shortly refused. He did not see her as she picked up a stapler and threw it at him just as he was trying to pull the pin on his last grenade.

The stapler didn't really harm the gunman but it stunned him long enough for another worker, a young man just out of college, to pick up their captor's gun and shoot him with it. In an instant other workers attacked their attacker and jumped up and down on him until he was dead.

By the end of the day, word of this clever ploy had spread out across the country. The media gave the deadly stunt a name. They called it *The Cleveland trick* and it became well known on both sides. It worked again the next day in Boston, where the largest portion of the population had believed the media's stories that there were no terrorists. It worked in Eugene Oregon as well. Because of the trick's element of total surprise both cities suffered death tolls approaching the Cleveland numbers, dozens more foolish citizens and brave first responders were killed.

Thereafter the trick lost its effectiveness. The Americans were not fooled by potential jumpers posing as aggrieved Muslims acting out of frustration with the callousness of the West toward their complaints against Israel and The United States.

In Milwaukee the response that had been crafted on the fly was first used. When the same scenario repeated itself and an Arabic looking man appeared on a roof ledge of a ten story residential building, a sniper shot him before he was able to play out his role. In Dallas a command level decision was made about what to do with people who were found on their streets in disregard of the President's order. The Dallas Police chief ordered her officers to arrest everyone they saw and drop the arrestees off at Texas Stadium. Volunteer retired military and police personnel who came forward in answer to the President's call for help guarded them.

MOBILE, ALABAMA

The May Street section of Mobile, Alabama is controlled by some of the most violent street gangs in one of the old South's main seaports. The gangs are comprised of Black teenagers intent upon trying to prove they are every bit as tough as the gangs in Chicago or Oakland. For the most part they do what gangs do. They sell drugs, they fight over territory and they delude themselves into thinking that they run the world.

When they do attend school many of them go to Louis Brown High School. Brown is a typical inner city school. Its test scores are low, its drop out rate is high and it is near the top of most violent schools in the state. Brown has a student population that is 84% Black; 11% Hispanic, mostly illegal aliens; 2% White non Hispanic and a small percentage of "others." The Hispanics have their own gang. They are not so much a criminal organization as they are a group brought together for self preservation. Among the others at Brown High were a handful of Muslim Middle Eastern teenagers who were themselves illegally in America.

The Muslim teenagers tried to keep out of the way of trouble. They were forced to take an enormous amount of abuse from the Black gangs. On a daily basis they were robbed if not beaten both in and out of school. These particular Muslim teenagers had to take what was dished out to them because they were not in America for an education. They were deep cover sleeper cell members who had to keep a low profile so as not to draw attention to themselves. They were constantly being reminded by their families that speaking to the police was out of the question. "No police, no attention" they were told.

On a Friday evening after services, one of the Muslim teenagers, Abdul Jaleel Hamud, walked home from praying at the Al- Islam Islamic Center to find that the violence of his May Street neighborhood came home with him. The woman who was posing as Hamud's grandmother was standing at the front door wailing and crying. She told him the little eight year old daughter of his handler had been killed in a drive by shooting. She was not related to Hamud, but he liked the little girl and loved her father, his handler. After listening to his grandmother Hamud knew who did the shooting. He knew it was the Five Pointers the smaller of the two gangs that was fighting for control of his neighborhood. He knew them from school. They were the same bunch that had beaten him and robbed him many times in the Boys bathroom at Brown.

Hamud's Mission

When news of the war against America hit the airwaves, Hamud was overjoyed. He believed that the Islamists would subdue America and as one of the deep cover operatives who had help bring the great Satan down, he would be rewarded with a big house and car taken from a 'fat, lazy' infidel.

He eagerly awaited his assignment and when it came he was even more excited. He was selected to drive to a police station and fire a shoulder held rocket into its front door as the officers filed out for their duties. His time had finally come. It was time to strike at the heart of America.

As darkness fell, on the first day of the war, Hamud was picked up by Najeeb, his handler who was accompanied by Mutaa, a 'brother' Hamud had never met. After a quick check to make certain they had a map and the supplies they would need, Najeeb showed Hamud the shoulder held rocket he would have the honor of firing. When Najeeb was sure Hamud understood how to use the stolen US Army weapon and all else was in order, they started toward their assigned target. They would have to pass through the gang controlled May Street section of town, but that meant nothing to Najeeb.

The May Street section was pure bedlam. People were running in the streets firing guns into the air, dancing to loud music, drinking cheap wine, and having sex on the garbage strewn lawns. They knew the police had been pulled away from their neighborhood to protect the nearby University of South Alabama campus.

They planned to loot the last few stores still operating on their main drag. Seeing them run around drunk and screwing in public like animals disgusted Hamud. Najeeb drove very carefully. Even though all was chaos around him, he was not going to draw unnecessary attention to his team. When he stopped at a signal light in front of the Five Pointers headquarters the trouble started. As they waited, one of Hamud's main tormentors crossed in front of them. Eyes locked on eyes. The gang member waved his gun at Hamud and smiled. As he walked toward his headquarters, he stopped and looked back at Hamud. Then he made a motion like he was shooting at him with a gun, blew the smoke away and did a holstering pantomime. Suddenly Hamud snapped.

He could no longer contain his rage. Months of being picked on and assaulted by punks he could have killed with his bare hands, would stay bottled up no more. He reached into the rear seat, grabbed the shoulder fired rocket from under a blanket and ran to the front of the headquarters.

Najeeb and Mutaa jumped out and tried to get him back into the van. Hamud wouldn't listen to them. His hatred for America would have to wait. He wanted revenge for his 'little sister.' He was tired of the insults. Without thinking, Hamud fired the only rocket they had for their mission. A weapon that his 'brothers' had risked their lives to provide to him was now gone and there was nothing to show for all the effort and planning they had put into their mission.

The house burst into flames. It was almost totally destroyed, but that meant nothing now. Najeeb was speechless. Everything they had planned was denied them by the thirst for revenge of one hot headed young man. To Hamud all the abuse, topped off by the death of the little girl, was too much for him to handle. He had let his emotions get the best of him. He had ruined his mission and many other missions to come. Now the Americans knew about their presence with nothing to show for it. Najeeb looked at Hamud for a few seconds while he tried to think through his next move. He thought back to the day he picked Hamud from a bunch of hungry boys on a dirty street in Damascus. All the hopes he had for the boy came to mind. He remembered the fire in his speech, the clear and purposeful glint in his eyes.

When he made his decision, Najeeb let his Tec 9 machine pistol do his talking. To show some small measure of mercy to the young 'brother' he shot him in the head so he would die immediately and not be taken alive by the remaining gang members. An angry mob was starting to close in on them. It was time to move on.

CHICAGO

In Chicago wars in the streets flared up immediately as America's Al Qaeda made its play to take control of the Windy City. Americans rallied at a WalMart in Oak Park a small bedroom town just outside of the City limits to buy or take as many weapons as they could. Liberals prohibited Chicago's citizens from carrying or even owning firearms, so those who wanted to fight for their lives had to look elsewhere for weapons.

This caused big problems for the citizen volunteers who were trying to fight back, but not for everyone in Chicago. Ironically, the first defeat the Islamists experienced in Chicago came at the hands of a large Black street gang. The Islamists made the mistake of believing that no one in Chicago was armed. They were also wrong about the reception they would get from the Black street gangs in the Windy City. Their lack of understanding of America fooled them into thinking Jeff Ford still ran the Black P Stone Nation. They did not know Ford was not running things anymore. They thought that since he had been willing to commit terrorists acts for Moammar Gaddofi he would gladly have his El Rukn, the term means cornerstone, gang join with them in their battles with the hated infidel. The fact that Ford was doing life in a federal super max prison escaped them. Things turned bad for them very quickly. El Rukn was gone and replaced by criminals who were better armed and determined to keep control of the city. When the Islamists killed a gang member who was selling drugs on a street corner and were immediately faced with many enemies they had no idea existed. The Black street gangs had superior firepower. The gang members drove their black SUVs to the mosque the Islamists were using as their headquarters. The fight was quick and violent.

When the smoke cleared there were no Islamists left. There was no mosque left either. Because the Muslims were bad for the drug peddling business in the neighborhoods they shared with the Black pushers, the gangs took advantage of their opportunity to wipe them out. They knew the mosque was the glue that held the Muslims together in their hood and they wanted them out instead of converting their customers to Islam and a drug free life.

Killing drug dealers was an easy mistake for the Islamists to make. To them all Americans were exactly the same: dirt under their feet. They made no distinctions between non-Islamists who were Black or White or Hispanic, Asian, liberal, conservative, young or old, male or female. They hated every American.

They did think that Jews were worse than any other Americans, but that made little difference. Recognizing Jews from non-Jews was yet another aspect of western living the Islamists had no grasp of. Fortunately, picking Jews out of groups of Americans proved to be just as difficult for these monsters from the seventh century, as it was for their Nazi heroes.

In Texas, a huge mosque on the edge of Houston was burned and blown up on day two. There were dozens of Americans killed on the campus of the University of Houston. The Islamists went there because after a series of unrelated shootings on college campuses around the country, the president of the school had made a major point of installing metal detectors at the doors of every building on his campus. He held a well-attended press conference at which he proudly proclaimed the University of Houston to be a gun free zone. The liberals in his audience cheered. The Islamists listened to his announcement and cheered even louder.

The sad thing was that the ban on guns on the University of Huston campus took place on the day before the Muslim world exploded. Whatever else that could be found on the University of Houston, drugs, typical anti-American activities, credit card scams, or forged documents: guns were absent.

The Islamists methodically swept through the grounds shooting grown people as easily as shooting kindergarten children. They killed and killed then killed again. The campus guards had no guns and were just as busy hiding to protect their own lives, as the students and faculty were.

There were no reports of the attackers asking anyone for his or her position on America's withdrawal from the Middle East before murdering them.

NEWARK, NEW JERSEY

In Newark, New Jersey, the fighting started at a Black Muslim mosque. Two of its members who were former United States Marines led a group from the Masjid Mosque in an assault on the federal courthouse on Walnut Street in Newark. It is called The Martin Luther King building, but that meant nothing to people who are intent on hating America.

The group of eighteen men and young boys charged the building in an attempt to free an Islamist who was on trial for plotting to blow up the Statue of Liberty. They came armed with shoulder held rocket launchers, Tec 9 small arms and five hand grenades. They were able to kill twelve security guards and easily take control of the ground floor of the building. They were still planning their next move when the New Jersey National Guard troops arrived. The attackers quickly learned the differences between Newark's street riots in 1967 and what they had committed to.

In their initial assault, they killed all of the guards and bystanders in the lobby, while losing just two of their troops. With the ground level secured, they planned to move up the floors and search for their objective. At the first sound of gunfire the three men safely locked themselves in the basement and alerted the guards on the upper floors.

Immediately a US Marshal who was trapped in the building while testifying in a bail jumping case took command of the resistance. In a calm authoritative manner, he coordinated the counter attack. The Marshal used an internal phone to order the elevators shut down between floors, but because of a faulty switch, one of the elevators could not be shut down.

The attackers devised a plan to separate so they could complete their mission. Fourteen of their troops would stay on the ground floor to fight off any counter attack while the remaining four would take the rest of the building. For the Islamists the single working elevator became a blessing. Since each floor's stairway doors were set so they only opened from the floor area into the stairwell, taking the elevator was a very practical way for the attackers to sweep the building.

Each time the single elevator crawled skyward floor after floor, the Marshal and those he was leading and protecting could hear them getting closer. When a building is silent and people are coming to kill you, the sound of an elevator is compelling. The Marshal was on the fifth floor.

With two floors to go, his cell phone rang. It was the National Guard Commander. "Sorry I haven't gotten to you sooner. A Newark cop, who saw the assault and was smart enough to count the attacking force, told us there were about fifteen to twenty of them. We count two dead on the floor and another dozen or so in the lobby.

"That means you might be facing one, but more likely you've got three or four to deal with. Be careful with these guys. Our information is that there are at least two and maybe four ex Marines among them. So we have to assume they know their way around weapons and will kill you unless you kill them first. What's your position and situation?"

The Marshal responded,"I'm the only one with a gun here. The rest, about ten people, are courthouse workers. The judge in my case led everybody up to the higher floors using the stairs. They're locked, but the court clerks have the keys. There's only one elevator working and they're comin' up. I can hear 'em searching then coming up to the next floor. I'm setting up an ambush so when the elevator door opens I'll start shootin,' How'd you get my cell phone number anyway?"

"Your wife called your office with it. She knew you were in the building and wanted them to warn you. It was a good thing she did, because with all of this shit flying around maybe nobody would have realized you were there. Is there a window behind you?"

"Yeah. There are three big old windows. Why?"

"You hear the copter? You're on the south side, middle bank of windows on the fifth floor right? Just watch."

Ten seconds later two heavily armed National Guardsmen repelled from an attack helicopter and came smashing through the windows. The Marshal waved them to his position behind a large metal desk and the room went quite. The Marshal whispered to the civilians to crawl away and move down the hallways to either side. Then the three American fighting men got set.

Tension filled the air. This was a very serious step they would be taking. None of them had ever been in combat, let alone planned an ambush of other Americans, even if they were traitors who were coming to kill them. Now they would be shooting and killing other people for the first time ever. In minutes the elevator doors would open and they would start firing. Getting mentally set to kill other Americans, even those who had gone over to the enemy, was a tough assignment.

Their hearts were almost pounding their way out of their chests. Suddenly they could hear a series of loud explosions from the direction of the plaza in front of the building. The National Guard had fired a tank round into the lobby. That raised the stakes for both sides. The two rogue Marines knew the United States military was pounding its way into the building. They knew the forces against them were overwhelming and they were now on a suicide mission. It immediately made them ten times more dangerous. Talking a good game about dying for Allah and actually doing it are two different things as they came to realize. The Americans knew the attackers would now be suicidal as well. They swallowed hard and prayed for help.

In the lobby the attackers fought as best they could, but with no leadership and no familiarity with military weaponry, the fight was brief and bloody. Most of it was over when a young boy trying to arm and throw a grenade fumbled it and killed almost all of his comrades.

Their Marine leaders had left the grenades with him with instructions to use them only if it became absolutely necessary. "These are very dangerous weapons. Be very careful when you handle them. Allah wants you back, but in one piece."

There was no time to even think about the explosion from downstairs somewhere. Seconds later the elevator doors slowly opened. As per their plan, the Americans waited until the four attackers were just outside of the car. The last two out were the Marines. The first two carelessly stepped to the side to defer to them. As they did, they turned away from the three Americans who were waiting for them. It made all four of them perfectly framed targets.

Two rapid bursts from the machine guns held by the Guardsmen and the Marshal's side arm stopped the attackers. The first two went down like sacks of bananas, flopping from side to side on their way to the floor. The next two were the rogue Marines. They were wearing bulletproof vests, so initially they were only knocked down, but as they were falling they passed face first through a stream of bullets being poured on their position. Both were bleeding from neck and face wounds, but managed to get to their feet to fight back. Their vests saved them long enough to allow them to briefly return fire, but the combination of receiving heavy fire and trying to fight back against shooters with the sun at their backs, kept them from doing much harm.

One of the Guardsmen was grazed in the right ear lobe and the Marshal took a round to his left shoulder, but all would live. The two Marines turned active Islamist enemy of America ended the action flat on their backs face up. One was stretched out with his head half in and half out of the elevator. When the gunfight winners surveyed the area, they had something to marvel at. The automatic doors of the elevator car kept slamming on one of the dead attacker's head; opening back up, then slamming on his head again and again. The repetitious beat of the doors as they strained to close in spite of the dead man's head, was the only sound in the room.

The Guardsmen looked at him and smiled.

"Dude!" One said as they touched fists and smiled.

PHILADELPHIA

In Philadelphia, there was a spectacular attack in which a crazed Islamist dove from a fifth floor window to crash himself into the windshield of a bus. It killed the driver and caused the bus to crash into a storefront, where it burned and exploded. That one attack killed twenty-seven passengers, another eight people on the sidewalk and six more in the store.

Surprise, the only advantage the American sleeper Islamists had, actually cut both ways.

They could run through crowds, shooting and killing people, in quick hits, but organized attacks were a totally different matter. As much as Qiryat Shemona caught the American people off guard, it found the embedded and generally autonomous individual Islamists largely unprepared to select targets, let alone strike them. Because America had been on high alert for virtually the whole year leading up to Qiryat Shemona, the advantage went to the Americans.

Because they were in deep cover, most Islamists had some training, and some Islamists had extended training, but only a few had rigorous detailed training. More than this, even the best-trained soldiers carrying the best most up to date weapons, would not have much impact without leadership and a cohesive plan of action. This has been a fact of warfare across the millennia.

History tells us that the Union Army, at the start of the Civil War, was very well trained by the standards of the day. Under General George McClelland, the Supreme Commander of Lincoln's Union Army, tens of thousands of well trained, equipped and fed troops had been whipped into fighting shape by the fall of 1862.

Nevertheless, while McClelland was a great drill instructor, he was not a leader of men. All of their brand new rifles and shinny boots brought nothing in the way of help to the Union's war effort. McClelland's army never was effective, as he had constructed it. This is not to say that there were no Islamists terrorists living in America who were prepared to bring the fight to America, because there were many of them. There were enough hidden Islamist troops across the country to strike America and hit her very hard. It was the lack of leadership that hamstrung them from the beginning.

Because deep cover American terrorist cells had always acted in complete autonomy they were relatively safe from discovery even when one of their members was arrested. The theory that what a man does not know can not be tortured out of him, however, proved to be a major obstacle to the type of large scale actions they would need to take to win any battles on American soil.

As both sides learned, divided cells are easier to conquer. Both also learned that al Qaeda's instructions that local cells should act on their own had limited value in the kind of conventional war they had been forced into. Almost without exception the most successful attacks carried out by the terror cells were those made on targets of opportunity.

When roving bans of Islamists, bent on murdering Americans, found groups of people who didn't think the warnings about staying indoors or at specially guarded shelters applied to them, things got bloody. They were pounced on with the full force of the frustration felt by Islamists who were not really able to do major damage to the institutions of the country they hated so much.

Most of those caught on the streets were curious teenage boys. Thousands of teenaged boys were killed in their own neighborhoods because they would not/ could not resist the temptation to 'see for myself.'

In some cases, such as in Paterson, New Jersey, dark skinned Hispanics who were not able to convince their attackers that they were not Arabs ducking their 'duty to kill infidels' were taken away and tortured to death to satisfy Islamist blood lusts.

CATCH AND KILL SQUADS

In preparation for the war he could see was coming, Andrews approved catch and kill squads, a measure never before officially sanctioned by an American administration. Everyone hoped the most extreme measure would not have to be taken, but the direr circumstances of the times demanded that it had to be used. America still had enough steel willed men and women to carry out the ultimate in required savagery. When the war started, killer squads were sent out to hunt down, find and splat the brains of the deep cover Islamists whose locations were dug out by clever American teamwork. The kill squad's general orders and new secret rules of engagement were simple: "No deep cover operatives shall be taken prisoner. Deep cover operatives are hereby declared enemy combatants. You will engage and kill every enemy combatant on sight."

The rules of engagement for hunting down Islamist leaders were different. Because they could be assumed to possess valuable intelligence, they were to be captured and taken to secret locations for interrogation. To keep them secret, President Andrews flipped a coin each day to select a new location.

The orders regarding the treatment and interrogation of the few captured Islamists deemed worthy of transfer to a holding facility were not complicated. There were no restrictions on the interrogators, save for those which were self imposed by their own personal value systems.

Specialists in efficient torture methods were brought in from Allied countries. In cases where Islamists leaders appeared to have been trained in ways to resist the type of interrogation techniques employed by agents from America, specialists from other countries where immediately rotated in and given a green light to do whatever his or her specialty was. The interrogations were purely results oriented operations with no holds barred.

CHAPTER 42

WALEED SINKS HIS TEETH INTO SOUTH AMERICA
AN ENEMY OF AMERICA IS A FRIEND OF MINE

"AN ENEMY OF AMERICA is a friend of mine." From his first day in power Mohammed Waleed followed this rule. His plans always included getting a foothold in Central America and/or South America. He had to find a safe place from which to stage a ground attack on the United States if he was ever to realize his demented dream of destroying the world. To get this safe base, he had to deal with South America's resident chief America hater, Andreas Rios the strongman dictator of Venezuela. Rios was a mirror image of the evil Waleed.

Rios was a classic South American dictator. He had led a group of unpaid army officers and enlisted men into a long, bloody coup and took control of the country. His first acts were to declare himself president for life and order the confiscation of all civilian held firearms. When these moves were accomplished he dissolved the legally elected congress and appointed a new House and Senate. The new congress promptly passed a bill giving Rios the power to force the members of his Supreme Court into retirement. Those that refused were placed in protective custody to keep them safe from the supposed wrath of the people. Soon all of the judges agreed that retirement, not protective custody was the best way to spend their remaining years.

All of these moves had taken place in such a short period that Rios caught the world be surprise. There was the obligatory *note of severe condemnation* from the big powers, the United States recalled its ambassador from Caracas, but nothing else happened. Basically the world yawned at 'Just another greasy little bastard in sunglasses taking over a South American country at gunpoint.

He'll be gone before we have to even learn his name.'

While the world was ignoring what was happening or meekly accepting that the deal was about oil, Rios, and Waleed were cultivating a friendship, which was actually an arms deal. It had nothing to do with oil because it really could not have anything to do with oil. Both leaders counted on ignorance and powerlessness for their success as partners.

Those who had a platform to speak out against this alliance, the world's media were either ignorant of the process of refining oil, or willfully blind to the facts of how high sulfur crude is refined into a commercially useful product. Those who understood what non sense the announcement was had no power to get the truth out. This was another example of the Western media being led around by the nose by anti American thugs, precisely because they were anti American thugs. Venezuela has oil but not enough refinery capacity to help Iran. Venezuelan oil is a high sulfur content commodity that must be refined using extra steps that are costly and time consuming. Iran has "light sweet" crude oil under her desert sands, but not enough refinery capacity to benefit from it.

Any partnership between the two countries, which was based on oil, would be a dubious one at best. There really was not much they could do for each other petroleum-wise.

The original announcement from Rios was straight out of an old style South American dictator's playbook. He made a five hour speech during which he banged his fist on a table and blustered against American 'Imperialism,' accusing Washington of planning to invade his country. He bragged that he would be ready for an American invasion because he reached an agreement with his comrade 'Mohammed Waleed of the great Republic of Iran' to build defensive installations on Venezuela's coast. When he heard about this, Waleed was furious and he almost canceled the deal. He did not want to remind the Americans that he was building a military base so close to American soil. It was one thing to build the base and have America ignore it, but it was quite another thing to brag about it. That would certainly draw a response from 'the Great Satan.' Waleed was not ready to deal with such a response at that point. For a few tense hours the deal was actually dead.

It took a personal intervention by Osama bin Ladin to smooth things over. Bin Ladin brokered an agreement where by Rios would stop mentioning military bases and Waleed would stop calling Rios an idiot. Both sides kept their mouths shut and the dust was finally allowed to settle. They issued a joint statement about their new peace and freedom pact, which was eagerly printed by the American and Western media. The New York Times put the story above the fold and ran follow up pieces praising the forward looking agreement for the next three days.

The fact that it was word for word the same as their original statement meant nothing to those news outlets. They changed the date on the press release and ran with it. The cynical thugs in Caracas and Tehran intentionally left the original date on the release so they could laugh at their dupes in the American print media who meekly changed the date on the new announcement and made no mention of that fact in their reports. The friendship between Waleed and Rios was not one based on OPEC prices. It was based on AK 47 prices. Waleed offered hundreds of thousands of small arms military style weapons to Rios at a very attractive price: All he had to do was allow Iran to build and maintain an air base in Venezuela manned by tens of thousands of Waleed's troops.

The deal to build Venezuela's *Protectores de la Libertad,* "Protectors of Freedom" Iranian Air Force base was worked out very quickly. Both sides thought they had gotten the best of the other. Both sides were right. The Venezuelan and Iranian engineers built the air base on the Paraguana Peninsula near Punto Fijo, a town of more than 200,000 people. Paraguana Peninsula is a small piece of land jutting out into the ocean off Caracas.

Being so near to so many people gave the military installation a shield against Western attacks. Both Rios and Waleed assumed that fact would stop the Americans from attacking it for fear of harming innocent civilians. Using the latest runway construction methods and materials, they practically completed the air base overnight. The location was perfect for the scam. Punto Fijo was built around a series of oil refineries, constructed by Standard Oil and Shell Oil in the 1950s. The idea that Protectores de la Libertad Air Base was placed there made the whole oil deal cover story very plausible.

CHAPTER 43

RALPH MAC NEAL

FINDING A MEANS TO IDENTIFY the top leaders of America's Islamist enemies was a major step forward. The next step was just as important. The Intelligence Community had to find a way to determine how many deep cover agents the terrorists had in our midst, and where they were living and working. That meant finding the best computer hacker the government had and putting him or her to work.

Once the upstate New York Islamberg camp had been successfully penetrated by a specially trained Black Canadian Mountie, the analyst were getting regular information about what was being discussed inside the compound, but the most valuable information was still out of their reach. The compound had a sophisticated computer room with a bank of the most state of the art machines American money could buy for the Islamists. They had used a skim off from the Muslim People's Committee, (MPC's) Let's Fight Hunger (LFH) money to buy everything they needed. The embedded agent could get close enough to the room to know that whatever was passing through its computers was important intelligence, but no further. The only way into the computer nerve center in Islamberg would be to hack into it.

A review of properly skilled and available computer experts, with the proper clearance, showed that there was only a handful in all of the proper agencies. Most of the really qualified experts were already on some important mission and could not be spared for a fishing trip that could be time consuming and still lead nowhere.

Even President Andrews was aware of the super secret search for a skillful hacker. One night the White House hosted a dinner party that finished with a screening of one of the President's favorite movies, *Catch Me if You Can*. At the end of the movie the government is employing a man who spent his life as an impostor posing as many different people in many different professions. The purpose of employing the man was to have him teach FBI agents how to spot frauds. As the world's best impostor, he was the best man they could hire to teach them what frauds looked like.

Harlan Andrews got an idea after watching the movie. The next day he called the FBI director.

"Say Bill, I think I have a way to find the hacker we need for the Islamberg investigation. How about searching federal prisoner records for computer criminals and see who we might make a deal with and use to get this job done? Of course there might not be anybody, but I think it would be worth a look. I'd give the official legal permission in any kind of agreement we might come to with the prisoner and his attorney."

"I'll get right on it Mr. President," FBI Director William Pollock replied as he rolled his eyes.

The computers of the Federal Bureau of Prisons found seven inmates that matched the criteria for selection and the reduced sentence agreement that would come with the offer.

After careful interviews the FBI Field Agent in charge of the search selected two men for final interviews. One of the men came across as being too much beyond the level of untrustworthiness they thought was acceptable. The second man was a free spirit type with a long ponytail and a wild look in his eyes. He was Ralph Mac Neal or Reverend Ralph Mac Neal, as he liked to be called. The 'Reverend' Mac Neal was not an ordained minister of any known religion.

Mac Neal was a drifter turned street preacher who had settled down and spent several years running a storefront church in Topeka Kansas. Mac Neal had not always been a street preacher running his own church. At one time he had been a computer criminal making millions of dollars a year cheating people out of their money. He was very good at what he did and was never caught in any of his scams. His life was full of parties with drugs and willing pretty girls. Then everything came crashing down on Mac Neal. A team of men, hired by one of the people he had cheated, found him and almost beat him to death.

During the four months he was hospitalized, Mac Neal found God and promised Him he would never again use his hacking skills to commit crimes. After he was released from the hospital and several weeks of physical rehabilitation, Ralph Mac Neal the criminal hacker stepped out of a rehab facility and into his new life as a street preacher. To his surprise he was successful. After a few months, a small group of his 'congregation' pressed some money in his hand saying 'Reverend' Mac Neal use this to rent us a place to meet and worship.

When more and more people came to Mac Neal's 'church' looking for help with their bills and feeding their families, the temptation to use his criminal skills became overwhelming. It started small at first. He just skimmed a few hundred dollars from the bank accounts of people who were, very old, had over $50,000 in their accounts and had not checked their balance for over a year. He would have been safe except that he forgot that one of the reasons his plan worked was that the victims were very old. Very old victims tend to die and their affairs tend to be managed by other people who are not old. Finally he dipped into one too many accounts. He was prosecuted in a federal court because it was determined that his actions had constituted an interstate crime.

Ralph Mac Neal was sentenced to fifty-seven months in a low security prison near Duluth Minnesota. In spite of the general laxity of the institution, it was still a prison. During most of the year the prison was very cold. The only exception to the norm was during the brief summer, which was very hot. It was cold and damp or hot and humid, and seemed to rain most of the time. Ralph Mac Neal hated being there. He was ready for a deal, but his flakiness made the FBI think twice about him.

On the day of the final interview, Mac Neal was put in front of a computer that had been especially modified for the purpose at hand. Using it, Mac Neal could prove he knew what he was doing, but he would not be able to take advantage of anything he developed. The FBI was not going to help a computer criminal commit a crime, at least not for his own benefit.

Mac Neal was everything his records said he was. He was like a concert pianist in front of a Steinway. He would do. He would have to do. Nobody with near his talents could be found on such short notice. The deal that was struck was simple. It had been negotiated for him by another inmate who was formerly a high powered lawyer, but was now serving time for stealing from a widow whose son happened to be a US District Attorney.

The jailhouse lawyer was told nothing about why the government wanted Mac Neal's help. Mac Neal himself knew nothing about the investigation except that he was told he had skills he could trade for reductions in his sentence depending upon how valuable his assistance was deemed to be. Under the agreement, Mac Neal would be given a twelve-month cut in his sentence as soon as he stepped onto the government's airplane. He would get another twelve months cut off his sentence if he provided what was described as "material assistance" to the government's investigation.

A complete pardon was possible if he found whatever the government was looking for in a reasonable amount of time. If he was released, he agreed to be closely supervised for ten months in a half way house, commit no further crimes and remain silent about the matter for the remainder of his life. Two days later Mac Neal was put on a plane to start his journey to FBI headquarters in Manhattan where he would be working.

Each night he would be brought to a special cell in New York City's federal short-term detention facility, The Metropolitan Correctional Center (MCC). At MCC, Mac Neal had a cell that looked more like a hotel room compared to his quarters in Minnesota. The room had a television and a refrigerator, its own shower, an easy chair as well as its own lighting system controlled from within. Mac Neal could stay awake and read all night if he wanted, but he never did.

He usually went to sleep soon after eating his evening meal, which was brought in, from a nearby restaurant. He wanted to be fresh everyday so he could give his best efforts to the investigation. Once he understood exactly what they wanted from him, he wanted to succeed as soon as possible. He knew that if he found his way through the maze of firewalls and passwords, the Islamist's were using to protect their secrets; he would taste full freedom again. He also wanted to help his country, because he honestly did care about people.

Day after day he worked two hours on and then one hour off. When he decided to work three on and one off, the Bureau cheered him on. At one point after working at the hunt for five weeks he was able to work his way into a minor program that contained the plans for a Brooklyn police station that were down loaded from the New York City Department of Public Works. The text with the building plans described how to use the attached schematic of the wiring system so a major fire could be started.

It was a step-by-step tutorial on how to cross enough wires to cause such a blaze. It was deemed worthy of another twelve-month sentence cut.

A Big Break Through

With the Brooklyn police station break through, Mac Neal became an accepted member of the FBI's hacker team. The government nerds accepted Mac Neal even if he was a convict. They could see him as one of them, and the nerd brotherhood was stronger than most people thought.

The new relationship helped move the hacking project along. Ralph Mac Neal had become *Ray-Mac* to the pocket protector gang. He was no longer isolated at his workstation. When he arrived the next day he was greeted by the hacker team and it became obvious that he had informally become their leader. The intensity of the team's efforts increased everyday. Ten days later the big break through was reached.

Mac Neal was able to breakdown the last firewall that had been protecting the Islamist's secret list of social security numbers. Although he was not able to get all of the numbers, he was able to access the portion of the list in the Islamberg's computers. What he dug out was a document containing "page 87 of 257 through page 121 of 257."

At first the data had the agents stumped. The list included 1,360 numbers, but it gave no further information about how many other numbers were being used; or who was using them for what operations.

HOW THE NERDS SAVED THE OPERATION

Mac Neal's nerds threw a pizza party for themselves. They talked computer issues and delighted each other with the relaxed unguarded conservation that made its way around their room. It was not often that they were able to enjoy being the heroes in an investigation. Classical music served as their base sound as they recounted the painstaking process of figuring out the passwords to beat the last two obstacles protecting the list. Like most puzzles and riddles, the answers looked obvious in retrospect; they always do. To unravel the password mysteries, the team decided to put itself in the mind of their counterpart; the Islamist computer genius who they had never seen, but knew was out there somewhere. At first they referred to him as Mister X. Then in a bit of nerd humor, they started calling him Abdul X. Nerds laughed at this. They really did.

They reasoned that Abdul X would be under enormous pressure to set up his system as quickly as possible. The team members had all been there. They had all been put under high pressure from bosses who did not understand what they did, but always wanted to tell them they could be working faster. They also recognized that working for the FBI and working for a terrorist organization were very different propositions. Their bosses could only fire them, but Abdul X's bosses could chop off his head. When they were all thinking on the same page, Mac Neal posed a question that got them reasoning out loud: "Okay let's see. What would we do under that type of pressure?"

"He's looking at two immediate problems: set up a system with sophisticated locks on the one hand, and make it user friendly for your average seventh century asshole on the other," said Irving Schimmel a computer genius who always wore a yarmulke and brought his own kosher lunches with him everyday.

Sanjit Patel, an observant Hindu, spoke next, "I think he looked at the imbeciles around him and decided on passwords they can remember. I think he knew that if they forgot the passwords they would blame him and maybe kill him for being too Western or something like that."

Morris Tifton, a small African American man, tried to speak next, "I

Th-th-th-think. I th-think they ew-ew-used..." In frustration Tifton grabbed a pencil and pad and wrote 'I think they used: M-A-L-S-I and A-C-C-E-M!!!!!!!!!" Islam backwards is MALSI and MECCA backwards is ACCEM. The simplicity caught even these brilliant minds on the team by surprise. When both passwords worked, they seemed simple enough that anyone could figure them out. That was how they were figured out. They were simple enough for even a seventh century mind to grasp. At the end of the party, the hacking team cleaned up, and was starting to leave when they noticed there was no celebration coming from the analyst's room.

Patel opened the door to say good night and found them silently staring at an overhead projection screen. They were looking at a slide that read: "page 87 of 257 through page 121 of 257" and a handwritten note asking, "How many total?" Patel smiled and shook his head as he walked in and sat down.

"Here! Here are your answers! There are 34 pages and each has 40 numbers listed on it, that's 1360 social security numbers. But you know that already. Now if there are forty numbers on each page with no deviations on the pages we can see, then it is a fairly safe guess that there are forty numbers on all two hundred and fifty seven pages we can't see. Allowing for an incomplete list on the final page, the grand total is probably between 10,241 and 10,280."

That he had done the calculation in his head amazed no one in the room. Having the list of 1,360 social security numbers and fairly good grounds to believe the grand total of maybe 10,200, was a great start toward finding the people connected to these numbers, but there was still much work to be done to get every ounce of benefit out of this data.

True to its agreement, the American government released Ralph Mac Neal soon after the team solved the passwords problem. Within a short time he was living in Harrisburg Pennsylvania. He had founded another Church and seemed to be doing well. He never told any of his flock he was a former "FBI computer expert." The FBI wanted to hire him as a permanent employee but Federal law prohibited them. The idea to ask for a waver was considered but put aside because doing so might draw attention to the operation he had worked on.

MAKING THE LIST WORK

As soon as the list's size was determined, Special Agent Melanie Wilson, the commander of The Islamist Desk at FBI Headquarters Manhattan, called in a team of IRS field agents. She shared the list data with them and asked for their thoughts on how best to handle the information. The IRS agents had no second thoughts. They were experts at making the lives of ordinary American citizens miserable by tracking their social security numbers. They could and would do the same to the terrorist deep cover agents working here under false names with otherwise legitimate social security numbers.

The IRS agent in charge, Bill Samuelson ordered a computer search of the numbers on the list. Every single one was being used at least twice. Most were being used by as many as six different people. "In all of these cases one person is innocent and the rest are involved in some kind of criminal activity. Now not all of the activities are likely to be in the nature of terrorist activities. It may turn out that many of these people are illegal aliens who paid for the number. They might be picking tomatoes someplace but that's not what you're looking for. I realize that," Samuelson said.

"How do they get these numbers, I mean so many of them....?" Wilson asked.

"The world champs at stealing American personal information are the Nigerians. They have it down to a fine science. My guess is that since Nigeria has such a large Muslim population, these numbers falling into the hands of people who are trying to destroy us can't be an accident. I'd say this was the work of Nigerian Islamists almost certainly. Most of their identity thefts are so they can drain their victim's bank accounts, so I'm sure there is some of that going on although I don't think they're doing too much of that stuff," Samuelson said.

"Why not?" one of Wilson's agents asked.

"They wouldn't want to attract attention to themselves for any amount of money. They don't want our money they, they don't want our lifestyles, they want to kill us anyway they can," Samuelson said.

"Yes I know. It's too bad more Americans don't want to accept what's going on. Now how do we figure out who's who here?" Wilson asked holding up the printout of the list.

"We'll check to see who has used one of these numbers on a return. Once we get that list, we'll match those against whose employer has used the number in his paperwork. The numbers that come up on both lists are the legit guys."

"The ones that never file a return, but have social security taxes withheld aren't leaving that money in our hands because they want to; they're doing it because they have to. They can't file and get their refunds because they're illegal. That still won't give us the terrorists in the group, but it will help us avoid messing with the innocent taxpaying American citizens who will have enough grief to deal with when the multiple use problems start to surface. Of course we can only check into the 1,380 names we have, but when we start flipping over rocks we're bound to find others we think are terrorists as well."

"Will you tell the legits about their problem?" Wilson asked.

"That's not my job, or yours either," Samuelson answered.

For the men and women whose daily job is protecting America from savage enemies like the Islamists, Racial Profiling is a genuine tool.

They may be officially prohibited from racially profiling in the course of their duties, but that doesn't mean they don't do it. Wilson understood what *find others*, meant. The FBI and the IRS jointly developed a plan. It called for agents to quickly spread out and investigate the workplaces of the people who were using the flagged numbers. In one week a list of locations employing suspected terrorists was complied.

If used properly, the new list could point agents in the right direction when surrounding up deep cover Islamist operatives. When the Islamists started their war on America, the immediate roundups took many of them off the streets. Even in the crazy swirl of urban combat, the news of these roundups quickly traveled through the Islamist communities. For the innocent Muslims, the news went in one ear and out the other. For the deep cover operatives it was indeed important and chilling news that demanded attention. It helped make them easier to see by forcing them to actions they were not always ready to take.

CHAPTER 44

AMIR AL HAQ

AMIR AL HAQ was the most important target in the northeastern United States. He was clearly the brain behind many of the most devastating attacks America had sustained on her home soil. He planned every detail of an attack that sunk a Staten Island ferry. He blew up cars at opposite ends of the Holland Tunnel, an underwater roadway between New York and New Jersey, and then had his men machine gun those who were trapped in the cars between the explosions. That attack went so well that all of his men escaped except the suicide bombers who blew up the cars.

UNIT Z

A special super-secret unit was created to hunt Haq down and capture him. The unit was simply called Unit Z. Even that became just Z as people familiar with the unit's true mission started to call it. Z's mission was to do all of the things ordinary soldiers or even trained and authorized spies would not do. They killed in cold blood and worse. Their orders were to kill their way to Amir Haq and bring him in alive if at all possible. They were authorized to use any method they saw fit. The jobs Z did were dirty and mean.

Z was made up of volunteers from a number of agencies. Homeland Security had to search long and hard to find volunteers willing to do the things that Unit Z members would be called upon to do. The average person would be very surprised to hear where Z got its members. Unit Z's recruitment policy was simple: If you were willing and had skills the Unit needed, you got the call.

Intelligence reports on al Haq said he was a 37 year old engineer from Pakistan. He was not married and he was very close to his mother. Al Haq was so close to his mother, Fayzah that he smuggled her into America and put her in an apartment on New Lots Avenue, a seedy section of Brooklyn. Five large soldiers of Al Haq's Glory to Allah Brigade guarded Fayzah constantly. Fayzah al Haq, 58, was a widow whose husband and children except for Amir her oldest son, were killed in a bombing raid carried out by the Indian Special Air Operations Strike Force. She was not the usual ignorant peasant woman one could have been expected to find in the small Pakistani village the al Haq family came from. She wanted more from life and saw to it that all her children got an education.

It was because of Fayzah's dreams and desires for his future that "Hacky," as Z came to call him, was off at university and safe when the bombing destroyed their home. Now she was traveling with him as he carried out his jihad against the world. Fayzah was a bitter and angry woman who was very capable of helping to plan Amir's attacks. She was not known to most intelligence agencies outside of the Indian sub-continent and had only come to Z's attention when the CIA discovered the connection between mother and son.

Fayzah freely traveled the subway system of New York City hidden in a Burka and veil. Picking her out from among the growing number of Muslim women who were traveling freely throughout the city was difficult at best. Fayzah used this advantage and did the scouting for her terrorist son. She did, however, have one very distinctive characteristic: her voice was high pitched even for a woman's. Although not many people had heard her speak, those few agents who had, reported she sounded almost bird like.

After carefully studying Hacky Z put a plan together. The Hacky plan was ugly, but had to be done. They would lure him out of hiding by kidnapping and raping his mother Fayzah.

Then they would mail multiple video copies of the rape to the Islamberg computers the FBI had hacked into and humiliate him. Z had no hard intelligence that he was there, but they knew he would hear about the rape wherever he was. The plan was to use his humiliation to push him to an emotionally triggered mistake. When he made that mistake and showed himself, they would snatch him up and bring him to their headquarters for interrogation.

The CIA's intelligence was very solid on Fayzah Haq's address. They had confirmed information that she was posing as Fayzah Farrah, a widow living with her five sons who were legal immigrants from India. The team staked out the building, learned how many *sons* she had and when those sons went on and off duty. They picked up the seams in the coverage. Z noticed small periods of time where they could snatch Fayzah up and have to fight and kill just two guards. They were ready in three days. The team had to hurry. Word had come down that something very big was about to happen and capturing Hacky became the highest priority for Unit Z.

The Farrah family was the only non-Black family living in 31351 New Lotts Avenue. Team Z used Black agents for the operation. Dressed as common laborers able to blend into their surroundings, five agents approached the building. One stayed at the ground floor appearing to smoke a stick of marijuana. Three went to the hallway outside Fayzah's second floor apartment. The last team member went to the floor above to stand guard. They all wore black jeans, a black jacket and carried black ski masks in their pockets.

On a signal from the leader the team members on the second and third floors pulled on their masks. Through the apartment's porous old door, the agents could hear three people, two men and a woman. The woman had a very high-pitched voice, which confirmed it was Fayzah. The leader slid a flexible cable, equipped with a television camera, under the door and watched. He signaled there were just two guards. Without speaking, he first pointed right and held up one finger, then pointed left and held up two fingers. He passed his hand over his face to signify a burka and pointed right. They had to move quickly so they could get in and out without killing innocent Americans who might happen by as they did their job. The leader held up one finger, then two and when he raised his third finger they smashed the door in and quickly killed the guards.

Fayzah picked up a .45 and was bringing it up to eye level when she was zapped with a jolt of electricity from a stun gun and knocked unconscious.

In seconds she was gagged, wrapped in a rug and slung over the leader's right shoulder. The third floor man joined them, they all took off their masks and walked out the door onto Brooklyn's streets.

At a safe house about two hundred miles away, the Team methodically set up a camera and repeatedly raped and sodomized Fayzah al Haq. Somebody suggested putting it up on Publixtube.org a website that would make it all but certain that al Haq would see the assault. That idea was rejected because too many Islamists would see it. The risk of it unnecessarily stirring up trouble was too great. The question then became: what to do with the tape?

Z knew the Islamists maintained a phony computer address they were using to try to feed disinformation to American hackers. The Z leader saw an opening in that web address. He decided they would send a straight up E-mail with the rape as an attachment.

That would serve a few purposes. It would help flush Hacky out to avenge the attack on his honor, and it would let the Islamists know Z knew about the phony E address. That would force them to wonder what else Z knew and it would also force them to change their passwords, which would cause confusion among their seventh century warriors. The more Hacky and his technicians had to change the passwords to receive messages, the more confusion it could cause.

They theorized that when the Islamists in the field finally got frustrated enough, one of them would make a phone call and ask, in plain uuencoded Arabic, what the new passwords were. The behavioral section of Unit Z assured them the Islamists intolerance for frustration would bring about a breach in password security. After a day and a half it did.

As cool and professional as Amir al Haq was, he could not contain himself when he saw the video of the rape. He became blind with rage, and lost his ability to clearly weigh what his next step should be. In his world such insults demand blood. Only blood could expunge the stain on his honor.

The message traffic, believed to be coming from where the team thought Hacky was, jumped dramatically. Without al Haq's knowledge his chief internet technician, a white Anglo Californian convert to Islam named Adam Paulson, changed the passwords needed to access the daily messages from his headquarters. It was a minor decision of the kind that Hacky had given Paulson permission to make without checking with him.

No amount of effort could keep Hacky's field commanders from finding out about Fayzah's rape. Just the thought of Hacky's rage scared the field commanders.

They knew what such an insult would mean to a man like their leader. They knew that there would have to be some retaliation. None of them wanted to risk being responsible for causing it to fail because they were not able to access their daily orders. Fear of being blamed for a screw up that would cheat Hacky of his revenge drove them to throw caution aside and demand the new passwords while speaking plain uuencoded Arabic on unsecured phones.

Ordinarily the passwords were changed every fifth day and messengers forming a notification chain would transmit the new passwords only in person. Each of these messengers carried knowledge of only a single letter and a number. At their destination, the final messenger in a particular chain would only be able to say something like *M -9 and I - 4* which would mean the ninth letter in the new first password was *M* and that *I* was the fourth letter of the second new password. The very reason for the computerized notification system Hacky and Paulson had set up was to keep loose talk from coming to the attention of the Americans, but that was exactly what Team Z picked up. In a plain Arabic conversation, an older male was heard ordering one of Hacky's teenage soldiers to tell him the passwords.

"I am not going to be the one to cause our leader's retaliation to fail. Do you understand? Now I demand in the name of Allah the All Powerful Ruler of the Universe that you give me these passwords."

There is no word for *password* in the Arabic language so the gist of the conversation could not be clearer. The young man gave in and told the old field commander the passwords. Team Z got the same information in real time. The passwords enabled the team to listen in on Hacky's plans for the next twenty-four hours. If he wrote nothing of value in the next day or so, they would be out of luck, because opportunities like this do not happen often. The team waited and prayed for a break.

Fifteen hours later, at three o'clock the next morning, Team Z was in a special meeting. They had the break they needed. Using the new passwords, they had gotten the full details of Hacky's plan for revenge.

The team read details of Hacky's plan to attack the safe house where Fayzah was being held. That information chilled the team. Hacky had discovered where they were holed up. What made this discovery still more disturbing was that the team had selected the safe house at random and only a handful of trusted people knew where it was. Now the most fearsome and dangerous Islamist terrorist on American soil was personally leading an attack on their location. The ironic thing was that both the team and Fayzah knew al Haq was coming after her with as much zeal as he was coming after them.

Being raped had automatically marked Fayzah for death at the hands of her own son, Amir. Being his mother would bring her no mercy once he caught her and she knew that.

Where the al Haq's came from, the murder weapon of choice for avenging a man's honor was burning to death the *kari* or *black woman* as a raped woman was called. The team had no time to worry about the leak. A mole could have accomplished it or Paulson might have hacked into their communication system. They just had to trust each other and search for the hole in their security afterward. Saving themselves and catching al Haq were the most important items on their agenda.

The safe house was a small cabin on a lake in rural Columbia County New York. Six sharpshooter snipers were positioned on both sides of the two lane county road that served as the only approach to the cabin on its south side. To the North there were fishermen stationed in the lake that washed up behind the cabin. They were sitting in small boats ready to kill any of Haq's men who paddled across to attack from the rear. On the perimeter immediately surrounding the cabin, camouflaged agents were dug in and ready to kill anyone who slipped through the outer defenses. The team's orders were to do their best to capture Hacky alive if they could. After a few hours, four out-of-place vehicles approached the safe house. A voice crackled over the team's radio, "That's them! He's gotta be in the ambulance. They think we won't shoot at civilian vehicles. When I give the signal, let 'em have it but don't kill Hacky."

The Islamist's convoy of stolen vehicles consisted of an ambulance and three delivery trucks. The ambulance was in the lead and was followed by two stolen bread trucks and a stolen dry cleaning delivery step van.

At a point about a mile from the safe house, the vehicles reached a fork in the road. Trucks two three and four went northeast to the far side of the lake. The ambulance went southwest toward the target. Moments later they attacked the safe house. The fight was furious. The Islamists made three wild suicidal charges, but were stopped in their tracks. More than half of Team Z was killed. The attackers had shoulder fired rockets and incendiary grenades.

The main room burst into flames when one of the grenades crashed through a window. The team was able to quickly put it out and secure the immediate area. A few minutes after the shooting stopped, the after action inventory and review started. The team members on the far side of the lake had been over run and killed. When the attackers gained command of their objective, a small dock, they used inflatable rafts to paddle across and attacked the rear of the building. The waiting team members, who had to valiantly fight in a back-to-back posture in order win out, killed them all. When the fight was over the Islamists dead bodies were searched and photographed.

The team gathered together to count heads and get ready to move out, because the safe house was no longer useful. The leader was thinking through the withdrawal plan when a team member rushed in to the still smoldering cabin. "We've searched every body and matched the faces. Hacky's not here... we gotta get movin' this was a fake out and we were had."

At that moment the woods on the Western side of the cabin filled with fifty of Hacky's toughest fighters. They ran at the cabin giving their lives in bunches to kill the remaining team members. The leader grabbed Fayzah and pulled her down into the specially built sub-basement. It was a fireproof command center equipped with communication capabilities and food for four people for a week.

While the fight went on, the leader radioed for help and reminded his base that Hacky was in this second wave of attackers. The sounds of torture from just above his head made the leader fume with hate and anger, but he had to sit silently and wait. Every fiber in his body wanted to take action and kill his enemies. He wanted to somehow charge up the stairs and do something, anything, but that would abort the mission. He was ashamed of himself for being put in that position. All he could do was keep Fayzah quiet and wait it out. In his wild fury Hacky was screaming in perfect English, "Mother! Mother! Where are you? You whore, where are you?"

Haq knew he had to play up to his troops and their sense of *izzat,* the rights he had under the Pakistani system of honor killing. He knew he had to put on a show for them so he switched to Urdu, the language he shared with his troops. He called to his dishonorable mother that he would murder her under izzat and called her a *Sali Haramzadi,* which roughly translated means idiot bitch. He also called her a *maaderchode* which translates to an extremely foul word spoken on American streets in certain neighborhoods. *Maader* means mother.

His rage was wild and burning, but he wasn't so distracted that he could not remember to yell in English. Hacky was hurt and embarrassed by his mother's sin, so he reasoned that using English would keep at least some of his men from hearing his private family business.

Hacky searched the cabin and found a fireproof strong box. He assumed it would contain useful documents, but he had no idea it contained his mother's eyeglasses and case. When she was snatched she was wearing a housedress and her glasses where in her right pocket. After the rapes, with nothing else to put her in, the team gave the housedress back to her. Fayzah thought no one would notice the one hundred dollar bill she had secreted in the lining of the case. Her loving son Amir had given her the bill as emergency money. She was wrong. The team found the bill, soaked it in G Juice, and carefully replaced it so they could track her in case she broke free.

Fifteen minutes after the sounds of gun shots faded, the leader slowly dragged himself and Fayzah through an escape tunnel that came to the surface twenty five feet away on the cabin's east side. When he peeked out and saw he was alone, he handcuffed the now gagged Fayzah to a pipe and took a better look. A quick search of the area and the remains of the cabin convinced him that Hacky had taken the strong box with Fayzah's glasses and unwittingly took the soaked bill as well. He immediately radioed for two helicopters, one to pick up of Fayzah and other to search for Hacky.

"Send me the G *Juice* signal detector and have the New York State Police set up a road block. Have them look for several Middle Eastern looking males and... no wait. He's gonna be traveling alone and probably in a disguise. Have them stop any single male who looks like a he owns an all night gas station or a convenience store. I'll be in an open field to the West of the safe house. You know the coordinates. Hurry we've got to catch Al Haq before he crawls back into the woodwork."

The leader had work to do. His men were all dead, now he had to capture Amir al Haq so they would not have died in vain. Fifteen minutes later two Massachusetts Air National Guard AH-1 Cobra helicopters landed in the field and took Fayzah and the leader on their separate journeys. The pilot of the leader's copter motioned for him to put on a set of headphones so he could be heard above the din of the copter's register.

"The New York State Troopers are saying they might have our guy on a small road off route 9 near Stottville, just north of Stockport."

Pointing to the other bird, the leader asked, "They know where to take her?"

"Yeah"

"Okay. Let's get down to Stottville." The leader said as he lit a cigar and tried to relax for the first time in twenty-four hours. In sixteen minutes the leader was face to face with a man who looked like he could be a doctor in any major city hospital in America.

There was a small black bag on the seat next to him and the black SUV he was driving had New Jersey MD plates. The leader ordered the man out onto the shoulder of the road. He grabbed him by the neck, held his face up and matched it against an old picture of al Haq. The leader stared at the papers indicating the man was Doctor Dinesh Patel of Teaneck New Jersey, and thought about what to do.

"The G Juice signature detector, Damn!" the leader thought. In his fatigue and excitement he had not thought to turn on the detector that could immediately tell him whether he had Amir al Haq or not.

He reached into the Cobra and threw the switch. Before he could turn away, the machine went wild. The gauge went to 100% indicating the absolute positive presence of G Juice.

The leader wanted to yell with joy. He wanted to bellow, "Hold that son of a bitch. He's our man! I wanna cut his heart out!" But he couldn't and he knew he couldn't.

"Gotta make believe I figured out who he is by talking to him. I can't let him get any idea we have anything like G Juice, but how?" the leader thought.

His eyes swept around his immediate vicinity until they stopped at the G Juice signal detector.

"Wait a second that looks like a laptop, maybe I can..." he thought.

"Okay, look just play along with me. I'm gonna make believe I figured out who he is with a facial recognition program" the leader said to the State Troopers.

"Okay we'll pull him over to you and make it work."

The leader took a photograph of al Haq and then made a point of letting him see that the picture was being fed into some kind of a machine. After two minutes the leader closed the G Juice signal detector, looked at al Haq and said: "al Haq, I've got you." The leader used a plastic zip cinch, shackled al Haq's hands behind his back and dragged him to the waiting Cobra. "You know where to go?" he asked the pilot.

"Yes, we'll be there in about twenty five minutes."

Adam "el Baahir" Paulson

Adam Paulson was a blond haired green-eyed atheist when he arrived at the University of California at Berkeley in the early 1990s. He was an only child and while he was small and frail, he was extremely bright. On his fifth birthday his mother brought him to a testing center run by American Mensa, an organization of people whose IQ scores are in the top 2 percent in the world. He scored a 161 on the Sanford-Binet scale, which was substantially above the 132 cut off mark and was enrolled in a school for gifted children.

Almost from birth Adam was clearly different from other children. He went from a few sentences of baby talk to complete important thought sentences at two years old. He wanted to be the one who read the bedtime stories. His curiosity was endless. Each facet of adult life that he unraveled like a cryptanalysis delighted him.

He took things apart to learn how and why they worked. His memory was truly photogenic and always unfailing. If he liked a movie he would sit his parents down and make them listen to him act out the parts and lines of every major character, word for word.

As a child he almost never played with other children. He was always either too smart for them or when he did meet children who were his intellectual equals he was unwilling to share toys or the spotlight with them. He was absolutely fascinated with mathematics and soon bored with anyone who could not grasp numerical concepts. He tried to connect with other intelligent people by joining Mensa when he was a teenager. His association with the high IQ club lasted only a few meetings. At Mensa meetings he was not special. Not only did he not have the highest IQ in the room, there were many people who could speak about many subjects he knew nothing about. His basic low tolerance for failure made him turn inward and stop attending meetings he could not control.

He was just another genius in the room and he could not stand that situation. His brief brush with the real world behind him, Adam Paulson retreated into cyber space where he was once and for all lord and master.

He created his own world and allowed no other humans into it. At sixteen he enrolled in Cal. Berkeley's Computer Science program where he quickly excelled.

He became a teaching assistant to a brilliant young Computer Science genius from Bosnia who was also a devout Muslim. Paulson never thought about religion let alone one that was practiced by "swarthy wild eyed men and veiled women." At first Professor Hakim Bolavic's Muslim practices meant nothing to Paulson.

Bolavic was nothing like Paulson envisioned Muslims to be or look like. He was over six feet tall with strong muscular hands, green eyes, sandy hair and a square jaw. If anything, Bolavic looked more like a WASP Highway Patrol Officer than a Muslim college professor.

Paulson was in love with the logic, reason and the manly appeal of the exciting young professor. Up to his meeting with Bolavic every other teacher he had was a timid looking mouse who tried harder to excuse himself than extol the virtues of science. Bolavic was different. He made science come alive and those that mastered it feel very special. Paulson had not felt "special" the way his mother made him feel special for a long time. The Muslim professor from Bosnia gave him back that feeling.

Over the months he worked with Bolavic, Adam Paulson fell under the spell of the Muslim with the square jaw. Soon Paulson began to ask general questions about Islam and its place in the world. Since no one in Paulson's family had ever been religious, his mind was a virtual clean slate when it came to spiritual matters. He believed everything Bolavic told him about being a Muslim. To his credit he taught Paulson about the need for Islam to dominate the world. Bolavic sugarcoated nothing. He did not shy away from instructing him on the *Verses of the Sword.*

From the beginning, Paulson embraced Islam as his personal call to subjugate the world. Believing that he was smarter than everyone else made him believe he was better than everyone else. Islam gave him a validation of his narcissistic insistence of superiority over anyone he met. A billion people all over the world would now be agreeing with him that he was the smartest guy in every room he walked into.

Adam Paulson, once the atheistic little nerd who was nobody in high school, became a self-important Muslim follower of the *Verses of the Sword.* Soon he insisted upon being called Adam *el Baahir* Paulson or Adam *The Brilliant* Paulson.

The flame of destructive rage that burned within Paulson's heart turned white hot. It quickly surpassed any evil in the heart of Hakim Bolavic. Soon *el Baahir* came to see his mentor as soft on the question of an Islamist's duty to commit violence against the infidel world.

His frustration with what he saw as his professor's "accomodationism" built until he could no longer contain it. After a particularly fiery sermon at his local mosque *el Baahir* withdrew all his money, packed a small bag and prepared to leave for training as a *Warrior for Allah* in a camp in Afghanistan. Before he left, he stopped to say good-bye to his friend and teacher, Professor Hakim Bolavic. When the young computer genius came to his door, *el Baahir* shot him through his left eye and calmly walked away.

Just before September 11, 2001, he slipped back into America through the woods on the Maine/Canada border. From there he found his way to the deepest levels of terrorists in America. Soon he was the computer genius for Amir el Haq's cell in the United States.

CHAPTER 45

AMIR HAQ'S INTERROGATION

PLAYING DIRTY SAVES LIVES

AS THE CHIEF OF ISLAMISTS OPERATIONS in the Northeastern United States, Amir al Haq would be the highest value capture made in the war. After Amir Haq was captured in a little upstate New York town, where Team Z outsmarted, he was drugged into unconsciousness and brought, to a bunker deep in the ground below New York City's Grand Central Terminal. Its location was the safest place to house him on the east coast. Almost no one knew it existed, let alone how to find it, successfully attack it and free Haq.

When the terminal was built in 1913 it was designed to be not only the hub of America's railway system, but an emergency control headquarters for events that could not have been conceived of one hundred years ago. Most of the millions of passengers, who have used Grand Central over the decades since it opened, had no idea of the six secret levels of subbasements they walked over everyday. In the type of intelligent foresight America had grown accustomed to seeing less and less of, the structure was not only built, but also built in complete secrecy. All of the suspicious continual digging was done at night by laborers who kept their vow of silence about the true nature of the project. The six sub basements were hand carved by immigrant labor that wanted to be part of America.

At the third sub level a special train station was constructed during World War II so Franklin Roosevelt could enter and leave the City without anyone knowing he had arrived or learning of his confinement to a wheelchair. That flair for presidential vanity became a very valuable asset for those charged with delivering Amir Haq to Team Z's subterranean headquarters. Only a few Americans and very likely no terrorists knew of it. Even if it were discovered, its location sixty feet below the streets of Manhattan, made the Team's headquarters almost impossible to attack and very easy to defend.

Team Z, a subunit of the Mind War team, brought in its best behavioral analysts to examine Amir Haq, the most important and dangerous terrorist leader known to be on American soil. Before asking Haq a single important question, the Mind War team's analysts examined him to gather information to construct a psychological profile of America's prize captive.

Initially Haq was left in a very cold room for eight hours. He was given a glass of water and one slice of bread to eat every three hours. That kept him alive, but hungry and distracted. He was then stripped naked and forced to eat his bread and drink his water while sitting on a stainless steel bench with no back.

When the interrogator thought he had gotten as much out of that method as he could, he gave Haq a hospital style gown and form slippers and left for another twelve hours. Before he left he turned on a strobe light that flickered continually, and lowered the room's temperature to 60 degrees. When the Mind War team's leader returned, the sparsely furnished room was cold and drab except for the yellow bile filled vomit Haq had deposited on the floor. He silently stared at Haq for ten minutes, never breaking his gaze on his eyes. When the staring stopped, the interrogator hit another switch and bright glaring lights came on. High overhead an old sweep hand clock that was engineered to run six minutes an hour slow, ticked loudly while nothing else happened.

When he was ready to start, the interrogator began to speak into a tape recorder, "Amir Haq presents as diminutive dark skinned male of approximately 60 years of age. He has graying hair and a stubbly mustache. He appears to be slightly over weight and suffers from myopia. He has small feminine hands with no obvious signs of ever having done manual labor."

The truth was that Haq was 41 years old, but the interrogator was using the older age to test the level of his vanity. Next another interrogator came into the room wheeling a chair and a portable Electroencephalograph (EEG).

Haq was connected to the machine and strapped into a chair. Then he was shown a series of pictures that were quickly flashed on the wall in front of him. The pictures showed dead babies, flowers, cargo ships, dogs, a blue sky, and a woman's body on fire. The pictures were rerun in different order so that he saw each one five times. At the end of this process the results were reviewed and a preliminary estimate of Haq's psyche was postulated.

He was questioned for another three hours during which he was given proper clothes and a traditional Pakistani meal of curried chicken in a source made from garlic vinegar, onions and spices. There was a side dish of cauliflower and carrots. A small loaf of whole wheat bread and a glass of lemonade completed the meal. While still connected to the EEG machine, Haq was allowed to eat. As he did the interrogator talked to him about the pictures. Haq was asked if he could describe them. Speaking in a singsong Paki accent he accurately described each image he was shown. His emotional reactions never changed during the actual showing nor did they change as he spoke about them while sipping his lemonade. He took the opportunity to challenge the estimate of him as approximately 60 years of age.

"*Bingo, his vanity is showing through!*" the interrogator thought. As the interview went along, a picture of Amir Haq as a sociopath became clear. The interrogator noted that Haq's persona contained all of the classic signs of a dangerous psychopath. He was actually very charming with a quick wit and easy laugh, but as everything else about him it was phony. Haq was totally devoid of genuine emotions and not able to experience any genuine emotional concern for the welfare of his family or Soldiers let alone strangers. He professed to be a devout Muslim, but was determined to be lying about his religious fervor.

He acknowledged being glad his father had been killed in the bombing that killed his younger siblings, and added how disappointed he was that his mother was not killed. He offered his mother's rape as proof that he was right about not trusting her all his life.

At one point he smiled and said he would have killed his mother if he had found her, but not for reasons of honor.

"Such backward superstitions are for peasants," he said. "I would have killed her because so many of my 'shit heads' (as he called his men) expected me to. I would have enjoyed it because she needed killing, but I really do not care about this 'honor' bullshit. Blaming her for being raped is stupid," Haq added. The interrogator recognized this as another sign of the psychopathic personality: persuasive, charming and disarming speaking patterns.

He told the interrogator he had threatened to kill his college roommate in order to get him to move out so he could live alone. At every point the qualities of a classic psychopath found in Haq, became clearer and stronger. His desire to live the fast and dangerous life of an international terrorist outweighed his innate yearning to be alone. Forgetting what he had said originally, he said he was "shocked at the deaths" of his family members and decided to use his skills of persuasive speaking to join the killing squads in his village when they raided border towns in India.

When he was not immediately elected captain of his paramilitary company, he shot and killed the man who had been elected to the position. After that he was the undisputed leader of a larger and larger company of men. Although it meant associating with other people who were far inferior to him, he decided the power and lifestyle of a terrorist leader was worth the inconvenience of leading the "shit heads." He acknowledged never giving any thought to the consequences of his actions, because, "I wanted to do everything I did."

Once the diagnosis was settled upon, a method of effective interrogation was selected. Talking to Haq would be a waste of time. He was very intelligent, and a confident speaker as well as a very accomplished liar. Trying the *Reid Method*, which is a technique of digging out information from prisoners totally by use of talking, would not work with a man like Haq. The Mind War team had to acknowledge that he was much smarter than they were.

The way to break Haq was to punish him when he lied, and reward him when he seemed to be telling the truth. Thereafter chemicals and tag team interrogations could be employed. The questioning had to be non-stop. On signal from the interrogator, Haq's next glass of lemonade was laced with sodium amytal a substance that helps bring about increased suggestibility. He was exposed to white noise and kept awake for twenty hours before he was questioned again. None of the interrogation restrictions introduced in the period immediately after the Western media had helped the Islamists close Abu Grab Prison, were of any concern to anyone who was trying to break Haq. If he broke, the majority of terror cells in America could be found and destroyed. For Team Z, breaking Haq was more important than worrying about following the latest New York Times approved rules for interrogations "Tag teams" of interrogators used sleep deprivation, flattery, room temperature extremes, hanging upside down and water boarding to break Amir Haq.

He was very tough to break, so after using everything else, the Team went to their ultimate bad-guy-breaker. A masked Team Z member came in with a short red handled bolt cutter. He said nothing as he first punched Haq to the floor and then ripped off his foam slippers. Haq began screaming, "What do you want to know? I'll tell you! I'll tell you!"

The bolt cutter man said nothing. He knelt down and snapped off Haq's left little toe. Blood gushed from the wound and the terrorist leader wailed in deep unrelenting pain.

"Why? Why? I would have talked! Why would you do this? I would have talked! Don't you believe me?"

"I believe you now. Please begin to talk so I don't have to do this again." Bolt cutter man said without an apparent trace of emotion. Haq was cleaned up, bandaged and given a shot of morphine. He began to talk, but at a point about an hour later, he began to sound evasive and his statements stopped making sense. Without another word, bolt cutter man snapped off his right little toe. Haq made perfect sense after the second snap. He realized they were serious and were not going to worry about the Western media's rules. As Haq writhed in pain, the interrogator whispered "Believe it or not, you will come to thank us for this second snip."

When Haq decided to talk, he had a few simple demands. If they were met, he would tell the Team whatever he knew. The team only had to promise him that no one would ever hear of his break, and he would be housed in a single bed cell in a warm safe federal prison with Paki meals and a color television. The Team agreed and cleaned him up and let him sleep for three hours. That would bring back the pain in his feet and he would have to beg for the drugs they wanted to give him anyway.

WHAT AMIR HAQ REVEALED...USING WHAT WAS DRAWN FROM HAQ

Once Haq started talking he was hard to stop. It wasn't that anyone wanted him to discontinue giving information and it certainly wasn't that his information was proving to be disinformation. They wanted Haq to slow down because he was giving so much information that they could hardly keep up with what he was saying. Of course this was a happy problem the Team's interrogators had caused. They had Haq doped up on amphetamines and almost allowed him to slip into an amphetamine psychosis. This required a great deal of attention to Haq, but he was worth the manpower. The America's streets had been turned into battlefields by marauding paramilitary Islamist troops who were killing hundreds of civilians a day. Pain from the area where Haq's snapped off toes had been was still exquisite. To get his continued cooperation, they would have to keep him high on drugs.

At times the attack plans Haq revealed were chilling and terrifying even for the tough as nails interrogators. The details Haq had on military installations and mobilization SOP (standard operating procedures) regularly stopped the sessions cold. So hot were some of the threatened attacks, that at times they were disrupted just hours before they were to take place.

Haq told of plans to blow up the Brooklyn Bridge. He detailed plans to attack and take control of two National Guard Armories in New Jersey.

From just his memory, Haq drew a diagram of the residence of the Catholic Cardinal of Boston and accurately named streets to be used for the escape route after the church leader had been assassinated. Time and again, his narratives were proved out either by being slightly too late or so vivid that when the information was forwarded, the counter strike forces were able to employ the data in real-time planning to stop the attack. He described a simple but serious and potentially important terrorist strike on Richmond Virginia. The aim of the attack was to have el Qaeda saboteurs dynamite the supporting pillars of an overpass for Interstate Highway 95 and tie up traffic for weeks. That would make it difficult for American troops responding to subsequent attacks on the city and nearby.

Because Haq's information was so detailed it was unmistakably the truth.

Of the I 95 attacks, he said, "The plan to disrupt the north/south flow of traffic on your highway number 95 will be carried out this way; C-4 plastic explosives are stored in an old coal box at an abandoned coal company. I think it is something like South Coal Company. Anyway it is very near the Franklin Street exit number 74. It will be blown up to stop you from stopping our real target which is the Philip Morris Company just down the road.

"You see we have a man in there who told us all about the chemical you use called G Juice. He is a Paki like me…a petrochemical PhD who has worked on its formulation. We know exactly where in the complex it is being made and we would blow it up if we could."

"What else do you know?" he was asked.

"I want another pain pill first."

"Okay, but if you stop singing you'll need more than one pain pill. You understand?"

"We will again strike your road number 95 to cause confusion a few miles away from the plant. "After we hit the plant we will use the diversion to go after your soldier's hospital nearby. My people will bomb a very high bridge something about Viet Nam is the name. When it comes down we will strike." Bolt cutter man picked up his tool and started to smack it into his palm as he paced around the room.

"Haq, I think you're full of shit. How can you know all of these places? You could not have personally inspected all of these locations." The interrogator looked at him with a pained expression of exasperation. He knew what Haq was going to say and he knew it would make bolt cutter man look foolish.

Haq said nothing for a while until he made eye contact with the interrogator, whose expression told him to answer but to *be gentle and remember he's got a bolt cutter in his hands.*

Haq wisely decided not to look at bolt cutter man as he spoke for fear of unconsciously revealing the contempt he had for the computer illiterate American.

"I was sent video through my computer system. They were as good as being there myself, so I feel almost like I have been everyplace we planned to attack," He spoke in a voice that was as flat as he could.

"My people also have more plans for road number 95. In Jacksonville Florida there is a location where the road actually comes down to a single lane under another highway. We will blow up that overhead highway and paralyze all traffic in the area.

This time the plan is to use doctors we have planted in a large hospital a few hundred feet away. They will take out a walkway connecting two buildings of the hospital."

The interrogator's head shot up on hearing this information.

"Are you saying you have doctors working for you? I mean medical doctors in some hospitals?" he demanded.

"We have over one hundred soldiers of Islam (jihadis) who are medical doctors and technicians working right now in the US, Europe and Canada. Yes that is what I am saying."

"Do you know where they are?"

"I only know an area of your country they are in. I only found out about those brothers on a need to know basis. I have no further need to know about other doctors so I have not received information about them. I know the others exist because I have been told they do. My orders are to wait for them to contact me for instructions. Until they contact me I do not know anything about them or their whereabouts."

"What are the names of the doctors and the hospital in Jacksonville?" The interrogator demanded. "I will write them for you. You will not be able to speak their names."

"How do we access your system?"

"I only know my own password "Amaso" which gets me in so I can pick up my messages. With all that has happened I would guess they have gone deeper underground now."

"Or popped their head's up ready to fight. 'Amaso' you say... How do you spell that word?"

"A M A S O"

"That is true, but Adam Paulson is the one you want. He built our whole system. He knows every part of it. He is an American you know. He calls himself"el Baahir." It means "The Brilliant."…. another shit head I am forced to work with. Imagine el Baahir! The balls on that man!"

"That was an amazing piece of information," the interrogator thought as he struggled to stay calm. He did not want Haq to realize that this was news to him. If Haq did get onto the truth, he would start playing the "Paulson" revelations for further concessions.

"Look we'll talk about this 'Paulson' guy a little later. Let's finish up what you know about planned attacks around the country.

"As you have already come to recognize, I know only just what will happen in my sector, the Northeast …. only from Maine to Florida along road 95. I can't say for sure but I would assume that you should increase your guard along all of your major roads especially where they come down to choke points that can be blown easily and cause a maximum amount of disruption. You see the real aim we have is to keep you off balance fighting shadows until we can rally enough jihadist brothers from around the world to crush you like a bug."

"Okay, you've made your propaganda speech now continue singing or else," bolt cutter man said slapping his toy in his left palm.

Perhaps the most important threat uncovered by the interrogation of Amir Haq, was the planned small plane attack on a warship in dry dock at the Norfolk Naval base. It was based on information that had been amassed by local Islamists living and working in Norfolk. In one instant a spy for Amir Haq actually worked as a maintenance man on the base.

He also described an operation that was to take place at Newark Airport in New Jersey. Haq provided the name of a native born American who was going to steal two dozen blank airport identification cards. The scariest part of this information was that Haq's agent was a red haired green-eyed former Catholic named Sarah McCarthy who looked exactly like a 'Sarah McCarthy' and nothing like an agent working for the most dangerous terrorist in America. She was armed with a stolen hand grenade when she was approached. She pulled the pin and took three FBI agents with her.

The arrest and kill totals from Haq's narratives rose into the hundreds. In the early days of the Islamists' war on America many innocent citizens died, but many, many more were saved.

The Team's biggest prize was information on Amir's computer genius. They knew the man existed, but up to that point, they had no solid data on who he was or what he looked like. After a solid week of non-stop questioning him, the Team had gotten Haq to talk about, the man known as *el Baahir.* This was a major break.

USING THE SHIT HEADS

When they were satisfied that they had squeezed everything they could out of Amir Haq, at that point, the Team sent him to Swan Island. The Team arranged for five of Haq's captured fellow Pakistani *shit heads,* to be sent there along with him.

The chopped off toes gave him a cover story. It enabled him to maintain that he had not been broken. If he lost one toe, the *shit heads* would have thought that he had broken before losing a second toe. The second missing toe cinched it for them. They believed Haq when he said he did not break. The Team's plan for Haq was to store him where they could reach him, but he could not be freed from. They could take no chances on the media reporting his capture and location. They wanted to be able to question him again and use the promise of a cell in a warmer climate to get more out of the terrorist leader.

They put the *shit heads* with him and leaked the news that Haq's mother was also being housed on Swan Island knowing it would drive them crazy. The distance to the Falklands covered the first requirement. Sending five Pakistani *shit heads* with him and saying they had put Fayzah Haq in the same complex covered the second requirement. When Haq wasn't moaning and begging for painkillers, the Pakistani *shit heads* were constantly urging him to sneak over to the women's prison. They wanted him to murder Fayzah to avenge his family honor. He was not able to enjoy a single clear thought during his time on Swan Island. Of course Fayzah Haq was nowhere near Swan Island.

President Andrews insisted upon being told everything about the handling of Haq. He wanted the interrogators to know he stood with them and would publicly admit he ordered everything that was done. He knew that doing this would reassure them that they could do whatever was necessary to get the information that Haq had. Andrews well understood that America's streets had been turned into battlefields by marauding paramilitary Islamist troops who were killing hundreds of civilians a day. He wanted to stop these attacks by use of any weapon he could employ.

Chapter 46

Cowpens:
Warfare American Style

FBI computer experts took the information that Amir Haq provided and began to fight back immediately. They used the Cowpens program to trace back to many computers in Haq's network and destroy their capabilities. They quickly replaced the programs set up to coordinate al Qaeda's terror attacks then patiently waited as agents and deep cover terrorists reached out trying to get their instructions from Haq.

This attack was especially effective because it turned the anonymity of the hidden terrorists around on them. As totally autonomous cells, small groups of terrorists knew nothing about each other. When one cell after another was fooled into revealing itself, other cells never heard about their capture.

The medical doctors Haq referred to either were too smart to volunteer their presence or they never existed to begin with. Only three doctors, all Egyptians who worked in the same small hospital in Scranton Pennsylvania, were snagged by the FBI's trap. When they "checked in" for instructions they were told to quickly make their way to Philadelphia in order to be part of a plot to blow up the Liberty Bell.

The FBI agents that wrote the message actually used it to entertain themselves. In the Bureau's experience there had never been a serious anti-tgovernment group, from the Klan to the Black Panthers that did not want to blow up the Liberty Bell. Mentioning that particular target would be irresistible and as one agent put it "almost unfair" to use as bait.

Haq's doctors were told go to Philadelphia and make their way to the corner of Market Street and 4th Street to look for a large blue van marked

Norman's Bakery. They were to knock on its back door with three short wraps. Once inside, they would be fitted with suicide bomb vests and sent down the street to blow up the historic symbol of American freedom. It was a perfect trap for Islamists who burned with hatred for America.

The hardest part of the operation, for the Bureau, was finding a way to clear the Philadelphia police from the area so as not to scare their prey away. Thereafter it was leading lambs to slaughter.

When the trio of would be bombers arrived, the FBI agents were amazed at how meek and unassuming they were. Each was still in his early thirties. Each was small and frail looking with wire rimmed glasses crowning small delicate features. When the first one was taken into custody he sat quietly and seemed dazed as he listened to his captures.

When the second doctor stepped into the van he was immediately jabbed with a hypodermic needle and knocked out. Watching the second doctor being captured sent the third one into a fight to end his life. He ran at the backup agents waving and wildly firing a .38 revolver. Seconds later he got what he obviously wanted. He was shot through the heart and died before he could hit the ground.

Cowpens was used in many other trap and kill operations. In almost every case its results were kept secret even after the day to day fighting on America's streets ended.

Finally after weeks of successes both large and small, the Cowpens program was outted.

It was featured in a story on the front page of the Baltimore Sun. Every detail of why Cowpens was developed, along with a fairly accurate description of how it worked and some of its successes was laid out point by point by the newspaper.

Because of the heads up from the media, Paulson changed his system's data storage cards, which plugged up and ended its vulnerability to hacking. Because new data cards enable a hacking victim to dodge detection, the terrorist computerized message system was saved. When a target system changes its data cards, it moves and disguises its Internet Provider (IT) address making it almost impossible to hack back into its computer work stations. In short the alert caused Paulson to change his data cards and shield his system from further intrusion by the FBI's hackers.

The remaining terrorist's website that the FBI knew about shut down. It changed its opening page to a picture of a man's bare ass and a banner that read *Thank you Mr. Baltimore Son.*

HOW COWPENS WORKS

The Cowpens anti hacking program used a classic honey-pot trap. It was designed by Sanjit Patel to catch the Islamists computer hackers and keep them from either stealing sensitive data or distorting the information contained within the FBI's network. The effectiveness of Cowpens came from its central feature, which was making certain servers in FBI's computer network appear to be vulnerable and therefore attractive to potential hackers, and creating a tunnel for hackers to try and run to get to the honey-pot. To achieve this disguise and make the FBI's system look like an easy target, Patel isolated his computer from the rest of his network in a manner that made detection as such, impossible for a hacker.

Once this surreptitious isolation was completed, each successive attempt to penetrate the system's security shield provided additional information about who the hacker was and how he could be thwarted and captured.

Patel knew that Haq's people were trying to gain access to his honey-pot by tunneling through several FBI subnet systems on the way to his honey-pot. He suspected that his use of the computer network at a nearby college that he had recently taught at and had access to might have been the gateway for the attack. His reasoning was that since the hacker would keep trying to access the ultimate honey-pot in Washington; as the administrator of the target system, he would wait and watch as his hunter came progressively closer and deeper into a network he did not perceive was trapping him.

Patel's computer was a set-up honey-pot, and seemed to be the only computer that would grant access to the main FBI storage servers: America's most sensitive secrets. In reality, Patel's honey-pot was really an isolated box that only seemed to hook into the FBI storage servers.

Once Patel had gathered enough information about the source of the hacking attempts, Cowpens created an Internet pathway from the source computer to the destination computer and monitored all interactions along that pathway. Then by employing an intelligent algorithm to filter out normal traffic based on usage patterns, it identified which computer the hacker was using.

From there, Cowpens used its zapping feature and Patel struck back. When he did this all of the computers that the hacker ran through to hit the honey pot started blasting corrupt TCP/IP packets to the hacker's computer, creating a Denial of Service. As a result the terrorist's American computer network was shut down.

CHAPTER 47

HAMTRAMCK

THE ISLAMISTS COMMUNITY of Hamtramck, Michigan, was one that was not caught without a plan to attack America. Once the Islamist across the country started their attempts to blow up America, the Darul El Taweed Muslim Center pulsated with activity. Nevertheless, there was no confusion about what its members felt they had to do. Hamtramck is an oddly situated city. It is almost totally surrounded by Detroit. In the early 1920s when the automobile industry drew them, thousands of Poles moved to Hamtramck, and it is still about 20% Polish descent.

But like the city that swallowed it up, Hamtramck's people have changed. Since the mid seventies large numbers of immigrants from Muslim countries have arrived and stayed. The new arrivals from two of those countries, Yemen and Bangladesh, have brought with them a virulent strain of Islamist thought. More than 40% of Hamtramck's people were born outside of America. Most of the remaining 60% are either second generation Muslims or old Poles who have no power to keep the town's Islamists in check. Meetings among Hamtramck's young Muslims are most often little more than anti-west/ anti-American gatherings. Hamtramck is a hotbed of Islamists activities. As word of war spread, Hamtramck's Islamists gravitated toward their local mosque. They knew what was expected of them. At least one hundred had been trained at Islamberg a terrorist training camp in upstate New York.

Islamberg had been allowed to continue to operate so the FBI could monitor its activities. Taking that approach had created a dangerous two-edged sword that some in the Bureau had counseled against, but more powerful forces had argued for. Now the moment of truth was at hand. The Islamberg trainees were tough dedicated haters of America and everything not Islamic. The men at the Hamtramck mosque divided themselves into five teams of twenty. None of the cells knew anything about the mission of any other cell. All they knew or cared to know was that their time had come and they were on their way to an eternity with seventy two virgins willing to submit to their every sexual demand.

At 10:30PM of the first day, each group was given its orders. Each man then lined up for outfitting with weapons and maps. Within an hour the evil swarm left to destroy America. They were filled with zeal and hate. It was only after all but a handful of coordinators had left that the real planning began.

Rashid El Jihad was the main planer. He had been a heavy weapons instructor at Islamberg for a year before he left to organize the "brothers" of Hamtramck. When he left, he explained that his true calling was beyond weapons training. As a physicist he realized his place was with the *Detroit brothers* as they planned the detonation of a nuclear dirty bomb. While everyone knew his real name was not El Jihad, no one knew his real name, but no one cared either. All of them used fake names.

He was really Mohammed Hassan an Egyptian national who had been the Commanding officer of his country's military training depot in spite of his scientific background.

Mohammed Hassan burned with hate for America. Hate was his wife, his children, and his family. Living alone with his hate was all he needed.

Mohammed Hassan

Hassan's radical Islamist roots started to take hold of him literally on the day he was born. His family had been active members of the Egyptian branch of the Muslim Brotherhood. The Brotherhood was originally founded in 1928 as a vehicle for achieving social justice in a country ruled by the British. As it grew and the pro British government in Alexandria became more and more alarmed over its activities, the Brotherhood became more militant. Acting on basic pragmatism borne of fear of severe British retribution, the Brotherhood caused no trouble for England during World War II.

That de facto cease-fire ended soon after the fighting stopped.

By 1948 the Brotherhood was a genuine threat to the pro British government and Downing Street ordered a crack down. During a raid on a Brotherhood vehicle, a copy of a plan to assassinate government officials was uncovered. Alexandria took action against the Brotherhood. Wide sweeping round ups were made all across Egypt and many young *brothers* were put in prison. Nevertheless, The Brotherhood would not be denied. In December 1948, a *brother* assassinated the Egyptian Prime Minister. That young *brother* was Abdel Meguid Ahmed Hassan.

In 1954, at about the time Mohammed Hassan was born, his father and two uncles were caught in a dragnet after they attempted to murder Gamal 'Abd al Nasser, the tough talking President of Egypt, even though he had just succeeded in kicking out the British who had been in control of the country since the early 1880s. The attack infuriated Nasser. He ordered that the treatment of those involved be brutal and lethal. Hassan never met either of his uncles or his father. Through the Brotherhood's spy network, he learned that they were taken to a re-education center where they were used as practice dummies by Nasser's men who were learning torture interrogation techniques from the American CIA. From that point on his grieving mother fed him a steady diet of hatred for America and the entire western world.

As a young man Hassan was an acquaintance of Osama bin Ladin when they were both students at a university in Saudi Arabia. Contrary to popular American media myth, bin Ladin was a radical Islamist even as a young student. Any talk about him originally working with America when he first came to prominence was just not true.

Even as a little boy, young Mohammed dreamed of going to America and blowing it up with a nuclear bomb.

As he grew up, he came to realized, first that he could not bomb America into the sea, and then he realized he could not destroy even an entire city with any dirty nuclear bomb he might actually be able to deliver himself. Since he would trust no one with his dream, he had to continually rethink his murderous plot. Becoming a physicist was part of his plan to make a dirty nuke and blow up Americans.

Growing up, even in Egypt, he was a very low profile man. Hassan was actually quite nondescript. His features, his coloring and his manner were very much the same as any of a million Middle Eastern Muslim men. He was usually one of the last people anyone would believe harbored such murderous designs on America. Hassan was a disciplined man. He never allowed himself to reveal his true thoughts about America and the West. He never told anyone what the CIA had done to his family. He never even talked about America unless a companion raised the issue, and even then he would limit his remarks as much as possible.

To all but a very few close associates, Hassan seemed to be unconcerned with politics. That was just as he wanted it. He had no intention of being drawn into idol chitchat with part-time-Islamist-dabblers, as he thought of those who seemed to get a vicarious thrill out of discussing the latest terrorist attack on the West.

"*They'd never send their own son or daughter on a suicide bombing mission; never get their own hands dirty... cushy lives are too good to give up. We'll never see them taking up the Sword of Allah,*" he would think as he listened to people like that speak.

As soon as the other fighters left for their battles, Hassan got his inner circle of just two other men aside. They were going to have to quickly put the real plan together. The real plan they had was to arm and deliver a nuclear dirty bomb in the heart of Detroit.

The plan was to cripple the city of Detroit by crippling its Police Department. Hassan and his team intended to gladly give up their lives to make that happen. They would drive an SUV into whatever barrier was erected around the main building housing the nerve center of the DPD. The target was on Woodward Avenue in the center of the city. Hassan had spent a lot of time observing the city's downward spiral into second-rate status. The slide started when the auto industry pulled out for better prospects in Mexico. After decades of trying, GM and Chrysler followed Ford and set up shop south of the Rio Grande. The Big Three had finally given up trying to work out a livable contract with the Auto Workers Union.

He had spent hours listening to local Muslim converts like Kunta Jabbar, a retired Detroit police officer, telling of the ineptitude of the city government and concluded the city would not be able to stop his dirty bomb nuke attack.

The first teams out were told only to stay away from the center city area. They were being used as decoys they understood this, and where glad to give their lives as ordered. They knew nothing about Hassan's real plan, but did what they could to further whatever he had in mind. The timing fell into place.

By watching local television, listening to radio and word of mouth reports Hassan was satisfied that the least well policed area of Detroit was its center where its government buildings were.

CHAPTER 48

DETROIT BECOMES AMERICA'S FIRST NUKED CITY

THE WAY TO THE POLICE HEADQUARTERS BUILDING was not an easy ride. In his busy final preparation, Hassan missed something important. The President's announcement had called for a curfew, but the first reports in Detroit said the city would not enforce a curfew because it saw doing so as an unnecessary provocation.

A little too eager to hear what he wanted to hear and a little eager to believe his own estimation of the incompetence of the local police, Hassan missed the follow up message that the President had called Detroit's mayor and personally instructed him to enforce the curfew or be arrest and jailed himself. Hassan and his two men found themselves out on city streets that were empty except for the military and police vehicles that seemed to be everywhere. Immediately things started to go bad for him and his team.

The black SUV they were in looked official enough, and Hassan's insistence upon ignoring the stop lights along the way, gave his vehicle an air of officialdom that allowed him to get within two blocks of Headquarters before a P.A. system ordered him to pull over. The weight of the bomb plus the effects of the radiation sickness that was over taking him made him swerve from side to side which made it clear he was not an official, but rather someone who should be questioned.

A truly dangerous nuclear bomb would weigh about five tons and be too hot for "backyard" handlers to deal with. The only way a dirty bomb could be dangerous would be to make one that is greatly reduced in size and weight. Hassan's bomb, even in its greatly reduced and diluted configuration, still weighed about a ton. In order to load it in the specially fitted Pathfinder, the three Islamists had to carefully set it in the rear area using a stolen folk lift. All three men knew they were dying from radiation sickness as soon as they tore off the lead outer cover of Hassan's bomb. He himself had already begun to look and feel like a very sick man even before they packed up their box of death.

The diminished size of the weapon meant that its killing potential was diminished as well. If conditions were perfect such a "mini nuke" would be able to kill about 2,500 people. That projection was based on crowded city streets and proper wind currents, but now Detroit's streets were empty. When he realized he was discovered, Hassan gunned his engine and readied himself and his followers to meet Allah as His chosen heroes.

As the SUV sped forward, bullets ripped through its skin. One of his helpers was wounded and the other was killed, but not before he had fully armed the bomb. In seconds the Pathfinder smashed its way through the wooden 'horses' that were serving as barriers in front of the building. More rounds poured into the SUV. This time they were from three machine guns fired by the DPD's special weapons and tactics team.

Hassan was dead by the time the bomb exploded. The toxic cloud of nuclear materials cobbled together from sources all over the world and smuggled into America through the Canadian woods bordering Montana, immediately began to poison the air. In just seconds, clouds of gaseous death began to spread out around the city's government buildings area. In a very short time hundreds of people, mostly Windsor Ontario Canadians, who thought they were above the war on terror, would be dying from radiation poisoning. A Detroit Police Hazmat (Hazardous material) Unit was parked down the street. The crew was waiting for orders they thought would not come. They expected to be pressed into service controlling looters and rioters, but never seriously thought they would have to deal with a nuclear explosion, especially not sitting in their own rig parked in front of Police Headquarters.

Without any discussion, they jumped to action. There was not much they could do about the explosion and toxic materials that had already escaped, but now they had to act. They were a well-trained, well-schooled and disciplined unit. Each of the four men, two black, one Hispanic and one white, knew that they too had probably been killed by the blast. They knew there was likely nothing anyone could do to save them, but they acted anyway. They gave the people of Detroit and their neighbors in Canada a chance to live. Each man quickly ran toward the danger that others where running from, then gathered and smothered as much radio active material as they could.

The blast knocked over two local TV remote broadcasting vehicles situated just across the street. Both crews were killed except for Leslie Johnson a female on air reporter. As the Hazmat Unit moved in to start its work, Johnson worked her way out of her nearly flattened mobile studio. She was taking pictures of the mushroom cloud with her cell phone when two men in specialized protective suits, knocked her to the ground. They were DPD detectives who were specially trained by the FBI in counter terrorism methods. They knew the real danger from dirty nuke detonations was the panic and loss of morale they were designed to create.

"We'll take that. Now stand up and turn around so we can put this protective suit on you," one said.

Johnson started screaming, "First amendment, police brutality, interference with the people's right to know," and all the standard media lines.

"I really wish you hadn't said that. Now we have to take you in. You're under arrest for inciting to riot and sedition under the Patriot Act. Let's go." The cell phone was bagged and tagged in the holding cell area in front of Johnson. Letting her see that they were not just smashing the phone and throwing it away was a purposeful move.

They knew who she was. They had often watched her on local television slamming innocent cops for doing their job. The color and race of the cops in her reports made no difference. If she could find a way to attack the police because of what a Black or Hispanic cop did, she would run with it. For a cop hater like Leslie Johnson, waiting around for a misstep by a white cop was not an option. There just were enough of them on the Detroit force. They wanted Johnson to see what they were doing so she would understand this was not just another roust of a "sister trying to make it in the white man's world."

They wanted her to know this was not one of the assaults on minorities she imagined she saw everywhere. This was trouble with the United States Government caused by her seditious act. When she was stabilized Johnson was placed on a military helicopter with two armed guards. It landed at a nearby National Guard armory that had been pressed into use as a hospital and make shift detention facility.

There was no way she would be allowed to start attacking American institutions during this war. There was no way she would be allowed to report having seen a mushroom cloud. Of course the emergence of the cloud would get out by word of mouth. Those charged with smothering the news knew that, but without a TV story covered by a well-known reporter, the story could be suppressed until after the blast damage had been accepted and was in the past tense.

Leslie Johnson was released a week later, but only after signing a waver of claims against the government and a legally binding promise not to report anything she saw for three months under pain of re-arrest and being put on trial for violation of the Patriot Act. The United States Attorney handling the case wanted a total and complete prohibition against her ever reporting what she saw, but was forced to yield to pressure coming directly from the Attorney General's office.

The Homeland Security Agency's after action report for the Detroit area, cited the brave actions of the DPD Hazmat Unit, "In that by placing what materials they could in the special containers they had and then finally using their own bodies to cover what else they could, the Detroit Police Department's Hazmat Unit saved a least several dozen lives, both in Detroit and Windsor Canada."

Once again America's police officers had stood tall when their nation needed them the most. The final death totals for both cities was estimated to be about two hundred, but it would have been much higher had it not been for a small group of brave police officers who acted without waiting for orders because they knew no one else could step up and do the job. The orders to stay indoors may have done most of the job of keeping the death tolls down, but the selfless courage of the Detroit Police undoubtedly saved many lives.

CHAPTER 49

THE TYLER EXPOSURE

FIGHTING BACK AGAINST BIOLOGICAL WEAPONS ATTACKS

FEAR IS ALWAYS THE MAIN WEAPON in the terrorist arsenal. They constantly work to build then increase and maintain fear among their target populations. When people who look, for all the world, as normal as anyone else suddenly blow themselves up on a crowded city commuter bus the end result is death, but more importantly fear. The sting of death subsides after a while for most people unless they were directly affected by the loss of a relative or close friend. The fear of the next attack, however, becomes like the ripples in a pond. Fear spreads and spreads until it reaches the furthest edges of a society. Drenching a target population in that paralyzing fear is the aim of the terrorist.

Among the most fear inducing weapons the Islamists had was an array of biological agents that had been engineered into a weaponized state. Virulent strains of diseases ranging from lethal forms of pneumonia to the medieval super germ called the Black Plague and others not known in civilized countries had been put into a transferable state. They made the Islamists very dangerous enemies.

In addition to these germ warfare weapons, Mohammed Waleed's terrorists had anthrax, a deadly respiratory disease causing agent that was easy to spread, only in low non lethal dosages. Yet even this served the terrorist's aims. An infectious disease, Anthrax is caused by spore- forming bacteria. It is common among people who work with shaggy animals as the spores thrive and grow in warm, woolly environments. In some parts of the world Anthrax is called *wool sorter's* disease.

It is a perfect example of the fifteen hundred year old mentality of the Islamists being turned against modern America. Anthrax is their disease. They wallow in the dust and dirt with their sheep and camels. They are well acquainted with wool sorters disease or Anthrax. They made Anthrax the *punji stick* of the 2000's. Using Anthrax in a way that would actually kill people in large numbers was desirable, but not necessary to reach maximum fear effect. In 2002, when a small number of people, in the Washington D.C. area, came down with some of the early symptoms of Anthrax, fear spread rapidly. Seeing friends and neighbors with even a few cold like symptoms that also appear in those sick with Anthrax, convinced many Americans that it was time to panic.

Natural fears mixed with media reports insisting that the administration was unprepared or frozen in fear, and therefore unable to protect Americans against Anthrax. These reports caused some rioting at pharmacies as supplies of the necessary medicine, Cipro began to dwindle.

Over the ensuing years, successive administrations had seriously addressed the problem of countering biological weapons attacks.

Government laboratories put together teams of infectious immunologists, civil engineers, mechanical engineers and psychologists as well as city planners and big city police officials to address the problem of germ warfare attacks.

Working in close coordination the team produced an amazing network of virus-sniffing sensors that could detect every know germ/biological agent Waleed could send to America.

The sensor boxes were named *smart boxes* by the psychologist because she wanted to instill confidence in people that the machines could in fact'sniff' the air and detect dangerous elements in the atmosphere. After the great Anthrax scare of 2002, the Postal Service had removed almost all of its street corner mailboxes. The reasoning was simple and solid. Those boxes could have been used as places to introduce dangerous chemical agents into America's mail system. A psychologist argued that putting the smart boxes in the spaces where the old mailboxes had been would send a very strong, but subtly reassuring, message that America might have been knocked down but now we are fighting back. The smart boxes went into duty on a long Fourth of July weekend and caused hardly a stir. People accepted them even if they had no idea how effective these trunk size machines were at keeping them safe.

The Tyler Exposure

On the fourth day of the fighting in America's streets an independent Islamist cell made its move to infect the streets of Tyler Texas with a strain of highly contagious Smallpox virus. The smart box did its job. It was set up unobtrusively at the corner of North Bois D Arc Avenue and East Locust Street in front of the town's Greyhound Bus Station. The attack was planned and carried out by two Jordanian Islamist students studying Mechanical Engineering at the nearby University of Texas, Tyler Campus. Both of them were from oil wealthy families with long ties to the Muslim Brotherhood. They used the money they made from their paid jobs in the Muslim Ministry Office on campus, to travel to Europe on their Spring Break. In Budapest they connected with a former Soviet Germ Warfare Officer who sold them a vile of Smallpox virus.

When word of the fighting reached the two Jordanians, they immediately began to plan how to use their evil weapon. Since the war had caused a general unrest on campus for both the Americans and the resident Muslim students, many students were withdrawing from classes and traveling to their homes or wherever they felt they should be. The team noticed that many Muslim students were attempting to fly home, but many of the Americans were taking Greyhound buses to their destinations.

The two bio-saboteurs deduced that the bus station would be a very good target for spraying water they had laced with Smallpox. By putting Pox laced water around the building they could infect hundreds or thousands of people and watch them travel away to far corners of the Southwest to infect tens of thousands, maybe hundreds of thousands of their families and friends in their hometowns.

At 10: 30 PM they made their way to the station and, using two common household plant misters, sprayed the entire Greyhound building. They started inside the men's room spraying toilet seats then moved to the waiting area and sprayed railings and other places people would touch. They sprayed counter tops and the panels on the shuttered newsstand. When they were finished inside, they went outside and sprayed the door handles of the virtually empty terminal. They walked around to the rear lot where they found two empty running buses. The doors where opened and the cargo compartments were opened as well. They dashed up into the open buses sprayed them, and then sprayed into the cargo holds. With their remaining diseased water they sprayed every door handle on every car and shop on East Locust Street. Four minutes later the drivers came out and pulled away with a few weary passengers. The buses carried Smallpox to half of Texas and as far away as San Diego.

The whole attack took less than eight minutes. The few people in the station at that time of night took no notice of them. They were very efficient merchants of death. Twenty-two minutes later and 640 miles to the east of Tyler the National Center of Controlling Infectious Diseases (NCCID), the nerve center for the smart box network, picked up a major breach signature. The (NCCID) quickly responded by alerting local emergency response teams to shut down the entire town of Tyler and evacuate everyone in a five block radius around the bus station. They also dispatched a Hazardous Material Control Team (HAZMAT CON-TEAM) to the scene.

The Tyler Police Department quickly managed a panic free relocation of hundreds of people to the University's campus then cordoned off the proscribed area. They had everything ready when the (HAZMAT CON-TEAM) arrived. Traveling in a US Army helicopter, the team of three scientists reached the Greyhound Terminal just after 2 AM. The counter bio-warfare team was able to stop a widespread Smallpox pandemic, but in spite of their best efforts, many people across the Southwest became infected and died from exposure to the virus.

The idea of connecting the infectious material to a major mode of transportation was a very powerful stroke of genius. Cases of Smallpox traceable back to what became known as *The Tyler Exposure* were discovered as far away as Little Rock Arkansas, San Diego California and Portland Oregon. When they were diagnosed most of what could be done for the victims was just high doses of Cipro and doxycycline to hold off secondary infections. Beyond that, isolated bed rest was the main prescription.

Not surprisingly, bus travel in the whole Southwestern United States was disrupted for months. Bus travel in general fell to half what it had been before the attack. It was a month before the bus station could be re-opened.

In the confusion, the Jordanian students quietly slipped out of Tyler a few hours after the attack. It was not until a fuller investigation could be completed a week later that they were even missed. Most of the Muslim Arabs on campus fled so two more that left without notice weren't missed. They were never captured or even identified.

Around the country a strange sociological phenomena took place. Americans started taking grease markers and writing thank you notes on walls near smart boxes. They didn't think their country was incompetent. To the contrary, people started to scrawl things like:

"Way to go NCCID!" and "God bless the NCCID."

"Smart box for president"

One even said: "Hey Waleed take that and stick it up you ass!"

There were bio attacks in Omaha, Tacoma, and Miami, over the following three weeks. Each killed several people, but none killed as many Americans as they might have without the alarm messages sent out by the smart boxes. Although final death counts could not be accurately gathered because of the essentially idiopathic nature of this a bacterial disease, the best guesses were that between 40,000 and 52,000 people died directly or indirectly from The Tyler Exposure.

Nevertheless, the fight against Waleed's bio/chemical weapon attacks went better than could have been expected. The experimental smart boxes saved untold numbers of average Americans and gave the country's morale a major boost in the first critically important days of the fighting. There were still many things the terrorists could do to strike fear into the heart of America, but at least for the moment unleashing bio weapons was not one of them.

PART FIVE
VICTORY ON AMERICA'S TERMS

CHAPTER 50

A NEW SHERIFF IN IRAQ
TURKEY SAY "NO"

THE POLITICALLY MOTIVATED WITHDRAWAL of American and Allied war fighters from Iraq caused a predictable collapse into a savage civil war. Given that everything in Iraq is "exactly the same as it is everywhere else, only a little different" as the very apt description of the country went, the civil war was a crazy quilt of sides that changed with the winds. The Sunnis fought the Shiites. Both sides hated the Kurds and killed them as the opportunities arose. The Kurds attacked the foreign Islamists who poured in to Baghdad the day after the last Americans left.

The foreign Islamists were well trained, well financed and well led. A week after the last western military presence was gone from the Iraqi capital, Osama Bin Ladin and Mohammed Waleed arrived in a huge stretch limo. They moved into the old Green Zone where the United States Army had been headquartered. While they ate a big lunch, Bin Ladin's troops celebrated with AK 47 rifle salutes and Waleed's technical experts setup the necessary computer workstations. When the eating and the shooting were over, the real celebration started.

Waleed ordered a round up of all of Baghdad's local officials. They were to be "invited" to a late lunch with the men who had saved them from "American oppression." Everyone from police commanders to the mayor to the head of the school board was escorted to Baghdad's government offices complex. A poorly led and out of tune band was playing marching music as Waleed's forty-one "guests" were herded toward the Iranian madman's desk on the sidewalk outside of the mayor's office. For a long time Waleed said nothing. He busied himself by writing something on several pieces of paper he was tearing out of a notepad. As each of the men, and the three women, in the group stepped forward and said and spelled his or her name, Waleed wrote on his pad. When all of the invitees had stepped back into formation, Waleed shuffled the loose notepad sheets and without an error handed each the one with his or her name written on it. Ever the showman, Waleed wanted Bin Ladin to take notice of how sharp his memory was, and it did impress Bin Ladin.

When the collection of guests read the paper they had been given, they saw the word *ahmand* the Persian word for liar under their name. No one in the crowd said a word. The only sound that could be heard above the murmuring of the guests was the sharp report coming from the Islamic Revolutionary Guard flag crackling in the wind over their heads. Waleed began to wail and chant Muslim incantations asking Allah to bless him in his quest to purify the world. He begged the Almighty saying, "Only blood can cleanse blood." The sound of fearful heartbeats filled the tightly packed formation in front of him. When he finished praying, Waleed ordered his men to arrange his guests in a group picture pose, placing the name sheet under each one's chin.

When the pose was just right, Waleed brought out his personal photographer and several shots were taken. After he finished his ritual, Waleed grabbed his personal AK 47 and sprayed them with dozens of rounds, and his men cheered and chanted, "Death to America" between screams of "Allahu Akbar!" (God is great!) A few, who were acting on secret orders, chanted "Al Mahdi. Al Mahdi, Al Mahdi," although few joined them.

Waleed and Bin Ladin's reign over Iraq was short lived. In less than a month the Turks had seen enough of the mess Iraq had become since America's latest cut and run maneuver. While it was true that they hated the Kurds, the Turks knew they were fierce fighters who could be reasoned with based on the new circumstances both had to deal with since the fall of Baghdad.

After striking an uneasy truce with Kurdish leaders, Ankara sent one hundred and sixty thousand of its best-trained and equipped troops into the northern regions of Iraq. The Kurds were assured they were not the targets of this invasion and for once in the long history of hatred between the two ancient peoples, the Turks meant what they said. If the Kurds would agree not to try to form a state without consultation with Ankara, and aid the Turks in their effort to kick out Waleed and Bin Ladin, they would be left alone. The Kurds could establish a separate country when the fighting was done. Both sides kept its end of the agreement. Without having to look over their shoulders, the modern Turkish Army was able to fight the Islamists to a standstill in Iraq. It quickly became clear that Iraq would become a re-run of the twenty-five year civil war that had destroyed Lebanon, but the Turks didn't care about that development.

They ended up taking the place of the Americans and although they came to Baghdad with different goals and wishes for their war torn neighbor, they were at least able to keep the Islamists from controlling the Iraqi oil fields. The Turks became the bombers of the oil fields and kept them idle and did to the Islamists what they had done to the American backed Iraqis.

Nobody could make a drachma or a lira on the oil fields and that was just what Ankara wanted The combined efforts of the Turks and their new best friends the Kurds, pushed the civil war fighting half way down Iraq toward Basrah. They forced Waleed and Bin Ladin's troops to keep moving southward until they were able to finally stop the push and set up a headquarters in Kabala.

The Turks were content to remain the prosperous middleman sitting on the east/west trading routes between Europe and the Arabian states, as they had always been. Over the centuries, they had become both an Asian and a European mixture. They liked their position and saw themselves as the model for balancing the demands of traditional Islam with the influences of the modern world. The Turks were not going to let rabid mouth-foaming Islamists drag them back to life in the seventh century.

Turkey enjoyed a long history of being able to work with, and fight besides, Western Christian nations. Going back to their heroics at Gallipoli in the First World War, the world had to grudgingly grant Turkey's claim to respect as a modern fighting military.

Turkey had been recognized for her willingness to be part of the Western world when it committed troops to the United Nation's war in Korea. Seeing the toughness and skill of the Turkish fighters, NATO brought them into its membership as early as 1952. Unencumbered by an anti government media, the Turks did everything in Iraq the Americans should have done and avoided doing the things they should not have done. One of the first moves they made off the battlefield was to warn both Syria and Iran to shutdown their borders with Iraq. They made it clear that Turkish and Kurdish soldiers would be killing anyone who tried to cross into Iraq.

The next thing they did was advise all of the world's news gathering agencies to immediately pull their reporters out of Iraq because 'their safety could not be guaranteed.' Finally they used diplomatic channels to make it clear to the European Union and NATO that they would not be listening to their hand wringing complaints about how the Turks were conducting war it Iraq. Their message was:

"Do not confuse us with the Americans. Bin Ladin was right about them. They did not have the stomach or the balls to do what has to be done. We do. Shut up and stay out of our way." The loss of Turkey as an ally and member of NATO would have been too much for Europe to risk. The European Union wisely said nothing about the "Iraq/Turkey situation."

The world had long acknowledged the clear difference between the backward tent dwellers in the Middle East and the Turks. During the Korean War the Turks were initially given menial tasks. They served as POW camp guards and in other slots that would not regularly put them side by side with American troops in combat situations.

For Americans, fighting next to Turks was out of the question. In its hubris fueled belief that the war in Korea was another "white man's burden," America would not allow the Turks to do more than guard prisoners. When the Chinese and North Korean POW bodies started to pile up, it became clear that the Turks were serious when they asked why prisoners had to be taken and kept live. Left to their own rules of engagement, Turks do not take prisoners; they kill them. When the Turkish troops fought their way to Baghdad, they made a point of reopening Abu Garb prison and staffing it with Iraqis who had formerly worked in the infamous prison. Enemy war fighters who could not be immediately killed on the battlefield were brought to Abu Grab and tortured before being shot. The nightly traffic of trucks loaded with dead enemy fighters leaving the facility never stopped.

AMERICA'S DECLARATION OF WAR

On day one of the war, when President Harlan Andrews called Turkey's Prime Minister Dilek Ekin to explain the reasons for declaring war against Turkey he was met with a stream of curse words of the type that might be heard in a waterfront barroom. As the purpose of the call from Andrews became apparent to Ekin his anger grew. He listened as politely as he could while he was being talked down to like a schoolboy found smoking in the restroom, but could not hold his anger in check.

When Andrews got around to the part about declaring war so America could legally enter Turkey as per the Geneva Convention, Ekin could hold his tongue no longer. President of the United States or not, Ekin was not going to simply smile and agree to have Turkey's sovereignty violated for any reason. The mildest thing Ekin said was, "Go to the devil, you insulting dog."

Ekin explained that Turkey was not a nation of peasant rug merchants herding goats in the desert. "Mister President Harlan we are this moment preparing to do what your country did not have the balls to do in Iraq. If you insist on this declaration to serve some stupid political correct motive which is important to you, I must warn that Turkey will not take a declaration of war with, as you say, 'a wink and a nod,' not even from the United States of America. If you do this, you stupid bastard, we will treat it as a serious matter and target your soldiers wherever we find them. To us this will be a real war, not a phony one as you and your media run countrymen wish it to be. Open your eyes mister Harlan. See what you do not wish to believe. America has many enemies in this world, but Turkey is not one of them unless this is what you want! If so then you are a very poor leader to not see the truth."

"PLEASE MISTER PRIME MINISTER, I..."

"No you please Mister Harlan. Your runaway left a security vacuum for us. We had to clean up your mess. We watched you do this before. When you ran from Viet Nam it was nothing for you. Some brown people died, but you said 'So what?' Mister Harlan we are now that 'so what!' Turkey now has to fight to stay alive because of you. We will fight and live with or without your help. If we have to we, we will fight you when we finish with Waleed and Bin Ladin or at both the same time. We will survive Mister Harlan because we are now the country with the dream you once had. We know who we are, but you no longer know who you are. Please do not talk this fool threat to us. We want nothing more than to be what you used to be but you turned your back on."

"Minister Prime Minister, no plan is foolproof. We are working as hard as we can to achieve goals that I'm sure you and I share. As I have laid it out for you, I think you can see that we have to all act in a manner that best fits our own circumstances. Now that I have thought about this I agree that it would be a foolish mistake for America to treat Turkey as an enemy instead of as a friend merely because you are a Muslim country. We're all a little stressed out here sir..... I guess we acted improperly in your case. You have my word that this matter is closed."

"And your formal apology will be coming. When?"

"I've said all I am going to about this issue Mister Ekin."

"Mister President Harlan, Turkey demands a formal apology, when will we get it?"

"You just got as close to an apology as you are going to sir."

"Yes but when will formal apology be coming?"

"When hell freezes over, you little twit!"

Both men hung up at the same time. The Turks went back about their business. They ruthlessly crushed Waleed's militiamen and Bin Ladin's al Qaeda troops and kept an uneasy peace in Iraq. Because of the Turkish/Kurdish alliance, Iraq was taken out of the equation of the American/Israeli war against the Islamists. Waleed could not seize the oil rich fields in Iraq. He would not be able to use the resultant petro-money to fight on, as his troops were defeated in theater after theater.

CHAPTER 51

THE SAUDI PEACE PLAN

THE CONNIVING PRINCES OF THE DESERT SHOW THEIR TRUE COLORS

THE RAPID DESTRUCTION of the major components of the Iranian, Syrian and Jordanian Air Forces was a surprise to no one. American F-22s Israeli F-17s and British Harriers had systematically ground up the MiGs that the Islamists had been able to put in the air. Sending ill trained pilots up in old Soviet planes against the best of pilots flying the best fighter planes ended as could be expected. The huge advantage the Allies had in the Mach 2 dog fights over the sands of the world's ancient Holy Lands led to certain death for Waleed's airmen.

The Islamists had fought back with everything they had. Using smart bomb technology they were able to destroy many of the Israeli Air Force's (IAF) airfields. To keep up the pressure, the American nuclear powered aircraft carrier USS Gregory Boyington, affectionately called *The Pappy* by her crew, and a British small carrier battle group were pressed into service as temporary air strips for the IAF's fighters until repairs were made to its own facilities. Once the problem of landing and takeoffs was solved, the huge armada of Allied air power was free to strafe and destroy targets of opportunity across the entire Middle East. When Waleed rallied Islamists for a ground assault on Israel he was stopped cold by the ferocious fighting skills of the IAF.

In the busy early hours of this most unique war, where each enemy country was given the option of fighting or surrendering from day one, the question of how Saudi Arabia would respond was shuffled to the back of the line of pressing matters. By day three the Saudis had not yet responded to the declaration of war and its accompanying offer of an instantaneous surrender.

When given the choice of surrendering immediately and saving herself from a savage beating or actually engaging the United States in a shooting war the Saudis begged for time. They wanted to negotiate a deal. They offered a third choice.

When the Saudis finally answered they did so through their OPEC office, which raised eyebrows in Washington.

Their OPEC Minister Prince Sultan Bin al-Khatab called and asked to speak with Vice President Walter Hodges. Hodges knew him well. Al-Khatab was his roommate at Yale. Both were in the class of '71.

"Katty how are you? Boy it's been a long time. How are Liffie and the kids?"

"Well Walt we've been better; to be perfectly honest. We haven't been hit yet and of course, that's what I'm calling about. Let's see if we can't work something out shall we?"

"Okay Katty sure, but let's go through our respective positions so we can get on the same page?"

"We're bent over a barrel here at this end. We really don't know what to make of your declaration of war. What can we do about this? You don't have any reason at all to declare war on us. We are your strongest ally in this part of the world after all."

"I believe that spot's been filled by Israel, but let's grant that for the sake of argument. We declared war on more than 20 countries, there's been so many I can't keep track myself. Anyway..."

"Yes, but why us?"

"Damn it Katty didn't your people tell you anything about this situation before they put you on the phone?"

"Yes, but I can't believe what I am hearing. We have always cooperated with you guys. All you had to do is ask us for our help. We would have let you come in to search and destroy the camps. This is just shocking!"

"And it would have been just 'honkey dory' for us to push past your border guards, charge in and start kicking ass right? Just like that, and your people would have smiled and waved to us as we drove out to the desert. Is that about right? We're trying to help you with your internal problems. If you just surrender like the other legitimate countries we'll do our strikes surgically and none of your people will be harmed. You have to see that, right? You have my word on that."

"Our internal problems are exactly what the problem is. We are under enormous pressure to stand up to you. You are after all 'The Great Satan' to half of the crazies sitting around collecting oil checks over here. We can't do anything about them if they decide to pull off a coup and take us down. We may have to fight back for appearances but we're not idiots. We know we can't hold you off for two minutes if you really want to come in. Can't we phony up something that saves our face and gets you into our desert to clean up Bin Laden's camps?"

"What are you offering?"

"Can we hold this action up for say three days? Then when we get rolling we can give you some meaningless targets to kill? We'll round up some criminals from our prisons shoot them and put their bodies in a few bunkers on the frontier with Jordan near the Israel border. You can do what you guys do best and blow them to pieces. Then we can claim we tried to fight you but 'lost.' Once we do, we can talk about how we both handle it from there."

"Make it tomorrow Katty and we might have a deal."

"Walter my friend, we are seven hours ahead of you. It is already 6:30 in the afternoon here. Can you do anything about the time frame for this? Even we can't round up and execute a few hundred prisoners for this show in just a few hours. Can we say we'll be ready for you by 7 PM our time tomorrow? How does that sound? We have a border outpost near the point where Jordan and Israel squeeze together. I'll give the orders as soon as I get off the phone."

"What else do you have to offer? Remember we played a lot of poker in college. I know you wouldn't be calling if you didn't have something else up your sleeve. They would have had somebody from the King's Office call if that was all there was to it. So what do you really want? Why you, the OPEC Minister?"

"You are right my old friend, we do have something else to put on the table. We have no doubt that since you have baited that fool Waleed and his partner Bin Laden into a conventional war, a brilliant stroke I might add, you will pummel them back to the seventh century… The question will then be: where will we all be after this cleansing storm?"

"We see this situation as a major opportunity for both of us to benefit for many years to come. You have your priorities and we have ours. We believe you will come out of this victorious. We believe that once you do, there will be a power vacuum at the top of the Muslim world. We want to fill that vacuum and be the new leaders of the Muslim world. We believe you would want us to be that leader as well. We trust that 'Bible Bud Andrews' is a religious man and not the kind of leader who would make war on the holy places of Islam."

"Well of course not. We both know we wouldn't bomb your holy places unless we had to. But I'm sure it would never come to that. Where are you going with this? I'm pressed for time. Get to your point."

"We have an offer for you that will allow you to refrain from doing something you weren't going to do in the first place and get a great reward for not doing so."

"Damn it Katty, get to your point!"

"Very well. If you agree not to bomb Mecca and Medina, the most holy places in the world, which we both acknowledge you will not do anyway, the Saudi government has something for you in return. If you let us tell the Muslim world that we used our previous ties to you to convince you not to bomb these holy places, when things get stabilized we will agree to sell you discounted oil. We will ship you the same amount of oil that you have purchased during the last fiscal year at a permanent twenty-five percent discount."

"The discount will be against the daily worldwide market price as set by the London Oil Trading Market. Only you and those you designate will have this discount. And we agree to keep this price reduction on for you for the next twenty- five years. That should give you a huge advantage against every other economy in the world. You would have the breathing room to find your alternative fuel while enjoying great prices and we will still make our money. There are enough barrels of oil and buyers of them to pay top dollar and keep us very comfortable until we figure out how make our money after oil. Our kingdom won't stave. Our analysis of the oil market has convinced us the party will be ending within twenty to fifty years. We're looking at this as our 'golden Parachute.' We can stay very wealthy and run the Muslim world if we ourselves can shape the future. We trust this economic weapon in only your hands. What do you say?"

"All of this just for play acting with you on the Israel border and not bombing Mecca and Medina? You just want one day and a statement?"

"Do we have a deal?"

"I don't know. I'll run it by President Andrews and get back to you, but until I do you have my assurance that we won't hit you."

"I'll get my end going right away and..."

"And Prince al-Khatab, don't you ever refer to my president as 'Bible Bud' to me again. Do you understand?"

"Yes Mister Hodges, I do."

CHAPTER 52

TURKEY'S PROPOSAL

After the conversation Harlan Andrews had with Turkish Prime Minister Dilek Ekin just a few days earlier, it seemed unlikely that they would be speaking again anytime soon. Nevertheless, Ekin called back with his proposal for how the world should look after the current Islamists attempt to end it was stopped. Ekin would only speak to Andrews. He wanted to make certain that if he got a commitment from America it came from as solid a source as he could get, given America's long record of breaking her word. Ekin had watched American politics from his days in grade school when the young President John Kennedy turned his back on the Cuban freedom fighters at the Bay of Pigs.

Ekin had been among a small group of Turkish university students that secretly loved America. They loved everything about America, her freedoms, the civil rights movement and of course American music. They believed America was the greatest country Allah had ever made in spite of what they were being told on Friday afternoons in their mosques. When the United States left Viet Nam for internal political reasons, Ekin and his friends idealized vision of America was all but destroyed. Ekin's final illusions about America's heroic status died when the United States merely watched as Saddam gassed tens of thousands of Kurdish men women and children. By that point, the Kurd murders disappointed, but did not surprise Ekin.

Dilek Ekin had no love for the Kurds, but seeing them gassed and dumped into mass graves went well past his level of animosity for his country's ancient enemies. Trusting America's word for anything would not come easy for Ekin.

His former heroes had been disappointments too many times. Andrews started the exchange with a streak of caution in his tone.

The conversation started with a stiff and formal tone, "This is President Andrews Prime Minister Ekin; I understand you have a proposal for a post war Middle East. Is that right?"

"Yes, Mister President I have a vision of how this corner of the world should look and I think you will find it interesting. I think you will agree the United States and Turkey have much to gain from a dialog on how to declare an end to hostilities. We now have no doubt that you and your allies will prevail and push the extremists who sully Islam back into their holes for many years to come."

"Yes, the latest reports show we have pretty well pacified all of the Middle East except for Iran and Syria. Your troops have done marvelous work in Iraq. Our Intelligence teams are saying you have ground our common enemies into dust throughout your theater of operations. I hope that with the possible end of the fighting coming somewhat closer, you're not back to ask for that apology again for some internal political purpose because..."

"No mister president that is an issue now best handled by history. We are men of the here and now. Neither of us has time for things of the past. To the contrary, I am thinking more about how we can work toward mutual future goals of safety and security in this most tempestuous world. If you were willing to make just a few public remarks about the nature of your conduct of this war as it concludes, I believe both of us could come out of this situation with major gains."

"A few public remarks eh? Let me guess.... You want me to acknowledge we were going to bomb Mecca and Medina and maybe a few other Muslim holy places... but that you, Dilek Ekin used your influence with me to dissuade me for doing these terrible things. Therefore Turkey should now be recognized as the leader of the modern Muslim world."

"Mister Andrews President you are a wise man. Please take no offense from my clumsy attempt to negotiate this matter in this less than forthright manner. You have my word sir; I was getting to the part about our Intelligence agents having picked up a free floating conversation between your Vice President Mister Hodges and the Saudi Prince Al-Khatab. The Prince foolishly spoke on his cell phone and our men were able to easily capture his conversation with Mister Hodges. We were very surprised at Prince Al Khatab's imprudence but we could not very well disregard what he was saying merely because he is an idiot."

For the first time in many weeks, Harlan Andrews allowed himself a small faint smile. "No I don't reckon you could have ignored information like that. Okay what's your proposal Mister Ekin?"

"We both know that the engines of America run on oil. Without oil the world's economies will come to a stand still. This makes the Saudi's offer very attractive. But being able to even count on a price, even if it will be a high price, is a big advantage to economic planners. A constant twenty five percent discount for twenty-five years is a very difficult offer to turn aside. But one has to ask: 'How valuable will the cheap oil be if constant wars and terrorist acts keep you from access to it?' The Saudis may be serious about their offer, they may not be, we do not really know for sure, but I think we can agree that they will have no way of protecting their own pipelines, wells and refineries. They have no military so you will have to remain in large numbers in this region. When you do you will be targets and you will be held up as an occupying force, which you will be. Your troops will be killed in numbers large enough for your Left fellows and your media to pressure you to pull out. When, not if, that happens all of this will be for nothing and the Islamists will get their hands on the oil we both want to keep them from. This will be bad for you and worse for me. We were already in Kurdistan cooperating with them in a joint drilling and refining venture... we have worked side by side with Western companies Canada, Norway and Switzerland.

"We can not guarantee you anything but a fair price, but we can guarantee that Kurdistan remains a free state able to continue to do petro business with you. There may be as many a twenty five billion barrels of oil in the grounds of Kurdistan and, that sir is a sizable amount."

"That would almost match all of our present reserves." Andrews thought.

"Go on sir."

"Once we pacify Iraq, we will leave a small presence of our troops in the lower two thirds of the country but maintain a heavy presence in Kurdistan as its hired protectors"

"Hired protectors?" Andrews thought with a blank stare.

"If you make these admissions and credit us with convincing you not to harm Islam's holy places, we can make an even stronger case to become the new leader of the Islamic world, then our Saudi brothers could make. The world already sees us as the bridge between the Christian world of Europe and North America and the Muslim world. The main complaints about our arrangement would come from Iran and Syria and terror organizations. Those complaints would fall on deaf ears. And Mister President we can guarantee none of them will be able to do anything about their unhappiness with our arrangement. With these countries permanently out of any future wars, you and your allies can handle the rest of the Islamists should they rise again. And as you fight them you will have all the oil you need, not at a discount, but at a fair price with a 'never stop' guarantee of the supply."

"And you would guarantee the political integrity of Kurdistan?" Andrews asked.

"You need only to make the acknowledgement sir and the wheels will begin to turn. We would keep the Iraqis in check. We would keep our foot on the necks of Syria and Iran for as long as it takes to crush them. We become the unquestioned leader of Islam and never allow the evil heresy of Waleed and his kind again. We increase trade with the West and help take away the lure of the terrorist ideology. You get a reliable military power as a new ally who stands as the leader of Islam. We will never encourage attacks on the West. We will always encourage Muslims to do for themselves and grow economically. When Muslims are living better they will not look to hate as a way to make themselves feel worthy."

"I see what you mean Mister Ekin. With a strong military to protect her from outside interference, Kurdistan could thrive and become a wealthy nation with at least a nominally positive view of America. But with the history between the Turks and the Kurds how can you...."

"Nothing in life is a sure thing, ever. I will understand your hesitation, but I give you a word that Turkey is committed to the future and we are ready to put the past aside. Looking forward has always been the Turkish way of life. We recognize that clinging to the past has been what has brought us to the edge of this canyon. So, yes and we would continually grew our relation with the Kurds. We would encourage such positive views toward America. Kurdistan could join us as the co-leader of the region. The Kurdish brothers would also be free of oppression from the Iraqi parliament. Sir, at least something positive would come out of your disengagement from Iraq; you would not be blamed for Kurdistan's refusal to honor the outrageously unfair oil revenue sharing agreements that were rammed down their throat."

"You paint a very attractive picture, but with Turkey's long history of antagonism toward the Kurds, well I just don't quite see it happening..."

"I hope you can come to believe me sir, this is a serious proposal that would benefit both of our countries. Our Kurdistani brothers would be out from under the scandalous, 'Enough Money for Everyone' oil revenue sharing plans that robbed them of their money. We would not do that to them. We would not force them to honor those contracts. Our goal would be to make them strong trading partners. Once security is assured in the region, foreign capital will come in and the basic industrial nature of the people of Kurdistan will take over. That would benefit, as you Americans say, 'all boats' in the region. But none of this happens without security. We can provide security. The Saudis can not."

"Well sir you make some important and salient points. We still have plenty of war to fight and details to work through so I can't give you an answer now. I will take your offer under advisement and respond when it is appropriate to do so. In any event, I'm very glad we could put our differences aside and begin to focus on our mutual interests. Thank you for the fine job your troops are doing in Northern and Central Iraq. I'm glad somebody has turned the tables on Waleed and Bin Laden. Good bye sir." Andrews outlined Ekin's proposal to Hodges over two fingers of Jack Daniels and cigars.

"Well I'm certainly glad I didn't say anything that would come back and bite us in the ass in that conversation with Katty. I'm sorry about that slip Mister President. I should have done more to ascertain what kind of a phone he was using. I never thought he would be dumb enough to call on an unsecured line, but he did. Then again he always was a 'C' student at Yale if you remember what that meant." Both men allowed themselves a moment of laughter between the serious items they would have to weigh in considering the Turkish proposal.

"Walt, he makes some damned good points. These Saudis can afford to make any kind of pricing promises they can dream up. Once we make that acknowledgement we can never take it back, but the day after they sign their cheap oil contract, they can throw up their hands and tell us we have to fight a new war to get to it."

"Okay but how is Ekin supposed deal with the 20 million Kurds he has in his country? I mean what happens if he starts killing them to keep them from pouring into Kurdistan as their promised land?" Hodges asked.

"The Turks have always been very good at making people do what they want them to do. The Kurds have about a hundred thousand troops themselves and they just stepped aside when the Turkeys ran in and kept on going, chasing the Syrians all the way to southern Iraq. They must have worked something out, even if it wasn't much more than a threat."

"It comes back to security. Without military muscle in the region we can't rely on the Saudi oil and at this point putting a virtually permanent force in the area to secure the flow of oil would open us up to every attack about 'blood for oil' the media could throw at us, and they wouldn't be all wrong at that." Andrews said as he stood up and walked around his desk. He raised his glass so its rim could touch Walter Hodges glass.

"So far, so good, Walt. We'll decide which one we go with when this is over."

"So far so good Mister President," Vice President Hodges answered.

CHAPTER 53

THE AFTERMATH

THE WAR TOOK the lives of millions of people around the world. Huge numbers of Islamists who truly wanted to die met Allah. Britain suffered the loss of nearly 200,000 of her people. Most of them died in a single instant when Waleed's nuclear tipped missile smashed into the middle of London. Western Europe, especially in France and Luxembourg, was a heap of death and destruction. The disaster was cataclysmic. The nuclear strike at Gonesse and the carnage that followed Waleed's arrival left the French countryside, shredded and strewn with rotting bodies. The bodies, those men women and children as well tens of thousands of military and police personnel went unburied for weeks in many towns. Nobody was left to dig the holes.

The crushing disaster in Luxembourg was stunning even to its very old citizens who had seen the dead pile up when the Nazis steamrolled across the continent in World War II. The cruelty and willingness to descend into an animal like state to survive made some European liberals openly question if death was not a better choice than such behavior.

The fires the Germans used to trap and kill the Islamists attackers charging through the Black Forest toward Stuttgart smoldered for weeks. Due to the radiation from the Davy Crocketts, the European Union countries had to violate their own environmental laws and let them burn. For the first few weeks, finding workers who would fight the fires as well as tend to the rotting half burn bodies of the jihadists was too difficult.

Rebuilding France was the European Union's top priority. White

Christian Europe could not afford to redirect native European white workers from the reconstruction projects. At last Europe understood the "cheap labor" they got by throwing their doors open to Middle Eastern immigrants was not cheap at all.

The Europeans learned a hard lesson about true independence. Their six-decade party was finally over. They had to face life after America. They could no longer be like carefree teenaged boys who could, "kiss Mom, promise not to drink and drive and ask Dad for the keys to his car and gas money." Acting like carefree teenage boys more concerned with fast cars and naked starlets than facing the reality of the Islamist threat, had altered their lives forever.

Gone were the days of laughing at America's "stupid cowboy mentality." Gone were the make-believe grounds for the European Union. Their having declared themselves to be equal to the United States in every way was exposed as the fraud it was. They were simply not up to defending themselves without American weapons and military know how. NATO was not a force that struck fear in the hearts of the Islamists. They had survived only by fighting a war of attrition of the type they could not afford to fight again. Erasing their borders and living like every night was Saturday night was over. Europeans would have to start spending money on their own defense.

They also had to accept that the United States would no longer pour out her young men and treasure on the soil of Europe. Stopping any trade with avowed enemies of freedom would no longer be something only America had to do. From that point on America would no longer shield them from the consequences of their own actions.

JAPAN AND SOUTH KOREA

The Japanese and the South Koreans had no fighting on their soil. They are not countries that are welcoming of immigrants and their Muslim populations do not extend much beyond visitors from other countries. Both countries watched the agonies of Europe and America and recognized they had to change their own ways of life.

For many years the South Koreans had allowed their students and Leftists to demonstrate for the removal of American troops and reunification with their 'brothers and sisters' in North Korea. At times American soldiers had to be confined to their own bases for their protection. The ignorance of the students and the duplicity of the Left appalled older Koreans who remembered the way America had saved them from being forced into Communism by the North Koreans and their Chinese masters.

Japan felt the need to change as well. Over the preceding decade, she had quietly whittled away are self- imposed state of military weakness. Seeing the threat of Islamist rule for what it is, the Japanese had concluded that they had done enough to atone for World War II. The countries they had been the most aggressive toward were now their closest allies.

During the war they had violated the articles in their constitution that prohibited their involvement in military operations and joined with South Korea to help with supply missions for American and Israeli troops fighting in the Golan Heights. After the fighting had been wrapped up, the Japanese Diet repealed most of the remaining restrictive articles and began to rearm for the next Islamist attempt to rule the world.

South America

The dictators of South America's socialist countries that had willingly rubbed America's nose in the dirt by helping Waleed and his terrorist were isolated when the Iranian madman fell flat on his face. Europe would not be trading with the South American thugs either. President Andrews did not have to tell Europe to stop trading with the countries on America's doorstep that had so willingly worked with Waleed's terrorists. Europe finally understood the Giant's patience and good will had limits that had been reached. Things had changed for everyone forever. The smile had been wiped off Europe's face.

The Islamists had succeeded in splitting the alliance between the United States and old Europe. The deeper thinkers on both sides of the Atlantic recognized the rare opportunity the war had presented. Europe would have to stop acting like America's worry free teenaged son, and the United States would have to rethink her knee jerk urge to jump to Europe's defense. The world had come to understand that the genuine threat to world peace and safety came from the Islamists and not from the Americans. Moreover the continent was forced to accept that the Islamist threat would never really go away. Europe had to process the reality that, powerful as America could be in another conventional war, the terrorists were not likely to allow themselves to be "Sucker Punched" again. There would be no more conventional wars with the terrorists.

Because the left in America was only temporarily defeated, as the Islamists had been, the United States could never fight a real war again. That meant America could never come to Europe's aid again.

Harlan Andrews and Ethan Gross both fully expected to eventually be exposed for what they had done. Neither one cared about that possibility. They did not care about history. Great men do not worry about history while they are doing the necessary and heroic things that make them great; they just do them.

CHANGES IN AMERICA

Across America people were stunned and shocked. The numbers painted a gruesome picture. Save for the states of North Dakota, Montana and Idaho every section of the country was touched and rudely awakened by the war. Most Americans did not believe they would ever see day after day fighting on their city streets. The unity that facing a war and the common recognition of 'all being in this together' was short lived. Bonds forged in time of peril fell apart like snowmen in April.

It was not long before those who had so publicly and vigorously mocked the very notion of danger from the Islamists, whom they insisted upon calling peaceful Muslims found themselves in great peril. Families and friends of those lost in the fighting whether overseas or on American soil were in no mood for generosity toward the *Muslims are peaceful people* crowd. Some who openly held liberal views toward immigration and the handling of Islamists, had their homes burned and their cars turned over. A few were murdered. America had suffered the loss of nearly 400,000 civilians and police personnel at home and another 17,000 military war fighters in the various theaters of the war. In a nationwide movement that started in New York City, people started to stop overturn and burn delivery trucks of the newspapers believed to have aided and abetted the Islamists during the war. A Television station that ran nightly footage of American atrocities was stormed and trashed as well.

For a brief period the days of an anti American, American media ended. Circulation numbers for the country's largest papers fell to record lows because Americans had had enough of being told they are the cause of terrorism in the world. Across the county, Unity and Reconciliation rallies were scheduled for the third Sunday after the fighting ended. Stadiums in every large city opened their doors for these events, designed to heal the wounds of a divided nation. The stadiums that had any appreciable number in attendance were mostly in the big cities. They were filled with local leftists and politicians. The politicians thought they smelled votes in the toxic stew of racial and religious hatred that oozed out of every pore of the nation's body. These rallies flopped. When the cast of dignitaries rose to be recognized and receive their undeserved applause, they heard boos instead. When the obligatory local Imam was recognized, in most cases he was booed until he left the stage and in some cases was chased to his car.

As could be expected, the politicians saw their mission as calming people down and getting back to the status quo of the pre war days as soon as possible. They did not work for the people. They worked for Big Business, Big Labor and Big everything else except Big Voter. This time people saw right through the make believe. In the first days after the September 11th attacks, a series of similar Unity and Reconciliation rallies took place. In New York, people still in shock at the attack, went to Yankee Stadium hoping to hear something genuine being offered. When they heard prayers in every conceivable language praying to every conceivable God, most came away dazed and angry at the feckless display. People who intuitively understood that the 9/11 attack was a time for 'kicking ass,' not listening to somebody chanting, came away with a deep sense of resentment. After the Islamists War some politicians 'got it,' but others treated America's most genuine fears and concerns as 'childish retreats into darkness.'

The rallies after the war did do some good however, if only of the unintended kind. When Americans saw their leaders trying to pat them on the head as they had in 2001, the words self-reliance jumped to mind. Reliance on the government for anything beyond delivering the mail three days late was hazardous to the health, Americans understood.

The compact between the American people and the American government had been seriously damaged. People began to look past their government and its phony officials instead to looking to themselves. A new spirit of rugged individualism and watching out for your neighbors and family sprung up. People kept guns in their homes and dared beleaguered authorities to 'come and take them. Crime in many gun-toting locations fell dramatically. Within a few months the immigration patterns of many Muslim countries slowed, then stopped, and then turned to a net negative. The welcome mat at America's borders and ports of entry were pulled up. Americans demanded and got a concrete wall along the Southern border.

Soon the obligatory *law of unintended consequences* kicked in. Immigrants with high levels of all kinds of skills began in apply for and receive visas and green cards in record numbers. Because of America's new tough stance on immigration, decent people from every corner of the world who could immediately contribute to America in a meaningful way were welcomed in to the nation. They came in substantial numbers because they knew America was the only country in the world capable of protecting them from the next Islamist uprising. They knew their home countries were not up to the test.

In deep gratitude to their new country, many newly arrived immigrant families sent their sons and daughters to America's military forces. In certain circles of young American men, joining the military was seen as an obligation again. They put pressure on each other to contribute saying things like "Dude, if we don't do it who will? We can't depend on anybody but each other."

CHAPTER 54

PRESIDENT ANDREWS ADDRESSES THE NATION
STAND TALL, TALK LOUD, BE PROUD, AMERICA WINS, FOR NOW

The war had taken a great deal of strength out of Harlan Andrews. He was not in good physical condition at its start and ran on coffee, cigars and grit during its long dark hours. His pale and worn face was a stark testament to the perilous journey he had just guided America through.

As he stepped to the podium in the Rose Garden his demeanor gave no indication of the cautious announcement of victory he was about to make. The nation and the world knew he was not going to announce that a peace treaty had been negotiated. Although he had not said as much during any of his many reassuring chats with the American people, it was well understood that mere peace was not his goal. If America's aim in this war had been the reestablishment of a state of peace military operations could have been shut down after the first few days of the fighting.

Andrews never saw "peace" as his mission. From the first furtive talks he had with Israel he had made it clear that he would not bring America into any half hearted effort to place yet another band aid on the Islamist cancer threatening the world. It had been his firm insistence that the *fighting be hard fast and in every way to win from day one to the end*, as he wrote to Ethan Gross the Israeli Prime Minister. It was Harlan Andrews steely determination to *go all in* in this showdown war. Andrews had worked very hard to reassure the Jewish leader that at last God had given him the right American President to work with. The American people expected an announcement of victory not merely of peace. They were not disappointed. Harlan Andrews looked into the cameras and spoke in a strong firm voice that belied his true constitution. He talked about how the war had started when, "our one true friend in the Middle East, the State of Israel was viciously attacked by nuclear weapons of mass destruction."

He went on to outline the heroic deeds of America's fighting men and women in military uniform and her first responders. His original speech contained a list of other countries to be lauded for their contributions, but he personally crossed that section out. He explained to his staff that this was America's day. Other countries can pat themselves on the back.

"Today I will be the nation's cheerleader, because that's what our country needs right now. Plus I think we're all a little tired of making believe we couldn't have done this without help from Europe. Hell they're using our weapon systems; what does that tell you?"

The President continued:

"Today I am proud to say, as a nation we can once again: stand tall, walk proud and talk loud because our American war fighters have thoroughly routed our enemies. These enemies have been hiding and attacking us from the shadows and their cycle of attack and hide for another day has been broken. The military power of the United States of America has quieted our enemies for now. I say for now because we have every reason to think that they will be back again at some point. But you and I can be proud of the fact that our courage and fighting spirit have set down the blueprints for future generations of Americans when their time of trial comes. This struggle has been, is and always will be one of good versus evil. We have not fought our war against Muslims and Islam. We have fought our war against evil men who have used their Muslim religion to justify murdering those that do not believe as they do. We Americans will never accept having anyone force us to worship God in a way we do not agree with. We enjoy the most religious freedom in the world and we will fight to keep this treasured freedom.

"So while it is true that this war is now over and we have won a victory and not just a peace, we can never again let our guard down. We Americans are a peaceful people, but we will never lose sight of our duty to vigilance again. Providence has entrusted America with the duty to protect and defend the freedom of religion. We will never hesitate to fight for our freedom to practice our own faith as we see fit, each by his own set of beliefs and we will join with our world wide neighbors to protect their rights to freedom of religion as well.

"We must never allow ourselves to be fooled as to the continued purposes of the radical Islamists we have just defeated. They want one thing and one thing only: the destruction of the world so they can find favor with their God for doing His bidding in bringing about the end of days.

"They will never ever stop but we will never ever let them defeat us and murder us to satisfy their perverse fascination with death. Because of these basic truths, this struggle is a never ending war between good and evil.

"Americans in recent generations have been faced with a similar insidious problem when they had to make a judgment about the dangers of Communism. They had to decide whether the malignancy of Communism was a threat to be dealt with or ignored. Like the Islamists of today, certain segments of our society became self appointed apologists for the Communists.

"Americans were told that socialism and communism were nothing more than alternative systems of government designed to fit the needs of people who could never survive under their own self governance. Talk and propaganda like that kept the stultifying socialist Communists countries propped up long enough to murder tens of millions of innocent people whose only crime was a desire to live in freedom. We Americans have learned from our struggle with Communism. We now understand that there great differences between systems of government.

"We can see only too clearly that our freedoms are never free. We now understand that we will probably have to move forward into the unknown of our future sure only of the fact that to live as we wish to live, we will have to remain ready to fight those who would murder us and our families for being different then they are.

"We know that even now, they are licking their wounds in some dark hiding place and planning to come at us again. Those who would deny that are fooling themselves.

"Fourteen centuries of history tells us they are plotting to do what they have just failed to do. Wishing this was not so won't keep us safe. Dealing with reality will. The reality of our world is that those who have tried to murder the world for the sake of their religious beliefs will never stop until they are victorious or we are victorious. As your president, I can promise you the Islamists will never defeat our nation.

"We will stand ever ready to meet force with superior force as long as every American contributes to our common goal of peace only through military victory. They will never stop, so we will never stop.

"Now let me speak directly to our enemies, those who have declared war on America: 'As you consider your next move keep in mind that the defeats you have just suffered will be only the beginning of the lessons we have to teach you. Many of your apologists here in the West have stated that 'We don't know anything about the Islamists and we don't understand them.'

"Well that may be true, but you know nothing about America and do not understand the first thing about the American spirit. You can learn from what just happened or you can get yourselves another lesson. That is up to you. If you wish to live out your lives in peace we will do likewise. If you insist upon bringing war to America we will destroy you. Regroup and come back at your own risk.

"We have shown the enemy the power of America's military might once and we will show it to them again. America is a nation that was founded on love of freedom. Those who dwell in the shadows plotting our destruction may win individual battles, but they will never defeat America. They have been made to see that America is not just a country but an idea that can never be stamped out. We are as much a state of mind as their twisted ideology, only America is tougher and smarter. Some may cringe at those words, fearful that they will generate more attacks. This position badly misses the point. These monsters from the depths of evil need no external motivation to hate America. They need no particular igniting spark to want to come here and kill us.

"A burning desire to kill Americans is their way of life. Should they ever prevail, they will not distinguish between their victims. They will murder us all, even their homegrown apologists. We will all be much safer when every American accepts this reality.

"So my fellow Americans, let me say this very plainly: The threat we faced from the Godless hordes of Communism was not half as dangerous as the one we face today from radical Islamists; not from Muslims but Islamists striking at us from behind the veil of Muslimism.

"Let every American accept, here and now that, just as Communism was a serious danger to our existence, the radical Islamist movement is still more dangerous to us. And let me say also that fighting against the ideology of the Islamist is not fighting against a religion. Religions do not teach hate and murder. Religions do not command their followers to spend their lives scheming up ways to torture and destroy other human beings to appease a God. Religions, all religions teach peaceful care and concern for all humans without qualification. True religions teach peaceful, caring, and respect for all, not death. We Americans recognize the differences between true Islamic teachings and the teachings of the Islamists.

"True religions command their followers to do the most good they can during their brief stay on earth. The hate the Islamists preach is no more a religious doctrine than the hate the Ku Klux Klan preaches is a genuine political point of view. Death is contrary to life. The God we worship as Jews and Christians and members of all other true religions recognizes this.

"Now for the sake of truly living in peace and future religious freedom, I call upon the Muslim community in America to face up to those who have poisoned their own religious dialog with hateful words and actions. I ask for their public repudiation of the fringe elements in their fold. And I promise the full support of the American people if you show this courage.

"This is the American way. When we make a mistake we own up to it. Other religious communities have owned up to their mistakes, it is now time for you to do the same.

"This horrific war we have just concluded has taught us many lessons, not the least of which is the new definition of being an American. It ought to be very clear to all of us that being an American means cherishing and fighting to protect our freedoms in whatever ways we are equipped to contribute. Each of us must resolve that being an American can never again be considered a spectator sport.

"They will kill us to take these freedoms from us. We can never ever make them stop coming for us by negotiating with them or retreating from them. The Islamists are a constant challenge to us to step up and fight. We can never afford the risks of cowering and turning our back on them.

"To continue to thrive and prosper as a people we require contributions from each of us as individuals. To survive we must constantly busy ourselves thinking of ways to help turn back their murderous intentions. Young Americans should carefully consider securing their own future by joining our military. Others should join efforts to teach the truth about the intentions of our enemies and challenge anyone in or out of the public eye who attempts to spread misconceptions and falsehoods about the basic nature of our enemies. Older Americans might consider writing letters to our war fighters to cheer them and remind them of how special we think they are.

"I also call upon Congress to put aside political differences to move legislation on immigration reform and further strengthening our borders. It is evident now that we allowed many enemy agents to slip through our border defenses. This carelessness on our part brought death and injury to many Americans and must not be allowed to continue un-addressed. To that end I have ordered a special joint session of Congress to outline the changes in law I believe are needed to protect our nation

"Finally, I have ordered the Attorney General to prepare indictments for charges range from espionage to treason against all individuals and corporations he believes have, released and or published the secrets of the United States Government leading up to and during the just completed war. The prosecutions, coming from any indictments in this new process, will be tried by a newly created branch of the Attorney General's office. I have made a written request to the Chief Justice of the Supreme Court to request that these trials be held before an assigned Justice of the Court. I have made this request in order to expedite any appeals which may follow any convictions. At this hour, Agents of the Federal Bureau of Investigations are arresting and detaining a number those who are considered flight risks and not likely to appear as ordered to stand trial.

"America is the finest country the Almighty ever put on this earth. He has allowed us to work our way through a maze of competing ideologies to forge us into His chosen nation. He has shown us that peace is not just the absence of war; it is the guarantee of basic human rights of freedom that no man can take away.

"We now know that freedom is never free and that the only way to guarantee a free and genuine peace is to be constantly on guard and prepared for war.

"With this announcement all extraordinary limitations and government ordered closings of schools workplaces and other points of congregation are hereby lifted. Take tomorrow off America then let's get back to work. We still have a nation to protect, and may God continue to bless us all as we do. Good night and God bless America.

Afterwards Vice President Walter Hodges and President Harlan Andrews sat alone in the Oval office and watched a beautiful Washington sunset.

"Walt, you know they'll be back at us again." Andrews said.

"Yes Mister President, we've won for now, but it will be up to every generation after us to fight them as we have. It's the only way for us to survive."

Within a few years the Islamists began regrouping and planning to defeat America.

-The end, for now -